PENGUIN BOOKS

WALTZ IN MARATHON

Charles Dickinson was born in Detroit, Michigan, on 4 June 1951. He graduated in 1973 with a degree in journalism from the University of Kentucky. His short stories have appeared in *Esquire*, *The New Yorker*, *Atlantic Monthly*, *Grand Street* and the *Pikestaff Forum*. His story 'Risk' was included in the O. Henry Awards' collection of the best short stories of 1983.

Waltz in Marathon is his first novel. His second, *Crows*, will be published in the U.S.A. by Alfred A. Knopf.

Charles Dickinson lives with his wife and son in Palatine, Illinois, U.S.A.

Charles Dickinson

Waltz in Marathon

Penguin Books

Penguin Books Ltd, Harmondsworth, Middlesex, England
Viking Penguin Inc., 40 West 23rd Street, New York, New York 10010, U.S.A.
Penguin Books Australia Ltd, Ringwood, Victoria, Australia
Penguin Books Canada Ltd, 2801 John Street, Markham, Ontario, Canada L3R 1B4
Penguin Books (N.Z.) Ltd, 182–190 Wairau Road, Auckland 10, New Zealand

First published in the U.S.A. 1983
First published in Great Britain by Michael Joseph Ltd 1984
Published in Penguin Books 1985

Made and printed in Great Britain by
Richard Clay (The Chaucer Press) Ltd,
Bungay, Suffolk

For Donna and Louis

Waltz in Marathon

1

A man approaches Harry Waltz at his father's wake and places an envelope full of cash in his hand. Waltz puts the money out of sight in his coat pocket and presents the man a small smile of thanks. He does not care who witnessed this piece of business thrust amidst the routines of mourning. He's accustomed to it. It has been going on all night. His customers have seized the wake as an opportunity to come and see him, to see his house, to pay face to face part of what they owe, to get a feel for his life. The richest man in Marathon is Harry Waltz.

Daddy Waltz, dead half an hour after turning one hundred years old, lies in a mahogany box at one end of the dining room. He was a practicing physician in Marathon until the age of ninety-five. He played in a July 4th softball game at the age of ninety-seven. He is the latest in a long string of men and women in the Waltz family to live to one hundred. He had a twin brother, Ogden, who died in his eighties, and when Ogden passed away, Daddy Waltz told Waltz the seas were clear ahead to his hundredth birthday, there was nothing to stop him.

The Waltz family also runs to twins. Waltz has a twin brother, Aaron, not present at the wake. Waltz called to inform him of their father's death and could only get through to his wife, Molly, a woman Waltz knows only by her voice. Her voice has not changed appreciably in the thirty years Waltz has talked with her on the telephone. She said Aaron was too busy to make the flight from L.A. Waltz offered to meet their plane in Detroit. But, despite Waltz's words of disbelief, Aaron would not be attending his father's funeral. He had departed by bus for California at the age of seventeen with no hint he would never be back. He left in the shadow of his twin brother, Harry, who revolved alone in his father's light.

Aaron became a physician, trying to melt his father's heart from a distance. Waltz stayed in Marathon and lived in his father's house. He married Louise Parker, fathered two sons, Eugene and Monroe, and twin daughters, Carla and Susan. He lost Louise to a heart attack on the day JFK was inaugurated, and on the day JFK was assassinated he was struck by a car in the Marathon town square. The leg that was broken in that accident pains him more and more as he ages; he is sixty-one now. The car that hit him was driven by a man who owed him money.

People set drinks on his father's coffin. They tap ashes into the carpet or let their cigarettes burn too long on the coffin's edge and leave hot trenches they immediately distance themselves from. Waltz takes all this in and almost smiles. Daddy Waltz would laugh. Ashes on his unreal face, he'd find the humor in it. Three summers previous, he made his way to center field in a game played by his patients. None of Waltz's debtors participated. The glove Daddy Waltz wore was as old as he was, crafted of leather thin as cloth, and claw-shaped. The very first pitch was struck hard and flew out toward him. The left fielder, a young boy, came streaking over. Waltz feared a collision. His father would die three years short of his cherished hundredth year, camped under a fly ball. Or worse, the kid would pluck the ball away from the old physician, in all probability the kid's final act in life. (Waltz had seen his father, sitting old and still in a public place, flick out a hand like a toad's tongue to slap the cheek of a rude or unruly child whose birth he had overseen.) But the kid braked at the last instant and the ball fell into Daddy Waltz's old glove and when the story was related in town in the following days it came off the tongue like folklore.

Carla and Susan, twin tall beauties, arrive at the wake. They stand in the front hall and kiss the sides of their father's head. Susan's husband, Willy, waits behind them. Waltz snakes a hand between the two women and shakes his hand.

5

Waltz is so glad to have his daughters there he returns his attention to them to hug them; surprised, they squeal and draw looks. He won't have to go through the evening alone. Carla has always understood her father better than his other children. He reads this in her eyes. Susan is pregnant with the couple's first child.

Then, like that, they are dispersed by a crush of well-wishers. He feels the intrusion of these mourners as an assault on what closeness he has remaining. He wants to be alone with his daughters. He watches them moving above the shifting lake of heads, their dark golden hair, their strong, beautiful faces so full of Louise.

Their presence turns the focus from Waltz, though, and frees him out the back door. He feels propelled gently out a hatchway into space. With cigarette and glass of beer he floats weightless over the dark grass. A jet goes overhead without a sound, a small diamond shape of four lights, two red, two white. Behind the house is a long run of yard with a gazebo halfway out and a twelve-foot-high chain link fence marking the rear boundary of his lot. Daddy Waltz owned the land beyond the fence and in 1920 sold it to the state of Michigan, which erected the fence around the property and inside the fence built the Michigan State Home for the Retarded.

The Home's closed now. Waltz, taking a seat in the gazebo, still misses the smiling heads bobbling inside the fence, their happy acknowledgment of him as he was growing up and as his children were growing up. Marathonites fought the State Home idea when it was proposed, they imagined foaming mouths and twisted brains on their doorsteps. Daddy Waltz laughed at this prejudiced opposition. He knew the state would prevail when it wanted something bad enough.

Waltz, nine years old when the first resident, a shy mongoloid boy in white shirt and bow tie, arrived, remembers Daddy Waltz telling him earnestly, "Get to know them, Harry. Make them your friends. Develop a feel for what God's given you and for what he's denied you."

Waltz lights another cigarette. The Home windows are boarded over, the four-story red brick dormitories, the dining hall, the gymnasium, the bell tower all closed up with plywood sheets. A year after the closing, though, the Home grounds are still spruced. Waltz never sees anyone in there working. It is magic, maybe. Or night work. His own lawn looks tattered to him because the young men he hired from the Home to take care of it are gone; with the Home closed he never catches up.

His father's house, his house now, sits atop a hill with Columbia Avenue out front bending slightly at the northwest corner of the lot, then dropping down the face of the hill into the square. The square is actually a rectangle, its center marked by a famous cannon. The bus that carried Aaron to California still makes its same stop on the square after all these years. He can look down into the square from the upstairs western windows. He enjoys this limited vista. Things happen in the square; looking at it he gets a feel for his hometown that his line of work otherwise denies him.

Sitting in front of his house like hard-shelled candies are repossessed vehicles. They come and go. Waltz hires a guy in Flint to take them away. Waltz hates to see them because they are symbols of money not paid. He doesn't want his customers' cars. He wants the money they owe him. He wants them to experience the warm satisfaction of paying their debts on time. It is July, so more vehicles are present; in summer, people who owe him money are more likely to fall behind, thinking they can get along without a car in nice weather. Winter, especially winter in the Mitten, nobody who can possibly avoid it loses their car.

Waltz grinds out the cigarette on the gazebo floor. How long has he been out here? The Home bell used to toll the hour, so Waltz never wore a watch. He never started, even after the Home closed. Now he's always a little confused as to the time.

Waltz stretches on one leg, crane-like, in the dining room. Mourners and the curious turn uneasily away from this eccentric display. Waltz could reach out and touch his father's face. The tallest man in Marathon is Waltz. He is six and one-half feet tall, Aaron's size, not a dime's thickness of difference between them. Waltz has white hair he wears disinterestedly long; it unfolds over the collars of his shirts, and his friend Sam Boggins will cut it for him when Waltz thinks to have it done.

He wonders if Sam Boggins will attend the wake. He might be there already, lost in the crowd, the smoke, the chatter of good times. Their friendship goes way back. There was quite a long time when they were friends and did not realize it. This spell of time is sacred to Waltz; he fears asking Sam Boggins if it is sacred to him, too, fearing it is not.

He wants to slip upstairs to work but guesses it would be rude. His body is tired from the weight of all the envelopes of cash he is carrying. His JFK leg is sore from standing. He lights a cigarette and finds Willy in a corner.

"I'm going upstairs for a minute," Waltz tells him. "Tell one of the girls so they won't worry."

He unloads the envelopes of cash onto his desk. More such envelopes arrive in the mail each day, a name written on the outside of some, on slips of paper inside others. He takes off his suit coat and hangs it over the back of his chair and sits down. Through a window he sees downstairs light from the house spilling out onto the lawn. Guests arrive and approach the front door humbly. Waltz gets to work.

He takes the first envelope and slits it with a thin gold knife. Currency falls out, a total of $100 in tens, fives, and ones; there is an almost audible scraping together. It makes Waltz proud of these people who owe him and pay him back; he loves his string of customers for their punctuality and their adherence to honor.

The $100 is the month's payment of Paul Rivers, who is an unemployed auto worker in Flint. His name, no good with the banks, is fine with Waltz. Money is tight all over the state, but Waltz still lends. He finds the page in his records bearing Paul Rivers' account and meticulously marks the $100 payment.

Waltz cuts open another envelope. Among the limp bills are

pieces of silver taped in neat rows to both sides of a three-by-five card. Everywhere he looks, times are tough. He is in one of those not uncommon fields that profit from the misfortunes of others. He has been at this all his life. He has a talent for it, a gift, and he understands the souls of the people who owe him. They need the money, but they also need to prove they are able to pay it back. He is famous in Marathon. The crowd downstairs is there as much to see Waltz as to pay last respects to his father. He thinks of himself as beloved, in a fashion.

He decides he must go back to his guests. He locks his desk, puts on his coat, and leaves the room. From the top of the stairs he can smell the humid flowers that crowd his father. His daddy's face has a waxy, unreal sheen. He looks too peaceful, simplified, all the rough-earned creases on his face smoothed away. He never looked worse. Daddy Waltz lived to a hundred but in death has been returned to his sixties; the transformation annoys Waltz, time having been stolen.

Daddy Waltz, at the exact moment of turning one hundred, stood up out of the armchair in his bedroom and took a deep, precarious breath. He held a pocket watch in his hand.

Waltz asked, "Was it worth it?"

"I guess it was. I miss your mother. I wish she could be here with me."

Her name was May and she had died years before, and her husband's response was not so much one of grief as of disappointment that she did not have what it took to see a hundred years out with him.

"Regardless," Daddy Waltz said, "I made it and you're next, Harry. I was right about me and I'll be right about you. You watch."

He was silent then. He had made it to a hundred and he had to admit he was pretty tired. He remained standing for a half hour, then with the facility and absolute control of his destiny that marked him and was much of his legend, he folded up neatly dead in his chair.

As the moment of the wake's ending nears, Waltz experiences a palpable exhilaration. He will soon be free of all this. The funeral remains the following day, but it will be private, just Daddy Waltz and his family, with no debtors coming up and putting envelopes of cash in his hand, none of the gawkingly curious. His daughters will disappear back into their lives in Ann Arbor. His children have been away from home long enough so that he now thinks of them in fragments of image that quite often bear no relation to the truth: his daughters move in his mind in a parallel beauty, there is no telling them apart although Susan is pregnant and Carla is his favorite. Eugene is always heading inexorably for trouble. Monroe moves in a cloud of music.

Sam Boggins had come and said a few words to Waltz, words that somehow completed the night an hour before it ended. The house is empty now, and Waltz is back at his desk with his work before him. His work is mostly counting, he long ago decided. Indifferent to math in school, he now makes his living within a universe of numbers.

The desk phone rings. He snatches it up before the first ring is completed, he still thinks of his house as full of people whose sleep he must protect.

Aaron asks from L.A., "How did it go?"

"Not bad."

"You mad at me, Harry?"

"I think I have good reason."

"How's business?" Aaron asks.

"Good. These people come up to me within an arm's length of my dead daddy and hand me envelopes full of money."

"Better that than empty envelopes."

"Don't change the subject," Waltz scolds. "Why are you in L.A. when your father will be buried tomorrow in Marathon?"

"For your funeral, Harry, I'll come home. Or you'll come to mine."

Aaron is older by only twenty minutes, but through a coincidence of time and maternal effort his birthday is October 17 and Waltz's October 18. Aaron tells stories to his friends in L.A. of their dear mother May, laboring over twins, the first a physician and surgeon, the second a loan shark, and how she was eager to have the first but fought for a day to keep the second away from the world.

2

The richest man in Marathon is Harry Waltz, and to kill time and stoke envious hearts men sit in Sam Boggins' barbershop on the square and peer up at the Waltz house on the hill. Some time ago a customer came to the shop with a pair of binoculars and when he departed he forgot them. Sam Boggins does not recall the man; his work flows along in a featureless river of cut hair. But the man never came back for the binoculars and they sit in a drawer waiting and are put to interim use studying Waltz's house.

Sam Boggins loves Harry Waltz. He has owed him and repaid him and he loves him. In school together, Harry Waltz was a klutz, Sam Boggins deft with his hands, a shortstop; a future surgeon, said those fond of linking an entire future life to a child's odd gift.

Sam slides the binoculars along the face of Marathon: to the empty Home bell tower, up the hill where on rare occasions he will see pink womanly winks in the late-afternoon windows of houses and apartments, into blank-faced store windows, finally picking out the Waltz house. The house is fortress-strong, arguably the best house in Marathon, erected with care. A porch runs around three sides. Shades are drawn on the western windows as the sun comes down. These same windows will blaze orange for minutes at a time when the sun is right, frightening Sam Boggins with the impression of a fire contained within the house. The lawn could use work.

A flickering motion, like the tipping of the shadows on the edge of the binoculars' field of vision, draws his attention. A car has arrived at Waltz's. A Toyota, already rusting along the door panels. Sam was born and raised in Michigan and it breaks his heart to see Detroit choking to death on these Jap trinkets.

11

Dee Hirsch gets out of the car. She has come with money for Harry Waltz. The way she holds her purse with two hands in front of her signals her sense of value in what the purse contains. He wonders how much she owes, and for what she needed the money.

He does not understand her willingness to be seen paying her debt. Why open herself to that? When Sam Boggins owed Waltz he mailed his payments. He addressed the envelope and put on the stamp, then inserted what he owed. He refused to walk to Waltz's house in the line of sight of some phantom binoculars.

The $1,000 he borrowed from Harry Waltz was for a woman. She lived in Flint, he met her in a restaurant there when she waited on his table. She was smartly built, small-waisted, flirtatious. She wore a tiny diamond wedding ring. He learned her name was Tina and that her husband worked for Fisher Body. She was proud of him, she talked about him a lot. They had no children and she said this was fine with her. The earth and the air, to her way of thinking, were unfit for the young. Her beliefs put a chill in Sam Boggins. The air she spoke into was infused with poison.

She frightened him out of his reason for eating in that restaurant when he came to Flint. His only son, Tim, was at that time in Vietnam. A rifleman, he signed "Lucas McCain" to his early letters, and in those letters he counted for himself and his mother and father the time remaining until he came home. Tina's certainty of the deadliness of the world for children took away Sam Boggins' appetite.

When he did finally go back to the restaurant she was gone. "She got knocked up and quit," a sullen assistant manager informed Sam Boggins. This delighted Sam more than he would ever have expected. Her pregnancy signaled to him the safety of the world for children, his son in particular.

He told the assistant manager he owed her money and the assistant manager gave Sam her address and phone number. She came to the door of her apartment in a yellow robe. Her belly protruded, it made her look younger, childlike. Her compact form had squeezed upward to fill her face with a rounded, sallow weight. For an instant he saw she did not recognize him, then somehow she did, and she smiled.

"I see you took the plunge," Sam said, touching her belly shyly.

She laughed, but it was dipped in acid. "Yeah, great, huh?"

The girl settled her new weight on a sofa and lit a cigarette. He wanted to warn her that cigarettes were not good for the baby, but he saw that the baby had already lost, that it would be born into a poisonous world.

"How's your husband?" Sam asked.

"What husband? The asshole took a powder when I got pregnant. Not in his plans, he said. A kid was not in his plans."

Could a man do that? Sam wondered. He supposed so. It had been done. He said a quick prayer for Tim, for this woman, for himself. There was no protection. They were standing in Fate's sights.

"Do you need money?"

"Who don't?"

"He has to pay you something, doesn't he?"

"Oh yeah, he gives me a little. He lost his job right after he walked out. Serves him right." She waved the memory of this man away. "He's just an asshole. Better I should find out now." She smiled at Sam Boggins. "I'm a mess, ain't I? Let me get fixed up. I'll let you buy me lunch."

But when she was in another room, humming a Beatles song, Sam slipped away. He drove back to Marathon with the radio tuned to an all-news station. He wanted word of his son. A letter from Tim was waiting when he got home. Five months left. Sam wrote to tell his son to stop counting, to forget the time left, and then one day like a surprise they would let him come home.

Sam Boggins paid a visit to Harry Waltz. A pudgy mongoloid boy smiled, raking grass clippings in the yard. Sam appreciated that Waltz did not ask what the money was for. He thought that was the reason Waltz was such a success at what he did. Sam put up a collection of turn-of-the-century silver dollars as collateral. He signed a note. And from somewhere within that solid house Waltz produced ten $100 bills and presented them to Sam Boggins in an envelope.

Then Waltz asked, "How is Tim?"
"Fine. He writes a lot."
"You appreciate that."
"And how's Monroe?" Sam Boggins asked.
"Fine. Safe. He's a bugler in Saigon. I wish he'd write more. I tell him that from day to day he will be safe. I don't know if it helps."

Sam Boggins remembers the way he had with girls in high school, how his fingers played over their breasts, unfastening bras one-handed like snapping his fingers, slipping inside enclosures of lace. He walked the halls in springtime with his glove under his arm and his spikes around his neck. It was his most godlike time.

Harry Waltz was just the shy. He loaned money to students and seemed enthralled by the fact, almost a law of nature, of more money than he loaned being paid back. He was scorned, otherwise, being among children. The importance of his place in the social scheme was lost on them.

Waltz would sometimes sit in the bleachers after school and watch baseball practice. A boy or girl might come and sit beside him for a minute. They would talk, a note would be signed, and money produced.

Sam Boggins floated across the choppy infield with his glove low for the ball. He was too rapt within himself to notice Waltz doing business. Waltz's twin brother, Aaron, who played first base, a towering lean target for Sam's hard throws, would sometimes call across the field, "Don't sign your soul away to that shylock!"

Waltz never seemed to hear. In a week or so the kids who borrowed would pay back to Waltz a little more than he had loaned. No one ever accused Harry Waltz of being stupid.

They are children still and Sam Boggins finds himself walking a block behind Waltz in downtown Marathon. They walk at a similar idle pace, the distance between them never changes. It is a mild

Friday night in early winter. A basketball game is being played at the high school. The air is so clear and quiet that the pep band's tinny enthusiasms and the chattering of the crowd can be heard on the square when the gym doors open.

Harry Waltz never attends these games, though Aaron is often the star. Sam Boggins is just out walking. He had learned that afternoon that his grades would not get him into the University of Michigan, as he had hoped. His friends await his appearance at the game, but he lacks the heart to go. Between baseball seasons he finds himself drifting in the presence of others. He feels his mind slip free if he doesn't catch it. He has admitted to the ambition of becoming a surgeon, but only to avoid trouble. What he truly wants to do is play professional baseball. But in his clearest moments he recognizes he is little more than fairly good. He has the hands; he catches what comes his way. But he is not a very good hitter. He uses his hands mostly on girls, and lately on one girl in particular, her name is Melody, she fights him off like a panther, smiling. What will those hands be good for now? He stops on the sidewalk to examine these hands and feel sorry for himself.

Somewhere ahead, Harry Waltz has disappeared.

Sam Boggins walks another block. He had become accustomed to the shy's presence in front of him and with Harry Waltz gone he is off balance, menaced by the empty streets.

He hears glass break and down an alley sees the shadowy commotion of a fight. It is frightening without illumination; he is unable to form an allegiance. Then he recognizes one dark form as outnumbered by three others. No words are spoken; only the whistle and grunt of punches being thrown. The lone fighter is not helpless. He gets loose and whales. Sam Boggins runs toward them yelling and his words break the rhythm of this dark dance, three of them run out the other end of the alley, and Harry Waltz falls to his knees.

Sam helps him to his feet. Blood runs from his nose, from a mean slit in his lower lip, from somewhere in his mouth. Sam lights a match and Waltz swivels his head away from the flame.

His right eye has begun to swell and bits of gravel and ground glass stick to his cheek. He begins to laugh.

"You should see a doctor," Sam Boggins says.

"My daddy'll sew me up."

"Who were they?"

"Tom and Ray Dugan. Sal Bonaparte. It was attempted robbery, pure and simple."

"Did they get anything?"

"Not a cent," Harry Waltz says proudly.

Sam Boggins is cutting hair when word comes that Monroe Waltz has been killed in Vietnam. The fact of it takes an entire day to become concrete, and another day passes before Sam learns how Monroe was killed.

Harry Waltz is not seen. Sam Boggins puts part of his debt in an envelope, addresses it, and stamps it, but before sealing the envelope includes a short note expressing his condolences and his willingness to be of any help necessary. Two days later he has locked his front door and turned out the lights when a tall figure appears in the rear of his shop. It is Harry Waltz.

"Thank you for the note, Sam," he says in a dry voice. He crosses the floor, passing Sam, who has nothing to say, Waltz is almost a stranger, and takes a seat in a barber chair. Sam goes in the back to call Melody and tell her he will be late.

Waltz takes two bottles of beer from the inside pockets of his suit coat. He opens one and passes it to Sam and opens the second bottle for himself.

He says, "Cut my hair, Sam."

Sam Boggins swirls a pinstriped sheet around Waltz and fastens it with a safety pin. He appreciates Harry Waltz for placing this time they share squarely in elements he is comfortable with. Cutting hair: it is all he can remember.

"Monroe tells me there is no way of knowing who is who over there," Waltz says. "Anybody could be the enemy, he says. And that can change from day to day. What happened was, I'm told, is that Monroe finished playing his bugle at a ceremony on the U.S. Embassy grounds and when he was riding back to his base a little girl stepped off the sidewalk and shot him. Said it could've happened to anyone, they said. This little Vietnamese girl shot him and then just vanished in the crowd. Nobody saw anything, they said. Could have been a girl, they said, could've been an old man. Said they all begin to look about the same. Sappers, they call them. That's how they got Monroe." Waltz shakes his head, Sam Boggins has to pull the scissors back or he would have cut him. "Did I tell you he was a bugler?"

"Yes, Harry, you did."

"Saigon," Waltz murmurs. "I pictured it as a safe place. A city way down at the end of the country. It was at one time as beautiful as Paris, they say. My boy was killed in a city as beautiful as Paris."

Sam Boggins sections out wet hair with his comb and cuts it off. There is some light from the street, not much, but some.

"And how is Tim?"

"Tim is fine." Another letter had come that day. Against all his father's advice, Tim was still counting.

"Good," nods Waltz. He rolls his beer bottle in his hands like a potter. Sam Boggins is thankful for the motions of his work.

"And how's Eugene?"

"Eugene is in Flint."

"And your girls?"

"My girls are fine," Waltz says. He touches them in his mind, his surviving children, and the feel of them is insubstantial. In thinking of Monroe, he hears firm music.

He says nothing more until Sam finishes and swirls the striped sheet off him. A storm of hair takes place, invisible now in the dark room.

It is a month later, more or less, that Sam Boggins' son Tim is killed in a fire fight in a strange locale. Marathon visibly cringes. Bugle music from Monroe's funeral still hangs in the air. Sam Boggins sits in his closed shop waiting for Harry Waltz. He waits for two days, then the rear door opens and there he is. He has brought two more bottles of beer in the pockets of his suit coat.

He sits for Sam Boggins to cut his hair. When he departs he exercises the lone talent he has built his life around, he pronounces Sam's debt paid, pronounces them even.

3

A winter month of a much earlier year, a storm fills the Michigan air and Waltz keeps his children indoors. He likes to move among them and touch their warm heads. He watches the storm out a rear window. The snow appears to effectively erase from the earth the gazebo in his back yard. Winds blow traceries of snow through the white slat weave; the gazebo roof, a stubby cone of green shingles, is coated and vanishes. He can see the Home buildings where lights burn in the windows. He imagines faces looking out.

Waltz feels safe; his family is warm, his money is out earning money, he feels the brain within his skull ticking smoothly. He feels deservedly lucky. But in the next moment he seeks out a child, Monroe is the first he encounters, to touch his head for luck, and says a prayer, fearing he has used up a favor.

The following day is bright and mild, the packing excellent. The gazebo stands. A green net rises through the melting snow on the roof. His children's laughter awakens Waltz. He sees them through a back window hunched down behind walls of snow built like wings off the sides of the gazebo. They industriously roll snow into balls.

Beyond the State Home fence is a knot of retarded children. They closely watch his children's preparations for what Waltz is certain will be an attack upon them.

Eugene then stands and throws. He has an athlete's good form and release, but lacks power, and the snowball falls well short of the fence. Monroe throws one short, too. The twins' mimicking efforts barely clear the walls they have built.

Waltz, in his robe, smoking a cigarette and drinking a cup of coffee at a kitchen window, laughs to himself. Eugene has committed a tactical blunder. He has failed to take into account the quality of his troops; he has positioned them outside the range of their weapons.

Eugene is then struck squarely in the back of the head with a snowball. It hits so hard he is knocked forward a step and his stocking cap dislodged. The Home children jump and shriek. The boy who threw the snowball is actually a man. An olive knit cap pulled down around his head frames a rapt face stubbled with whiskers. He launches another shot. It rises high and strong over the fence and misses Carla's head by less than a foot. The man crouches and reloads; his motions have a bland concentration that touches Waltz with the sure knowledge that this man will throw snowballs for all eternity until told to do something else. His retardation has placed him beyond the reach of boredom.

Waltz studies Eugene. How will he respond to being behind, on the defensive? Waltz is already worried about his eldest child. Eugene is a boy still, and Louise tells Waltz not to worry so, but he suspects Eugene is a quitter if given the chance. A meanness exists in him, as well.

Eugene arms himself with a snowball in each hand. He says something to Monroe, then jumps over the snow wall. Waltz is pleased: A man of action. He is denying the Home forces the luxury of stationary targets. Monroe follows his older brother over the wall. The twins, Susan taking bites out of a snowball, go around.

The man in the knit cap abandons his arching shots and whips a snowball straight at Eugene. The intent and velocity of the throw startle Waltz and he opens his mouth to cry out. But this is a child's game. The missile disintegrates passing through the fence. Eugene and Monroe return the fire. Their rounds suffer the same fate. Compact projectiles when they leave their hands, they reach their targets in a negligible spray. It is a child's war, fought through a filter. Even twin little girls engage the enemy and survive.

Waltz is encouraged that Eugene is soon bored and wanders off. The fighting ends. A bell that Waltz hears as a faint shimmering in the house's floor summons the Home residents to something they must enjoy, for they turn like oiled toys and run off through the snow.

That summer, Eugene was slapped by his father for committing an act of pure cruelty. This took place on the first Saturday in August, Founder's Day, a blazing, humid day when Eugene was young and jazzed with excitement.

That morning Waltz gave Eugene twenty dimes and Monroe fifteen dimes, because he was younger, to use as they saw fit on the collection of cheap arcades and amusement rides imported for Founder's Day. "Spend them wisely now," Waltz counseled. "When you spend that money, you're done for the day." He gave his twin daughters ten dimes each, and the same speech.

Eugene blew half his stake in the first fifteen minutes attempting to throw wooden rings around the necks of pop bottles. Light a dollar, with the day long before him, he stood back and pushed his hands into his pockets and made them into fists to keep them there. He took a deep breath to shed the panic of poverty. He moved down the midway, an avenue shaped of striped tarpaulin tents and counters polished by the relinquishing of coins. He walked between tents offering balloons to be hit with darts, miniature steam shovels to excavate for treasures on the floor of glass boxes, basketballs to be shot at tight hoops, lead-bottomed bottles to be thrown at. All these temptations pulled like magnets at the money in his pockets.

He reached the end of the midway, where the stink from the pony rides hung. He counted his money and was stunned to see he had four fewer dimes than he thought. He could not remember where he had spent them. He checked his pockets for holes and found none; he felt sucked upon by a phantom.

In one pocket was a pair of Chinese handcuffs. He could not remember how they got there. A flexible tube woven of cheap colored reed, Eugene idly stuck a finger in each end. Trapped. If he pulled to escape, the tube only clutched his fingers tighter.

Eugene shook his head. For this he had paid forty cents? He set himself free and dropped the handcuffs back in his pocket. The day seemed endless now. His money was vanishing without his being aware of the pleasure of spending it.

He cut across the square toward home. He had gone out that morning without eating breakfast and now he was hungry. He would have lunch, then scout the house for stray coins; his mother sometimes left dimes and nickels in small china saucers, or at the bottom of clean ashtrays, mixed with buttons, sewing needles, and pearl-headed pins. Eugene never questioned whether she kept track of this careless bounty; his ability to find the coins and put them in his pocket made them his.

Some kids he knew were hanging around the cannon at the center of the square. Eugene stopped to talk. Lou Basil complained of a lack of money. The others agreed. The boys were thickly caught in that age where wealth was becoming everything and like cats they sensed the few dimes remaining in Eugene's pocket. Eugene played nervously with the Chinese handcuffs; to give himself something to do he allowed himself to be caught.

Joe Knox, the oldest boy in the group, asks, "Where'd you get that?"

"I don't know. I won it somewhere."

"You got money, huh?"

"My daddy gave me some dimes."

"Ooo," Joe Knox teases, "ain't you precious."

Eugene blushed. He wanted to feel a part of this loose cluster of boys. "I can lend you some money," he says.

Joe Knox was interested. "How much?"

"How much do you want?"

"A buck?"

"I don't have it."

"Half a buck?" Joe Knox says.

Eugene counted his money without removing his hand from his

pocket. The dimes went through his fingers like patrons through turnstiles.

"I can lend you thirty cents," he says. "But you'll have to pay me back forty cents by one o'clock."

"Shit," the older boy complains. "Where'll I get forty cents in two hours if I ain't got one cent now?"

Eugene shrugged. He enjoyed this; something was being made clear to him.

Joe Knox says, "Give me the three dimes."

Eugene took three dimes from his pocket. They were warm in his hand and sparkling in the sun. He put out his hand for Joe Knox to shake. "Forty cents by one o'clock," he repeats.

"Sure."

They shook hands and Eugene passed over the money. He continued on across the square and up the hill to his house. In the shade of a birch tree in the side yard he loaned his last three dimes to Lou Basil on the same terms, the boy having circled wide to lose his friends and intercept Eugene.

"I'll give you until two o'clock," Eugene says, feeling generous and lordly.

He ate the lunch his mother prepared for him. Louise was not surprised to see her eldest boy home; she suspected he would be the first to burn his money away.

Eugene found some pennies and a quarter on his parents' dresser, and two dimes and a nickel beneath the cushions of the house's armchairs and sofas. At fifteen minutes to one o'clock he got an apple out of the kitchen and walked back down the hill to the square. The day was hot and still. The midway was deserted. Most of the children had gone home for lunch. He saw Tim Boggins sitting astride the barrel of the cannon.

"Seen Joe Knox?" Eugene asks.

"Nope," Tim says.

Eugene walked three blocks up Alabaster Street, believing it was the way to Joe Knox's house. Already it was twenty after one. A car drove past with a stranger at the wheel. Eugene had no idea what he was doing; just walking stupidly in the heat.

He took a seat on a bus-stop bench in the shade. Looking around anxiously, he feared people had already begun to laugh at him, had already been told by Joe Knox how he had been suckered. He feared word getting back to his father.

The Marathon bus stopped on its way out of town. One person got off and it was Joe Knox. His head was lowered in thought; he had problems of his own.

Eugene was too amazed to stand. "Got my money, Joe?" he asks.

(It was a meeting and a question Joe Knox would describe to himself and to others many times in his life. "I got off the bus and Eugene was sitting waiting for me. Cool as mud. And he asks, 'Got my money?' It was spooky. The son of Harry Waltz, truly.")

Joe Knox repaid Eugene. Three of the four dimes looked familiar. He wondered if Joe Knox even spent the money he borrowed. "Thank you, Joe," Eugene says.

He waited for Lou Basil at two o'clock by the cannon. The town was coming around again. A baseball game began at the high school. Boys ran past and Eugene called to them, "Seen Lou Basil?"

He took a seat in the shade to wait.

A large truck arrived on the square and burly men disembarked. They worked to erect the canvas shelter for the Founder's Day dance that night. Food and ice would be provided. Beer would cool. Somewhere in Detroit the members of the band went about their day knowing they had work that night in Marathon.

Eugene took more interest in the erecting of the shelter than he would otherwise. His money was on the string and it was this money that kept him on the bench in the shade watching grown men perform menial work. He told himself the money was present, that he had not lost it, that it was owed him. He thought of Joe Knox stepping off the bus into his arms. Eugene was young and believed Lou Basil should come to him as easily.

He waited through the afternoon. At four o'clock he made a pass down the midway looking for his debtor. There was a snap to the day now; the worst of the heat had passed and adults were pushing onto the scene and taking over with their easy money. They felt the night growing in the distance.

Eugene saw Monroe but ignored him. He talked to some boys but none of them had seen Lou Basil. He left behind word that he was looking hard for him. He watched the baseball game played between adults. They were raucous, beery, semi-inept. Eugene sat expecting Lou Basil to tap him on the shoulder any minute.

When Eugene left the game at six o'clock the feeling he had was of sad completion. Much light remained but the day was irrevocably past. Darkness and fireworks lay ahead, and food and the music of the band from Detroit, and men and women dancing, but for Eugene the day was spent.

He took his seat on the square but the sun had swung the shade away. Lou Basil rode a bicycle on the other side of the square. He was pedaling hard; Eugene was sure Basil had seen him. He called out but Basil kept going. Eugene knew where Lou Basil lived but he would not go after him; it was Basil's responsibility to bring the money he owed.

A black Cadillac hearse drove onto the square and parked by the tent. Five lean men in seersucker sport coats and string ties emerged. They stretched and laughed and lighted cigarettes in the assurance of a night of music. Instruments were unloaded from the rear. Thin sheaves of chrome unfolded into music stands. One of the musicians put together a small drum kit. Another worked the slide on a trombone; others tuned. A pretty girl, the singer, would arrive later.

On the other side of this encampment Eugene saw Monroe, drawn like a bug to light, taking in the combo's two-bit aura. He also saw Lou Basil on his bicycle, and their eyes locked. "Come and pay me the money you owe," Eugene says, just loud enough to hear it himself. "Come and do the right thing."

But Lou Basil pedaled around the square and Eugene pivoted in his seat to keep him in sight. He would not chase him: It was not his place.

At that point on Lou Basil's orbit farthest from Eugene, he yells, "I'm not paying you back!"

"Yes, you are," Eugene says to himself.

"My dad says you're just a shylock like your dad!"

The men in the band looked out at the boy on the bicycle. The guitarist said something and the others laughed.

"You owe me money, Lou Basil. You shook my hand," Eugene says, but his words were softly spoken, he did not mean them to carry.

He waited another hour. The lights strung through the eaves and crown of the tent came on and the band returned from dinner. The singer arrived. Tuning filled the air. Pink strips of sunlight were stretched taut at the horizon. Men and women began to arrive, most paired, some shyly alone. The band kicked things off with "The Darktown Strutters' Ball."

Eugene could hear it all the way home. He hid in the gazebo. He heard his mother, then his father, call for him. He answered neither. He felt lost to them with his money on the string. He felt defied and cowardly.

The square burned like a jewel at Eugene's back. The night was perfect. His parents would dance a single dance amidst the people who owed his father money, then they would depart, bringing Monroe and Carla and Susan along, leaving behind word that should anyone see Eugene he was also to come straight home.

A pale face floated toward Eugene within the Home grounds. It was a young man in blue jeans with rolled cuffs, black shoes, and white shirt. He stopped at the fence and grinned when Eugene came out of the gazebo.

" 'Lo," the young man says.

"Hello," Eugene replies. He removed the Chinese handcuffs from his pocket. All day he had carried the stupid little reed tube he did not even recall getting. It was all he had to show for the day. He had money on the string and he had been called a shylock, too, but he seemed unable to do anything about it. The money would remain on the string and word would pass with it: Eugene Waltz, the touch.

In a sudden angry motion he screwed one end of the Chinese handcuffs down hard on the retarded man's pudgy index finger that curled through the fence. Eugene smiled to reassure the man everything was all right. The man held the finger up to his eyes; he sniffed the reed and grinned.

"This is fun," Eugene says. "Give me your other hand."

Fat fingers came through the chain link fence. Eugene took hold of one and uncertainty flickered in the man's eyes. Eugene smiled again. He says, "Fun." He pushed the man's finger into the open end of the handcuffs. It was so easy.

"There, you big goobie," Eugene says, and the mocking tone in his voice made the retarded man frown. He pulled against his fragile and deceptive bonds. Slow connections were made; a small but vital part of him was trapped on the other side of the fence.

"Don't go away," Eugene says. "I'll be right back."

A half hour later he was in his room when he heard the man cry out. It was not a frightened sound, only sad that he had been abandoned.

Eugene could see the man from his window. Each time the man cried Eugene heard his father move a little closer to the sound. First up from his desk, then going downstairs, then standing in the shadows near the back of the house. His father paused between these advances to listen, to take his bearings on that sorrowful cry.

Light washed over the back yard. Eugene studied his father stalking across the lawn. Another shylock, what did he do when the money he was owed was not paid back?

His father fussed at the fence a minute, then the retarded man ran free, the white tail of his shirt jumping like a scut in the dark.

Waltz went directly to Eugene's room and dropped the Chinese handcuffs on his bed. He asks, "These yours?"

"Yes," Eugene says. His father slapped him once on the face. It left a mark, a faint hand.

"That was an act of pure cruelty," Waltz says. "I've never been more ashamed of anyone in my life."

"It was a game. I was gonna let him go."

"If anything like this happens again you won't have any free time for a year," Waltz warns.

"It won't," Eugene says. He wouldn't touch the Chinese handcuffs. His possession of them a mystery, they haunted him.

"It better not," Waltz says. He took a deep breath; he was appalled his own son disgusted him. He says in a gentler voice, "I heard you loaned some money today."

Eugene looked quickly at his father. "Who said?"

"I talked to some people at the dance. I heard you charged interest."

"I did it just like you do. Make money with money."

"That's different," Waltz says. He sat beside Eugene. "Loaning money to your friends, you shouldn't charge interest."

"They weren't really my friends."

Waltz asks, "They pay you back?"

"One did. One didn't."

"What are you going to do about it?"

"I don't know."

Waltz says, "He has to pay you back."

"He said he wouldn't. He told me he wouldn't."

"You didn't make a gift of the money, did you?"

"No."

"Of course you didn't. You're not stupid. It's your money he's got. He's got to pay it back. Do you understand?"

"What should I do?"

"Go talk to him," Waltz says.

"He won't listen. He already told me he won't pay the money back. He called me a shylock."

Waltz says, "It doesn't matter what he calls you. Talk to him in the right way and he'll pay the money. He *has* to pay, Eugene. He's only a boy but already he has his honor."

4

Waltz telephones Tipton to ask if he has the money he owes and Tipton promises that he does. Waltz drives up Route 15 to Vassar, where Tipton lives in a cottage on the Cass River. A minute after

Waltz arrives he knows Tipton does not have the money. He can tell by Tipton's pained, deadbeat expression.

"I'll have to take the Sony," Waltz says. Out a back window he can see the river. He can't understand wanting to live so close to an instrument of nature. He asks idly, "Aren't you afraid of floods?"

He sees Tipton's face fill with hope at this human element in the shark before him. Talk of floods, nature, gives Tipton air in his constricted chest to turn and breathe. "I don't think about it," he says. "I got flood insurance."

"Do you think about the four-fifty you're late with?" Waltz asks.

"All the time."

It is the truth, Waltz knows. It is something he noticed from the start in the men and women who owe him. They think about almost nothing else. Not husband nor wife, not sex, not work, not even that which drew them into debt in the first place. They think only about the note Waltz holds with their name on it.

"I've got thirty," Tipton says. Three tens he presents, damp and sordid, looking fished from the river.

"That does me no good," Waltz says.

"Then what happens?"

He expects violence, Waltz understands. He expects Waltz, a man of sixty-one, a peaceful man, to break his legs. "You tell me," Waltz says.

"I can give you thirty. I heard you take a little at a time."

"The four-fifty you owe *is* a little at a time, compared to the total you owe. You want to pay a little on a little now?"

"I get paid in a week. I can pay you then."

"How will you eat? How will you buy gas to get to work?"

Tipton shrugs miserably.

"Go get the Sony. You have any coffee?"

Waltz sits at the kitchen table. Being off his feet is a luxury. His legs ache, not all the time, but more than he would like, and his left leg never really got over being broken the day JFK was shot. His daddy set it and cast it and he can walk on it, but it has never felt exactly right since. A piece of coldness, marble-sized, is how he pictures the ache; a piece of cold got into the broken bone before it was put back together and now this cold is inside there, with him for life.

Tipton puts a cup of coffee on the table and leaves the room. Waltz sips the coffee and smokes and looks out at the river. Ducks land on it, bouncing in on their downy butts. Two girls paddle by in a canoe. He might learn to like living by a river. A house might be safe if built up high enough. He refills his coffee cup. Tipton makes soft noises moving in another room. Waltz is patient; he is not about to leave without his money or a reasonable facsimile.

A silver boat ties up at Tipton's dock. A tall woman in canvas pants and a checked flannel shirt pulls an outboard motor clear of the water. A slim woman, nearly hipless, she loses her balance in the boat for an instant and Waltz thinks she will go over into the river. But she recovers with a clever shift of weight, wipes her hands, and springs up onto the dock.

The woman's presence confuses Waltz. In the basic research he did on Tipton this woman did not appear. Tipton lives alone, he works in Saginaw, he is good for the money, he is not going to get crazy if pressed and shoot somebody.

The woman is out on the cottage's back porch a minute unlacing her boots. She lets herself in with her own key. White hair is tied in a shock behind her. In her forties somewhere, Waltz guesses, though the white hair makes her look older.

Waltz stands, a mannered reflex, but also from discomfort with her authoritative height and her sense of belonging.

She sees Waltz but looks past him to the door where Tipton disappeared. She asks, "You the loan shark?"

"I'm Harry Waltz. Who are you?"

"I'm the fool's sister." She pours herself some coffee. She refuses Waltz's offer to light her cigarette. "Where is he?"

Waltz points to the doorway.

"How much does he owe you?"

"Today, four hundred fifty dollars."

"Does he have it?"

"He has thirty," Waltz says.

"What interest do you charge?" Her eyes are canny and patient. He guesses she has never married, or married young then shed the man like ill-fitting clothes; she is not one for the false.

"I charge what the market will bear," Waltz says.

She shrugs, squints through smoke. "In times like these," she muses, "with interest rates so high, I would think any derelict could borrow money from legitimate lenders. They're so anxious to give their money away at seventeen, eighteen percent. Why bother with you?"

Waltz smiles wryly; he feels he has to sell himself to this woman. "I'm flexible. In times like these I can give my customers little breaks here and there. I can take a little off the going rate. I'm unofficial. I don't ask what the money's for. I have a heart. Why, do you need money?"

She goes to the phone without answering him. For ten minutes she makes calls that Waltz absently listens in on. She cancels someone's gas service, newspapers, and electricity.

"You moving?" he asks.

"Helping a client sell a house. The phone's already out. That's why I'm here. They're in a hurry to get off the river." Then she is quiet. Calm becomes her. Waltz feels excited by the coffee and this woman's presence. He needs to piss badly.

"Go find him," he finally tells the woman.

"He'll be out. He only hides so long."

"I have to get going."

"What happens now? If he can't pay you, what happens?"

"Tell him to come out here and we'll arrange something."

"Are you going to beat him up?" she asks. Her tone is faintly humorous, almost hopeful, as though common sense and frugality can be beaten into her brother.

"No," Waltz says. "Please go get him now."

"He can hear us. He's hiding just around the corner."

As if shamed, Tipton reappears. "Hello, Mare," he murmurs. He carries the Sony, the plug trailing on the floor.

"Are we even now?" he asks.

Waltz sighs. "No. You've still got the rest of your debt."

"That's an expensive TV," Tipton complains. "You could strip me clean."

"Other people in my business would break your arm for the same thing." Waltz shudders; he feels falsely sinister with the inflections his voice takes in these situations. Is it for the woman's benefit? Her brother called her Mare.

"I don't threaten," Waltz says carefully, "and I don't hurt people. But one way or another you've got to pay me what you owe."

Waltz sits back down at the table. His bladder is so full he thinks if he pulled up his shirt he could see it through his skin. The woman has gone to the window looking on the river. White hair hangs almost to her waist. She is lean like Waltz; he has her fainthearted, dim-witted brother on a string. Mare? Short for Mary?

Waltz writes a fresh note. "You want to hold on to your TV?" he asks.

"What do I have to do?"

Waltz explains, "I can lend you the money to cover what you owe today. I'll have to raise your rate a bit, of course, but it will settle us for now. You'll owe me more next week but you won't have to miss any of your shows."

Tipton bites his lip and grinds a tear out of his eye. He looks to his sister but she has abandoned him, she has gone outside for her boots and kneels by the door lacing them up. Tipton has no choice but to sign the note; it will give him a week more to worry. He takes Waltz's pen, a fountain pen that scratches like olden times over the paper, and signs the note. Waltz blows the inked strokes dry and folds the note away in his pocket.

A quarter mile from Tipton's cottage Waltz turns down a small lane he hopes will take him to the river. He follows sensations, the pull of the river on the taut lake of urine sitting in his very center. He had thought to ask to use the bathroom at the cottage but his chance passed when Tipton signed the note; with that act Tipton bought a week's immunity and arrogance to use on Waltz.

The vehicle Waltz drives, a 1980 Ford Bronco, once belonged to a man laid off in Flint; it is a sign of the times. It moves easily down the lane. After fifteen minutes of winding among thin pines and shadowy houses he comes to the river. He stands on a fallen tree and unzips his trousers.

This is how the white-haired woman comes upon him. She is in her silver boat out in the center of the river and only when Waltz sees her looking at him does he hear the low mutter of the outboard, like someone blowing through a straw into a glass of water. He stands at the edge of the river pissing with the sun on him. He is not half finished. Her eyes are calm and fixed upon him. She does not look away. She even pivots her head to watch him as he finishes, shakes himself, and tucks himself away. He blows her a kiss. Her head snaps around then and he knows he has hit her perfectly.

Waltz makes some calls when he gets back to Marathon. No Mary Tiptons anywhere. He tries his acquaintance in Saginaw, the man who put Tipton's name forward as a potential customer. Waltz begins by complaining about Tipton's inability to pay.

"I'm surprised," the man says. "I didn't think that was going to be a problem."

"It's no problem," Waltz says. "I just would have liked to avoid the wear and tear."

"I understand, Harry. I'm sorry."

"He signed a second note to cover the first."

The man groans. "No brains."

"Fewer than that. His sister had it right when she called him a fool."

"Mary was there?"

"Tall? Long white hair? She said she was the fool's sister."

"That's her. Hard to believe she's his kid sister," the man says. "She's a lawyer in Saginaw. Has a house on the bay."

"Is her name Tipton, too?"

"No, she uses her married name. Hale."

He opens his mail, gathers the money from his debtors, marks his books. He dials information and is told Mary Hale's number is unlisted. This is half taken as a personal rebuke. Then again, he is asking after a married woman and this dead end he strikes is something of a relief; he will never be required to put himself forward. Nevertheless, he is charged with a suitor's anxiety. He decides to press the matter, he tells himself he might need the practice with a future woman. He dials information a second time and is given without question a work number for Mary Hale, attorney at law, in Saginaw. He copies the number on a scrap of envelope and puts it in a slotted block of wood he uses to hold letters. The phone number sits alongside an unopened letter from Eugene. The letter, and Mary Hale's number, arm that section of his desk with emotion. He works steadily for another hour, sorting through potential debtors, recommendations, pleas, his web of strings. But he works conscious of those two small bombs on his desk. He might touch them and set them off. With Eugene's letter he knows he is relatively safe, he has been working around his son's letters for so long he has created a sequence of actions that protects him. He is safe until Eugene's next letter arrives. Mary Hale's number, though, is raw and volatile. He has to think back years to pick out memories that help him understand it. It makes him so nervous he finally snaps off the light and leaves the room. He is not ready for this yet.

In a week it is again time to drive to Vassar. He wants to see the white-haired woman, so he does not call ahead; he needs a reason to make the trip and fears Tipton will foil him, saying the money is in the mail.

Tipton has a surprise. He hands Waltz fresh bills. Waltz counts them and it's exactly what Tipton owes that week.

"Who'd you borrow the money from?" Waltz asks. He has been made to stand on the cottage's small front stoop. Tipton blocks his entrance; the rooms over his shoulder are dark, keeping their inhabitants a mystery to Waltz.

Tipton angrily replies, "It's none of your damn business where I got the money."

"Your sister?"

"I've paid you what I owe today. I want you to leave now."

"No offer of coffee?"

"No. Beat it."

"Can I have a light?" Waltz puts a cigarette in his mouth. He darts into the cottage behind Tipton. No silver boats are tied at the dock. Only the river moves, and Waltz must study it a long moment to verify its motion.

He lights the cigarette and shakes out the match. Tipton herds him toward the door like a sheep dog. Waltz makes an appointment for the next month, then departs. He expected the woman to be there. He expected her to remember the hour of his arrival from the previous week and to come at that hour today. Waltz takes the same winding lane to the river. He pisses off the same fallen tree. The texture of the day is different. Rain has not fallen in a week and the river is down. Sticks pivot slowly by.

No boats. No white-haired women. He takes off his shirt, then his shoes, pants, socks, underwear. He stands naked daring her to appear. His body is nearly as white as her hair, common as age, and excited by his stand there at the river's edge. But the river is flat and unoccupied. A kingfisher plucks something golden from the water. Waltz thinks he hears this caught thing scream and his sense of things out of place is complete.

5

His life with women was one of emotional espionage. He had been a spy in another life. There had even been a long period of time when he approached his own twin daughters only covertly, when he watched them hidden from a distance.

Twins ran in the Waltz family. Daddy Waltz and his brother Ogden, Waltz and Aaron, twins deep back through the generations. And Carla and Susan. The two girls early on created the balance in their duality. Carla was the protector, Susan the lump of beauty. Carla considered her twin sister the more beautiful and so took it upon herself to guide Susan through life to preserve that beauty. Carla selected her sister's clothes and in the morning sliced a banana into her bowl of cereal. Returning from school one afternoon they were caught in a hailstorm. Carla threw her coat over Susan's head, took her by the arm, and led her home like a horse from a fire. She feared the hail would pit Susan's face.

Waltz put an end to Susan's reliance on her sister when he learned Carla had been doing Susan's schoolwork for her. It was the year Louise died, the twins were thirteen years old, and their mother's death precipitated a closing together within themselves; they became the two halves of a perfect sphere.

Waltz put his arm around Carla one afternoon and walked her out to the gazebo.

"How long have you been doing Susan's schoolwork?" he asks.

"Who says I have?"

"Me. Daddy Waltz. Grandma. How long?"

"About two years," she says.

"Why?"

"It's easy for me."

"But Susan doesn't learn anything."

"Neither do I."

"Don't be a smart-ass," Waltz says. "You've done more harm than good."

"She counts on me," Carla says. "She'll be a favorite all her life."

Waltz says, "Her grades are good. She must be learning something."

Carla slyly grins. "I took her tests, Daddy. We *are* identical twins."

Waltz sees a scheme unfolding. Each facet is a small weight hung like an ornament on his image of Susan. "What if you both had tests at the same time?"

Carla laces her fingers on her lap. Waltz sees she is proud of herself. These are questions she expected him to ask.

"Picture this," she says. "Susan and I both have a test third period. We wear matching outfits, right down to the shoes, jewelry, the works. We comb our hair the same way. Third period arrives, Susan goes to my class, I go to Susan's. I take her test and get an A. Susan, as Carla, pretends to get sick just before the test is handed out. Carla is a straight-A student, she contributes in class, turns in all her homework, so the teacher doesn't think twice about letting her go to the nurse. Carla recovers and takes a make-up test after school. Gets an A. It's foolproof."

Waltz sits thinking in the gazebo's slatted shadows, they rest like a net thrown over his shoulders. He recalls tales of Daddy Waltz and Ogden, and tricks he and Aaron pulled, each event turning on the frictionless jewel of their identicality. It was a way of being in two places at once; it was like living two lives.

But those were harmless stratagems played for laughs. This with his daughters cut to the root of what sort of life Susan had ahead of her.

"You can't live her life for her," Waltz says. "What happens when Susan is an adult and has to do things for herself?"

"Oh, Daddy . . ."

The back door swings open. Waltz and Carla turn and spy through the gazebo's web at Susan on the back porch in the sun, which casts her in gold. Carla draws in her breath. "Isn't she beautiful?" she whispers, proud, and smug, too, for they are identical twins, after all. "She'll always have someone to look after her. She'll always be a favorite."

When his daughters entered high school something of a siege of boys began. Carla had been right: Susan was the favorite. Boys clung to her trail like scouts. They dogged her through town, knowing they must summon the courage to approach her before she reached the imposing house on the hill, with its ever-changing configuration of automobiles out front, for that house was off limits to Marathon's children.

Also, Susan moved in public always in Carla's presence. A boy would have to possess the gumption to approach twin beauties in order to get to Susan; and quite often the boys could not be certain who was who until Susan's quiet docility flowed forth, less assured, less threatening, and hence more appealing, than Carla's frank confidence in herself.

Without Carla taking her tests Susan slid into the lower middle ranges of academic standing. Waltz watched her fall and waited for her native intelligence to halt the slide. He believed the system of dependence built in her would break down at some point, and then he would begin to help her put something of her own together. He helped her with her homework every single night of high school. They grappled like cats over the kitchen table. Waltz thought of it as a chipping away; he could not imagine what Susan thought of it. He did not dare back off, saying, "Come see me if you have any questions," for fear of never seeing her again. Also, he fought the impulse to take Carla's place and do the work for her. "You must learn to think for yourself" was the litany he repeated over and over.

When the hour of the evening's date arrived Susan left by the front door and met the night's boy at the corner of the Waltz property. On warm evenings she sat on the grass smoking a cigarette, believing that keeping her body between the cigarette and the house would hide the fact of her smoking. It touched and saddened Waltz, watching from his office, that she did not take into account the smoke rising off her, that she was evidently that dumb.

Her beauty was legend in Marathon. On some days she received more mail than her father. The envelopes were thick with lockets, many-paged letters, bracelets woven of clover, shy mementos. She and her father sat down over her schoolwork at five o'clock and concluded by eight o'clock. Susan then underwent a quick ministration at Carla's hand. Into a dress, fresh make-up, then out the front door she went, always home by midnight.

On a particular evening Carla stood in the front foyer watching Susan get into her date's car at the corner. In Carla's hands were lipstick, eyeliner, hairpins, compact, a comb, and a brush. Waltz watched beside her.

"This is when I miss Mom most," Carla suddenly admits. Waltz nods. Carla says, "She's changed so much since you put your foot down."

"There was no choice, Carla. She'd have been lost someday."

"I don't know."

"She still needs you to do her make-up. You tell her what to wear."

Carla comes away from the window and burns her father with a pained look. He follows her upstairs to the bathroom, where she puts away the cosmetics. She has a cigarette going in a blue dish. With her father watching her she takes it up and draws off it. Waltz sees no point in fighting her. He is living with strange women. He lights a cigarette for himself off hers.

"Why don't the boys come to the door?" he asks.

"You can guess."

"No, I can't."

"Their folks tell them to stay away. Our house—your home—is off limits."

"Because of my job?"

"Because of how you make your living. They're afraid you'll get your hooks into their children."

"That's absurd," Waltz declares. He looks at his hands; hooks. He is pictured hovering in the shadows of his own house with offers of money at attractive terms for his daughter's suitors.

"How many people owe you money, Daddy?"

"It varies. Some borrow fresh and some finish paying what they owe. It changes day to day."

"How many right this moment?"

Waltz disappears for an hour. His daughter's question waits all that time. He could tell her the number; he knows it precisely. Relating it to Carla, however, would make him uncomfortable. Part of it is shame, he supposes, that his work is not something that allows his children's friends to approach the house. And part of it is a fear his answer will be appealing and lure his daughter into the same line of work. Eugene is already in it. When no music comes from Monroe's room or from the piano downstairs, Waltz worries he, too, is plotting his rate of return.

Carla comes into his office and stands by his desk. The question will form again on her lips, he thinks, but she surprises him, telling him something he has known a long time: "Eugene is lending money."

"He has for quite some time."

"What do you do to people who don't pay you back?"

"Everybody pays. It's that simple."

"But what would you do if someone didn't pay you back?"

"I'd talk to them," Waltz answers. "I'd take what they put up as collateral. I only deal with adults, Carla. That's why it's silly for your friends to stay away from here. Their parents know where to find me."

A moment later, Carla asks, "What's a shylock?"

"Is that what they call me?"

"Some do."

"Does it hurt your feelings?"

"I don't know what it means. It hurts me that they have a name for you."

"Shylock," Waltz says, "is a character from Shakespeare. *The Merchant of Venice.* He loaned money. So, ever since, people who loan money have been called shylocks, or shys, most often by people who borrowed the money in the first place."

"I heard," Carla revealed carefully, "that Eugene beat up a boy who didn't pay him back on time."

"Is that true?"

"It's what I've been told," Carla says.

Susan returns from her dates before the stroke of the new day. She is punctual in that way; it is a matter of trust Waltz cherishes. Waiting in the dark, he watches the headlights of her date's car swing off Columbia and up the driveway. The boy comes around the car to her door and for the few moments it takes Susan to emerge and the door to close she is bathed in faint, warm interior light. And in this light he tries to read her moods from a distance, how she likes this boy, what he means to her.

Even at midnight, with only the porch light on, the shy asleep inside, the boys won't bring Susan to the door. They plant kisses on her by the car and she walks the rest of the way alone. Waltz is sometimes tempted to go outside and help her home. When she is safely inside Waltz gets up and meets her downstairs, feeling it is important she knows he waits up for her.

Carla enrolled at the University of Michigan in the autumn of 1966. Three weeks later Susan packed and followed her sister to Ann Arbor. She rented a small apartment on the edge of the campus. Carla kept her dorm residence but spent her nights with her sister.

They were a sensation, those beautiful twins. Other students from in and around Marathon (Flint, Davison, Clio, Columbiaville, Imlay City) transported their history. Waltz, in the retelling, became evil. His daughters became the offspring of a gangster. Tales flourished of men killed for money borrowed and unpaid, of chopped thumbs, of unexplained disappearances. Their living together in an apartment was further evidence, as was their being so beautiful. The apartment became the site of mythical gatherings, gangster orgies, night shootings. Blood was reported on the windows Sunday mornings. Naked women were seen running through the lamplight.

In truth, there were no men in the lives of Waltz's daughters. They had made a home and ventured outside only to shop or for Carla to attend class. Susan stayed home reading her sister's textbooks. At long last, her father's lessons had taken hold. She was in Ann Arbor because she loved her sister and missed her when they were apart. But she was on her own, finally. She felt at peace, her mind growing effortlessly.

Men, boys really, did not approach the twins because of who they were rumored to be. The stories attached to them were so complex, pervasive, and imaginative that they bore the weave of truth. And frankly, the boys at school in that year lacked the motivation to pursue mysterious beauties. They had problems of their own. They were most often hard at work avoiding the war. They lacked the spirit to take on the troubles of a gangster's beautiful twin daughters.

• • •

A year passed and in 1967 the war the college boys struggled so diligently to avoid took Monroe Waltz. Carla and Susan went home to Marathon for two weeks. Eugene, now a denizen of Flint, came and stayed two days, sleeping on the couch, never going upstairs. He was twenty-two years old, nearly as tall as Waltz, and his father was unaccountably afraid of him. When Eugene returned to Flint, Waltz wept, that he had said barely a word to his only surviving son; but he was tremendously relieved that he was gone, too.

Carla and Susan returned to Ann Arbor after the two weeks had passed. They had taken a larger apartment. Like old veterans of an endless campaign, they resumed their charade of identicality. This time, however, it was Susan taking Carla's place, braiding her hair and donning jeans and silk blouses and going to class.

The balance between the sisters was serene. Susan, in response to her brother's death, found she wanted to get out in the air and sun again after a year of interior life. Carla, for the same reason, felt shell-like and sad. She wanted to sleep, and when awake she wanted to avoid sensation. She blessed Susan and sent her forth. Neither woman was surprised when Susan did work as fine as Carla.

In the aftermath of Monroe's death Carla and Susan decided they had no desire to see their father. Perhaps he reminded them of Monroe, perhaps they resented their father's inability to protect Monroe, arguably the family's best, while Eugene, arguably the worst, survived. No formal declaration of separation was required; the women just never left Ann Arbor. For two years they did not see their father.

Waltz was patient. Although lacking specific reasons, he understood the basic emotions keeping him from his daughters. The space around him after Monroe died felt cramped and sore even to only himself. The one person whose company he could stand was

Sam Boggins, they met frequently after his shop closed to drink beer and talk, or to get Waltz's hair cut.

He was not sure which daughter was attending classes. He paid the bills and waited. On days he felt strong he drove south on Route 23 and parked in the shade across from his daughters' apartment. He packed a lunch, a container of coffee, cigarettes and matches, the day's paper, and spent eight hours. It was like a job he loved. Circumspect about these trips south, he feared arrest as a voyeur or a spy. The car was repossessed, so his daughters would not recognize it. He in turn feared not recognizing his daughters.

Three windows of their apartment faced the street. One was vertically shaded with an American flag. Plants in orange pots lined the sills. Fragile diamond shapes of cranberry glass hung from the latches on line so hair-fine and taut they seemed to levitate. A hand slipped through drawn curtains to retrieve a cup and saucer. Waltz ducked away as though the hand had eyes. But whose hand was it?

He saw Eugene, in from Flint, enter the building and stay the afternoon. Waltz feared for his daughters. He left when his son did. Carla and Susan were safe again, and he felt horribly excluded, cut off from the remainder of his family like some lame animal while they continued life in this fantasy college town.

Now and then he saw one of his daughters, Carla or Susan, he could not say which. They were still tall and beautiful, their hair was a darker gold than he remembered, and worn very long. They wore calf-length dresses and heavy, workmanlike leather boots. Had they always looked so grim? Waltz thought they were too pale. He wanted to see them walking arm in arm in the sun to be convinced of the existence of them both.

On a day whose memory Waltz supposed would be with him always, he fell asleep in his car and awoke an hour later within a quiet river of people—students, kids, men, and women—marching past him. Nobody noticed him, he was not harassed, but he felt vulnerable and exposed; they might have been marching past his bed at home.

He opened the car door and slipped out. The river nearly

pulled him along, a few strangers grabbed his arms and urged him to join them, but he broke free and made his way to the front of the car, and from there climbed onto the roof.

Up and down the street for as far as he could see, people marching, absolutely quiet. Some carried candles in small paper disks to catch the wax. Others wore peace signs painted on their faces. The mood was of condemnation. Placards were few; there was just marching, a tightly focused coming together. No longer was there a need to name the purpose.

Waltz sat on the roof of the car with his feet on the windshield smoking a cigarette. A green-faced girl called to him to join them. Someone jeered when Waltz smiled and shook his head.

A door across the street opened. His eyes were drawn to the motion. A daughter of his emerged holding the hand of a young man taller than herself. His hair was curly, he wore a tie. His daughter kissed this man on the mouth and this single action, the angle of her head, the slight rising on the balls of her feet, some memory of all those nights spent watching her return from dates, confirmed to Waltz that this was Susan. She was twenty-one years old, a phenomenon of time that astounded him.

She was looking at her father now. Waltz had glanced away to take in the march and when he looked back she was watching him. He raised his hand to her, embarrassed at being caught, and to be caught sitting atop his car.

She smiled, which thrilled him, then spoke to the man she was with. Then she went back inside the apartment.

Waltz looked up at the three windows facing the street. He understood this was where the next brief contact would be made. In a moment a hand drew back the flag and one of his daughters looked out. Waltz did not know which one. He had not intended this reunion but now that it was proceeding he did not want it to fail. They know I'm here, Waltz thinks. Am I so abhorrent they will continue to shun me?

The young man waiting by the door watches him. His demeanor is good-natured and assured. From a distance, Waltz likes him. He thinks he reads in the young man the fact he will never owe money. He is of a better cut than those individuals Waltz deals with.

The march is thinning. The people bringing up the rear seem less intense. They laugh, talk, pass joints, sing, do cartwheels, walk on their hands. A few elderly people hurry along as best they can; their disgusted countenances convey that they do not want to be at the tail of this column of protest, in league with these stoned children, but that immutable physical laws prevent them from advancing any faster. Waltz thinks they are missing the point.

Susan is across the street again, holding the young man's hand, and calling to her father.

"Did you come for the march, Daddy?"

Waltz shakes his head. His impulse is to be stubborn, to not speak a word until she crosses the street to him.

"Why are you here then?" she calls.

"Come closer," he says, waving them to cross.

"We have to go," and she points up the street where the body of the march is disappearing over a hill; this is important to her, Waltz realizes. If they wait too long they will be separated from the marchers, they might be just another empty-headed couple on their way to the movies. They need that tie to the movement.

"Where's Carla?" Waltz asks.

"Upstairs."

"Can I talk to her?"

"Of course you can, silly," she says. Waltz is embarrassed and annoyed; no one has ever called him silly before.

"Who's your friend?"

"This is Willy," she announces. Like a candidate for office, this young man breaks away from Susan and dashes across the street. He is nearly as tall as Waltz, though on the car Waltz towers over him, and runs with an athlete's ease. His action surprises Susan and puts a pained look on her face, which pleases Waltz and makes him like Willy even more.

He shakes Waltz's hand. "I'm Willy Conover," he says. "Don't tell Susan or Carla, but I'm asking for your daughter's hand in marriage right now."

"Which daughter?"

Willy laughs. "Susan. I know this is abrupt, I don't expect an answer right away. But I hope you'll give me a chance. This is like fate. All the time I've known Carla and Susan I've asked to meet you. I asked again today. Now here you are. Here we are."

"She looks angry," Waltz says.

Willy does not look back. "I know," he says. "Keep me in mind, Mr. Waltz."

"Call me Harry," he says, but Willy has pivoted and run back across the street.

So Waltz settles to wait. The car is warm beneath him. The day is perfectly crafted. With the silent river gone past, everything is somehow better. The marchers were too self-aware, they projected a sense of watching themselves march. He has lost a son; that is protest enough.

He lights a cigarette. A breeze pushes a curtain of his daughters' apartment aside. Nothing to be seen there. It is all shadows within.

Waltz is conscious of his waiting now. Before, when he was a secret, it was a vigil without a frame of time. Now he is clearly waiting. She knows he is down there. He has set himself up to be disappointed. Even in his mind he dares not place an ultimatum before her (ten minutes, an hour, before sundown) that she must appear within. Such a barrier of time would only agonize him when he was forced to revise it.

If he had a stone and a good arm he could throw the stone at their window, a juvenile suitor's tactic. He has only his cigarettes. He could drop one lit down the gas tank of the car and jump back. The explosion would get her attention. It would have a revolutionary feel to it; a bit of the war brought home.

But he lacks something to get him started. He is too law-abiding. Consequences come to him too clearly. How would he get home? And what if even after the explosion Carla still did not appear? What if after all this time she had turned mean?

So he lights another cigarette and waits. He passes time counting the people who owe him money. The number has been higher but times are good for the nation at the moment. The economy percolates with war. He is a student of human needs and he understands his business will rise and fall according to the way the world conducts itself. But he also knows the line of work he has chosen is solid and nearly eternal, people always need money, and in every town there are people who need more money than they can get their hands on (it stupefied him, when he was just starting seriously in the business, how many of these people walked the earth) and for this multitude Waltz exists.

He never went looking for business. He did not advertise. He was simply a success. Newcomers to Marathon were shown his house; realtors driving by said, "There's the home of the local shy." He has lent money every day of the month, so every day of the month he has money coming back in. He is proud that he has never forced anyone to sign one of his notes.

Waltz guesses at the hour. He has to be getting back. He estimates an hour and a half has passed since the march ended.

He climbs down off the car. Gone stiff in the back and in his JFK leg, he groans and twists, standing in the street trying to get loose again. And not even fifty years old, either; not even halfway there.

If Carla is watching from deep in her rooms he wants her to know he is preparing to leave. He is giving her a last chance to show herself. Waltz tells himself he did not really expect it. He is the intruder. When she wants to see him she will come and see him. Carla has never been one to proceed on terms other than her own. They are both, Carla and Waltz, still mourning Monroe, though two years have passed and he suspects his grief might be getting morbid. Also, he hates to see Carla folding away. Mourning does not require her own spiritual death as well. He wishes he could see her to tell her this.

And when he opens the car door and gets in, Carla is sitting there in the passenger seat with a cigarette of her own going. She smiles, and says, "Still as self-absorbed as ever, I see."

"How long have you been here?"

"Since the march went by."

"Why didn't you say something?"

"Surprise."

"Jesus. You did. How did you get in without me seeing you?"

Carla smiles, a smile filled with wit, brains, and wisdom. Here is my favorite now, he thinks. "I just went out the back way and circled around behind you," she says. "The door was unlocked, so I just got in. You were in that ozone you frequently inhabit." She shrugs elaborately. "It was a piece of cake."

"I'm lucky you weren't the Cong," he says.

She frowns, her motions of lighting another cigarette are brittle. He has moved too abruptly out of the safe wood. He is imagining, also, what would have happened if he had followed through on his idea to blow up the car. He shudders, then leans over and kisses her on the cheek.

"I'm glad to see you," he says.

"Let's you and me go to Marathon," Carla suggests. "Susan will be with Willy all night. I'll call her later and tell her where I went."

"You're sure?"

"Yes, I'm sure. This is the first time since Monroe died that I've had the nerve to leave this town."

"Do you want to pack?"

"No!" she says, becoming exasperated. "I want to be moving."

Waltz and his daughter do not talk on the way home. They smoke and watch the sun go down.

At home, Carla reaches Susan at Willy's apartment.

"I'm in Marathon," she says. "I don't want you to worry about me. I'm safe."

Carla listens for a minute. Waltz watches her. Daddy Waltz is there. Carla gives her father a quick, inspecting look, then says, "Yes, he's human. I don't know exactly why I came back here. When I think of a reason I'll let you know."

She listens some more. She makes a bored face at the other people in the kitchen; with her fingers she forms a chattering mouth. Daddy Waltz laughs.

They have turned, Waltz thinks. Now it is Susan on the watch for danger, Carla the sheltered.

She covers the mouthpiece. "Can I count on you for a ride back to Ann Arbor?"

"Sure."

"He says, 'Sure,' " she tells Susan. "I don't know when. A day or two. I'll call you tomorrow. Say hello to Willis." She listens again. "I will. Don't worry. I will. Bye."

Carla stayed a month. She was a quiet woman; Waltz would often lose her in the house, or come upon her in unexpected places. She smoked and read, mostly. She helped with the house and the cooking. She visited Daddy Waltz at his offices and stayed through the afternoon just talking and listening. She called Susan collect every day.

"She's becoming frantic," Carla reported one afternoon, a week into her stay. "She thinks I'm being held against my will."

"Invite her up," Daddy Waltz says.

"Her and Willy," Waltz says.

"They won't come."

Daddy Waltz asks, "Who's Willy?"

"Willy is Mr. Right. You'll like him. I do."

"I do already," Waltz says.

"He's a teacher," Carla says. "What sort of work do you do, mister?"

Waltz grins, spreads his hands, palms up. Carla smiles back ruefully. "Same old thing?" she asks.

"Always and forever."

"Once a shark, always a shark?"

"Yes," he says curtly. He resents her for bringing this up. "Are you still embarrassed to tell your friends what I do for a living?"

Daddy Waltz stands and folds a towel closed. He walks out of the room.

"See what you did?" Waltz asks.

"No, I didn't. He knows how you make your living. He wouldn't run from that. As for my friends, for the last two years I've seen Susan and Willy, nobody else."

"Susan and Willy," Waltz says. "Silly."

"Maybe. But it was my time to use as I pleased."

"It seems to have brought Susan out."

"There's that." Carla nods.

"Have you learned anything from your two-year hibernation?"

Carla frowns; it appears she has learned something. "I love Willy," she says. "I love Mr. Right."

"Is that a problem?"

"It could be," she admits.

"If you had seen other men in the two years . . ."

"Maybe Willis wouldn't look so good by comparison?"

"Maybe."

"Daddy, I had him first! I picked him. I went out in a snowstorm for cigarettes and aspirin one night at eleven-thirty. Susan was on a date. I trusted the storm to keep the people away from me. I walked two blocks up the street to a drugstore. And who should be working behind the counter to make a little extra money? Him and his damn lovable face. That smile he gives you. I tried to get away—I knew I was in danger—but he was bored and kept talking. When he closed at midnight I was still there. My headache was gone. I brought him home with me. A lousy half hour, that's all it took me to get hooked." She shakes her head. "Goddamn Mr. Right."

"And now he's with Susan . . ." Waltz says.

"I told him I lived with my twin sister. He had enough style not to make the usual stupid remarks we always hear. I liked that about him as much as anything else. He and Susan met the next morning. She liked him right away, she told me later. He could tell us apart right away, too, which is something else I liked. He took enough of an interest to keep us separate. We tried the old switcheroo on him once. Susan went in my place on a date. I was going to meet him at the drugstore and we'd leave from there. Well, he caught on the second she walked through the door. But they went on the date anyway and that was that. They didn't even have to explain it to me. They look so good together. I think it was all the time I spent by myself. The light was out in my face while it was burning brighter than ever in Susan's. She was succeeding in my classes, really stoked on herself. I think that's what drew Willy."

Waltz says, "She's always been a favorite."

6

In his youth, a particular time, his seventeenth year, a conjunction of events led many people in Marathon to predict a life of crime for young Harry Waltz.

Through the winter of that year a burglar stalked the town. He was sly and never caught. He became known as the Shoe Burglar because residents awoke to find any spare cash, plus a pair of men's shoes, gone.

All agreed this was a clever ploy. In the deep snow of that winter tracks were easy to follow and the Shoe Burglar left behind dozens of clear prints of stolen shoes.

After the Bradley house was robbed of $49 the imprint of Chester Bradley's boots appeared two nights later at the burglary of $28 and a pair of work shoes at Robert Seth's house, and, according to Bob Seth and the sheriff, these same stolen work shoes were worn to the Carl Tyler burglary the next week, where $22 and a pair of galoshes were stolen. The winter went on like this.

The Shoe Burglar stole less than $500 the entire winter, it being 1937 and spare cash uncommon (in fact, in many houses visited by the Shoe Burglar there was nothing to be had *but* the shoes), and never hurt a soul. He was, everyone agreed, good for conversation, a progressively dwindling commodity in Michigan winters.

The sheriff spiced the humor when he began measuring the feet of the burgled men. No shoes smaller than a 9D were taken while a pair of 14EEs were the largest. The sheriff thus theorized the Shoe Burglar was a size 9 or 10, since the average person will put up with shoes too large before he will shoes too small.

The lone official sighting of the Shoe Burglar was made on a bitterly cold January night when Frances Beckett awoke to discover a tall man in a white poncho, white knit cap, and white trousers going silently through the things on her dresser. Her scream kicked her husband, Bill, out of bed still asleep and sent the burglar flying down the hall and out into the frozen night.

Bill Beckett, now awake, followed. He stood barefoot in the back doorway holding his shotgun, praying he would see nothing. The landscape was plump with deep snow, moonstruck. Another four inches had fallen that night.

A line of tracks led away from the house. They were lengthened by haste. Another line, more precise and put down with care, coming from such a direction as to form a V with the other set at Beckett's door, showed where the burglar had approached.

Marathon loved the idea of the white costume. It was the perfect mythic detail. Bill Beckett, in the light of his celebrity, soon came to firmly believe that it was he as well as his wife who saw the Shoe Burglar. He also reported to anyone within earshot that as he looked over the frozen land outside his door he detected a tic of movement in a snowdrift out by the road and only realized later this was how the Shoe Burglar hid so well; he became part of the landscape.

Inevitably, talk in Marathon turned to the question of the Shoe Burglar's identity. Nobody had any real faith in the sheriff's catching the thief, so the belief was that guilt would have to be determined by the citizenry.

They were not so hardhearted as to parcel this out prematurely. The trial by innuendo, speculation, and circumstantial evidence stretched through the winter.

The one solid clue was a tall male; probably young, judging from the quickness demonstrated in vacating the Beckett house.

And clever, Marathonites decided; the Shoe Burglar would have to be clever to think of the white costume, both as winter camouflage and as a nod to legend.

And wealthy, too. He would need money to go out of town to

buy the white poncho, far enough away so that he would not be recognized or his purchase remarked upon.

So the clues: a tall, young, clever, wealthy male.

"Has to be a Waltz," Marathonites said.

And Harry had to be the one. Bernard, their elder brother, was a sophomore at Michigan and Aaron was already in California, never to return in his father's lifetime. Harry, a lonesome-looking, solitary boy, six and one-half feet tall, skinny, lending money at every opportunity, fit the clues perfectly. He was suspect for having no friends. His movements thus went undetected. The adults in the case did not trust him because he had no place in particular he had to be.

Daddy Waltz came home one night that winter and went to Waltz's room. He wore a wry smile. He was an intelligent man easily amused by the world in general. Daddy Waltz was the richest man in Marathon then, and by the day he died only his son Harry was richer.

He shook snow from the cuffs of his pants onto the hardwood floor of his son's room and dried the puddles when it melted. Waltz sat at his desk working on a series of figures. Throughout his career as a lender of money he would keep impeccable books. The room was long and dim at the end opposite the desk lamp. He would bring his wife, Louise, to this room when they married. He would move his office down the hall.

"Harry," his father begins, still with that wry smile of something held within that he does not understand, "the people of our fair town have asked me to have a talk with you."

Daddy Waltz took a seat on the corner of the bed.

"They believe you are spending too much time alone," Daddy Waltz says. "They believe you should take lessons in something, have someplace to go in the afternoons."

"How did this come up?" Waltz asks.

Daddy Waltz says, "I don't know, really. It's something I put together in the course of the day. It was kind of amazing, really. Four separate and distinct patients broached the subject of your free time. Then three other people I just ran into in town brought up the same thing, roundabout of course. Everyone was concerned about the quality of your free time."

"I'm fine," Waltz says, resenting being the center of anyone's business but his own. "Tell them that for me."

"Why are you angry?"

"Why did you tell me this?"

"I thought it was amusing," Daddy Waltz says.

"That your son is considered strange by the majority of the populace?"

Daddy Waltz waves a hand in the shadows. "That never occurred to me. They're just busybodies."

"Seven busybodies in one day?"

"Busybodies think alike, Harry," Daddy Waltz says. He got to his feet, performing an elaborate shudder, a shaking of his entire body, capped by a gaping yawn. "A long day, Harry. Everybody's sick of winter and come to me for the cure. Where's your mother?" He had reached the door.

"Somewhere in the house. You'll have to track her down."

"Thanks," he says. He waited a beat in the doorway. His mind can concoct no preamble for what he wants to ask, so he just asks it. "Harry, why don't you have any friends?"

"I've got friends," Waltz cries.

"You do?" Daddy Waltz is genuinely hopeful. "How come I never see you with them? I see other boys in town, but never you. Who are your friends?"

Waltz picks a name. "Sam Boggins."

"You're friends with Sam?"

"Sure."

"That's great. Who else?"

"You don't have any friends," Waltz accuses. "Maybe I don't have any because you never taught me how to make friends."

"There's truth in what you say, Harry. I'm not an easy person to like."

"Yes you are, Daddy."

"I'm a pain in the ass, in the general public eye."

"You don't bullshit," Waltz says. He is anxious to leave this room of feelings. "Why," he asks, "do you think all these people are suddenly so interested in me?"

"The fact is, Harry," his father says, "the people in town seem to believe you're the Shoe Burglar."

"No," Waltz says quickly, "that's Bernard."

"Is that true?" whispers Daddy Waltz.

"Think about it a minute. He's got a good car, he can get up here in no time at all. Everybody thinks he's out of town. It beats waiting tables."

"He doesn't need the money." Daddy Waltz scowls. "I give him all he needs."

"He likes to pay his own way."

"Robbing our neighbors' home? Bill Beckett said he almost shot him! Crime is paying your own way?"

"It's exciting," Waltz says. "It requires cunning. He's a big man on campus because he makes this secret money. He's a man of mystery."

"I don't give a damn for mystery!" roars Daddy Waltz.

His wife comes up the stairs. She has a book closed on a marking finger and holds a cup of coffee. She kisses her husband and says, "What's for dinner?"

"May, did you know Bernie is the Shoe Burglar?" Daddy Waltz asks.

She laughs. "That's nonsense," she states. "Now what's for dinner?"

"Harry says he's the Shoe Burglar."

"I thought you said Bernie was."

"Harry says Bernie is. He says he does it for the money."

She looks sternly at her son. "Stop spreading nonsense about your own family, Harry. There's enough nonsense in this town as it is."

"Go visit his dorm room," Waltz says. "His closet will be filled with stolen shoes."

"That's ridiculous," May says. "Bernie is too smart to leave evidence like that around. He'd throw them away."

"Then the white poncho," Waltz persists. "You'd find that."

"He'd keep it hidden," Daddy Waltz says, "in a place he could get to easily but which couldn't be linked to him."

"Right," nods May.

They stand for a moment thinking like thieves, covering mental tracks, then May's stomach growls.

"You're right," Daddy Waltz says, "they'd never catch him."

And they never did.

But Waltz remained in the town's view the Shoe Burglar, and one fresh spring morning the sheriff came to work and found his car hung like a Christmas tree with stolen shoes. A pair hung by tied laces from each door handle and from the radio antenna and five pairs from each bumper. The men whose houses had been burgled were called to come and claim their shoes, but not before a nice picture was taken, which ran in the newspaper and served to fossilize in the memory of Marathonites everywhere the fact the Shoe Burglar did nobody any harm and seemed to have a sense of humor about himself.

"I think we've seen the last of our friend the Shoe Burglar," the sheriff was quoted in the story that accompanied the picture. "I read this as his way of making peace, now that winter is over."

A majority of Marathonites considered the sheriff a fool for these remarks. He was just inviting the Shoe Burglar to strike one more time. And as happened often in Michigan, a snowstorm struck in mid-April. The Shoe Burglar robbed the house of a dance teacher of $1 and a pair of tap shoes, size 4.

Marathon thought this was hilarious. If a vote were taken then, the results would show Marathonites in favor of the Shoe Burglar never being apprehended, but remaining at large as a town legend.

But rumors swirled as the month of May arrived that the sheriff was still hot on the case. And on May 6 the sheriff left his office and drove once around the square and up the hill to the Waltz house. Though no one was so bold as to follow, all eyes were on the progress the sheriff made. They watched him go to the Waltz's front door and knock.

May Waltz answered.

"Is Harry home, May?" the sheriff asks.

"No, he isn't," she says. "Is something wrong?"

"I wanted to talk to him about some things," the sheriff says.

"What sort of things?"

"This Shoe Burglar case, May. Just something I wanted to get cleared up. I tell you what—when Harry gets home, have him stop by the jail. Won't take any time at all."

Then the sheriff got back in his car and drove down the hill to his office. Marathonites said knowingly: Harry's not home.

In the cumulative way rumors have, the way they roll up like clouds, this visit by the sheriff blew into a full-fledged arrest of Harry Waltz as the story made its way through town circles; all that was lacking was gunfire, and that would have been added given another twenty-four hours. The arrest sounded so convincing some citizens were shocked to see Harry Waltz on the street in the afternoon; they were sure he must have broken out.

At four o'clock in the afternoon Waltz went to the sheriff's office. He had been at home when the sheriff came to the door but his mother, in a reflex of protection, denied his presence. Waltz had been upstairs reading, about to fall asleep, when his mother told him the news.

The sheriff was a rumpled man with a dirty white mustache. Three years from retirement, he had stopped carrying a gun when he turned sixty, hoping this would give him some edge of defenselessness that would see him to the end of his tour. His dreams lately were full of visions of himself gunned down the day he was to retire, one last case gone wrong. His wife had worried herself to death over him. The Shoe Burglar case was too eccentric for him. He hated the Shoe Burglar for outfoxing him and holding him up to ridicule this late in his career. He hoped to God Harry Waltz was the Shoe Burglar.

Waltz walked in the jail. The sheriff set aside his paperwork. Sitting at her own desk was Louise Parker, the sheriff's secretary; at a time in the far future, Harry Waltz's wife.

"Have a seat, Harry," says the sheriff.

Louise Parker was a crackerjack typist. She rolled paper into the carriage and commenced at a machine-gun pace. She ignored Waltz and the sheriff, but as she worked a fine tint of embarrassment shaded her cheeks and Waltz was sure she was listening for something.

She was twenty-six, nine years older than Waltz, a petite, auburn-haired woman with steadfast blue eyes. When Waltz first met Louise she was already halfway through her life, a fact that only struck him later, years after she had died on the day of JFK's inauguration.

"Harry," the sheriff says, "I've asked you here to talk about the Shoe Burglar case."

"Yes, sir," Waltz says.

"You follow all the particulars?"

"Particulars?"

"I mean, are you familiar with the case?"

"Well—I live in town, so I've heard all about it. I guess I know enough about it."

"You know about the shoes being hung on my car?"

"Sure. I heard about that."

"Saw the picture in the paper, maybe?" the sheriff asks.

"I saw it, yes."

"You know Louise here?"

Waltz turned, glad of the chance to openly study this woman hard at work beside him. She stopped her typing long enough to give him a full-faced, totally false smile, just a baring of teeth that chilled him by its emotional distance from him. This woman would never be his, he understood.

"We've never met," she says crisply, and resumed typing.

"But you've seen her around, Harry?"

Waltz nodded, blushing.

"Louise is a marvel," the sheriff says. "I hear people say Louise Parker runs the sheriff's office and they aren't far wrong."

Waltz listened and waited.

"Louise puts in long hours, she's not afraid to work hard," the sheriff says. "She's frequently here long after the rest of Marathon has locked up and gone to bed."

"O.K." Waltz nods.

"She was working the night the shoes appeared on my car," the sheriff says.

"And she saw someone?" Waltz asks, beating the sheriff to the point.

"She saw something," the sheriff says. "I think it was the Shoe Burglar."

"It wasn't him," Louise declares.

The sheriff's dirty mustache fell like an old dog that has died in its tracks. Waltz felt sorry for him; an old constable whose last case was unsolvable.

"Take a look at him, Louise," the sheriff pleads. "You didn't even study him good."

Waltz turned again to the woman. Her typing had not diminished; it filled the air like a good, hard rain. Her jaw was set and her hair was clipped back out of her eyes with a pair of brass pins.

"Louise—look at him."

She stopped and turned her eyes grudgingly on Waltz.

"What did you see that night?" Waltz asks her. He loved this; he was re-evaluating the meeting; for the moment, he had her. Forced by the law to examine him minutely, Waltz believed, the goodness he was convinced resided within him would shine through and enflame this woman. Her fast hands thrilled him; he was seventeen, an age when lust was nearly boundless. He produced long, ropy flights of semen daily; his penis seemed erect for the great majority of his waking hours. To have this twenty-six-year-old beauty stare into his eyes was almost too much.

She tells the sheriff, "Just a flash of white out back."

"I figger that was the Shoe Burglar's damned white poncho," the sheriff says.

"That's all? Just some white?" asks Waltz.

Louise says to the sheriff, "It's not him. I mean, he very well could be the Shoe Burglar, but I couldn't tell you."

"This is great." Waltz laughs.

Louise says to Waltz, in almost a tone of confidentiality, "This was his idea."

In a minute, Waltz was back out on the street, and at a loss for a reason other than crime to approach the woman Louise.

• • •

She had never fit in, Louise. She had lost her parents when she was seventeen and this sudden orphaning left her eyes with a solitary coolness and self-reliance. She never needed anyone ever again. Waltz was eight years old then and remembered the incident that killed her parents as a roar and flash in the distance, a running of people toward the source, a bedlam of bells, sirens, and flame. Louise was already working in the jail. She came running. She stood apart from the efforts to put out the fire and Waltz even had a memory of her there; a small, strong-faced girl weeping, a shy beauty in a plain dress with ash in her hair.

She took a room on the square. She kept her job at the jail and posted cards around soliciting typing work. Waltz remembered most clearly of all his memories of Louise the callused firmness of her fingertips the first time she touched his skin.

Waltz was twenty-four years old in January 1945 when he returned from the war. Louise was thirty-three and her auburn hair was already run through with filaments of white. She was, by then, an institution at the jail. Some thought she should be made sheriff to save the cost of two salaries. She carried a small pistol in her purse and had a larger weapon in her desk drawer at work. She was friendly with everyone, but apart, too. She had saved her money and bought a house. Each day she passed the Waltz house going to and from work and that was when Waltz first saw her after coming home. He was on the front porch with his daddy's twin brother, Ogden, smoking cigarettes, ruminating in the winter air. Both men were wrapped thick as bears in coats and scarves, and Waltz was drunk. It was the fourth straight day Waltz had been drunk. It was all he could think to do with his time, was all he presently desired to do. He smoked cigarettes, he drank, he slept in deep half-day increments; he enjoyed the rhythm of this schedule and the seamlessness with which time passed.

He saw Louise going home in the dark. She passed beneath a streetlight on the corner and he saw her warm in a cream coat with a fur collar, a dark stocking cap, gloves. She carried a satchel of work, not at her chest like a woman, but at her side, like a man; it was her most admirable trait in the eyes of Marathonites: her ability, willingness, and desire to work hard. She did her own work, most of the sheriff's, and the free-lance typing she had solicited and which had grown considerably in volume. She was witnessed in the light of her house late at night working at a table in the dining room. She worked at a huge, black, high-backed typewriter. This was something else about her: She kept every light in her house burning.

Waltz glimpsed her profile as she went past that first night. She was in a hurry and this attracted him. In his young life of women he had always been drawn to women with somewhere to go; he liked that they didn't need him. He remembered the sheriff's ludicrous interrogation of him and Louise's humorless dispatch, the way she said, "This was his idea," pairing them against the sheriff's inanities. He remembered her beauty then, her age, and now she had come to this moment. The seven years since that moment came to him clearly as a slow revolution of experience culminating in her passing through the light out in front of his house for him to see and understand.

Waltz got carefully to his feet. He shrugged within his heavy coat and the bluish haze of beer to clear his head and align his feet. He drew in a deep, cold breath to call to Louise, but Ogden put a hand on his arm.

"Sit back down here," he whispered. He pulled Waltz easily back. "Let her go tonight. Don't approach her drunk, Harry. That'd be the worst thing you could do with Louise Parker. She won't see the humor, what there is. She can have all the drunken sailors she wants. Approach her seriously. Approach her when you're ready to be serious."

So he let her go then. But an hour later he followed her, first assuring Ogden he would not approach her in his present state. Her house was small. It was a shrine to light. He stood across the street and watched her. She was dressed in a heavy blue robe and her auburn and silver hair hung heavily on her shoulders, a pearlescent comb lodged like a blossom over her right ear. She sipped something from a cup and worked at a long table. Waltz was reminded of a museum diorama: woman at work. He wondered why she did not draw her curtains. He wondered why she did not extinguish the upstairs lights when she came downstairs. She might be lonely, he thought. Perhaps she had nothing to hide, or didn't like surprises.

In the weeks that followed, Waltz stopped his drinking. Ogden, who had taken off work to be with Waltz during his time of reentry from a society of war into a society of peace, judged Waltz sufficiently settled and returned to selling machine parts. Waltz missed having Ogden close at hand. Nobody had Ogden's gift for adopting another man's bad habits in order to be friends. Waltz could pester Daddy Waltz only so long; he had patients to tend.

Waltz was twenty-four years old then. He felt uneasy and insubstantial. He had liked himself better as a boy, as a young man. The war had fitted him against a larger scope and diminished him. Where he once imagined himself passing his life alone, the wolf, he now dreamed of himself as a family man, with a beautiful wife and beautiful children. He needed these elements, these strangers, to give flesh to what he lately regarded as himself.

Waltz began to haunt the typist, Louise. He did not think he was obvious about this. Quite often he went days without her catching sight of him. He was working toward his future.

After dark he would wait for the streets to quiet down, for Louise to walk by on her way home. Then he bundled up (it was a frozen early March) and walked to Louise's house to watch her through her windows while she worked.

In Marathon, he was impressed with the answers he received to his seemingly innocent questions about Louise Parker. Nobody was fooled. They thought his impulses sweet, but secretly doubted his chances with a serious-minded, hardworking woman nine years his senior. They had fixed the image of Louise alone and had no imagination for other combinations.

He worked to the subject of her in ways he considered circumspect. Louise Parker was just one in a lengthy list of people he asked about. He was possessed of the role of the returned sailor trying to bring together the history of his hometown since he went away to war. He would barter information with stories of his own, stories of tossed ships, the roar of fired rounds, tedium, strange brilliant friendships. He cached these memories and spent them like silver, buying others' impressions of Louise Parker.

He feared ill thoughts and dark stories about her and then was a little dismayed when none appeared to exist. Louise Parker was thirty-three years old, a looker (he could see that for himself), silent about the occupants and the doings of the jail, a hard worker, loyal, distant, a loner, probably shy. She dressed simply but attractively and was conscientious about her personal hygiene. She had no evident social life. She was never seen entertaining male callers at her house. She seemed to gain her greatest physical pleasure from typing, which she did faster and cleaner (it was judged by no one who knew for sure) than anyone in Michigan. The implication was that she was a virgin; most expected her to die in that state, as well.

Eventually (it in fact took a month, moving into an April still dogged by winter) he reached that point where no further evidence existed save what Louise Parker could teach him herself. He had picked the brains of every likely person in Marathon and in return had come to be regarded as something of a drudge with his war stories. He now knew as much as anyone about Louise Parker. Every Marathonite knew he had a crush on her. Only Louise, of anyone in town who gave a damn or mattered, was uninformed of this fact. Her solitude and cool bearing kept her out of the lines of information that wove through town.

With his research completed he was again at a loss how to proceed. He took to sitting on the front porch drinking beer. Minutes before Louise appeared, going home, he would get up and climb to the second floor to watch her pass. He planned his day around this brief sequence of moments and thus wasted a majority of his summer. He was like a man waiting for a letter from a lover he has no faith in; the moment he knows the letter is not in that day's mail he begins to wait for the next day's mail.

He was sitting on the porch one night when Daddy Waltz came out carrying his black bag, on his way across the side lot to his offices. He was sixty-four years old then, tall as Waltz, full of a vigorous impatience with his youngest son.

"You do nothing all day but drink and moon after that jailer," he observed.

Waltz shrugged. He had been drinking bottles of ice-cold beer since noon. A mist of pollen and dust seemed to hang in his vision.

"You've been home eight months now," his father said. "For a while, I thought you were doing fine. Now I'm not so sure."

Waltz waited, appearing patient, but anxious, too. Since he had been a small boy he knew when he could benefit by letting Daddy Waltz figure something out for him. This was such a time.

"You doing any work?" his father asked. "What about the people you had on the string when you joined the Navy?"

"We agreed to put a hold on things," Waltz said.

"All right. That's decent of you. You've been home almost a year now, though. Why don't you go talk to them?"

"I will," Waltz said. He was suddenly frightened. Talking to Daddy Waltz, he had forgotten to get out of sight and there was Louise Parker coming up the sidewalk in front of the house. She walked looking straight ahead. Long pale arms swung loose from her sleeveless blouse, one hand clutching the briefcase full of work for the night. Daddy Waltz turned to watch her pass and Waltz grabbed his father's wrist before he might open his mouth. Waltz studied Louise until she was out of sight, wide shoulders and hips, narrow waist, long legs, all that auburn and silver hair tugged into tenuous order with ribbons and pins. Even after she was gone he could still hear her heels on the sidewalk like code.

"That's a handsome woman you have your eye on," Daddy Waltz acknowledged.

"Thank you," Waltz said. She had not looked at him; not even a glance. But was it a studied ignoring of him? He thought it might be just that.

"Why not go over and talk to her?"

"Shy," Waltz said.

"Is that why you're drinking so much?"

"Could be."

"People tell me you've made no secret of your interest in the jailer."

"I ask a lot of questions." He had grown hot. He had no purpose or desire to be on the porch any longer, so he went into the house. Daddy Waltz followed. Waltz took another bottle of beer from the icebox and opened it. The night seemed endlessly long and it wasn't even dark yet. Later, he would go stand outside Louise's house. In hot weather she worked in a light cotton shift and let her washed hair dry in the air. He longed for winter. It seemed to take forever to get dark now. In winter he could be over there already.

Daddy Waltz said, "I hear you've been spying on her at night."

Waltz went out the back door and across the lawn to the gazebo. Daddy Waltz kept after him. They sat smoking and watching the retarded kids play raucous, ruleless baseball.

"I hear you spend most of your night hours outside Louise's house," Daddy Waltz persisted. "I hear you spend more time there even after she has turned out the lights and gone to bed."

"Who says?" Waltz asked. His father had it wrong; Louise never turned out all the lights.

"Friends," his father said. "People who see you walking down the street at crazy hours. Your own mother followed you one night."

"It's the closest I can risk coming to her right now," Waltz said. Standing outside her house it never occurred to him to go knock on her door; that was an act of courage unfathomable to him.

"Why?" Daddy Waltz asked. "She's just a woman. She can talk. She won't bite."

Waltz smiled out toward the State Home game; is all fear of women gone by the age of sixty-four? "She may," he said.

Daddy Waltz grumbled to himself a moment. One of the retarded kids—in truth a man, with a boxer's muscles—hit the baseball over the fence and off the gazebo roof. The noise thumped in Waltz's ears. Daddy Waltz went out and threw the ball back over.

"I've got it," he said, turning back to his son. "Hire her to type something."

"Now that's sly," said Waltz, though intrigued.

"Start on a purely professional basis. Work from there."

"What do I have that needs typing?"

"Oh, Harry! Don't be thick. It doesn't *matter* what it is. The fact of it is what's important."

Waltz thought a minute. He resented his father's good idea; it removed the comfort of having no resources to make contact with her. It forced a decision on him.

He wanted to run but there was nowhere to go. A good hour of daylight remained. When had his mother followed him?

"I could get myself arrested," Waltz mused. "I could put myself in proximity to her that way."

Daddy Waltz frowned. It was a characteristic of his to take seriously everything spoken to him. "I think that would be a monumental mistake," he warned. "I think the big obstacle you have to fight against now is that one time you were called in for questioning on that Shoe Burglar case."

Waltz folded his arms. "I'll talk to her when I'm ready."

Daddy Waltz stood to go. His son wanted him to stay to prod him further. Waltz was afraid he would sink deeper into his fear of Louise without his father's encouragement to keep him safe.

"Don't wait too long," Daddy Waltz said. "I think certain women who can take care of themselves—Louise Parker, for instance—reach a point beyond which they are untouchable. They become so self-sufficient there is no chance for a man to break through and prove she needs him. I don't know, Harry. Louise may be reaching that point. It would be a shame if you waited too long."

Waltz was left in the gazebo with his beer and cigarettes. Even into the darkness the retarded kids played baseball and their excited voices skipped like white figures to him.

The night Louise's water broke for the twins she shook her husband awake and rained kisses on his sleep-swollen face and down his long body to his penis and thighs.

"Are you awake?" she asked huskily. "It's near time. My water just broke."

"Yes," said Waltz. He sat up in bed. He felt jerked awake with leading promises. Louise was maneuvering out of bed, the process a series of weight shifts toward an end. A wide wet spot that smelled of the ocean was centered on her side of the bed.

In a moment she was back beside him.

"Promise me you'll still love me and the baby if it's retarded," she whispered.

"I promise."

"Promise me we'll raise the baby ourselves, and not put him in a home."

Waltz swallowed. "I promise," he said. Her strident concern spooked him. He waited for her to go on but she only kissed the side of his head and moved away. She was smiling peacefully. He was pleased with himself that he could so easily put her mind at rest.

He dressed and hurried down the hall to his parents' room. He knocked and in a minute Daddy Waltz came. Behind his father, Waltz saw his mother sitting up in bed holding a candle.

"Her water broke," Waltz reported.

"O.K.," his father said. He reamed something out of his ear, studied it on the tip of his finger. Waltz patiently waited for his father to awaken.

"Don't let her eat anything," Daddy Waltz said. "I'll go next door. You bring her over in fifteen minutes. No rush now. I'll call Abby."

"Don't worry now," May said, coming to the door. "She's young and strong."

"I know," Waltz said. He did not want to break away from the triangle they had formed; here he was a son, down the hall a father and husband. He wanted to remain for a minute in the door to his parents' room, weightless of responsibilities. His father unselfconsciously stripped and searched naked through his clothes for something to wear. His body was cream white and decrepit in the candlelight his mother held; it pushed Waltz away from the nest he sensed he wanted to remain within, back down the hall to his room.

He sat on their bed in the dark waiting for Louise to come out of the bathroom. Twice he went and tapped on the door to be sure she was all right.

There was no point in waking Eugene and Monroe. They would only snarl and get in the way. He heard his father on the hall phone call Abby Drinkwater, his nurse for twenty-three years. Then he heard the front door open and close and out the bedroom window he saw the dark figure of his father crossing to his offices.

His mother came into the room. Her hair was down and long for bed.

"She's worried the baby is retarded," Waltz told her.

"The baby will be healthy, bright, and beautiful," May said, and folded her hands on this pronouncement.

She had followed Waltz one summer night to Louise's house and after an hour came from her hiding place and stood beside him. They could both clearly see Louise Parker at work.

"Don't you think this has gone on long enough?" his mother asked.

"I've come to this point," Waltz said, "and I can't imagine anything beyond this."

"You can't imagine talking to her? Walking through town? Taking her for a ride?"

"No."

"She's just a woman. She won't bite."

He heard his father in her voice. In a moment she produced a slip of paper. She said, "I'm going to hire Louise to do some typing for me. It's not much. If she does a good job I'll give her some more."

"What is it?" Waltz asked anxiously. "Daddy put you up to this, didn't he?"

"I admit your father gave me the idea. The decision to put it into action was mine."

"What does the note say?"

She read: " 'Dear Louise. I am approaching you in this fashion because a paralysis of shyness grips me whenever you are present or the subject of you comes up, leaving me unable to form coherent words or thoughts. I would like to take you on a date—perhaps a ride or a walk. I am confident once the initial barriers are removed I will be able to talk to you. Having been brought in for questioning on the Shoe Burglar case at the age of seventeen, I can only hope you don't view me in a criminal light. I have grown up and will treat you with all seriousness. May I see you socially? Kindest regards, Harry Waltz.' "

Waltz said, "Nice try, Ma. I recognize the hand of your nefarious husband in this."

"He helped," May admitted.

"Go home. I'll be along in a while."

"Just take the note to her, Harry. If you just moon after her she'll go away and then you'll hate yourself. You'll always wonder." She pressed the note in his hand.

A telephone rang. Louise stood up from her worktable. May's mouth had a luminous, twisted shape to it, as though she could not believe something, or was trying not to laugh.

In a moment Louise Parker came out into the smooth light over the front porch. She had her hands in the pockets of her robe.

"Is that you, Harry Waltz?" she called.

Waltz turned to his mother but she had drifted back out of sight. He was alone with his called name ringing in his ears, and his mother's note.

Louise came down the steps. "I just got the strangest phone call, Harry. Someone told me you were standing out here trying to work up the courage to hire me to do some typing for you."

"That's not precisely true," Waltz called.

"Oh?" He felt her gentle voice, his mother's note, his father's phone call setting into him like hooks. "What is the precise truth, then?"

"I know how to type," Waltz said.

"Not as fast as I can, nor as well," she said. "Come closer."

He crossed the street. She pointed to the note. "Is that what you wanted typed?" she asked.

"It crossed my mind."

"May I see it?"

He came up the walk and handed her the note. He realized he liked being trapped; a decision had been removed.

She leaned slightly to the left, letting the porch light fall across her shoulder to read by. She was grave and did not smile.

"You came in for questioning?" she asked.

"When I was seventeen. The Shoe Burglar case, remember?"

She nodded. "Yes, I remember. And, yes, I would like to go for a walk or a ride with you."

"That would be nice," he said.

"Are you really shy?"

"Oh, yes."

"Come inside. I'll type this for you." She offered him coffee. "You smell like beer," she scolded.

She asked, "Do you remember that night?"

"What night?"

"That night you tied all the shoes to the sheriff's car?" she smiled.

"Yes, I do," Waltz said. "It was a beautiful night."

"I saw you as clear as I'm seeing you now," she said. He preceded her through the house to her kitchen. She was behind him all the way, turning out lights.

7

Waltz does good business in Flint these days, the auto industry is shot and his strings are long. The men he visits to collect are lonely. He suspects they delay their payments to force him to visit them. They miss the racket of camaraderie on the job, inviting Waltz to sit and drink with them and be their friend. He wants to tell them to get out in the sun more. They are turning pale and ghostly sitting at home in the TV shadows or the aquamarine light of taverns, as if this is camouflage for their present straits.

Flint is a sorry town. Waltz tells everyone, "Sorry, but you have to pay."

He has finished his Flint calls one Friday afternoon and is walking down the street toward his car when he suddenly has the feeling he is being followed. The premonition is slightly thrilling. The sidewalk is busy, full of people. Nobody has a job, to listen to everybody, but there is commerce in Flint. There is a rushing home. It is late afternoon and a weekend is about to begin. He sees small, anticipatory smiles on random faces.

Waiting at a corner to cross, he turns casually to get a look behind him. Someone meets his look, it is a man startled by the break in the flow of forward vision.

His car is on this block, a tan 1980 Cadillac Seville, someone's big eyes. It is a good GM car in a good GM town. He stands in the street by the driver's door, fiddling with his keys, stalling. A tall woman walks past. Her white hair is tied back with a black velvet ribbon. Her skirt is conservatively cut, her legs are nice and long. Waltz thinks he knows her from somewhere. Does she owe him? Her eyes had shifted away from him a split second before he saw her; she thinks she has been quick enough.

Like a good spy, she turns left at the end of the block and crosses to the opposite sidewalk. She has thus robbed him of his car as a following device unless he turns the car around, and by then she can have disappeared, or changed directions once again; she can run him like a fox.

She is studying something through a store's plate-glass window. Waltz imagines she is watching him and waves to her reflection. Her sheaf of white hair dances when her head twitches; it might be nothing, he is too far away to read her features, but he chooses to believe he has stung her. She knows he knows.

Although he sits in his car for several minutes watching her, she never leaves. She moves within a single block and though Waltz can never catch her he is certain she looks at him when she gets the chance. In one shop she purchases a bag of nuts or candy and in another a small oblong package. She stares for long moments into store windows. She so studiously wastes time that Waltz believes she must be waiting for someone, but just then she takes off hard in the opposite direction and in his side mirror Waltz very clearly sees her turn and look directly at him.

She has been lulling him, he decides. He puts the Cadillac in gear and slides out into the street. It is two lanes each way and he drifts across all four, through a propitious break in the traffic, into the mouth of an alley he picked out earlier as the best place for him to turn around. He puts the car in reverse and then for a moment his luck snags. Traffic released by the light up the block prevents his backing out. He is out far enough to see up the sidewalk but this is no help to him, there are too many people, the woman is too far ahead, she has given him the slip.

Moving again, he accelerates up the street, once nearly sideswiping a car coming out from the curb. If he crashes or is stopped by the police will she return and vouch for him? We are spies, she will say, we are in training to tail rival agents in foreign capitals.

He has to brake at a red light. Pedestrians cross in front of him, he looks beyond them to the storefronts, the shadows beneath the awnings, the dimnesses within stores, trying to find her. No, she is lost. She has slipped away.

Then someone loudly bangs his hood. He looks up and there is the woman crossing in front of his car. She isn't looking at him. She trusts him to see and understand that he has been outfoxed again. She wants him to know she can keep this up forever.

Waltz has to scout two square blocks to find a place to park. He is relaxed and excited. He understands now there is no rush to this. He parks and fishes a nickel from his pocket for the meter; he will give it an hour. He lights a cigarette and walks back to the field of battle.

He understands the woman will be waiting for him. She will be in a store or an entryway, proud of her sly maneuvers, perhaps still watching the traffic for his car. She would be disappointed if he stayed in his car, with all its disadvantages in the close dimensions they have chosen. She would lose interest, that he was so out of touch. She will have confidence in him, though, and watch the pedestrians closely. She will have covered her back.

71

Waltz returns to the avenue and sees that already it has begun to empty. Rush hour in Flint passes quickly. Some men out of work still venture out morning and dusk to keep up their end of the bargain, to remain grooved for a return to work. But now that time has passed and it is like autumn on a battlefield, all the leaves dropping away, taking with them the places to hide.

From the window of a magazine store he watches the opposite sidewalk. He is the only customer in the store and he moves with the furtiveness of a shoplifter. The man behind the counter wears suspenders and smokes a cigar. Waltz buys a pack of cigarettes. The man grunts; he's not impressed.

But buying the cigarettes gives Waltz the right to linger. He hangs in the window like a sign. He wonders if poking his hand out the door will draw fire.

"You work at GM?"

Waltz turns. It is the counterman asking.

"Sure," Waltz says.

"A Jap came through that door right now, would you kill him or wouldn't you?"

This man works for the white-haired woman, Waltz decides. She is everywhere, she and her minions. She has employed this man to drive Waltz from his place of sanctuary.

"Japs are killing this town," the man tells Waltz in an amiable fashion. "I say, kill 'em back. I'm praying for the day a Jap tries to rob me. I'll shoot him right between the eyes. I'll kill Datsun of a bitch." He laughs cruelly. "How about you?"

Waltz bolts before it is too late. He keeps close to the walls. It is all plate glass sliding past, a sheer, smooth flank, he dabs at it with his fingers to keep his equilibrium. He is clearly on the defensive. He is the one in the open and running, he is the one who can't see his enemy.

He dips into the store where the white-haired woman bought the bag of candies or nuts. Two women in pink smocks greet him simultaneously. "We're closing."

"I'll just be a minute," says Waltz.

The women return to polishing glass cases of candy. Plump cashews rotate on trays under orange lights. The air is lush with sugar, the pure white walls might be made of it. The women wear lace tiaras in their hair.

Waltz pretends to inspect the goods in the case, looking out on the street. He watches for an entire minute and not a single individual walks past the window.

"Chew dollars are good," one of the women says. She has come around in front of Waltz. She points to a compartment of orange, green, red, and yellow coin-sized candies with dollar signs stamped on them. The woman holds a red candy up to the light, which passes easily through it.

"They last forever in your mouth," the woman promises. "Can I bag a half pound for you? A pound? We're closing in a minute."

She is another one. Waltz smiles and the woman smiles back. She is speaking in code to confuse him, to pass a message to her partner swabbing glass across the shop. He smiles again to let her know he will not be taken lightly. She hovers over her cases of chew dollars, chocolate stars, butterscotch drops, sugar dabs, pink and white pistachios, peanuts in papery skins. When Waltz moves she moves, parallel exactly, and he guesses she is just doing her job, which is to obscure his view.

He is on the move again. Flint is shutting down. It is five seconds past six o'clock. Up and down the street he hears clear as gunshots keys turning locks. Lights will go out next. Flint will soon be at his feet and he will be standing with his back to this marble wall, unable to move. He is frozen by indecision. He feels he has failed that white-haired woman he thought he knew. Some set of rules has proven too obtuse for him.

He stands still for another minute, then just like that he starts for his car, lights a cigarette. The woman has gone home; he is free to go.

The woman steps out of hiding and follows him. They move through Flint a block apart. Waltz smokes and feels good. He has stepped back into his own skin. The woman stalks him with her head down, her ribboned hair swinging, her hands in her pockets. She has a car somewhere at her back but first this must be completed.

Something in the shape of the head of the man in the crowd reminded her of somebody. A head narrow and alert. The hair white and longer than that of most men his age, with waves in it that fell into the man's shirt collar. He was tall and walked loose and relaxed, obviously with nowhere to go. She thought he was just another Flintian auto executive getting used to having his days free, but then he stepped out into the street to unlock his car and she saw he was the loan shark. She turned away a beat before he caught her looking.

She thought of her older brother, of his helplessness in the world. He lived by a river praying to keep floods away. He fell into casual debt, then compounded his problems by signing other agreements that only delayed and heightened his troubles. He was her elder; this amazed her.

She lights a cigarette of her own and walks on after the man. She has seen his penis, from a distance, performing one of its two basic functions. The scene had a certain perverse elegance until he looked and saw her looking and embarrassment was created. She was stubborn, though, and refused to look away, but after she had moved on out of sight she remembered the loan shark with a certain fondness. She likes that he did not try to hide, that he did not make a mess of himself. She also likes that he has her brother in a squeeze. She is ashamed of this but it is there in her; her older brother who was once so special in her eyes, this loan shark has his soul on paper.

And here he is in Flint.

The time on the meter has expired but no cops have ticketed Waltz. He wonders if Flint has become a more sympathetic town with all its troubles. Do the cops look the other way, knowing times are hard?

He unlocks the car door. The white-haired woman is watching him from the other side of the car. For some reason he expects her to be armed. He expects to see the gun that will finish him.

Then, like that, he remembers: "Mary Hale."

"You remember."

"Just now. It just came to me. I'm Harry Waltz."

She nods. They watch each other across the car. He remembers her on the river.

"Does my brother still owe you money?"

"Yes. Little by little he pays it off."

"And little by little it keeps growing."

"Yes. I'm afraid your brother and I will do business together a long time."

"He's not picky about what he signs," she says.

This seems very succinct to Waltz. It has the ring of an epitaph. "What brings you to Flint?" he asks.

"Business."

"You were good at giving me the slip," Waltz says. He likes that she smiles in agreement, that she does not pretend obliviousness to their game. "Did you see me . . . ?"

"Frozen on the sidewalk?" she asks.

Waltz nods, though he was about to ask her about that day by the river. How good were her eyes? Was he in shadow? How much had she seen?

"I put it down to camouflage," she tells him. "The building you were standing in front of was nearly the exact color of your jacket. Very clever."

He likes her answer. "I wish I had planned it that way," he says. "Can I give you a ride somewhere?"

"Yes. I've got a car. I'd appreciate a ride to it."

Sitting in his car, moving, Waltz asks, "Where were you hiding?"

"When?"

"Anytime. I imagined you had hired storekeepers to drive me into the open."

"My . . ." She laughs. "You're serious?"

"It was a game," he says. The first disappointment in someone is always so difficult; he wonders if she has had the same with him yet.

They pass a locked store on a corner. "There," Mary Hale points. "I watched you from there for several minutes. I watched and waited for that inevitable moment you got tired of the game. I was prepared to tip my hand a little to keep you interested."

"Oh?"

"Yes. I was having fun. Left here."

She directs him to a parking garage that looms up four stories, dark and dangerous. A black attendant sits reading in a glass booth.

"Is this safe?" Waltz asks. The ramp up into the garage is glittery with grease. Lights are missing.

"Probably not," she says with a bright, false smile. "I carry this," she says. She has a long, thin ice pick in her hand.

"Have you ever used that?"

"Only at parties," she chuckles. "Otherwise, no." She taps the ice-pick handle with a lacquered nail. "Knock on wood."

"Let me walk you to your car."

"I'd like that," she says.

Waltz parks, there is parking galore now, and she slips an arm through his as they take the elevator up to the third level. He wishes she would keep her hands free. He is counting on her and her weapon.

But they see no one along the way. On the third level Waltz counts only four other cars. One of these sits on its rims. The block walls throw her clacking heels back at them, she sounds like an army in stiletto-heel boots.

"Thank you for your concern," she says when she has her car started. The ice pick is gone. "I'll drive you back to your car."

The attendant who had been in the glass booth has vanished. Mary Hale and Waltz sit at the closed gate for a full minute waiting to pay.

"If my rate goes up because of this, I'll sue," she fumes, but grinning.

"Maybe he had to use the john."

"Could be. He should hang out a sign."

Another minute passes. A car stops behind them. When Waltz turns to look the man grimaces and loosens his tie.

"This is absurd," Mary Hale says.

Waltz discovers he is pleased by the delay. They are held motionless at a border. Beyond lie questions and decisions. He has an adolescent boy's fear of women and their power over him. He felt much safer with Mary Hale when she disliked him.

Another car gets in line.

"Maybe I should bust down the gate," Mary says, and shrugs at Waltz.

"No, give him a minute."

"I really don't have the time to sit here," she announces, and unlocks her door. Her hand slips into her purse for the ice pick. It is such an obvious arming of herself that it frightens Waltz; does she recognize something in this delay that he has missed?

She gets out of the car. Waltz gets out on his side. She crosses to a door marked EMPLOYEES ONLY. She knocks, then pushes it open. Her boldness startles Waltz. Nobody is in the room. A couch against one wall is covered with a dirty sheet, copies of *Sports Illustrated* and *Hustler;* a desk in the corner is by contrast tidy, a tray of papers, a phone, an ashtray, a small photo of a little black girl under glass; a calendar hangs on the wall with a rack of time cards and a punch clock.

There is a second door across the room. Mary Hale moves for it but Waltz stops her. He understands that she feels the man is behind this door, and she is probably right, but the door goes too deep into the layered soul of the place, something not meant to be seen. The room is like a home; he feels like an intruder. It is not worth it to see behind that second door. He wants to save the young black man the embarrassment of being caught sitting on the toilet with his pants down. Waltz smiles, thinking this is this woman's way.

"Why are you smiling?" Mary Hale asks, smiling herself.

"Nothing. Let's go. It's not worth it."

"Yes it is," she says, getting mad again. "We pay money to park here. Part of the agreement they make with us is to have somebody present to let us out when we want to leave."

Waltz leads her to the door going outside. "Maybe he's back," he says. "Maybe we can figure out how to get the gate up. We can leave the money. Come on."

She follows him out of the office. Five cars are in line now. The car behind Mary Hale's suddenly produces a blast from its horn. The sound can't seem to get free of the concrete enclosure; it goes on forever.

Mary Hale, at Waltz's side, says simply, "I'd like to ram this up his ass."

"Get in the car," Waltz says. "I'll try to get the gate up."

The car horn blows again. Waltz waves to the man to be quiet but either he does not see or refuses to, for he lets go with another long blast.

The attendant has been in the booth all along. He is stuffed down beneath the counter and a thin trail of dark red blood splits his blank face perfectly in two. Is he dead? Waltz wonders. The cash register is open and empty.

With the crime discovered, Waltz begins to notice other clues to the struggle. A clutter of paper on the floor, spilled change leading out of the booth, two quarters shine all the way out on the sidewalk, the attendant's newspaper ripped in the violence of the robbery and spattered with his blood. Waltz thinks the man could have used Mary Hale with her ice pick, she would have saved him.

Waltz runs into the office to call the police. He hears the car horn go off again behind him. For a moment he is foiled by the telephone. He can't get an outside line until Mary Hale appears in the door and says, "Dial nine."

He does, like magic gets a dial tone, then gets an operator, who puts him through to the police.

Then he realizes he does not know where he is.

"We need an address," the police dispatcher says dispassionately.

"I'm in Flint," Waltz says, and winces at his lunacy.

"Calm down, sir."

"Where are we?" he asks Mary Hale. She shrugs. She patrols the room in tight circles, her ice pick ready.

"It's a parking garage," Waltz says. "There's been a robbery."

"You've told us that. We need an address."

Through the block wall, through the closed door, through his bafflement and embarrassment, he hears that damn car horn. Why couldn't the cops follow that noise there?

Then it comes to him. It has been right in front of him all the time; it has been all around him.

"Metro Parking," he reads from a piece of stationery on the desk. "2227 West Cadillac. Got that?"

"Thank you, sir. A squad will be there in a minute."

"A man is hurt," Waltz says. "Maybe dead."

"Yes, sir. We'll take care of it." I'm just a panicky old man, Waltz understands them to believe. He has besmirched himself as a reliable individual by his failure to know where he is. And why not?

But the attendant is not dead. He is sitting on the cement walk outside the booth. He has touched the blood on his face and studies it on his fingers. He does not seem the least bit startled to see Waltz and Mary Hale come out of the office, to see a woman with an ice pick. Perhaps he is comforted.

"We've called the police," Waltz tells the man.

He nods delicately, cradling his wounded head. Five times before he has been robbed, but this is the first time he has been harmed. All the blood, the ache in his head, has violated the rhythm of the previous crimes. It's not his money. It's a job. This is just Flint. He had trusted in the robbers to understand all this, take what they wanted, and leave him alone.

The police arrive and a few minutes later Metro Parking's owner turns up. He is a stocky black man in a suit and tie.

He sees the blood and gasps, "Bobby! They beat you this time?"

Bobby looks wearily at the man, nods. He is exhausted, his shift is complete, he just wants to go home. He repeats for his boss the story he told the police.

"I was reading the paper. The rush was over. Somebody came up behind me and scared the shit outta me tapping me on the shoulder. When I turned around he smacked me one right on top of the head."

"Did you get a look at him?"

"He had a mask on. Covered his whole head. Jimmy Carter."

One of the cops laughs, turning away.

"A pity," the owner says. "Not simple robbery anymore, but beatings, too."

The car horn goes off. Everybody jumps.

"Somebody shut him up," a cop orders. "Tell him he'll be out of here as soon as we can arrange it."

Waltz is glad to help. The driver is reading a paperback book, he does not see beyond the fact the car in front of his has not moved. He touches his horn in reflex annoyance, like a pulse.

"Please don't honk your horn," Waltz says to him. "There's been a robbery. We'll all be out in a minute."

"I been sitting here for twenty minutes. I'm not paying for that time," the driver says.

"Fine," says Waltz. He starts to leave.

"You a detective?"

"No."

"Who got robbed?"

"The cashier."

"Justice triumphs," the man says, and he slides back into his book.

Another employee arrives. An ambulance arrives. A thick square of gauze has been taped to Bobby's wound. He is helped into the ambulance, moving easily enough, and he complains he just wants to go home. He waves, grinning, through a small window in the ambulance at the guy who has just come, and at his boss.

Seven cars are now in line. The police give hints of leaving. The guy with the horn, sensing the end of this delay, lays on the horn repeatedly. The new cashier is told to let all the cars in line go through without charge.

Mary Hale slides behind the wheel, starts her car. She had offered Bobby a clean handkerchief, then a cigarette, and been rejected twice. Subtle changes of color have come to her face. The black velvet ribbon in her hair seems freshly tied.

Time to go, Waltz gets in the front seat next to her. He will ride the hundred feet to his own car. In a moment they will pass back across the border; responsibilities, challenges will return to him. Time will resume.

The striped gate rises and they are free. The new attendant waves them through, then they have to wait at the curb for a car to pass.

Waltz tries to think of something to say.

There is a commotion behind them. Waltz turns to look, it is a jangle of horns and irate utterances. The car with the horn has a crazy lean to it; the fool driver is getting out. Now he is the snag in the remainder of the day.

Mary Hale has her ice pick out and she's laughing. Then she puts her ice pick away.

8

A letter for Waltz comes from Eugene in the mail. Waltz takes it up to his office. The mail also brings envelopes bearing cash. He spends a good hour doing his books. He draws the time out like a thread.

Waltz has backlogged Eugene's letters ever since Eugene went to prison. He keeps one on hand, unopened, and only reads it when another arrives to take its place. This way he maintains a distance. Nothing he reads in Eugene's letters is immediate because when Waltz reads them his son has survived to write again.

To keep the letters coming Waltz writes short notes on plain paper. These notes are vague, full of weather, nameless debtors, empty as the house. He neither asks nor answers any questions. He tries to be encouraging.

Eugene has been in prison long enough to report in his letters that time has stopped. He writes that he will wake up one day and a guard will unlock his cell and tell him to go home. Until then, he writes, he is not interested in time.

Eugene's going to prison was the culmination of a series of hard lessons. Until he was in prison he would have nothing to do with his father. Then a month after he went a letter arrived for Waltz. Waltz put it aside; he was afraid of it. Another month and a second letter; Waltz opened and read the first.

Dear Daddy—

I've been here a few weeks and I'm trying to get settled. They tell me the key is to get comfortable. They tell me the days roll off easier when a man is settled in a routine.

I've been in a couple fights, but nothing too bad. I'm told this is the way of the world. I'm told I'm being tested.

My routine is this: Sleep. Eat. Work. Eat. Work. Eat. Sleep. I play basketball in my free time. These games are like fights themselves. I work in the kitchen.

We are not encouraged to make friends but I have a couple anyway. Guys who aren't in one of the gangs. Which makes us kind of like a gang ourselves, I guess.

I'd like to carry on a correspondence with you. Please write if this would be possible.

Waltz once asked Mary Hale at what age you stopped taking the blame for your children.

Eugene was thirty-one years old, a fixture in Flint, when a stranger came to Waltz's door. He said his name was Paul Vermillion. Waltz guessed he just wanted to borrow money. Paul Vermillion said he wanted to talk to Waltz about Eugene.

"Your son is too rough," Paul Vermillion says. "He's too rough with the good people of Flint. He has no sympathy. You are well known in Flint as a gentleman who has sympathy for the less fortunate. Harry Waltz, everyone knows, is firm, but a gentleman. I am here to ask you to talk to Eugene."

"Eugene's on his own," Waltz says. "I don't give him advice anymore."

"He's beating people up," Paul Vermillion says. "He has no

patience. If things don't go right your son Eugene's first response is to beat the living shit out of the good people of Flint."

"I hold no sway with him," Waltz says implacably.

Paul Vermillion laced his fingers and sighed. He was a handsome man. He stood with perfect posture in the center of Waltz's house.

"It's hard, I know," Paul Vermillion says. "I have two boys of my own. One sixteen, one fourteen. A girl, thirteen. They're at that age where they know everything there is to know." He smiled and gently slapped his cheek. "A big pain in the neck often, yes? I bless them but I also look forward to the day they are adults like me and can see the world as it really is. I wish my children had some years on them so they would stop and think once before telling me I'm all wrong. The mouths on my three children! All mouth and plenty of brains, my kids aren't stupid. But rarely do they put them together." He laughed and Waltz smiled. "Someday they will and then there will be peace.

"But you—Harry—your son is at that age when he should be an adult, when he should respect what his father has accomplished and recognize the problems of being an adult in this world. He should listen to you, Harry, but you tell me he doesn't. Instead he beats people up. Why, Harry? Why are you such a gentleman and your son such a violent thug?"

Paul Vermillion departed without any answers.

Waltz wondered if it was Eugene's mother dying young that turned Eugene the way he was. Did he lack some womanly gentleness? Or was it a failure of values?

But Eugene lacked something Waltz blamed himself for not imparting. Some grace, or an affinity for his customers, was missing. He beat people up.

An acquaintance told Waltz that life was difficult for his son Eugene. He was having trouble with his business. His reputation for beating up people made potential customers wary of him, no matter how desperate they were for money. Waltz laughed and winked at his acquaintance. He said, "Send them to me, then." He said this about his son. Waltz asked his acquaintance to tell him more when he learned more.

A month later Waltz was told by his acquaintance that Eugene was extremely short of money, that he owed money himself, and was considering turning to crime. The report came complete with the thoughts and opinions of Eugene, as though his mind had been read and transcribed.

Waltz sent Carla to talk to Eugene. She made the trip to Flint and back in one afternoon.

She reported: "He wouldn't even open his door."

"How did he sound?"

"I can't tell you, Daddy. He didn't sound like any brother of mine."

"Did you say I sent you?"

"No. I was talking to a door, for God's sake!"

Waltz got in touch with his acquaintance.

He asked, "What is happening with my Eugene?"

"He's committing crimes, Harry."

"What sort of crimes?"

"Nobody is exactly sure. He has a little better cash flow, though. There have been a number of minor armed robberies lately. But it's an expected thing. This is Flint. People are hurting. Eugene may have nothing to do with those robberies. I'll keep in touch, Harry."

Paul Vermillion came to see Waltz a second time.

"Talk to your son, Harry," he says. "He's making everybody nervous."

"Eugene's an adult."

"Forgive me, Harry, but I have to disagree. An adult accepts certain responsibilities and certain modes of conduct. By those criteria, your son is *not* an adult."

"He won't listen to me," Waltz says.

"Just try. Tell him to stop beating up people. Tell him that stopping the beatings will only improve his business. He'll attract better customers and as he attracts better customers he'll have less reason to beat up people. One thing helps another. You understand this—you've never laid a finger on a man, Harry—talk to your son and make him understand."

"It would do no good," Waltz says.

For the first time Paul Vermillion's mask of imploring gentility slipped; for just an instant he became another man entirely.

"He's committing crimes, Mr. Waltz. He could get hurt, get in trouble.

"Talk to him. I don't ask that you convert him overnight. Just talk to him. Ask him why he does the things he does. Does he do it to be tough? For better business? For the exercise? I don't know. I can't make a lick of sense out of the way he acts. Maybe you can."

"Who *are* you?" Waltz asks.

"I am you," Paul Vermillion says with smiling graciousness. "Me, you, your son Eugene, many others, we are all the same person. I admit I operate out of greed. Your son hurts my business; he hurts all of us. Not you, Harry, perhaps, because you are the best, but the rest of us just trying to make a living. He scares off our clients. People get to be afraid to borrow money. They think we're all Eugenes."

Waltz drove to Flint and sat in his car outside Eugene's apartment. He hoped to talk to his son when he left or arrived; he did not want to be turned away at the door.

At ten minutes before midnight Eugene came out. He carried a dark athletic bag and was in his car and gone before Waltz could approach him. Waltz followed Eugene to a small house on a dark, narrow street. Eugene tapped his horn once, but stayed in the car. A man came out of the house and joined Eugene in the car. They drove off together. A mile on, they parked and Waltz watched in amazement as Eugene's partner broke into a Chevy parked at the curb, started it, then drove off followed by Eugene, then Waltz. Another mile on, they parked Eugene's car and Eugene rode in the stolen car.

Waltz traveled in a state of disbelief. He was not dismayed so much by Eugene's committing a crime as by his being witness to it. The absolute perfection of place and time that set him down in this dark Flintian scene made him feel plucked and deposited, a witnessing tool.

Eugene's partner was a fast, almost reckless, driver (a quality Waltz would think undesirable while in a stolen car) and twice Waltz thought he lost them. Thinking he'd been slipped, he braked at a light and saw to his left, twenty-four inches away, his son Eugene lighting a cigarette. Waltz put up a hand to hide his face.

The two men in the stolen car drifted for over an hour; they covered thirty-three miles. Waltz was amazed at their brass. Four times they passed police cars; once they traveled a mile with a police car between them and Waltz. They trusted the owner of the car to be asleep; they had all night.

At 2 A.M. they parked in the lot of a branch bank, snapped off their lights, and turned off the engine. Waltz went down a block and turned around. He found a place to watch from across the street.

Eugene and the other man waited slumped low in the car. The precision of their arrival at the bank at 2 A.M. impressed Waltz. Planning was involved in this crime; care had been taken.

A second car with two people inside drove into the bank at 2:15 A.M. Eugene and his partner waited until the car had passed from their sight and then the interior light flashed as their doors opened. Waltz saw a brief, clear vision of two masked heads, ghoulish features for being lawless, and then they were out and the light was gone.

The two men hurried around the corner of the bank. One of the men from the second car had emerged with a satchel that hung with a weight Waltz knew was money. He was moving toward the bank's night-deposit slot when Eugene stepped up beside him and put a gun against the man's head. A light for the convenience of night depositors shone down on this scene with the clarifying properties of ice. It was a vision Waltz never expected to forget: his son threatening another human being with a gun. Eugene had deftly shifted his body toward the street to block the crime from idle passersby, but too late. Waltz had witnessed. He had begun to cry.

Waltz was waiting when Eugene came home two hours later. He was sitting in the shadows of the stairwell. Eugene whistled softly coming up the stairs. He carried the dark bag, his step was buoyant.

"Did you kill those two men?" Waltz asks.

Eugene's hand dove into the shadows within his coat. He would come out with a gun and shoot his father. But then he saw who it was and stopped. An embarrassed grin cut across his drawn lips.

"Daddy, you scared the shit out of me," he says. "What are you doing here at this time of the morning?"

"I've been here most of the night, in Flint," he says. "I watched you tonight."

"Cut the crap, Daddy. O.K.? What is it? You want to borrow some money?"

"No."

Eugene unlocked his apartment and went inside. But he turned in the doorway to block his father's entry.

"The place is a pigsty, Daddy. I'll invite you back another time."

"Did you kill those two men?"

Eugene sighed. "What two men?"

"I'm not an idiot, Eugene! I'm not a madman. Please don't think I want to be here. I followed you tonight. I saw you pick up your friend. I saw him steal that car. I saw you rob that man. I saw you take the two men into the shadows behind the bank. Now I'm asking you: Did you kill them?"

Eugene shrugged and backed into the apartment. He threw the equipment bag on the kitchen table. He took off his coat and his gun.

"No, we didn't kill them," he says. "We gagged them and handcuffed them to a downspout. They'll be fine until they're found in the morning."

"Thank you for answering my question."

"Is that all?"

"How long has this been going on?"

Eugene had begun to count the stolen money. He organized the bills by denomination.

"How long has this been going on, Eugene?"

"Wait, I'm counting." He kissed his thumb as he worked. In a minute, he says, "Eight hundred ninety-one dollars. That's my share, Daddy. You want to borrow some?"

"Please answer my question," Waltz says.

"This tonight was our sixth time. Me and my friend do real well. We work well together."

"Who is he?" Waltz asks.

Eugene smiled and shook his head.

"Where did you meet him?"

"Around. He is the cousin of a guy who borrowed some money from me. We met in that way. One time, we were talking, we discovered a mutual desire and talent."

"What happens if you get caught?"

"Won't happen, Daddy," says Eugene. "Tonight was the second time we did this sort of job. We'll do something different next time. That's our secret. We only do something twice, then move on. Diversity is the key. The police never have a chance to learn your rhythm."

Waltz lit a cigarette. The sun would be coming up soon. He would drive home and undress and shower and sleep. His clothes hung on him with the feel of old paper. In the light of Eugene's apartment his hands looked dirty to him.

"Do you know a man named Paul Vermillion?" asks Waltz. Paul Vermillion should be his son, with his growing family, his eloquence and understanding of life, not this crook sitting before him boasting about his petty crimes.

Surprisingly, the name meant something to Eugene. His cockiness bled away a little. "A troublemaker," he says. "He works for a guy. They lend money. They resent my competitive edge. Paul Vermillion is a punk; trust me."

"He's come to me twice to talk about you."

"Yeah?"

"He says you're too rough. He says you beat people up."

"They don't pay," Eugene says. "What am I gonna do?"

"Take their collateral. Repossess their goods. Talk to them."

Eugene scoffed. "Talk," he says mockingly.

Waltz says, "I've never hit a man in my life over money."

"In Marathon you can make that deal work. Flint is another world."

"I do business in Flint," Waltz says. "Good people. People are the same all over. You talk sense to them. You make them understand they have to pay. Then they pay."

Eugene says, "They don't talk sense in Flint, Daddy."

"Do you have a lot of strings out?"

Eugene shrugged. He was going vague with exhaustion. Waltz heard morning birds. The night was turning lilac at the edges.

"Some." Eugene yawned.

"Paul Vermillion says nobody will borrow from you because you beat people up. He says you're committing crimes because you can't make money any other way."

Eugene got out of his chair. He had scraped the stacks of stolen bills and change back into the bag. "Well, Daddy, you can tell Paulie Vermillion to ram it. And you can tell him to mind his own fucking business."

"Watch your tongue, Eugene," Waltz scolds.

He left then, feeling like a father.

He went to his father's room and tapped on the door; he wanted to leave a wake-up call. His father answered the door in a beard of white foam, holding a straight razor with an opalescent cerulean handle that struck Waltz as the first beautiful vision of the day.

"Call me at six," Waltz says. "I'm going to sleep all day."

"That's laziness. Are you so rich you can sleep away one of God's days?"

"Yes," says Waltz. He had worked all night. "Call me at six," he says, then went down the hall to his office. He canceled his appointments. The voices of the debtors he spoke with on the telephone were infused with bald relief. Each was precise in his demand to be assured the extra day would not count against his debt. When his calls were finished he undressed in the bathroom. He took a shower and soaped his old body twice. He shaved in the shower by practiced touch. Then he was quick to sleep, dreaming how Louise would handle this situation.

Eugene, in his letters, would ask Waltz to visit him in prison.

"I would like to see you here some Sunday, Daddy. Do you

think that's possible? I would like it to be a surprise. That is something I miss about the world: surprises. So don't tell me when you're coming or even if you're coming and then I won't expect you. Then if you do come it will be a nice surprise."

Eugene, in his letters, sounded to Waltz like the quintessential obedient son. He sounded bled dry. Waltz wondered if this was some process of smoothing out his persona to exist in prison; fewer sharp edges to snag something coming the other way.

Eugene's hair was trimmed with silver touches and he had grown a mustache. His face had gone pale and lined. He sat down across from his father at the long counter divided into semi-private booths. He stacked his cigarettes and matches carefully in front of him.

They shook hands. They had thirty minutes; it seemed like a long time.

"How are you, Daddy?"

"I'm fine, Eugene."

"How's business?"

"Good. Business is always good."

"You and doctors." Eugene smiled. "Never a slump, huh?"

"Shys, doctors, and undertakers." Waltz smiled.

They lit cigarettes.

"I hear from Carla and Susan," Eugene says. "They write. Daddy Waltz writes."

"I should write more often."

"No. That's O.K. You write as often as you feel comfortable writing. I appreciate what I get when I get it."

"Were you surprised I came today?"

"No, not really," Eugene says. "I had a feeling about today."

He might have read his father's mind across all those miles. Waltz had made the decision Wednesday to visit. It had been so large in his mind, he had turned its emotions and ramifications over and over so much, they might have generated an energy of their own.

Eugene finished his cigarette and lit another. Nothing to talk about, nothing between them. The ashtray at Waltz's elbow was plastic, big and round as a plate, maroon with white print that read: PROPERTY MICHIGAN DEPT. OF CORRECTIONS.

Waltz guessed they did not last long in that room. Souvenirs of a grim afternoon, a snatch at something good out of all this, reaffirming the criminal element.

"I was talking to a woman who works here," Waltz says into the silence that looms as wasteful and blessed as it flays away at their thirty minutes. "She said you'd be out of here in 1982."

Eugene went cool; he became more like the man Waltz remembered. "Who was this woman?" he asks.

"A woman on the phone. I called about visiting hours."

"A nobody," says Eugene.

"She had access to your file."

"Did she have access to the key to this place?" Eugene asks angrily. Waltz realized he had brought time into the room.

"I'm sorry," Waltz says. "I should have kept my mouth shut."

"Forget it." Eugene was quiet a minute, just smoking, stacking and unstacking his cigarettes and matches. He says, "It doesn't pay to get too excited in this place."

They shook hands across the long table when it was time for Waltz to go. It was the moment his son seemed most imprisoned. "Can you come next week?" Eugene asks.

"I don't know."

"Don't make it a regular thing," Eugene says. He would use it as a device for counting time; his father's appearance would mean a week had elapsed.

"It will be a surprise," Waltz promises.

Daddy Waltz shook his son awake at six o'clock. Waltz had the feeling several days had passed, not just the daylight hours of one. He sat at his desk with a cup of coffee and a cigarette. He called directory assistance in Flint and learned Paul Vermillion's number was unlisted. He called his acquaintance in Flint.

"How do I get in touch with Paul Vermillion?"

"It's not easy."

"Do you have his number?"

"Are you in Flint?"

"I'm in Marathon."

"Can you come to Flint tonight?"

"Yes."

"Come to Flint. I'll show you Paul Vermillion's house."

He went to Flint and was taken to a house ringed with a fence on a small lake. A man at the front gate let Waltz through after passing his name ahead.

"I talked to Eugene," Waltz tells Paul Vermillion.

"Thank you, Harry. I appreciate it. Did you have any success?"

"My daughter had gone to talk to him," Waltz says, "and he wouldn't even open the door to her. I planned to wait for him in my car and catch him outside. He got away before I could approach him. So I followed. I watched him commit a crime."

"That must have been hard on you, Harry. Was it a common crime?"

"An armed robbery," Waltz says. "He and another man waited at a bank and robbed two men who had come to make a night deposit."

"From a Pizza Hut," Paul Vermillion says. "I heard about it. I'm surprised it doesn't happen more often. It is such an easy touch."

"I guess," Waltz shrugged. "I talked to Eugene when he got home. He was proud. Proud! Can you imagine that? Here he is, talking to his own father, and he is proud of the way he breaks the law. Proud that he and his partner never commit the same type of crime more than twice."

"He said that? They would be hard to catch."

Waltz asks, "Would they?"

"Yes. If they are careful and their bad luck is at a minimum, they would be hard to catch."

"Would my son go to prison?"

"Yes."

"He's never been convicted of anything else."

"For armed robbery you only have to be caught once."

"How long would he be in prison?"

"Five years. Seven. Ten? I could only make an educated guess. My advice is to stay clear of anything that might land you in prison. I'd tell your son the same thing."

"Could he be caught?" Waltz asks after a minute. He was proceeding within the boundaries of his emotions; what he had in mind felt right.

"The perfect crime has not been committed," Paul Vermillion says. "There's always a risk."

"Could you arrange for Eugene to be caught?"

"In the act of armed robbery?"

"Yes," says Waltz.

"Are you sure you want this?"

"My son is bad," Waltz says. "I can't explain why, but there it is. I saw this last night very clearly. You say he beats people. I saw him hold a gun to another man's head. Unless something changes, I'm afraid he'll be killed, or will kill someone himself."

"He's not liked," Paul Vermillion agrees. "There is considerable sentiment in Flint that the world would be a better place without Eugene Waltz."

Waltz shuddered. "You see? I like my idea even better after hearing that. It will be temporary removal. A way of clearing the air."

"You have no guarantee your plan will work," says Paul Vermillion. "He could come out of prison worse than when he went in. In fact, I'd say that is likely."

"I don't see a choice," Waltz says. "I love Eugene. I don't want him to die and that is the way I see him heading."

"All right, Harry. What you ask can be arranged."

A letter comes from Eugene. Waltz reads the previous:

Dear Daddy,

I've met a man here in prison who says he went to school with you. His name is Salvador Bonaparte. He says he can't get over the fact your son is in prison. Neither can I. Sal is doing life for killing two clerks during a liquor store robbery. He's a quiet man. He's very polite. He runs laps in the yard, then smokes like a fiend. He has been here thirty-one years, if you can imagine. He says his father once owed you money.

Sal Bonaparte, who with the Dugan twins once tried to rob Waltz in a Marathon alley, Sam Boggins coming to the rescue, was there.

Paul Vermillion had done his job too well.

Waltz wrote Eugene's name and address on a slip of paper. Paul Vermillion asked him to do this, and to sign his name at the bottom.

"I want to know that you want this thing done," Paul Vermillion says.

"I want it," Waltz says. "But I won't sign any notes. You have his address and you know I want this done. That's all you really need."

"Harry, I can't blame you."

"It's the work I'm in," Waltz says. "Never give another man your name. That's weakness."

"Sure, Harry."

Waltz went home to wait. He conducted business. He took a ride across the state with Daddy Waltz to talk to some customers. He watched the news. He listened for the phone. Finally, Paul Vermillion called.

"Harry, I've got to ask. Do you still want this thing done? I ask because it will be done tonight. We followed Eugene and his partner three nights ago. The word is that tonight they're going again. Everything is in place. They'll be arrested tonight for armed robbery unless you tell me otherwise. I just had to ask you one more time."

Waltz says, "It's what I want."

9

Waltz drives north, searching for Mary Hale. He has her work address and plans to follow her home from there; just as he had followed Eugene one night in Flint, as he had followed Louise to her lighted house, always afraid what might unwittingly be revealed.

He takes Route 15 to Route 46, at Richville, then turns west and drives into Saginaw. He knows the town a little, but stops at a gas station for directions. A young man, a kid with grease under his nails and a wise-guy look in his eyes, points the way. Waltz almost asks the kid what he should say to Mary Hale first; what do women want to hear these days?

It has been twenty years since he was interested in a woman. He thinks of himself in other terms now. He has seen many beautiful women in that time but he has always lacked the will or patience to learn them. In each woman he meets he sees unfathomable layers of emotion and experience. There is always so much there. It would take years to get to know each one. He thinks of them all in terms of Louise, thinks he must know them as well in order to love them.

The twenty years seem to him a second virginity. He was twenty years old the day he lost the first. The girl lives in Clio now and reads palms in her house. A sign hangs in her front window, a maroon hand upraised on a white board, it reminds Waltz of Michigan, the Mitten. He sees her on Marathon's square about once a year and is always hurt by her old age. She is a month older than Waltz, she affects a studied gypsy's eccentricities of dress to attract business; bright scarves tight on her skull, flashy spangles of gold jewelry, long black skirts, boots, dark expressions going gray. She fucked Waltz, then read his palm as a twentieth-birthday present. They had met in high school. She expressed worry about his short life line; she predicted his early death. He was glad they had already been to bed when she took this reading. He did not think he could enjoy himself with a woman incompetent in her chosen field. It would make him too sad. This palm reader never married and Waltz sometimes wondered if she foresaw that solitary state in the life stamped in her own palm.

Waltz drives to Mary Hale's office and parks with his back to the sun. A windowpane on the second floor is patched with a square of red paper. He waits, smoking, estimating the time by the march of shadows, and then Mary Hale emerges. She runs a hand through her hair, her eyes on Waltz. But she does not wave or smile and Waltz is relieved. She might not have seen him.

She lives in a house on Saginaw Bay. The house is built of cream brick and weathered wood, with a wide porch in back and a small walkway going out to the beach. The beach is dark sand. Across the asphalt road running in front of her house is a field of wild grass. If Waltz is daring he will park on a rise in the road and watch from there, across the wide field.

As always, he feels snagged on an aching shyness. His parents are not around to spring him loose. Mary Hale's house is perched on a gentle rise with the bay spread blue-gray behind it. He can go no closer to it. Words, possible phrases of introduction, break up in his mind. He drives home when the light fades too much to be of value, and, every time, a jolt of resolve and anticipation shoots through him; next time, he will approach her. Go right to the door and knock and say hello. But it is like any boy's love of anticipation. The next time, he only parks and watches. Nothing has changed.

Mary Hale watches Waltz from her house and wonders if she should rescue him. Six different windows face the road and she moves from one to another, keeping an eye on the loan shark. Between preparing dinner and working on material she brought home she will stop and go to the window and watch.

The car Waltz drives is different every time. But he parks in the same spot, usually at the same time of day, and his presence comforts her in a perverse way. On nights he doesn't visit she feels uneasy and wonders where he is. The bay water's coldness seems to radiate more easily into the house. She sees vague shapes moving in the wild grass. She is alone, and resents Waltz for leaving her that way.

They had played that game of spies on the streets of Flint, and sat together in the parking garage in the aftermath of a robbery. They had met when he came to collect a bad debt. Perhaps he makes no move toward her because he has seen her only in unseemly contexts.

That stalking game; it had thrilled her more than she admitted. He seemed to catch on so quickly. As if they thought alike. They both possessed a sly, serious playfulness. It had been years since she met a man who thought like her. Her ex-husband never had. In five years, most of it spent on the road between Flint and East Lansing, where she was attending law school, he had never caught on. Or she to him. She avoided sex with him their last year together. Knowing their time was running out, she feared being caught with a child, like a bell hung on her as she broke free.

She goes to the window and sees Waltz's car lights go on. It is almost dark and she knows it is time for him to leave. She could easily go to him. He spends entire afternoons just outside her door. But she wonders why she has to move first. And why she doesn't.

There is no light behind her, so she is invisible in the dark as he rides past. There is a boathouse down the road a quarter mile. Gulls, in daylight, hover and squawk above this place. Mary Hale thinks this is where Waltz turns around for the drive back. Her mailbox is out by the road. She could stand there by it, caught in his returning lights on an innocent errand, and with a wave hook him.

But she doesn't and he glides past. She is momentarily furious with him for being shy. Then she returns to her work in the back of the house, with a glass of cognac and a sweater over her shoulders to fight the bay's chill.

• • •

Mary Hale has a friend, his name is Dick Hisk. Going into private law practice she discovered a need for accessory personnel; a receptionist, then a legal secretary, later two more attorneys when her business grew. And, finally, Dick Hisk.

Dick Hisk was hired to find out anything her clients might not have told her. He was good at this, and circumspect. He was a bland-looking man, with lank hair, a pale face, dressing in olive-green slacks and a beige sport coat. He was basically a researcher, and Mary Hale liked his effectiveness and paid him well.

After the stalking game in Flint, when three weeks went by with no word from Waltz, she hired Dick Hisk to research the loan shark. He reported back in three days: Waltz was widowed, had lost a son in Vietnam, a second son was in prison on an armed robbery conviction; Hisk reported odd echoes emanating from this last fact. Waltz was the father of twin daughters. A respected and wealthy loan shark. Sixty-one years old. Never had problems with customers.

She thanked Hisk and paid him. She felt bad, having put the man on Waltz; he had somehow been reduced for a time to the level of a stickup man, or car thief.

She wonders why he won't come see her. He has come so far, why leave without speaking to her?

The following day, she thinks he has not come (he does not need to follow her home from work any longer; he is sometimes waiting for her when she returns). No car is parked across the field and she is disappointed. From day to day she has hope for him.

But then she is watering plants on the sun porch in the rear of her house and sees him on the beach. He is far enough away to obscure his face, but the wind turns his white hair into a flag. He is throwing stones into the bay. His motion is stiff, as though his joints are packed in slush, and with each release of a stone his head swivels around to take in the length of beach and the back of her house, which is already shadowed for the night.

Feeling girlish, almost asinine, she puts on a jacket and goes out the front door. She will rescue him, but not let him know he is being rescued. She trots up the bay road until she is out of breath. She walks until she comes to a narrow, sandy common drive that runs between two houses down to the beach. A policeman sometimes hides there to trap speeders; or sleeps away the dreary late hours of a shift. The lane is not empty now. A boy and a girl, high school age, stand pressed against the tall bushes that line the drive. They don't know her, but she smiles at them, and the girl smiles back. She looks like she is waiting to be kissed. There is a car parked farther down the lane. She guesses it belongs to Waltz.

Mary Hale comes out of the drive up the beach from Waltz. He is about one hundred yards away, still throwing stones into the water. His eyes keep turning, regular as a lighthouse, toward her house. She needs a prop and finds a staff of driftwood that is so smooth and straight it might once have been a broom handle. So she has been on a beach hike. She sets off toward Waltz. She hates this coy ruse, but sees no way around it. It is this, or be alone when she does not want to be alone. After she knows him better, after they are friends, she will make him pay in some small way for putting her up to this.

Ten yards from him, she calls, "Why, Mr. Loan Shark!"

He freezes his throw to turn to her. He holds the stone as if it is a last weapon, and his face when he recognizes her is gripped with a fear that nearly kills her enthusiasm. He looks so frightened in that instant. But then it slips under and he smiles, he looks merely flustered, and she begins to think she has done the right thing.

"What brings you here?" she asks, wanting him to pay already for making her do this.

He finishes his throw. The stone shoots into the curl of a shallow wave with a faint *thwip!*

"I've been following you," he says. With Mary Hale there, the link made and smiles exchanged, he is full of possibilities. He even sees his shyness as a tool of charm.

"I know," she says. "You aren't very secretive about it."

"Almost like I wanted to get caught?"

She nods. "So why didn't you come to my door?" She is suddenly angry at all the time he has wasted.

"It's not my nature," Waltz says. "Sometime I'll tell you about the courting of my wife, Louise. It is a legend in my family."

"Why not tell me now?"

He looks quickly at her; that expression of fright surfaces, then slips under. She is more curious about this man than anything. He does not really excite her; his skin is loose and pale. He is on the edge of being an old man. But she senses a boy caught in him, one he tries to rid himself of, but which stubbornly refuses to set him free to be an old man.

"I was afraid you thought of me in a criminal way," she confesses. She holds the long stick in two hands. The distance between them has remained.

"Why?" he asks, truly curious.

"The places you saw me. Once, when you came to collect a bad debt. Then on the streets of Flint, in that seedy garage, in the midst of a robbery."

"Your ice pick scared me."

"It did?"

"You were good with it," he says, throwing a stone. "Like you practiced."

"I only let the air out of that man's tires. And he deserved worse. I hate stupid people, and it's so rare you can get any revenge on them for their stupid acts. A flat tire, he could understand that."

"You seemed so sure of yourself," Waltz went on. "Why would you need me? My daddy told me a long time ago that there are certain women who learn they don't need men, and then there is no getting through to them. You struck me as that sort of woman."

She is flattered, though she doubts he meant it that way. "Thank you. I guess maybe I am."

"So you see"—he spreads his arms, a stone, one blue, one

white, in each hand—"why should I try to break through at this late date?"

"Do what you want," she says, impatient with his hesitance. Her eyes look beyond Waltz, at her house. It is a short walk. She is willing to make it alone. Does he know enough about women to know this is his last chance with her?

She is gripping the stick like a baseball bat, so Waltz winds up slowly, he wants to tip her off to his playful intent, and lobs a stone toward her. It travels in an arc and she swings too late and misses.

"Again," she says, setting her feet in the sand, bringing the stick up high, memories of her girlhood.

Waltz takes two steps back, winds, and throws. The stone is not round and he throws too hard for its angles and surfaces to pass unhindered through the air. It swoops in on Mary Hale. She has to jump out of its way.

"Again," she says, smiling.

He finds a stone most nearly ball-like. It is the size of a large marble, with faint silver flecks in its gray coat. He throws this easily, wanting her to hit it. She does, too. The crack makes Waltz turn his back toward her out of protection. The struck stone sings out of sight. Neither sees it land. As if that was the last ball in the game, they stop playing.

"Can I stay for dinner?" he asks.

"Do you want to? It might be dangerous."

He closes one eye to look at her. "Yes, I think it might be," he says. "But I'd like to stay anyway."

"Will you tell me how you courted Louise?"

"I might. Have we even determined we like each other?"

"I'm intrigued by you," Mary Hale says. "I'm not sure I like you, however. I'm tired of being the only one doing the mating dance."

Waltz smiles. "You *are* dangerous," he says. He takes her arm and they walk to the car parked in the beach drive. It is a short ride to the house, as short as their ride in the parking garage. But nothing is in their path to slow them and elation fills Waltz the first time he steps into her house.

• • •

Mary Hale is tan, with flashes of white underskin (palms, toes). She wears a yellow sundress, a gold bracelet, and a pair of sandals that slap against the bottom of her feet. She shares a couch with Waltz on her sun porch. She has stacked her work out of the way on a table. Somewhere in the stack is Dick Hisk's report on Harry Waltz; she wonders what Waltz would think if he knew. The room is full of plants that radiate a green coolness. She finds her sweater and settles it on her shoulders. He makes a motion to help her with the sweater, but she has it arranged before he can reach her, and he is left in an awkward space, his hands up as though to hang invisible wash. They both have a glass of beer. Neither has spoken a word.

"I said you were intriguing," she says, deciding to have the worst out, where she will know if the evening will break up before too much is invested. "I wanted to know more about you, so I had a man look into you."

Waltz stares at her. She notices how the beer bubbles shoot up the center of his glass; air pearls. Has he heard what she said? Will he leave without uttering a single word in her house?

"And what did he find out?" Waltz finally asks.

"Nothing to be secretive about. He told me you were a widower. That you have two daughters. That you lost a son in Vietnam. And that you have a son in prison."

"All true." Waltz nods. "My daughters are twins. I have a twin brother in California. My father had a twin brother."

"My," she says.

Waltz thinks: Look into you. As if his skin was glass.

"Who was this man?" he asks.

"He's a researcher for me. He's valuable in my line of work. Often people aren't generous with the truth. He is good at filling out the bits and pieces of what I know. He says you are sixty-one years old."

"Yes. How old are you?"

"Forty-two."

"Since I haven't had you tailed," he begins—although he did

check into her, learning only fragments; he just was not as thorough as she was—"maybe you could tell me something about yourself."

"I'm an attorney. Married once, divorced for . . . seventeen years now. No children. I love my work."

"What sort of law do you practice?"

"Cheap, tawdry, and lucrative. Bankruptcies. A small criminal trade. Divorces. Many divorces. It amazes me, all the couples splitting up to weather these bad economic times alone. It's something that makes me very sad."

"But you're alone," he says, almost accusing her.

"Yes. But your father—what he said—has merit, to a degree, with certain women. I'm not absolutely sure it applies to me. I've spent time with men the past seventeen years. I lived with one from New Year's Day 1969 to the Fourth of July 1970. Another lawyer. A prick." She shivers and sips her beer. She waits for Waltz to stand and depart. But he is unfazed by her emotion and her words. She likes him for this.

"And I didn't say being alone didn't make me sad sometimes," she adds.

"How long has your hair been white?"

"Since I was twenty-eight. My mother's turned at the same age. She remembers hers going white overnight."

"Maybe she had a bad dream," Waltz says.

They have begun readying a bed of coals in a grill out back. When they go together to check the fire's progress a cool wind pours up from the bay.

"My first husband took me out there"—she points to the darkening bay, its horizon distant and ill-defined—"in a rowboat. We were drinking wine. He got drunk and fell in."

Waltz listens for her meaning. She forms ground beef into rough disks and positions them on the black grill rods. Then she wipes her hands on a towel.

"My back was turned to him," she continues. "He was standing in the boat, pontificating about something, embarrassing himself. I turned away to discourage him. When I turned back he was just a head bobbing alongside the boat. He had the stupidest look on his face. Then he went under. I remember two things about what happened next. One, I remember thinking I could see his face with its silly expression looking up at me from underwater. That is impossible, of course. The water was—is—dark and cold. It was nearly dusk. We were fools to be out there. If I saw something I thought was his face, I was imagining it, or hallucinating.

"And the second thing I remember thinking was that if he didn't surface I would be rid of him, and if he did I would have to divorce him."

She drinks some beer. Her jaw, raised up to swallow, is lean, with just the beginning hint of a slackening. She does not look at Waltz.

"You were willing to let nature decide," he says.

She nods. "Then he surfaced. But a decision *had* been made. I manhandled him back into the boat, throwing my back out in the process, and he lay there throwing up water and wine while I rowed us in."

"And you divorced him?"

"Not right away. A year passed. But the wheels had been set in motion, at least in my mind. Whenever my back goes out, I think of him."

Waltz says, "How sweet," and Mary Hale laughs.

They eat in the kitchen; it is too cool to stay out back and too awkward balancing the plates of runny burgers and limp salad on their knees on the sun porch. There is a banked skylight in the kitchen ceiling and just a faint wash of light remains in it before dark.

"Why did you have me checked out?" Waltz asks.

"A need to know," Mary Hale says right away. "It's sort of a compulsion with me. I wanted to be a reporter before I went into the law. I was an information addict. But then I learned that a reporter only interpreted information. A lawyer could do something with it. At first, with you, looking into you, I was after something my brother could use against you."

"Some grain of scandal?"

"Maybe." She shrugs, watching him.

"Did you find anything?"

"Maybe," she says, and looks away. It is the first time Waltz thinks she is flirting. She asks, "How did you get my brother to owe you money?"

"It was easy. He borrowed. It happens every day."

"And when will it end?"

"When he's paid back what he owes." He wants to talk about that day on the river, and about the grain of scandal she unearthed. He says, "After I met you at your brother's house, you hated me, didn't you?"

"Yes and no." She smiles.

"You seemed so capable and self-assured," Waltz says. "I tried to find you for a long time afterwards."

She raises an eyebrow. "Then, having found me, you were too petrified to come forward."

"Yes. Do you remember when you saw me beside the river?"

She won't look away. "Yes," she says.

"When I couldn't find you I went back to that spot," he takes a breath, "and undressed completely."

She produces a hoot of laughter. "Why on earth . . . ?"

"In the hope . . . as a way of calling you back," he says.

"Conjure me up with the male form?"

Waltz laughs that he has come this far on his own. "It was so amazing that you saw me that time. I thought it might work a second time."

"And this is the man too shy to come to my front door and say hello?" she says. "Life *is* full of amazement."

They get through dinner and Waltz helps with the dishes. Out a window he can see the coals in the grill twinkling, a city in a bowl, when the bay breeze puffs up through the vents.

Mary Hale has tied her hair back out of the way with a gold ribbon.

"Tell me about your son," she says.

His drying of a dinner plate ceases. "I can't," he says. "I don't know you that well. I'm sorry."

She likes this, that he is not easy with his emotions. Men, the men she meets, the men she occasionally brings home, are always overflowing with the awful lives they have led. These men are sloppy, spilling.

"Why is he in prison?" she asks.

"Oh—" Waltz says. He thought she was asking about Monroe, but it is Eugene she is interested in. "How much do you know about Eugene?"

She thinks of that odd echo that surfaced with the fact. "A little," she says.

"Then why ask?" A sudden angry light goes on in his eyes.

"I'm trying to draw you out," she says. "I'm circling."

"Do you know why he's in prison?"

She nods, almost proud. "Armed robbery."

"So why ask?"

"I'm sorry," she says. "I should be more forthright. It's the lawyer in me. Men are always telling me I hold back something—one vital bit of myself—as if I expect to use it later to win some mysterious case. If I know more about you than you know about me, then I'm ahead. Do you see?"

Waltz hangs the dish towel on its hook and sits down at the kitchen table. He gets up again immediately and goes into the sun porch. Mary Hale thinks for a moment that he is getting ready to leave, that she has driven him away, and a sad spot expands in her chest. But he was only getting his cigarettes and an ashtray.

She feels better and lets him smoke in peace while she finishes the dishes. He is a distant smudge of light and shadow in the kitchen window.

She joins him at the table. He lights her cigarette. Feeling bold, she pursues that echo she got from Dick Hisk.

"There *is* something I don't know about you," she begins. "There's a lot I don't know, of course, but one thing in particular about your son in prison."

"Eugene," Waltz says. "His name's Eugene."

"Yes. My researcher told me something pretty hard to believe.

He said that in his research he kept hearing rumors to the effect that you sent your son to prison."

"It's true," Waltz says.

She leans forward into the smoke of her cigarette and blinks. "Why?" she asks.

"He was heading for trouble," Waltz explains. "Eugene is in the same line of work I'm in—but you probably know that—and people told me he was beating up people. And also that there was a chance he would be killed, he was that unpopular."

"So you sent him to prison?" she says incredulously.

"I arranged for him to be caught committing a crime. I saw him rob two men. I *witnessed* this. It was my belief that prison was the only alternative. I didn't want him to get killed. Or hurt. So I arranged for him to get caught."

Mary Hale shakes her head. "Do you want him out?" she asks.

"No."

"He's your *son.*"

"He's better off where he is," Waltz says.

"That's absurd. Do you visit him?"

"Yes. Not regularly. He likes to be surprised."

"Take me to visit him," she requests.

"That would be an odd date," he says, smiling uneasily.

"Harry, please?"

"Let me tell you about my boy who died in Vietnam," he says. She has turned Monroe's memory into the safer ground. He trusts her to understand he was his favorite.

10

Waltz once asked Monroe what he wanted to be, not when he grew up, but any time, and Monroe said, "A musician. One skilled in performing or composing music." He used his allowance to rent an upright piano for five dollars a month. Two men in a truck came and wheeled the scratched old thing into the house and up against the wall. A yellow-keyed creature, reclining maidens carved in its wood, with grooves of wear, stained with drink and burned with cigarettes, Monroe loved it. He loved to smell the smoky air trapped between the keys. He told his father he wanted a piano that knew its way around.

He was then twelve years old.

He had the hands and the ear. He would have been at that piano every hour of the day if he had not had to attend school. Still, he played for two hours before school and at least four hours afterward. At first he produced just ragged collections of notes and tortured scales that wore thin the nerves of the house. Eugene, violent being even then, threatened to shoot Monroe, or the piano, or both. Then just like that the notes began to gather into songs. Waltz wondered how long this had gone on before he noticed. He had adopted a patient deafness toward his son's piano playing; he did not listen, therefore he was not annoyed by the early boil of learning. It was a gift of concentration. So Monroe might have been playing songs for some time before his father noticed. Lines of melody began to stretch from the piano through the house. Waltz looked up from counting his money. The song was strange to him.

"What's that?" he asked, going to the room where Monroe played. The young man had made the room his own, staking it out with saucers, empty glasses, bits of sandwich, a sweater thrown over a chair, shoes and trousers and school books thrown aside.

"It's just a song of mine," Monroe said, playing.

"What do you call it?"

Monroe shrugged and played. "It doesn't have a name," he said. His father's attention was embarrassing. He often played under the illusion the music he formed did not travel beyond himself. He played, looked up at his father while he played. "I was only noodling," he explained.

"It's good," Waltz said, and backed out of the room, seeing his son so ill at ease in his eyes, but his hands loose and on their own.

Monroe came home from school the next day, pulled off his coat and shirt, took his place at the piano, flipped up the key cover, and only then realized it was a different piano. This new piano was polished black lacquer, the keys creamy, their touch energetic and alive. He played his one song and it was not the same song. Something had happened to it, something had moved in and blown further life into the song's corners.

Waltz remembered that piano as the one cruel act of his life. The piano was repossessed from a family that had been in arrears for several months, a good family with six children and three jobs worked between the parents. But they missed payments and Waltz only let them keep the piano because it was inconvenient for him to haul it away, he had no place to take it. Now, however, he had a son who wrote songs.

"You take it without warning?" the woman had screamed at him. The two movers Waltz had hired worked around them.

"You've had warnings," Waltz said. "For seven months I've sent notes of warning to your husband. You must pay, or lose the piano, these notes said clearly. Every one a warning."

"But just like that you come into our house and take it away?" she asked.

"Yes, just like that the piano is mine."

He sat in his office and heard Monroe come home. He heard him go across the floor, scrape the piano bench into place, heard the key cover open, heard his son's song.

Nights, Daddy Waltz and May came downstairs to dance. They called out requests for old favorites but Monroe would play only his own songs. He was fourteen years old by then, and he kept a guitar in the corner that he could play now and upstairs in his bedroom was a banjo and a saxophone. He played them all with startling ease. And every time Waltz came into the room his son seemed to be playing a new song he had just written.

Daddy Waltz once said to his son, when they were in the kitchen and Monroe was out front playing some sad song of his on the guitar, "Have you thought of having somebody look at Monroe?"

"Look at him?"

"Hell, yes, Harry. The kid has got—it seems to me—pure innate musical talent to an extraordinary degree. I'd be curious to have a professional evaluate him. He may get more from his talent with professional guidance than just teaching himself."

"He won't join the band at school," Waltz said.

"Why?"

Waltz shrugged. "He said he was not interested. He practices more than any kid in the school, I'm sure. From the moment he opens his eyes in the morning he's making music of one sort or another. I think he thinks the other kids in the band won't take it as seriously as he does."

"I just have to wonder, Harry. With that natural drive, that desire to play, I'd be curious to see what he'd accomplish with a real music coach."

"He plays four instruments already and he's never taken a lesson," Waltz declared. "He writes his own songs. Good songs, too, you can hear it. What is he going to learn from some dusty old teacher in back of a music store?"

"I don't know, Harry. I know nothing about music. But Monroe has something wonderful and a trained musician might bring even more of it out."

"I'll talk to him, Daddy."

Later, Waltz knocked on the bathroom door; he had heard music coming from within.

"Who is it?" Monroe asked.

"Me."

"Come in."

Monroe was sitting naked on the edge of the tub, he had draped a towel over his waist. He was playing his saxophone. Faint curls of black hair grew out of the hollow over his breastbone. His face bore a remarkable clearness, with sparse stands of dark whisker on his upper lip, chin, and sideburns. While he studied his father and waited for him to speak he kept the sax reed wet, licking it and puffing his cheek like some weird nocturnal lizard uncomfortable at being caught in the light.

"You were very good tonight," Waltz said.

Monroe lowered his eyes. His impulse was to blow a note of triumph. But instead, shrugging his bony shoulders, he said, "I was just noodling."

"I can't help but notice," Waltz said, "that you're always good. You really seem to enjoy it."

"I do," Monroe said.

"Any friends of yours at school play?"

"I met some guys," Monroe said, then stopped, frowning. "They went to a different junior high, which is why I'd never run into them before."

Waltz nodded, then waited.

After a time Monroe understood his father expected to hear more. "Anyway, these guys, one guy has a small drum kit. Another one has a passable voice and plays some guitar. And another guy plays guitar O.K. and thinks he can sing."

Waltz asked, "Are they as good as you?"

"I can't sing."

"But musically, are they as good?"

Monroe smiled and looked away and wet the sax reed. A soft note escaped from the horn's bell. "No," he finally said.

"Are you guys forming a band?"

"The issue has come up."

"Have you ever thought about taking some lessons?"

"I've thought about it."

"Interested?"

"Not really."

"Your grandfather took me aside tonight. He seems to think what you have in the way of musical talent is—and I quote—wonderful, unquote. He also wondered what you might accomplish with some professional training."

"I'm not interested, Daddy," Monroe said carefully, wary of the enthusiasm in the air. "Right now, it just comes out, I don't know why. I love doing it. I don't have to be pushed."

"O.K.," Waltz said. He touched Monroe's knee, then stood. "If somewhere down the line you change your mind, just let me know. I'll be glad to foot the bill. O.K.?"

"O.K."

Waltz afterward stood in the hall for the longest time listening to a soft sax song blown with relief, his son conversing with himself.

Two months later, on a Friday night, Monroe left home carrying his guitar and saxophone. He declined dinner and went off down the hill toward town, carrying an instrument case in each hand.

Waltz wanted to follow him, as he had been following his children all their lives, never getting caught, keeping them safe and in sight; he planned to stop when they were at an age when what he observed them doing might break his heart. Monroe was a sophomore in high school then, and nearing that age.

He returned at 1 A.M. wild-eyed with excitement. It was a look Waltz took for sex; he guessed his son had been with a girl. Monroe's testicles would hang gloriously aching.

"You're an hour late, kiddo," Waltz said.

"I know, Daddy, and I'm sorry," Monroe said. He was wetting his lips, his hands jumping about, sweet adolescent sweat pasting his shirt, rolling in the cracks of his skin. "But I want to talk to you about that."

"I allowed Eugene one infraction before I laid down the law," Waltz said. "I'll allow the same for you. Next time, you're grounded for a week."

Monroe listened to this, outwardly patient. He swept a hand through his hair.

"Can I talk to you about it, Daddy?"

"Sure."

Monroe took a check for a hundred dollars from his wallet. The check was made out to The "Noodle" Waltz Band from the Marathon school district.

"I am a professional musician," Monroe said, holding the check in both hands. "This will be divided four ways, but still, somebody paid me to play music."

Waltz took the check and studied it. He felt a boundless pride and longing. His younger son was sliding away from him already. He shook Monroe's hand. "That's just terrific," he said.

"And we have jobs next Friday and Saturday night," Monroe

said. "I wondered if I could have my curfew extended since I'll be working and making money."

"Where are the jobs?"

"Friday night in Davison. Saturday night in Flint."

"How will you get there?"

"Gary—our drummer—his mom has a station wagon. If we pack it right we can get all our gear in there. Gary's brother is nineteen and has a license. He's got no talent, he's got no job either, and he's out of school. He has kind of attached himself to us. He's the driver, he helps us set up, he got us this job in Flint. I think he wants to be our manager if we'd let him."

"Monroe . . . you're only fifteen years old," Waltz said. "Flint is quite a different story for four high school kids."

"It's a good job, Daddy," Monroe said intently. "Two hundred fifty dollars. A huge high school. You make it in Flint, you've got a chance of going somewhere."

"Davison is O.K.," Waltz said. "Flint I've got to think about."

Monroe nodded, satisfied with the night's progress. The Flint job, he would be there; he had no intention of defying his father, only convincing him.

" 'The "Noodle" Waltz Band'?" Waltz said, reading from the check.

Monroe grinned proudly. "That's us."

"Why that?"

"Because it's my band, Daddy. I got us together, I wrote the songs, I'm the heart."

"Why 'Noodle'?"

"It's what I'm called."

So they played in Flint and a fight did break out in the parking lot, but they weren't involved. The next weekend they were in East Lansing. He is moving west, Waltz thought, and sure enough, The "Noodle" Waltz Band played Battle Creek and then Kalamazoo early in January. When the time came for Monroe to leave for Vietnam, Waltz felt a fragile certainty that the times were auspicious; his son was heading west, embarking from California, and he would not be touched.

Musical notoriety came to Monroe. Young, silly, striking girls, strangers to Waltz, began to assemble at the house, the house of "Noodle" Waltz. They spent hours in the room with the piano, the first girl in line rewarded with a seat on the piano bench itself. All they wanted was for Monroe to play.

Monroe sometimes left them for an hour at a time to read in his bedroom. He hoped his rude behavior would drive them away. When the girls still stayed he seemed dismayed. Waltz thought to be the host and entertain these young ladies but he saw in their gaping looks that he was an alien form, an adult with an adult's boring stories, and a pale substitute for his son.

"What am I going to do, Daddy?" Monroe whispered to his father one day. Monroe was then eighteen years old by a week, he would graduate from high school in a month. He had filled out in the shoulders and calves, he wore his hair short while everyone else grew theirs to rebellious lengths. He claimed his band was the only one in the state of Michigan playing its own songs.

"What are you going to do about what?"

"All those girls."

"Enjoy them, Monroe. I imagine a time will come when you will wonder where they all went. So enjoy the attention they pay you."

"They're so young. And they're annoying as hell," he said with something like fear. "I can't play my guitar or saxophone upstairs because they'll come running up to my room. They're so nervy, sophomores. And I can't play the piano because they are *right there.*"

"Do you want them to leave?"

"Yes, I do."

"Then ask them to leave," Waltz said. "Be a gentleman and ask them to leave."

Seven girls waited for Monroe around the piano. Waltz followed his son downstairs and watched unnoticed from the doorway.

Monroe moved through them, touching one or two atop the head or on the cheek, as if he did not trust his balance. Years from now, Waltz thought, Monroe would want this moment frozen in time.

"One song," Monroe said, sitting down at the piano. He held up one finger so every girl saw and understood. "Then I've got to study. You'll all have to leave after that, O.K.?"

Then Monroe played four songs. He spoke soft words between each, though each song ran into the next, his hands just playing, and the girls stood in a half ring around him at the piano, hiding him from Waltz. His son was safe in there in a cloud of perfumed hair. They were slow songs Waltz had never heard. They had words the girls knew by heart; they sang, but Monroe did not. He finished upbeat and quick, whirling off the piano bench and breaking through the half ring of girls. He went straight to the door.

"Time to go, ladies."

"May we come tomorrow, Noodle?" they asked hopefully.

Monroe looked at them, perplexed. Didn't they have something of their own to do?

"Yes. You may come tomorrow. But remember, just one song."

The girls would smile and go away. The bravest among them, and they were all brave, kissed Monroe on the cheek, lips, or neck as they filed out the door. His father watched enthralled.

Monroe graduated from high school and moved into a field of dread certainty that lately occupied much of his father's thoughts. Waltz read the newspapers. His son was young, strong, and out in the open. He spent that summer in The "Noodle" Waltz Band and from mid-May to mid-September played a hundred and one dates, Monroe's share coming to about $15,000, a stupefying fortune his son only saw growing.

Also, that summer he made two key personnel changes. He fired Gary Midland, the band's original drummer, and Glennie Black, the band's first bass guitarist.

Firing Gary Midland was easy. He had become entangled in the trappings of minor Michigan fame. He missed rehearsals three times in two weeks, then missed a performance in Grand Rapids, during which Monroe sat in on drums borrowed from another band on the bill.

Monroe came straight home that night and reached Midland on the telephone.

He said, "You awake, Gary? I'm going to say something to you and I want to make sure you understand. Are you awake?"

Waltz listened from the next room. He sat in the dark smoking. Everything was silver, the air, the rims of his hands, his son's voice. It was a quarter to four.

"I don't care about the girl," Monroe said patiently. "I want your undivided attention. Yes, hi, Angela. Put Gary back. . . . I'm doing O.K., Angela. You? . . . Yes, the job went fine. Put Gary back on."

Quiet again. Waltz heard his son's sigh of exasperation.

"Look, Gary," he said, "I don't want to hear any of your lame excuses. This is a professional band and you have not conducted yourself in a professional manner. I gave you warnings when you missed the rehearsals. Missing a show, I can't accept that. I'm letting you go, Gary."

Waltz listened through the silence; he imagined the drummer's rattling plea for another chance. He was proud of Monroe taking responsibility all down the line. At the moment of dismissal he did not switch to the collective "we"; it was "Noodle" Waltz himself doing the firing, not The "Noodle" Waltz Band.

"Don't be that way, Gare," Monroe said calmly. "You're a good drummer. You can hook on with someone else if you clean up your habits."

Monroe listened, Waltz listened; when his son spoke again his voice had gone imperiously cool and flat: "You're not *that* good a drummer, Gary. You brought this on yourself. I'm not buying any of that guilt. I've got two or three guys coming in to audition. I can fill in . . . Hey, O.K. No problem. Sorry you're being this way. Good luck to you."

Monroe hung up the phone. Waltz heard him mutter, "Asshole."

The firing of Glennie Black took place in a rehearsal room in Marathon above a hardware store—a long, cavernous, wood-floored room Monroe rented for twenty dollars a week. He had the only key. The hardware store's owner stipulated only that they rehearse after business hours.

Monroe kept a rented piano there, as well as the band's amps, the new drummer's kit, the guitars, tambourines, mikes, mike stands, snaked cables, a coffee pot, a five-dollar couch; pictures of nude women cut from magazines with razors and pictures of the Beatles hung on the walls. Tall, thin windows looked on the square. Monroe could see his home from there.

The decision to fire the bass player again was solely Monroe's. It was a decision based on pure musicality. Glennie Black had been in the band from the beginning. A year older than Monroe, he was noted for his bass obsession, carrying his guitar to school and playing it for the seven minutes between classes, and writing strained, shallow songs Monroe nevertheless always gave a shot. Glennie was the first band member at every rehearsal, he was the first one ready to go to every performance. He had also named the band.

When he graduated from high school he turned down a good job at his father's company selling carburetors. He believed his destiny was in rock and roll.

But Monroe, much as he liked Glennie Black, had never been very happy with his playing. Through high school and the string of hops and bar jobs Monroe had been able to overlook Glennie's shortcomings and hide his inadequacies within the mesh of the music. Glennie had other qualities; he was dependable, he worked hard, he was enthusiastic, he was Monroe's friend.

But like Glennie Black, Monroe also believed in the impending success of The "Noodle" Waltz Band. Once out of high school it was obvious to Monroe he could no longer afford to carry Glennie's bass. The band was now Monroe's livelihood. Three very good bass players had contacted Monroe, each with basically the same pitch: "We both know Glennie is holding your band back. When you decide to shuck him, keep me in mind."

Waltz found Monroe in the gazebo one night in early June. Monroe was sipping a bottle of beer and smoking a cigarette. He was crying.

"I fired Glennie tonight, Daddy."

Waltz nodded and waited.

"It's been coming on for a while," his son continued. "I've auditioned a couple guys on my own. Either one of them will be a better musician than Glennie."

"How'd he take it?"

"Like I stole his girl. Like I shot him through his heart. He kept pushing me for a reason. When I was letting him go I laid it out like a real ham-handed bastard. I was trying to be easy on him and easy on myself. I wasn't honest with either of us. He kept pushing . . . telling me we were friends, that we were going to the top together. Finally . . . I just came out and told him he wasn't good enough."

"Ouch," Waltz winced.

"Yeah, it was bad. Firing Midland was a snap. He was a fuckup. Firing Glennie because he didn't measure up, that's the worst thing I've ever done in my life."

"Most difficult, maybe," Waltz said. "It was not a bad thing, though. You believe you can do better without Glennie. It was a business decision. Things like that happen every day."

Monroe shuddered. "Do you know Glennie's got a brother in there?" he asked, tipping the mouth of his beer bottle toward the State Home. "He's only fourteen years old. A gooby through and through."

"That's too bad," Waltz said.

"Glennie thinks it's in him, too. When I let him go tonight and he got ugly, he accused me of thinking he was a quasi-gooby. He's always explained his low grades that way. It's sad."

In the fall, Glennie Black was drafted. Waltz felt for him. Once outside the safe haven of the band, Waltz figured Glennie was a goner. He figured his son was safe.

But then Mitch Levering, the band's singer, got his draft notice. It scared Waltz and struck the band like something catching.

"I can't hold them together," Monroe told his father. "Without Mitch we've got no real singer, and everyone thinks they're next to go."

"What about you?" Waltz asked.

"What *about* me?"

"Being drafted. Why don't you take some college courses somewhere? Why don't you get your butt in out of the line of fire?"

"Not interested."

"Don't you read the papers, Monroe? Don't you see where we're going in Vietnam? This is our next war, and they will need lots of strong, young men like you to fight it."

"I can hire another singer," Monroe said, as if he had not been listening. "We've got dates through New Year's."

A twenty-year-old woman named Dundee Holland was hired to be the new singer. She had a good, strong voice and a sensual awkwardness onstage. The band never warmed to her in a professional sense. Within a month of her arrival, however, she had moved in with the drummer and was lusted after by the bass player.

"It's coming apart, Daddy," Monroe said. "My only hope is she gets drafted."

Waltz laughed. Monroe looked at him sharply; he had been serious.

"I have committed the unpardonable sin," he said. "I have introduced sex into a working relationship. I never should've hired a girl. Even the audiences react to us differently. Having a girl singer, I get the impression they don't know what to make of us." He ran his hand over his face. "I blew it. I'm the last original member of the band left."

"So start over," Waltz said. "Honor the dates you have left but don't add any more. Then get out and start fresh."

"I've been doing that. But truthfully, the demand has not been there. Only one job offer for all of January."

Waltz said, "You, on your own, could do better than any band."

"I got no pipes, Daddy," Monroe said. "If I can't sing, people won't pay to sit and listen to me play."

"How do you know? They might."

"Nah." He sighed. "I think you're right. Time for me to get an education. This has been sweet, but the feeling is it's quitting time."

"You're just down," Waltz said, alarmed by his son's easy despair. "Let it sit for a couple days."

Glennie Black came home for Christmas and appeared on Waltz's front porch. In uniform, his hair cut in a burr, he grinned at Monroe and presented a bottle of scotch.

"Merry Christmas, you dumb asshole," he shouted. "Invite me in for a glass of my own scotch."

They took chairs around the kitchen table, Glennie Black, Monroe, his father.

"I hear you hired a chick," Glennie said.

Monroe nodded, gloomy. "She's a nice girl and a good singer," he said. "But she is a wrench in the works. You wouldn't believe the rehearsals. Every ten minutes she and Ross are over in the corner giggling or arguing and Al is sore because he wants to be in the corner with her giggling and arguing. They're all like dogs, suspicious, sniffing around, dogs in heat."

Glennie swirled his drink. "So fire her ass."

"I should."

"Or are you interested too?"

"No. That would invite utter pandemonium."

"So what's your plan?" Glennie asked.

"I'm gearing down," Monroe said. "We've got three dates between now and the New Year. At rehearsal tonight I'm telling them I'm through after that."

"Just like that?" said Waltz.

"Just like that."

Glennie said, "That's pretty quick and dirty."

"Right from the beginning I've been the only one to treat it like a business," Monroe replied. "They'll have two weeks' notice just like any other job. They should've been saving their money right along anyway."

"Then what will you do?" Waltz asked.

Monroe shrugged. He had felt some cell of music within him go dry of late. The fault was his own, too, he believed; firing a friend, hiring the girl, he had made all the wrong decisions. He feared making others now; he felt carried away by bad momentum. His hope was to come to a complete stop, pause, then get started again in a better way.

"I've got some money saved," he told his father. "I can wait and see."

"No . . ." Waltz said, the old fear returning, but Glennie Black spoke up.

"You'll soon be off to see the world like me. First sunny California, then sunny Vietnam."

"You're going?"

"I'm practically gone," Glennie said. "An ever-increasing U.S. presence in Vietnam is anticipated. The rumor is a million more men drafted in the next year. I am infantry and infantry goes where the going is tough."

Monroe murmured, "Jesus."

"It's not such an awful thing," Glennie Black said. "They have trained me well. The feeling among the guys in my unit is that we've been trained, so let's put it to use."

"But this is a war," Monroe said.

Glennie said, "Yes. The troops are anxious. They don't see it as good or bad, only as an opportunity."

"But it's fucking war."

"There are elements of both, I hope," Glennie said, and smiled at something he alone knew.

Monroe's turn came in an official letter delivered on a Saturday in March. Waltz was watching a basketball game on TV when he heard the mailman, the squeak of the slot opening, the dry-leaf sound of letters falling to the floor. The mail brought owed money and Monroe's draft notice. Waltz searched for good omens to piece together. There had to be a sign. His son's future could not be so random.

Monroe tore open the envelope and read the contents as raptly as a love letter. His guitar was laid across his lap and when he put the letter down it set the strings to humming faintly.

"It seems I've been called," he said.

"It's an honorable thing," Waltz said, reading the letter himself. "It seems every generation of men has a war, sad to say. Our leaders seem to think it is necessary."

Monroe's left hand curled around the guitar neck. His right hand picked out music. He stared at the folded notice. Monroe was innate music.

"If only I could sing," Monroe mused. "I'd be famous, in the public eye, and I'd have lawyers who would keep me out of Vietnam."

"Don't talk like that," Waltz scolded. "You're better than that."

"No, I'm not. I'm not above any of that."

"Yes, you are. You have elements of a hero in you."

"Bullshit," Monroe said crisply, and walked out on his father.

Waltz made a call that night from his office. The door was shut, the blinds drawn, the room dark except for his desk lamp. Lying on the desk in front of him was a slip of paper. He made the call after midnight, he hoped to shake the person from his sleep, scare him a little, convince him of Waltz's seriousness.

His intent was not to free Monroe from his obligation to military service; he merely sought placement.

He got through and identified himself.

"Yes, Harry," the man said. "What can I do for you?"

"My son Monroe got his draft notice today," Waltz said.

"I know, Harry. I have more bad news. We may call Eugene before the year is out."

"A push is on?"

"Yes."

"My son is musical."

"That is well known, Harry. If I've heard it once I've heard it a thousand times that Monroe Waltz is a born musician."

"Until the first of the year he made quite a good living at it," Waltz said. "For nearly five years he was a professional musician. Only when he could not find other players as serious about their music did he stop. I told him: Start fresh. Take his time and start fresh. He's written a thousand songs. He says he would be famous if only he could sing."

"I've heard that, too," the man said without impatience. He was waiting, sitting in the dark on the edge of the bed, his wife listening behind him; he waited for Waltz to request a favor the man could not grant.

"Now this . . ." said Waltz.

"It is an unpleasant fact of life," the man agreed. His wife shifted behind him. The man could see her under the sheets, humped like drifted snow, his wife of twenty-four years, she had blessed him with only daughters.

"I want to ask you something," Waltz said.

"I know, Harry, and I can't do it. The thing is out of my hands."

"Wait. I'm not asking that Monroe be exempt. I expect him to be treated like everybody else. I only ask that he go somewhere that he can use his music."

The man covered the phone and laughed softly. He heard his wife turn at the sound.

"He could be a bugler," Waltz said. "He could pick that horn up the first time he laid eyes on it and play it."

"It's out of my hands, Harry."

"I know, you said that." Waltz touched the slip of paper before him, realigning it with the desk's angles, his own ambitions; he was surprised when it flew an inch, powered by his exhalation. "All I want to say," he continued, "is that anything you can do to help Monroe will be appreciated. We can even put a cap on the business between us."

"Harry," the man repeated, getting angry, "it is out of my hands."

"You said that," Waltz said. Then he said, "Good night."

"And do you know," he says to Mary Hale, "Monroe went to Vietnam as a bugler?"

"Amazing."

"He sent me a tape of his playing," Waltz says. "I've played it three times in my entire life. And never since he died. I don't have the courage for that even now. He plays 'Reveille,' 'Taps,' 'Call to Arms,' 'Hail to the Chief,' 'Boots and Saddles.' All the classics, he called them. He talks a little between numbers. It's like he's on-stage somewhere."

"Maybe we could listen to it together," Mary Hale says.

"I don't know." Waltz shakes his head. "Am I ready for that?"

"I'd like to hear it. Where is it?"

"In Marathon, thank God. From this distance I can tell you I am not ready."

He remembered more than he thought possible after all that time. The man Waltz called the night Monroe was drafted denied all connection with Monroe's becoming a bugler. He was genuinely outraged when Waltz declared their business completed and for some months afterward sent him money in the mail.

"You talk so much about what a wonderful musician he was," says Mary Hale, "yet I never had the chance to hear him play. That tape is my only chance."

"He was never as good on the bugle as he was on the guitar or piano. You can tell his heart's not in it."

"Still, it's him playing music."

Waltz took a deep breath; he would agree, then hope she'd forget. It might be weeks before she got to Marathon.

"You may listen to it," he says.

"Will you listen with me?"

His fear curls cold in his stomach. "All right," he says. "I have to warn you, though. He doesn't sing."

"Of course," she says. "He's a musician."

11

They sit together in the quiet of her house. It is very early in the morning, Waltz's throat is dry from telling his story. He wants to sleep, not necessarily with this woman, but to just pack himself away for long hours. The musical facts of Monroe's life, coming from him for the first time, have the ring of an investment he must trust Mary Hale to protect. He has been emptied and she has been weighted with his most precious words. They hang from her like musical notes. Her eyes are closed and her hands are folded in her lap.

"Mare?" he whispers.

She smiles at him without opening her eyes.

"It's late," he tells her.

She says nothing to this. She does not move, does not open her eyes. He senses her waiting. He needn't tell her it is a long drive home. To do so would sound artlessly roundabout, a juvenile way to get her to suggest he stay.

"Can I sleep on your couch?" he asks.

She opens her eyes at this. They are moist and sleepy. "You can do that." She nods. She almost tells him he is welcome to sleep with her, but doesn't. He has left her off balance with his talk of dead sons and sons in prison. He is the only man she has ever met who she thinks might be dangerous to her. She feels there is wisdom in slow progress with this man; she thinks of the river.

Mary Hale brings sheets, blankets, and a pillow from her room. She makes the bed while Waltz stands outside watching the bay. It is nearly three o'clock in the morning. He thinks he can see a change in the light toward dawn. He wonders if, after all this, he will be able to sleep.

"Harry?" she says from the door.

All the lights are off in the room except a small lamp at the head of the couch, where Mary Hale has plumped the pillow.

"Don't feel you have to run off in the morning," she says. "I'll make us breakfast."

"Don't you have work to do?"

"Sure. Don't you?"

"Yes."

"Well—we can loaf together. Share the burden of the guilt of sloths."

He smiles. "All right," he says.

They kiss good night. For a first kiss, it is not momentous, just a connection of dry lips, two small puffs of smoky breath colliding.

Mary Hale hurries to her room. Waltz lies awake another hour listening to the bay, happy he has come so far in one night, but wondering if she had not expected him to pursue her further.

At some hour of the morning Mary Hale walks back through the dark house to watch him sleep. There is little light and she is afraid she will kick something over and awaken him. But she has not slept and her eyes pick out details like an animal. She moves unerringly. At last she can see his shape stretched out on the couch, under the blankets. His head is dark on the pillow. She will be exhausted at some point in the day if she doesn't sleep, and she wants very much to slide in alongside this sleeping man.

He rolls over, as if he heard her thinking. He scares her. She feels plans have been made; some goals have been placed in their future which they must work toward. This gives her hope.

Waltz stays two days. There is something like reciprocal amazement in their eyes. They wait to get on each other's nerves. Mary Hale catches Waltz studying her when they take a walk up the beach. They don't hold hands; they barely talk. Waltz skips stones on the bay. But he will look hard at her for as long as she will let him, and when she finally demands to know what he is seeking he is stumped.

They find a crook of sand out of the wind and sit in it smoking cigarettes.

"What if I could get your son out of prison?" she asks. She wears sunglasses with blood-red lenses. Waltz has on his clothes from the night before.

"Don't do me any favors," he says.

"I can do it. I know people."

"Let it go, would you, please?" He wants to enjoy her company and she keeps ruining it with Eugene.

"I don't have any children—" she begins.

"You already told me that."

"But if I did, I'd think I'd want to do what was right for them. Let me get him out."

"No."

"Let me at least look into it," she says.

"No!"

She gets to her feet and sweeps the sand from her behind. Patches she can't reach cling to her back. She shouts, "You're being a prick about this, Waltz!"

"Because I won't do what you want?"

"It's a horrible thing you've done."

Waltz says evenly, "You didn't see him hold a gun to a man's head. I did."

"So forgive him. Is that so difficult?"

"If he got out, what would he do?" he asks. Nothing comes to mind. "He'd go right back to lending money and beating up people. He's stubborn. He won't change."

"You don't know that," Mary Hale says.

"Trust me."

But she doesn't, and comes to a decision. This makes her stop on the beach, it is such a simple revelation. She has been on her own so long she is not accustomed to conflicting points of view. She can't remember the last time she weighed a man's opinion in her life.

Waltz has gone several steps ahead of her, then stopped.

"What are you thinking about?" he asks, only half interested.

"Nothing. You."

He laughs. "Thanks."

She feels free to put her arm through his.

There is a lifeguard chair up the beach in the other direction from her house. It pokes up like a fire tower from the dark sand. Initials, within hearts, or without, obscenities, names, have been carved into its white wood base.

Mary Hale looks up at the high platform. "Let's sit," she says. "Maybe we'll see a shark." She is agile going up. Four steps and she is above him, smiling down at him, her face full of color. She sits to one side of the seat and pats it for him to join her.

Waltz takes his time climbing. His shoes feel slippery on the painted struts. The structure seems an icon to youth, with its slick steps, its insolent messages of young lust, the way it sits perched for looking out at the future.

His head is at the level of the seat. The tower is taller than he thought. He feels he is gasping for breath. Mary Hale has not taken her eyes from him.

"Is there room?" he asks.

She pats the seat again. "Plenty."

He tries to climb on, but the seat looks dangerously narrow to his eye. He must execute a turn of his long body to sit beside her, and he fears either bumping her off the other side or falling himself. His bad leg aches. He can see his white hair out of the corner of his eye.

"Are you O.K.?" she asks.

"Scared," he admits.

"Go back down," she says, putting her hand on his shoulder. "I'll follow."

"No. I'll come up."

"You don't have to. Not for me."

He pivots and slides his thin rump onto the slick painted boards of the seat, hops into position beside her, and they are safe. The bay spins before him, he grips the chair edges. The seat is tilted forward at a slight angle and there is only one board for a back. They don't want the lifeguards getting comfortable; their job is to watch for imperiled swimmers, not to sunbathe.

Waltz feels exposed, a flagpole sitter. A cold wind comes off the bay. It is late summer already, no swimmers to be seen anywhere.

"Having fun?" Mary Hale asks, teasing.

"I'm worried how we'll get down."

"You *are* a worrier," she says.

"Only about some things."

"How did you get into loan sharking?" she asks.

"I've just always done it. From about the age of fourteen. I had this magical experience where I lent a dollar to a man in town and the next day he paid me back a dollar and a dime. I asked him what the dime was for and he explained interest to me. I was hooked. It was simple, elegant, straightforward, honorable." He sits back. Talking, getting excited about his work, he had almost fallen off the tilted seat. How will he get down from there without breaking his leg?

"You go first," Mary Hale says.

"No. You. I want the seat empty so I can maneuver."

"O.K.," she says. She turns and climbs down the side opposite the side she went up. She calls up to him, "Are you hungry?"

"A little," he says. Mostly, he feels stranded. She is down and safe. She has lit a cigarette and smokes while he tries to find his way.

"You need help?" she asks.

What can she do down there?

"Hold out your arms," he says.

When she does, he jumps, and she screams and drops the cigarette from her mouth.

It is not much of a jump, but he is sixty-one years old, and the absence of alternative routes to the ground that left only jumping startled him. He has panicked. He lands on soft sand, jarringly, and rolls onto his knees, then his face. The sand is cool, not so dark up close. Stray grains are sucked up his nose before he can stop them. They stick to the tip of his tongue. He feels first for a fresh break of the bone in his JFK leg but it feels fine. Nothing else feels out of joint or alignment.

Mary Hale's voice comes from above him. "Harry?" She sounds worried. "Are you O.K.?"

He gets to his feet. He wipes his hands, his knees. He spits out sand. Mary Hale reaches and with her fingertip dislodges grains suspended in his eyebrows.

"Well, that's one way down," she says, her eyes bright.

"How did I look?" Waltz asks.

She shrugs. "Like a man jumping from a lifeguard tower."

"Not like a bird?"

"*Nothing* like a bird."

But he remembers the short flight as they walk back to her house; details come to him, as though they were flying in behind him and only just caught up. He recalls how the light seemed to flash past, and the coldness of the air, and the way the air filled the spaces in his clothes, holding him up.

He feels the absence of clothes then later as a weight that holds him to the bed and makes it hard to breathe. All sense of flight is gone. He and Mary Hale fumble against each other; one's starting of something impedes the other, they are foiled, and must begin all over again. They are self-conscious of their bodies (though light is scarce), the slack skin they carry, their perceived lack of grace. And they are shy about even being there at all. Waltz wonders if he knows Mary Hale well enough. Mary Hale only wants to sleep, and participates out of a sort of curiosity, confident that nothing will break in either of them, and that reward waits on the other side. They touch each other respectfully. No lust drives them. Rain falls against her bedroom window. Waltz looks up. Mary Hale's eyes are closed, her head tipped back, her neck a bridge. He kisses her here. There. She says, "Oh!" as he slides into her. It is a relief for them both. Her eyes open just as his close. She thinks of him flying off the guard tower; she lands with a thump.

They make love a second time in the morning, though Waltz is reluctant, he is sure she emptied him the night before. But Mary Hale is wide awake, insistent, and expert. She proves he is not empty; and then he is again.

"I wanted to make up for last night," she says.

"Last night was fine."

"But I was looking forward to sleeping," she confesses. She pulls on a green silk robe. "You didn't have my undivided attention."

Waltz says, "This time, this morning, I was thinking about my work. So you didn't really have mine."

She frowns exaggeratedly. "I didn't? It seemed like you were paying attention."

"Not one hundred percent."

"It's never that," she says, stretching. Her thin arms rise out of their green sheaths; she makes fists in the air and pivots them on wrists that crackle softly.

"I think about *my* work," she says, "and your son Eugene, and things you've said, and thoughts I've had, and how clumsy we both were climbing that tower."

"It's a wonder either of us got any enjoyment out of it at all," Waltz says.

"So you should be getting back?" she says, making it a question at the last moment.

"I would think you'd be thrilled," he says. "A goof-off in dirty clothes, not much to talk to or look at."

"Don't fish for compliments," she says sternly, standing up. "Get dressed in your dirty clothes. I'll make breakfast."

He showers and dresses in his wrinkled shirt and stiff socks. She makes eggs, toast, and coffee and he eats it to be polite; he isn't hungry. Her eyes, he thinks, mirror his edginess. He feels their separation approaching. They both have lives they have set aside that call them back.

Waltz feels pulled back to Marathon. He has never been gone this long before. He fears his empty house has fallen into irredeemable disarray.

"You should be getting back to work," he says.

"If you want to leave, leave," she says, testy, surprising him. "But leave for your own reasons, not for what you think I want."

"All right. I've got work to do."

"I know. I do, too."

"Can I visit you again?"

"You may," she says. "Will you come to the door or just sit in your car out by the road?"

Waltz laughs, and wonders if he should be leaving at all.

Mary Hale asks, "When can I expect you?"

"Day after tomorrow? Are you free?"

"I can be," she says. "Bring a change of clothes."

His house stands even without him. The floor beneath the mail slot is snowy with envelopes. He gathers them up and drops them on his desk. Then he goes from room to room throwing open windows. One window on the west side gives a view of downtown Marathon, the square, the high school, the neat rows of houses, everything bathed in haze. Out a rear window he sees the State Home buildings. The place looks no different than it ever has, just nobody there. He is always surprised how much he misses the retarded kids.

The telephone rings and he takes it at his desk, thinking it is Mary Hale.

"Daddy? Where have you been?" Carla asks.

"Visiting a friend," Waltz says; he likes the mysterious vagueness of this answer, he likes the abraded numbness of his penis, the use it was put to on the sly from the rest of his world.

"I want you to come to dinner," she says.

"Who'll be there?"

"You. Me. Susan and Willy," she says. "Who's your friend?" She asks this question out of step with the topical rhythm of the conversation.

"She lives on Saginaw Bay," he volunteers.

"Is she like Mom?"

Waltz says, "I don't think so. I don't know. Why?"

"I was just curious. I just wondered what sort of woman you would choose after all this time."

"I didn't choose her," Waltz says. "We just kept running into each other."

"Bring her to dinner."

"No. I came home to get away from her for a little while," he says; this admission surprises him, puts a negative sheen on Mary Hale. "What time is dinner?"

"Eight o'clock. If you don't bring a date you'll be the fifth wheel."

"Who's your date, Carla?"

"A man I've been seeing."

"What's his name?"

"Don't laugh. Homer Cross."

"Really?"

"Yes, *really,*" she replies, laughing herself. "He's a very sweet, understanding man. He even understands my love for my sister's husband."

"Is that still going on?"

Carla says patiently, " 'Going on' is not the proper phrase. It's just there. I sometimes ask myself if I'd even be in touch with Susan if she weren't married to Willis."

"Sure you would," Waltz says, afraid. "You're twins."

Carla grunts doubtfully. Her quick silence clarifies his distance from her. He wants to see her face, he is certain he could read her feelings if only her face was before him.

"This love for Willy," he ventures, ". . . does Susan know about it?"

"What's to know?" she demands. "She knows Willy and I were together before she intruded. And sometimes, when they come over, she'll stick her head in the door and call, 'Willis is here!' So what can you tell me from that?"

"Is it a problem?"

"No," she says adamantly. "It is not a problem."

"Fill me in about Homer Cross."

"See for yourself," she says, and she hangs up.

He reaches Mary Hale at work.

"I have this problem," he says, "and I wonder if you have any advice. I have twin daughters and one twin is in love with the other twin's husband. They dated before the other twin came along. She says she wouldn't bother keeping in touch with her sister if she wasn't married to this man she loves."

"Is adultery involved?" Mary Hale asks.

"I don't know. I don't think so."

"Well, think so. It usually is. Are the married twin and her husband happy?"

"I guess," says Waltz.

"Is the other twin letting this love affect her life?"

"Hard to say. But I worry because I have a twin brother I never see and I'd hate that to happen to my daughters."

"Let events run their course. Right now, you are operating

strictly on parental concern, which is expected. But you'll only cause trouble if you butt in where you perceive something taking place when in fact it isn't. My advice is to find a beautiful woman, preferably a lawyer, and spend the night with her. That will be one hundred dollars, my secretary will bill you."

Homer Cross surprises Waltz; he is a contemporary, a handful of years younger than Waltz, with thinning gray hair, a brush of white mustache, and peaceful brown eyes. He rises politely from his place on Carla's couch to shake hands with Waltz and Waltz sees he wears a wedding band.

"Willy and Susan aren't here yet," Carla says unnecessarily, for Waltz can feel the emptiness of the apartment behind the room where they stand. It has been some time since he has seen her; she is still beautiful, he supposes this is a constant now. Her golden hair sweeps down her back and the weight seems to pull her eyes wide and alert.

In her kitchen Waltz gets a beer from the refrigerator. The air there is very warm, nearly hot, rich with smells of cooking. He holds a beer out to Homer Cross and the man shakes him off like a pitcher, but with a smile.

"What do you do for a living, Homer?"

He answers with a quick fluttering of hands that Waltz flinches away from as if they were the advance guard of some form of attack; it is sign language.

"He's deaf and dumb," Carla says. She has heard Waltz's question and turned from working at her sink. She does not laugh. She touches Homer's cheek, he kisses her mouth.

Waltz sees in the man's eyes that he is not stupid or retarded, or a fool, all characteristics Waltz feared were present, evidenced by his inability to hear or speak.

"Homer makes woodwinds," Carla says. "Flutes, clarinets, oboes, bassoons. He makes them all by hand. Right now, UM is paying him to work here for a year. Next year he'll be someplace else."

Homer Cross stands serenely studying Carla's mouth. He will

be someplace else in a year; is that his attraction to his daughter?

"How can he hear when the notes are right?" Waltz asks.

"Ask him," she says.

Waltz squarely faces Homer, sets his feet a little wider apart, seeking a special careful balance he feels he must have. He repeats the question clearly.

Homer smiles and holds out his hands. They are yellowish with callus. He moves his hands gently in front of him; they are like wash on a line. What is he saying? Waltz nearly panics. But Homer's eyes are closed. His head is tilted at a listening angle, he is searching for the answer.

After a moment his eyes open and he gets a spoon from the drainboard by the sink. He taps the head of the spoon on the counter. The tone is flat, then gone. The sound is there, a homely clink, and then it is absorbed in the fragrant, warm air. Homer repeats the tapping. He taps the spoon, then holds it out in the air. At last he puts the spoon in his mouth and smiles.

With his hands he speaks to Carla. Carla says, "He says that everything has its own inherent music. Some days the music is correct . . . good . . . some days it's all wrong. When he is making an instrument he can feel the music in it trying to get out. The closer I am to finishing an instrument, the closer the music is to the surface. I can feel it getting anxious and warm. I feel all this with my hands. I can see the music there just below the surface and I know when I am completely finished the music will leap free. But not a moment before. So there is no rush. The music will always be there."

Everything sounds correct. Homer's hands settle in his lap. They might be catching their breath.

"Where do you live?" Waltz asks.

The hands rise, speak. "I have a small room off the studio the university supplies for me. It's very comfortable. I eat out a lot."

Waltz nods and waits for more. He is watching only Homer's hands now. He glances at Carla and catches her in an amused, scolding look at Homer he understands he was not meant to see.

"Where's your wife?" Waltz asks.

"She lives with our children in the Smoky Mountains. Her

name is Bess. Our children's names are Ted, Clarence, Whittaker, Holly, Wallace, and June."

"Busy," murmurs Waltz to Carla, but Homer is adept at his reading of lips, and responds.

"She is a lovely woman."

Waltz wonders: Does he mean his wife, or Carla? Carla seems unsure herself. She quits her role as translator to stir a pot of spaghetti sauce. Taking off the lid releases a cloud of richly spiced heat.

"Whoo!" Waltz exclaims, and wipes down his wet forehead with his beer can.

"Go in the other room," Carla says. "It's cooler. I'll be in in a minute."

Homer does something with his hand, almost like waving goodbye. He heads for the bathroom.

Waltz feels freed.

"What's going on here, Carla?"

"What do you mean, 'going on'?"

"Who's this old charmer with the quick hands and the fourteen kids? And the wife back home in the Smokies?"

"Homer's just a good friend," she says.

"Why does he seem so at home? Why the joke about eating out?"

Carla turns furiously on her father. "That is absolutely none of your business."

"Yes, I know," Waltz says, feeling like a fool. But he can't stay out of it. She is too beautiful to be alone this far into her life. "Where's the future in falling for a married woodwind-maker?"

Carla says, "Willy and Sue aren't here yet. There's still time for you to leave. The night will survive your absence."

"I want to stay," Waltz says. He won't apologize for his protective impulses, though.

"Anyway," she says. "You're imagining things. We're just buddies." Leaving the kitchen she swivels her hips with burlesque exaggeration, shakes her golden hair at him. "You're nuts," she tells him.

Waltz thinks: She is thirty-three years old; so what if she sleeps with married men? She is of age. But her solitary life hurts him. And if this man's wife, why not her twin sister?

When the front door is opened to admit Willy and Susan a current of air is formed that cools Waltz and sets a hanging cluster of wind chimes in the kitchen window to playing like fanfare for royalty. Waltz pulls his shirt away from the wet small of his back and goes to greet them.

Susan, her baby a large ball round in the center of her abdomen, has cut her hair and curled it up at the ends. Waltz hates it, but says nothing. She looks plainer than Carla for some reason; her face in its serenity seems to have sacrificed all hints of experience. She is caught gladly in the momentum of what she is producing.

She kisses Homer Cross, then Carla, finally Waltz, and Waltz rushes rudely through her greeting because he is anxious to see Carla and Willy together, and thus misses everything. He turns back to Susan, feeling bad for her, and gives her a firmer kiss and a smile. He puts a hand on the taut upper curve of her abdomen. "Twins," he proclaims.

"Bullshit." Susan smiles.

"Not in this family, it's not."

"We have pictures, Daddy. No twins."

Willy comes to shake Waltz's hand. He has added a little weight to his face, a little silver to his longish, curly hair.

They create a few moments of firm direction getting drinks, finding an arrangement of seats where Homer will be included in every conversation. Waltz is the only person in the room without some understanding of sign language, and is thus more isolated than Homer.

"Daddy has a girlfriend," Carla teases.

"Her name is Mary Hale," Waltz says forthrightly.

"He spent the night with her," Carla presses.

"Consenting adults. And it was two nights."

"What sort of example are you setting for your children?"

"It's too late." He smiles falsely into Carla's eyes; he sees she is still burned. "You are hopelessly corrupt."

"That's hope*fully,*" Willy cracks. Everyone laughs, even

Homer Cross, whose silent dissolving of his face into shapes of laughter fascinates Waltz.

"Where did you meet her?" Susan asks.

"In Vassar. I had business with her brother."

"She went to Vassar?"

"No. Vassar, Michigan. Her brother lives on the Cass River. I was there to collect some money and she showed up. She hated me at first."

"That," Carla proclaims, "is the source of some of the best relationships. The people I've been most in love with, I hated first."

The remark is too transparent. It sits in the silence blatant as flatulence and Waltz rushes in to save his daughter.

"She's an attorney in Saginaw. She lives on the bay. She carries an ice pick for protection."

"Good for her," Susan says.

Carla turns to her sister. "Do you know Sally Worthington?"

"I do," Willy says. "She's a buyer for Hudson's now."

"Right. Went to UM? Pretty girl? Dark hair?"

"Whatever," Susan says. "What about her?"

"She was back in town a while ago and stopped in for a visit. The conversation got around to self-protection and from out of her purse she pulls the cutest little gun. She said it was a twenty-five caliber and that her boyfriend in Detroit bought it for her. It had a pink handle."

"Has she ever had to use it?" Waltz asks.

"No. But I got the impression talking to her that she thought it was inevitable that she would."

"Stay away from Sally Worthington," Willy says. "That's my advice."

"I carry some of that spray that is supposedly ten times more potent than Mace," Susan says.

"I heard that stuff is less than worthless," says Waltz.

"It probably is. I'd also have to tell my attacker to hold on while I got the damn thing out of my purse."

"He sees that belly on you," says Carla, "and he might tell you to take all the time you want."

"Ooo, *bitter,*" Susan coolly answers.

Carla gathers to spring; Waltz is startled how easily he recognizes it. Years have passed since he lived with his daughters, yet their patterns of attack and reconciliation have not changed. He inwardly roots for Carla, who loves the man between them, but lacks him.

"Twins," Waltz interjects even as Carla opens her mouth to respond. "That's why you're so big."

Homer's hands jump into the conversation. Carla, as hostess, is obliged to interpret for her father; Waltz likes Homer a little more.

"He asks if there is a history of twins in our family."

Speaking clearly, Waltz tells Homer, "Twins and living to be a hundred years old. Carla and Susan are twins, of course. I have a twin brother. My father had a twin brother. My father's father had twin sisters, Truth and Felicity. And the generation before that, there were twin boys. Also, my daddy lived to a hundred and so did his father and his father's father. And I plan to, too."

"One person from each generation," Carla says, "hangs around insufferably long."

"It might be you," Waltz says, and Carla makes a face, as though he had put a curse on her.

"Jesus, I hope not," she says. "Tell Homer your theory."

"My daddy had a theory," Waltz says. "Credit where credit is due. He was very high on himself, conceited in a charming way. He believed God recognized the superiority of the Waltz family and so every generation produced a set of twins to increase the population of Waltzes in the world."

With his hands, Homer says, "A two-for-one deal."

Everyone laughs, even Waltz, who believes in the theory.

Carla excuses herself to check her dinner. In a minute, Willy excuses himself and follows.

"Is Willy teaching?" Waltz asks Susan.

"No," she says, frowning. "He was low man in his department. He got let go. Or rather, not hired back."

Waltz gulps, for himself that he is so out of touch, for his daughter and her husband with no job and a child on the way. "Is he working at all?" he asks.

"He's self-employed," Susan explains, patting at the sweat at the base of her throat. "Carla's apartment is always so goddamn hot. He paints. He's a handyman. He drives a cab some days. He works part-time at a chicken place." She shudders, glances miserably down the hall toward the kitchen. "I'm sick to death of chicken. He brings it home. Buckets of it. The smell of fried chicken gets in his clothes, his hair, his mustache. My baby will come out in white feathers." She laughs harshly.

Waltz can see Willy standing easily on one foot in the kitchen, cocked against a bank of cupboards. His arms are folded and he is talking to Carla, who is out of sight in another part of the kitchen. He is a handsome man viewed through a long, tapering glass. Carla comes into sight with a jar of pickles for him to open; Louise did that, giving Waltz responsibility for anything that had to be unscrewed.

"He's beautiful, isn't he?" Susan whispers.

Waltz nods. He moves away before Willy looks and sees them watching. Susan rearranges her loose smock around her baby. She brushes a hair out of her eye.

"I'm happy you found a woman you like," she says to her father. "I was afraid you'd be alone the rest of your life."

"It's nothing like that," Waltz says.

"Still, it's nice," she says. She sits watching Waltz, and he thinks she looks at him to keep from looking down the hall at her husband. She smiles absently at Homer Cross; she tucks her hair behind her ears; she smooths her clothes.

"Could you get me another beer?" Waltz asks.

She frowns at him; he has badly misread her. "Not just now," she says firmly.

"I'll get it myself."

He expects her to block his path but she lets him go. Willy has moved out of the line of sight the hallway provided and Waltz is suddenly reluctant to proceed. But Susan is watching him and he can't retreat. Willy is at the kitchen table cutting the tops off radishes. Carla is draining spaghetti. A meaty-smelling sauce simmers in a pot on the stove. Willy sees Waltz enter and smiles. Waltz's heart is warmed, he believes it entirely possible Willy is ignorant of the storm he generates between these two women.

"Sit, sit," Willy urges, smacking a chair.

Waltz gets a fresh beer. "I can't leave Susan and Homer out there," he says.

"Sooz!" Willy yells. "Come in the kitchen! Bring Homer!"

Carla turns away from the sink with the dripping collander held in both hands. Her cheeks are steamed bright pink.

"Dinner's about ready anyway," she murmurs. She has a cold eye for her father.

Willy says grace over the meal. He asks for the blessings of friends and loved ones present. Everyone holds hands. Waltz holds the right hand of Homer Cross, the left hand of Carla. Carla with Waltz and Willy. Willy with Carla and Susan. Susan with Willy and Homer Cross. Waltz likes this linkage. He feels tension, love, hunger, flowing around this circle. When he finally lets go (Willy's grace is rambling and personal) he is surprised there is no snap of blue lightning between their fingertips, no smoke.

Carla has their plates stacked in front of her. She loads spaghetti on the top plate and passes it to Willy, who ladles on a sauce swimming with hamburger and fat, slick mushrooms. Two wicker baskets hold garlic bread wrapped in dish towels. Salad is passed in a green bowl, the salad made of Willy's radishes, unpeeled cucumber slices, dried mushrooms, quartered tomatoes, lettuce, chopped celery, kidney beans. Red wine is poured into glasses. Bread sticks stand upright in a narrow red vase.

"Wonderful," Waltz proclaims. "Wonderful."

Homer Cross stands and puts a hand on Waltz's shoulder. An orange spot of spaghetti sauce round as an eraser head already gleams on his shirt. He grins and raises his glass of wine.

"A toast," he says through Carla. He sets the glass down again, to give himself room.

His hands work the air. They draw Waltz in. He says, "Here's to the goodness in all of us. Here's to the goodness in the earth that it brings forth food so delicious and friends so fine."

"Hear, hear," Willy says.

Homer blushes, offers his glass around for the others to touch, then drinks. Waltz reaches over and shakes his hand.

"To twins and old age," he then says, and spills wine in his enthusiasm and belonging.

They finish everything. Waltz fears falling asleep in his chair. He sweats with the hot food in him and the thick air of the kitchen. He looks and Willy is slowly massaging the back of Susan's neck, her head comes forward inch by inch, as though he is dissolving the nerves, the muscles, and the bones that keep her head erect. Carla takes in this act with bright eyes.

Carla brings a cigarette out and Waltz, craving motion, scrambles out of his seat to light it.

"A beautiful dinner, honey," he says, kissing her temple.

"Thank you, Daddy," she says. "Anyone want coffee?"

Waltz scouts, in his imagination, the rooms of the apartment for a place to stay the night. The road back to Marathon seems endless and perilously narrow. He doesn't move from his seat. Conversations, the activity of clearing the table, water running in the sink, encircle him. A breeze rises. The window frames music. Homer Cross is asleep. Can he hear in his dreams? Is he an orator of great power?

Carla touches Homer's shoulder and this sensation brings him up long enough for Carla to lead him into the living room and onto the couch.

"He's out for the count," Carla tells them when she returns. "In the morning he'll be gone. In the afternoon he'll send flowers."

Willy says, "Sweet."

Waltz envies Homer his secure station for the night. Why doesn't he sleep with his date and leave Waltz the couch?

"Coffee," he pleads, "before I snuggle up to Homer."

Carla pours hot black coffee into a mug with a face. The mug has a bushy mustache and nervy eyes. A shock of fired clay hair scrapes Waltz's lips when he drinks.

"What time is it?" Willy asks. He speaks in a whisper; they are all thinking of Homer Cross asleep down the hall, forgetting.

"Nine-thirty."

Waltz groans. He had hoped it was later.

"Why don't you ladies take a hike," Willy says. "I want to talk to Harry."

"What about?" Susan asks.

Waltz wishes she knew. He is bothered that this is a secret between them. Is Willy about to ask for his other daughter's hand in marriage? It has a circular logic. Will Willy fill Carla with twins, then disappear?

"Personal stuff," Willy says, winking, smacking his wife on the fanny.

"Don't *be* that way," she whines. "Tell me what you want to talk to him about."

"I'll tell you later."

"Now."

"Later," he says, and Susan sees what Waltz sees, that Willy has been pressed as hard as he will allow on this issue. Susan whirls in a blown cone of billowy cloth and stomps down the hall. Carla shrugs, dries her hands, takes her cigarettes, and follows.

Willy, perhaps knowing Waltz is as curious as his wife, says directly, "I want to borrow some money."

"How much do you need?"

"We're in bad shape, Harry. Sooz's obstetrician is bugging me for the first half of his fee. Four hundred fifty dollars. Then that much again when the baby comes. Then the hospital. I clear about one-eighty a week, but I work sixty hours to do it. We're hurting."

Waltz rubs his eyes. He did not want to know. He liked Willy, less so now. He says, "I just want to hear a figure."

"Five thousand. If that's too—"

"It can be done."

"At what rates?" Willy asks; try as he might, suspicion getting in.

"No rates. When you can, you pay me back. No points. No strings." He put his hand out and Willy shakes it. "There," says Waltz.

Willy glances away, then begins to cry. Waltz is wide awake.

He has to be getting back to Marathon. He pats Willy affectionately on the back of the head.

"Don't cry," he says softly. "If I turned you down, then you'd have something to cry about."

Having loaned money, he feels his usefulness, his welcome, at an end. He has burdened somebody once again with the responsibility to pay him back and now he has to get away. Willy will begin to hate him soon.

12

Waltz's plan was to repossess Hesperia's truck, then drive it to collect the woman's refrigerator. Hesperia would be hired to drive the truck and help Waltz with the lifting. He was perfect. He had a thick, strong, beer-fed build and the dull eyes of a pack horse. When Waltz arrived to get the truck Hesperia met him in the driveway with a double-barreled shotgun. His left hand was wrapped in dirty bandages.

"What happened?" Waltz asks. He ignored the shotgun, though its barrels had circumferences round as quarters.

"I caught the damn thing," Hesperia says, studying the bad hand.

"Caught it where?"

"In the damn truck door."

"Bad luck," Waltz says.

Hesperia shrugs and spits. "Ain't luck, good *or* bad," he contends. "Just happened." He shifts the shotgun. Unmarried, and only twenty-six years old, he looks forty to Waltz. His face seems to require perpetual sleep. In addition to the pickup truck, Hesperia is also on the string to Waltz for a full-size Sony Trinitron. It will go next, probably soon.

"I wanted to hire you," Waltz says. "I needed you to do some lifting for me."

"Well, you can see I ain't going to."

"I didn't know you'd hurt your hand," Waltz says gently. "I've also come for the truck."

"*My* truck?"

"Yes, Hesperia. You haven't been paying your debt."

"I'll pay you, Mr. Waltz. I'll get the money together any day now."

Waltz sighs. He lights cigarettes for himself and the man who confronts him, then he puts his hands in his pockets and waits.

"I'll be working again any day now," Hesperia says.

"It's been six months," Waltz says. "I've given you extra time because I like you. I wanted to give you this little bit of work today. But I'm still taking the truck."

Hesperia shifts the weight of the shotgun. Waltz ignores it.

"Is your hand broken?" Waltz asks.

Hesperia says sullenly, "No."

"Can you drive?"

"Course I can drive!"

"I'll pay you five dollars to drive my car back to my house," Waltz says. "That'll be something, anyway."

"*Then* how the hell do I get back home?"

"I don't know," Waltz says impatiently. "Walk? Hitch? I'm trying to help you out."

"Five bucks? You call that help?"

"This really isn't my problem, Hesperia. You signed the note and you've been delinquent on your payments. The truck is mine. If you were dealing with anyone else they'd have taken the truck the instant you were late. They definitely would not have tried to line you up a little work."

"I'm sorry, Mr. Waltz."

"Call me Harry. Give me the key, Hesperia. Do you want to drive my car home or not?"

"How 'bout I leave it on the square?"

"My house is only a little ways past the square."

"The square, or nothing."

"Give me the key to the truck, Hesperia." The man goes into the house after it. Waltz takes a five-dollar bill out of his wallet; the action makes him feel expansive, foolish.

"The clutch pedal sticks," the man warns, surrendering the key. "And it needs gas."

"No problem," says Waltz. He gives the bill and the key to the car to Hesperia. "Park it in front of Sam Boggins' shop. You know where that is?"

"Course I do."

"Give the key to Sam. Tell him I sent you. Tell him I'll be by to get it later. O.K.?"

"Sure. I can do that."

"Thank you, Hesperia."

Waltz bought five dollars' worth of gas at a Sunoco station in town. He studied the men he saw there, seeking someone big enough and strong enough to move a refrigerator. Hesperia's bad hand had fouled his plan. He twice circled the square but nobody was around. He stopped and went into the Marathon Restaurant. The owner looked up from where he sat having coffee in a booth and blinked at Waltz. The room was otherwise empty. Waltz got back in the truck and drove out of town toward the woman's house.

Elaine Schoolcraft, barely thirty, was a widow of tenuous circumstances. Her husband had drowned fishing for muskellunge in Lake Superior and his body had never been found. Elaine Schoolcraft took a job in Marathon as a switchboard operator, quit it, ran through her savings, and now worked part-time nights as a barmaid in Clio. She had no children. Her husband had been gone two years.

She lived in a house on Genesee Road and she was waiting for Waltz at the front door, yanking it open before he knocked. She wore jeans and a man's old dress shirt. Her hair was wrapped in a silver scarf.

"The dreaded Harry," she says, holding the door open for him. A faint rottenness of spoiled food hit him and in the kitchen he saw why. She was emptying the refrigerator, arranging everything on a table over spread newspapers, cookie sheets, folded towels. Frozen packages of string beans, niblet corn, Mexican-style vegetables, and a carton of butter pecan ice cream were melting in bowls; she also had a cantaloupe, seven nectarines, half a head of lettuce, three apples, a bottle of salad dressing, a quart of milk, four cans of beer, and a pound of ground beef.

"I've been depleting my resources," she says, strangely chipper.

"This is too bad," Waltz says.

"Don't worry about it, Harry. My fault. I should have paid."

He takes a tape measure from his pocket and measures the height, width, and depth of the refrigerator. It is what he expected, a tall, broad-shouldered monster. Even empty it gives the appearance of immovability, of squatting serenely in the bounds of gravity.

"Do you have help?" the woman asks. Waltz doesn't answer. He measures the back door. A quarter inch of clear space will exist to each side of the refrigerator.

"Smooth," the woman observes without malice.

Waltz shrugs, rolls up his tape. "It will be tight," he allows. "But nothing serious."

"Not seriously tight," she says. She asks again, "Do you have help?"

"I was planning to hire Hesperia," Waltz says. "You know him? But the poor fool caught his hand in the truck door."

"So you have got no one to help you."

"You're a strong girl, Elaine," he says.

She smiles wryly. "I am, Harry. But not *that* strong."

Waltz goes to the truck for the dolly he put there. He takes his time. A solution to his problem exists, it is only his inability to recognize it that foils him. Elaine Schoolcraft must weigh 140 pounds, but she would be of no help in getting the refrigerator into the truck. He needs muscle; he needs a wide back.

The woman is in the rear of the house when Waltz goes back inside. He thinks he hears her talking. She returns in a minute with a cigarette and a John Deere ashtray.

"Think of something?" she asks.

"I admit I am stumped."

"Then can I put my food back before it all spoils?"

Waltz shakes his head. This all seems connected in some way to Hesperia. His dull face fills Waltz's mind; his bad hand, his indignation at being called to accounts, his sour luck, they all have passed to Waltz. Maybe he spent too much time in Hesperia's presence; he feels blocked and frustrated, snagged every way he turns.

"You want to wait," the woman says, "the fellas delivering my new refrigerator will be here in an hour or so. You can help each other."

"You've got another refrigerator coming today?"

"Of course, Harry. You're taking this one. A house has to have a refrigerator."

"If you can't pay me, how can you pay somebody else?"

"Easy credit terms," she says, and winks. "My monthly payments will be lower. I should've gone to them in the first place."

Waltz says, "They're official, though. You fall behind with them and it's on your record. Me, I'm unofficial. You only deal with me. I don't haunt you ten years down the road."

"Why, Harry," Elaine Schoolcraft says, "that sounds like a sales pitch."

"It is, I guess. I can lend you the money to buy your new refrigerator outright. Or we can refinance this one."

"At a slightly higher rate."

"Only slightly," Waltz says. "You have to pay some penalty for shirking your obligations. Nobody wants to face up to their mistakes these days."

"Why should I?" she asks. "I've got options. With options, I don't have to do anything."

"If you miss payments," Waltz says, selling himself and his way of life again, "I can come and take the refrigerator and that is that. We're still friends. Sears or Monkey Wards, though, if they repossess you—"

"No, Harry," the woman interrupts. "I'm not stupid. Get that thing out of here. It's cluttering up my kitchen."

After a minute of thought, Waltz tells her, "Square one."

"That's where we are, yes."

"How about one of your boyfriends?"

"Why, Harry," she says playfully, "whatever gave you the idea I am less than faithful to the memory of my dear husband?"

"It's to your advantage to have this refrigerator out of here when the new one arrives. Space considerations, for one. And what will these people think, seeing you with a practically new refrigerator being repossessed?"

"It's none of their business."

"It is until you've paid for theirs in full," he says.

"I'll tell them this one is a lemon," she says.

"They won't believe you. This is top of the line. I'll bet you even bought the same brand."

"I did," she admits.

"Well, there you go. Call one of your big, strong boyfriends."

"I don't have any boyfriends."

Waltz takes out a cigarette and lights it. He looks at his watch. With Elaine Schoolcraft's help he ponderously dances the refrigerator out of its bay an inch at a time. The unveiled floor beneath is caked with an oily black dust, ancient crumbs, a scrap of paper, and three pennies. The refrigerator hunkers down in the middle of the kitchen floor. Now that the refrigerator is out where Waltz can see all sides it appears even bigger, it has taken on an added dimension.

"So what do we have?" he asks. He has taken a seat because his heart is slamming ferociously in his chest.

"You're killing yourself," the woman says. She brushes hair from her eyes. Exertion has filled her face with color.

"No boyfriends?" Waltz gasps. "A pretty, available woman like you?"

"I am not pretty available." She laughs. In a minute she asks, "Can you keep a secret, Harry?"

"With the best."

She disappears into an adjoining room and comes back with a pad of paper. She writes a note, a document binding Waltz's word to the secret she will reveal.

"Sign this, Harry. This secret is so secret you can never tell anyone. Not trusted friends, not loved ones, not one single, solitary soul."

"Do I want to know this secret?" Waltz says. "This is what I'm asking myself now."

"If you do learn this secret, it will help you get this refrigerator out of here."

"Won't you just take my word?" he asks. "I'd rather not sign anything."

"This is *some* secret," Elaine Schoolcraft promises. "Look, I'll go first." She signs her name at the bottom of the note. "Now, it's your turn, Harry. I must insist."

He takes the pen and signs his name. The woman folds it away and leaves the room again. She is gone twenty minutes, longer than he expected. He drinks a glass of water and smokes two cigarettes. Occasionally, from the rear rooms of the house, he thinks he hears human voices, pitched to an argument. He thinks he knows the woman's secret: Not only does she have a boyfriend but he is living with her, too. It is not much of a secret; he knows of four unmarried couples living together in Marathon. The town is large enough so that no one cares. Elaine Schoolcraft is also given credit for being young, attractive, widowed, childless; her situation, in fact, would put her at a premium among single Marathon men looking for a suitable mate. She has been married before, therefore she is sexually experienced, she is not burdened with another man's children, and two years have passed since her husband drowned in Lake Superior, ample time to get over her grief; in short, Elaine Schoolcraft is a plum.

She finally returns to the kitchen leading a man by the hand. He is a bashful, bearded man who will look only at the floor. Dark brown hair falls to his shoulders. His skin is very pale but his arms are heavily muscled. He nearly flinches when Waltz says, "Is this your secret?"

"Come on," the woman says anxiously, "let's get this over with."

With the man's help (in truth, Waltz helps the man, who is strong and agile and does the heavy lifting) they get the refrigerator secured on the dolly, then slipped through the doorway without incident. The man then brings six long two-by-twelve planks from the garage and lays them from the bed of the truck to form a ramp. He and Waltz then work the refrigerator up this incline and the job is half finished.

Throughout, the man does not say a word, nor does he look Waltz in the eye.

"Can I hire you to help me unload this monster?" Waltz asks.

The man shakes his head. He darts back inside the house, and when Waltz follows, the man has disappeared altogether. The woman is sweeping out the refrigerator bay.

"He was the big secret?" Waltz asks.

"That was him," she says. "Please leave now. And remember, you signed that note."

"I know I did. But what's the secret?"

She leans on her broom and stares at Waltz. "You really don't know?"

"Humor me."

She laughs and shakes her head. "No. This is better. This is perfect."

"Can I hire him to help unload that thing?"

"No. I barely talked him into doing as much as he did."

"Let me borrow the planks then."

"Sure," the woman says. "I can rent them to you. Five dollars per plank per hour."

Waltz winces, then pays her the money. "I'll be back in an hour," he says.

Driving over to Alabaster Street, working with the refrigerator's new owner to get it off the truck and in the house, hooking it up, all along he wonders about the secret he has been told but does not understand.

He returns the planks to Elaine Schoolcraft three minutes past the hour. She says, "That's another thirty dollars, Mr. Waltz."

He pays without complaint. "Call me Harry," he says. "Tell me the secret."

The woman laughs. In the hour Waltz has been gone her new refrigerator has been delivered. Her food is safe and cold again.

"Harry, you've been told."

"But how could I if I don't know what it is?"

"I didn't realize you were so dense."

"I'm not," he says. "I'm just uninformed."

"It's best this way," the woman says. "Believe me."

Feeling cheated, he heads for the square. It is like getting someone to sign their name to a debt but then giving him no money. It is no way to do business. And he *signed;* against all his better judgment and lifelong habits, he signed the note. He picks the secret over in his mind, looking for something of value in it. Always he ends at the pale, muscular, silent man; he seeks a piece of intelligence he has missed or overlooked; but then he gets to the square and forgets all about the secret.

A crowd has formed in front of Sam Boggins' shop. Hesperia is there with his bad hand and his shotgun. Waltz sees four or five people who owe him money. He parks the truck.

Sam Boggins hurries out to him. "You'd better just go home, Harry," Sam says, wound up like Waltz has never seen him.

"Why?" Waltz says.

Hesperia calls in a calm voice, "I only brought the two shells, Boggins."

"The sheriff is on his way," Sam tells Waltz.

Waltz scratches his head. He has stepped into another secret. "Tell me what is going on, Sam."

"Didn't you hear the shots?"

"Shots?"

Sam Boggins leads Waltz like a sleepy boy through the knot of people to the front of the car Hesperia had been hired to park on the square. The windshield, on the driver's side, has been blown in with a shotgun blast, the front seat is thickly dusted with fragments of aquamarine glass, part of the steering wheel is gone, a hole the size of a basketball has been opened in the seat back. Hesperia's other shot went into the engine through the front grill.

Clean shots, efficient, Waltz wonders why he did not hear them. He does not bother to open the hood. He does not look at Hesperia; no chance, he guesses, of getting his five dollars back.

The sheriff arrives and Waltz tells him without any particular venom that he will sign any complaints against Hesperia. Nickel handcuffs are produced and fastened around Hesperia's wrists.

"Are those necessary?" Waltz asks.

"A weapon's involved, Harry," the sheriff says.

"He didn't shoot anybody."

"He shot your car. He discharged a firearm within city limits. Destruction of private property." The sheriff looks at Hesperia, grins, and says, "This is one *dangerous* individual."

Waltz, feeling mocked, starts to leave.

"Harry," the sheriff says, "this is still your car, shot wreck that it is."

"Use it for evidence."

"It can't sit here forever, Harry. It's dangerous. It's an eyesore."

"It's one of GM's finest."

The sheriff winks, taps Waltz on the arm. "Come on, Harry. Be reasonable. Just get it towed around behind the jail. We'll impound it as evidence there. Just get it off the square."

Waltz drives the truck home. He feels marked. The first thing he does is call Mary Hale.

"I need a good lawyer," he tells her.

"I'm a good lawyer."

"I want you to come down here."

"Business or personal?"

"Both. I need your help. I need your strong, young back."

"Terrific," she says without enthusiasm.

"All this ties together," he promises.

When the time comes that he is sure she is on the road he worries she will be tainted by the remotest link to him, that she travels beneath the same cloud that has frustrated him all day.

Then, sooner than he thought possible, Mary Hale is at his door. He kisses her, gets her small bag moved into the front hall, then takes her on a tour of his house.

"It has the feel of a woman," she notes.

"Louise," Waltz says. He has not bought or discarded a single piece of furniture in all the years since she died. Some of her toiletries are still deep in the bathroom cupboards.

Quiet comes over them; it has nothing to do with Louise, Waltz thinks. The strange house presents Mary Hale the responsibility of getting comfortable with Waltz all over again. He is again awkward and shy, where once they had made such progress.

He takes her bag up to his room while she sits smoking in the kitchen with a glass of beer. He cooks them a simple meal, but before Mary Hale takes a bite, she says, "Harry, I went to see Eugene yesterday."

He sighs. Bad luck presses everywhere. "Why?" he asks softly.

"Because it is wrong what you've done. What you're doing."

"I can't stop you from visiting him," Waltz says.

"No, you can't."

"But you'll need me to get him out," he says, "and I won't be party to that."

She takes a bite of food. She chews it a long time. Reluctantly, Waltz asks, "How's he doing?"

"He's doing fine. I know some people at the prison, so we were able to talk for almost two hours. He's a very sweet man, Harry. I like him."

"Did he say anything about me?"

"He thought you sent me," she says. "He was elated."

Waltz rolls his eyes. "Nice try, Mare. I hope you burst that particular bubble."

"He said to thank you and say hello."

"You're just getting his hopes up," Waltz says.

"I know a lot of people in prison, Harry. Many of them belong there. You can tell as soon as they open their mouths. But Eugene doesn't belong in prison."

"He robbed two men," Waltz says vehemently. He keeps having to cover old ground with this woman.

"It happens," she says. "But he still doesn't belong in prison." She lays her hands flat on the table. "I've said enough."

"I need a lawyer," Waltz finally tells her, "to press a case against another man."

"What has this man done?"

"He shot my car . . . a car I had title to. He's in the Marathon jail right now."

"He's the one who needs a lawyer," she says. "The city will provide a prosecutor to take this guy to court. Who is this man? Is he richer than you?"

"He owes me money," Waltz says, disappointed in her. "I repossessed his truck. I had planned to hire him to do some work for me, but he had injured his hand. I paid him five dollars to drive this car to the square and park it. So he shot the car twice with a shotgun."

"My," says Mary Hale.

"And *I'm* the richest man in Marathon," he says, and feels petty even as he says it.

"My, my," she says. "When are you coming to see me again?"

Waltz says, too sharply, "You're here now. Why does it have to be there?"

"My house seems empty since you left. I miss the togetherness."

Waltz kisses her on the cheek. "I'll come visit within forty-eight hours of your leaving here," he says. He almost expects her to produce a note to that effect for him to sign.

"Good" is all she says.

They sit in the gazebo for an hour, smoking and drinking beer, and Waltz is amazed it is still not dark. He needs darkness, he confides to Mary Hale, for the completion of his day's business. "This day had such promise, such a form to it," he tells her. "And now I'm scrambling to salvage any of it."

She wordlessly rises, unsnaps her jeans, and rolls them down over her long, slim legs. Her pubic hair, a furtive, matted wedge, glistens when it catches the last light in the right way. Waltz, seeing this woman before him, thinks of the residents of the State Home, what they would have thought if they had seen him, who as a boy masturbated in this octagonal place, now as a man is pursued by a white-haired woman. When he moves to be accommodating she stills him with a hand and does everything herself. He only has to raise his hips so she can get his pants down. She sits astride him, facing him, her smoky mouth buried in his neck, jerking to an amazing cadence. He can see beyond her, through the high fence, and he imagines running figures and googly faces at the fence, watching.

Just like that, when they finish, it is dark.

Without either of them moving, he explains his plan.

"Commandos," she whispers, intrigued.

"We'll clean the glass off the seat," he says, "and all you will have to do is steer. I'll push."

"Can you push a car all by yourself?"

"I can with a truck. And it's not far."

Still they wait another two hours. He wants the darkness to take a good hold. At half past eleven o'clock they get in the truck and drive to the square.

Waltz wishes he had not come. He should have waited until a minute after midnight, until the turn of the day, when his luck would be his own again. The destruction Hesperia began has been continued by persons unknown. Waltz wonders if they were people who owed him, or feared owing him in the future. The headlights and taillights have all been beaten in. Every piece of glass is crushed. The ground beneath glitters as though the car were shedding scales. The tires have been cut open. A sledgehammer has been taken to the body, ripping it like heavy paper, and as with the two blasts from Hesperia's shotgun, Waltz wonders why he did not hear any of these blows falling, there had to have been thousands.

He sweeps a spot on the seat clean of glass. Mary Hale has not said a word. Can she love a man so hated by others?

He covers the seat with a folded towel and carefully sits behind the wheel. No slivers of glass pierce him. He slides the key into the ignition. He does not expect the car to start, he is only curious about what will happen. Born and raised in a state founded on the automobile, he has never cared for them, or understood them, and he has always wondered what an automobile can do without and still function. The human body is full of spare parts. He wonders if the automobile is the same, or if it is so finely packed that one function undone stops the whole.

He turns the key. Nothing stirs. He feels better.

"What are you doing?" Mary Hale asks through the window.

"Collecting my thoughts."

"You're a popular guy in this town."

"It would appear so," Waltz says.

"What are you going to do?"

At a public phone lit like a blue tower at the edge of the square, he calls Sam Boggins.

"Sam, what happened to the car?"

"You should have seen it, Harry. They were in a frenzy."

"Who was there?"

"Marathonites. Your neighbors, Harry."

"Did anybody make any money?" Waltz asks.

"How do you mean?" Sam Boggins asks with distaste.

"Did anybody charge, say, fifty cents for three swings of the sledgehammer?"

"Heavens no. That would have gone against the spirit of the event."

"I see," Waltz says. He asks, "Sam, what time is it?"

"Just past midnight."

"Thanks, Sam." He hangs up. He is pleased to have survived that particular day.

The car is in almost the exact spot where, on the day JFK was shot, he was accidentally hit by a car driven by a man who owed him money. He can remember that more clearly than just about anything else in his life; his run across the square in the cold rain, the loosed schoolchildren a current he moved against, the car lifting him up, the bone in his leg coming apart.

He will leave the car where it sits. He will not fight them for it. His friend Sam Boggins will understand, he hopes. Otherwise, he has never been liked. Loved, yes, but never liked. He lets Mary Hale drive him home and wash the gas smell off him in the shower. For no good reason she claims he is her hero.

13

They come to the door of winter together and like an event out of place, or out of step, Mary Hale is pregnant.

She tells Waltz, "I had a feeling. Signs. But it was too unbelievable."

"Now it's a fact?" Waltz asks. His voice sounds scared, ready to flee.

"It's a fact." She nods, chewing her lower lip.

They are together in Marathon. His house is chilly and needs airing, it is thick with memory that makes everything clammy to the touch; the images he sees through the dirty windows are all slightly askew, and not to be trusted.

He puts a hand on her belly. Through the silk of her blouse it is loose and inviting to the touch. But she is white-haired, after all, and his semen, though incongruously abundant and easily drawn forth by this woman, is sixty-two years old. When passing his house's back windows he avoids looking at the State Home grounds; they make him think of goobies, through and through. He invites Mary Hale to take a walk into town, convinced they have conceived an idiot.

They walk in the cold down the hill to the square, then across the square to the Marathon Restaurant, where they take a booth by the window. Waltz can see Sam Boggins, the shape of him, arms raised like a conductor, through two thicknesses of fogged glass, cutting someone's hair.

Coffee is poured. They order. Waltz lights a cigarette. Mary Hale asks for one and he annoys her by refusing her request. She is suddenly full of mystery and responsibility. He feels the need to give this child whatever slim edge he can.

He swallows coffee. The cigarette smoke, tugged deep and held, sends him on a swooping high. He has to shut his eyes and hold the seat; it reminds him of the lifeguard's perch. On October 18, he had turned sixty-two, and made a birthday call to Aaron. Later that day he and Mary Hale made love. Was that the night it hit home? He asks her this.

"No," she says, almost smiling. "Too recent. My doctor says I'm about two and a half months along. You know when it was? That time in the gazebo. I'm positive. I was feeling very receptive toward you that night. I liked that you called me to you. It felt nice to be needed for something other than getting someone out of jail."

"Two and a half months?" Waltz says. "Didn't you suspect anything?"

"Sure," she nods. "I said there were signs. I throw up a lot. It's been official for almost a month now."

Waltz drops his eyes from her. "Why didn't you tell me?"

"Chicken," she says. "How well do I really know you?"

"Well enough," Waltz says.

"But look at what you do to your only son. Stick him in prison."

"That's not fair," he exclaims.

"Yes it is. It's part of you. I have to take that into account when I decide if I'm going to have this baby."

Waltz is stunned. "You mean you might not?"

"It's an alternative," she says. "I'm not ecstatic about the prospect of raising a child at my age. My law practice is going great. I'm selfish enough to admit I don't want to give that up."

"Yes," he says.

"It's just the *last* thing I want to do right now," she says, and he can tell by a rising note in her voice she is close to crying.

"You want an abortion?" Waltz asks.

"I don't know." She finds a cigarette of her own and lights it. She glares at Waltz, "Any kid growing up in my old wreck of a body is at a loss anyway. One cigarette won't hurt."

"You've got to be careful, Mare," he says. "That robs the baby of oxygen. He needs . . . a baby of ours needs all the help it can get."

"Why?" she asks softly.

"I'm sixty-two, you're forty-three. We're old for this. The kid is the product of two people advanced in years."

She holds a sheaf of her hair out where she can see it. "White hair," she says ruefully. "A white-haired mother."

"All these factors have to be taken into account," he says.

"What do *you* want to do about this?"

"I don't know. I'm scared to death. I can't get the image of a mongoloid baby out of my mind."

"Don't think about it," she simply says. "It's not a factor."

"You're determined to get rid of the baby?"

"Did I say that?"

"You were listing all the reasons," he says.

"Sure, there are reasons. I'd like to hear something from you."

"I'm looking in my past for experiences that would help me here," Waltz says. "And I haven't come up with anything."

"All right. What else?"

"Did I ever tell you how I met Louise?"

Mary Hale sits up straight and crushes out her cigarette, the motion brisk with impatience.

"My mother and father practically courted Louise for me," he says.

"You told me they arranged your meeting."

"I'd still be out on the sidewalk watching her if my parents had not meddled. I don't want someone making my decision for me here."

"All right." She nods, then watches him closely.

He says, "I've got a son in prison, a son who is dead, and two daughters out of town."

"And you want to try again?"

"It's a rare chance."

"You'll have to do better than that," she says. "I'm not having this baby just because you think you failed as a father the first four times. What other reasons do you have?"

He looks around, at a loss. For a moment Mary Hale wonders why she is there, how she walked into this mess. She thinks she can feel the baby impatient for an answer within her; and this odd old man across from them without an idea in his head. But she stays. They have been together enough for her to know a rich emotional life exists in Waltz. She need only draw it forth.

The restaurant window is lush with frost along its base. There is nothing to see outside. The square is empty. Even Sam Boggins has disappeared.

The place mat is a challenge: Write the capitals on a map of the fifty United States. Waltz does Michigan, Indiana, Ohio, Illinois, and Wisconsin in his head. Iowa stumps him. The chain of contiguous states whose capitals he knows reaches only that far to the west; to the east, he can go all the way to the Atlantic; south, he makes it to the Gulf of Mexico.

When he looks up from his travels he is almost surprised to see Mary Hale there. Her eyes have liquid rims.

"Sorry." He grimaces. "I got lost here." He taps the place mat forcefully. He asks, "What about you and me?" He points to Mary Hale, then to himself, and she smiles at his need to be clear.

"That's another question," she says.

"Do we get married? Do we move in together? What?"

"I like where I am," she says. "I wouldn't like moving. Most of my clients are in Saginaw and Bay City."

Waltz says nothing, just nods. He looks toward the kitchen, its swinging door and round window, and he wonders what is delaying their food. He carefully aligns his knife, fork, and spoon atop his paper napkin.

Mary Hale sighs. "I feel just like Louise."

"What do you want?"

"I want a little response! I'd like to know how you feel. Is that too much to ask?"

"You want to stay where you are. I want to stay where I am. That's that."

She says impatiently, "I was stating a desire. It's open to negotiation. I was expecting something from you in return."

Waltz says, "O.K. Here is what I feel. I want you to have the baby, though I'm afraid it will be retarded. I want to stay in Marathon, and I think we should get married."

Mary Hale takes a deep breath. Waltz had truly only wanted to get the notion of marriage out in the open; the other things were only a way to build momentum.

"We're not having a retarded baby," she says. "Believe me."

"How do you know? Now they say it's the semen that may cause Down's syndrome. Old semen. My semen is old."

"Jesus. This is—" She is stopped by the waitress with their food. "This is the dynamo who said he was going to live to a hundred?"

"Who told you that?"

"You did, Harry. A dozen times."

"I did?" He thought it was a secret ambition. Is it a sign of aging that he does not remember the things he speaks of?

"Yes, you did," she says. "Ten minutes after I met you I knew your ambition was to live to a hundred."

"You hated me when you met me," Waltz says.

"Only a little."

"Well, I'm sure I wouldn't tell you my goals if I sensed you hated me."

"Forget it. The point is, you're not that old. The kid'll be thirty-eight when you kick off. He'll be glad to see you go."

"Thanks."

"You'll be a drooling old fart too stubborn to go gracefully," she says, winking.

"My daddy played softball at the age of ninety-seven," Waltz says, stung by the implication his father had been a drooling old fart. "He was standing on his own two feet, without anybody's help, at the moment he turned a hundred years old."

"That's sweet," she says. "I'm sure you'll do as well." She squeezes his leg beneath the table. "You aren't too old, your come is not too old. You're a fine man. Do you really want to marry me?"

"Boy, I don't know," he admits. He holds up a hand. "I don't want . . . don't take this the wrong way, Mare, but before today the idea hadn't crossed my mind."

"Nor mine," she says with a gentle smile.

"We seemed too advanced for that," he says. "I liked the idea of you on Saginaw Bay, with your own house, your work, your values. I didn't have to prop you up." Waltz lowers his eyes. He does not know where he is going.

"I liked you, being with you," he says. "When we had sex it was just a part of it. It never occurred to me to classify that love of togetherness with a marriage license."

"And now?"

"Now it's different," he says. He realizes she has not taken her hand from his leg; it rests there, a calming weight, and he feels on safer ground that she has left it there.

"And Eugene?" she asks stubbornly.

He holds his head in his hands. The quiet of the restaurant becomes filled with tiny, magnified details. Cutlery, plates, water, his own harsh breathing. His voice sounds far away when he says, "Eugene is not a part of this."

"He is," Mary Hale says.

"He is not a bargaining tool. He is a grown man who must learn to pay for his mistakes. He has nothing to do with this child."

"It's—"

"And I wish you would stop bringing him up!"

Mary Hale touches Waltz's face. She thinks his skin looks grayish in the winter light. His hands are yellowed from the nicotine. He has a bad leg. It is a long way to a hundred and the thought of him coming up short scares her. She tips his burning cigarette into the ashtray.

"You won't make a hundred smoking these," she says kindly.

"Is this what it'll be like?" he asks.

"What what will be like?" she asks, though she knows.

"Marriage to Mary Hale. Will you seek to improve me? Will you keep bringing up my exiled son?"

"You don't need to smoke."

"I'll quit when you do."

"And Eugene," she persists, "is a sweet man who deserves to be free."

"Did you visit him again?"

"Yes. Four times now. Won't you visit him with me?"

Waltz, with all the venom in the air, still needs to know. "How is he doing?"

"He gets by. He sends his love."

"I'll bet," he says.

When their meal is finished he puts down a bill, confident it will be enough, and takes Mary Hale's hand and leads her back out into the cold. She puts an arm through his. Waltz feels she is with him now. Some affirmation has been made, or is approaching, which he patiently awaits. She is his second wife.

They walk once around the square before either speaks. They look into windows. At least one store on each side of the square is vacant; Marathon is starting to resemble Flint. The air is full of an icy, damp cold that coats their throats when they breathe. He wants to go home where it is warm but Mary Hale keeps making turns away from his destination and he has to follow.

She finally says, "Now *is* different. I think I would like to have this baby. For all the bad things, there are also many good things. But I would like to keep our personal relationship as it is."

"Wait—"

"Now, Harry, don't start on me. You asked. Now I'm answering. You admitted marriage hadn't occurred to you before, and I agreed. This baby is not *yet* reason enough. As long as I'm assured of your continued support and affection, I'd like to keep things the way they are."

A mean wind blows out of the north. Mary Hale rocks against him for warmth. The sidewalks have adopted a treacherous glaze.

"Can we go home now?" she asks, sounding exhausted.

Her arm is back in his. He is too old a man, he decides, to try reading a woman's feelings in the tones of her voice. He has emotional ground to recover.

Nearly a half hour passes and full night descends before they manage to get up the hill to his house. Mary Hale in her high heels scares Waltz with her precariousness. Twice she goes down hard and cries out; he is only able to slow her fall and the second time she pulls him over on top of her. He helps her up, holds her tighter, but his concern is for the embryo tethered in its sac of fluid; he wonders what her falls registered in there.

The third and final time she falls is on the walk leading to Waltz's front porch. As she falls they work together to keep her upright; it is a battle of small victories and defeats of balance lost and gained, and they get her descending momentum stopped when she is down on one knee. She howls up at the moon.

Her knees are scraped and in the morning they ache. Waltz feels her belly during the night while she sleeps. Nothing seems amiss.

Waltz telephones Carla in the morning and she answers just as he realizes the news he has is strangely unformed in his mind; it is just a fact, unpolished for the public eye. As Carla is saying "Hello" he puts the phone back.

He brews coffee, makes orange juice, scrambled eggs, toast, and puts it all on a tray and takes it up to Mary Hale. Her refusal to marry him is a nagging ache; she seems so at home asleep in his bed.

He notices a bruise on her chin. It is the size of a small button. Did she get it when she fell on the ice? Did he punch her in his sleep?

Sometime in the night she had struggled out of her nightgown. She might have been too warm, she has kicked off the covers and lies asleep on her back in just her underpants. Light falls on her stringy frame, her slack breasts, the narrow pool of her throat. Her white hair is nearly transparent.

Seeing her this way embarrasses Waltz; he might not know her. He flips the covers up and over her and this sensation of air and cloth across her body awakens her. He watches her rising out of sleep. He wonders if each morning hits her darkly, as they do him.

"I tried to call Carla," he says, "but I couldn't think of what to tell her."

She sits up and seems startled by her breasts; she holds the covers to them and asks for one of his shirts.

"Tell her the truth," she grunts. She drinks some coffee. "Do you have a cigarette?"

"Eat your eggs and toast," he says.

"I don't eat eggs or toast. A cigarette?"

While she smokes, leaning back against the wall, he eats her breakfast. She drinks the orange juice only after he insists. The baby is half his; this reassures him. Except for his broken leg he can't recall a single day of illness or physical pain. The baby has half his dumb good health.

"I found I was at a loss to explain you," Waltz says.

"Don't be silly, Harry."

"How do I explain you?"

"It's not fair, you doing this to me so early in the morning."

"It's eleven-thirty."

She is so surprised she demands to see the clock. "I've become slothful, in addition to being knocked up," she says.

"I'm just confused about what I should tell Carla."

"Do you want me to call her?"

"No. But I'd like to have her, Susan, and Willy to dinner. We can invite them, then when they're here we can spring it on them together."

"If you want," she says, distracted. She gets out of bed and hurries into the bathroom. Waltz sits in the warm sheets she has left behind and dials Carla's number. Waiting for her to answer, he hears Mary Hale through the bathroom door vomiting. Just as Carla picks up the phone Waltz again hangs up. He is frightening his daughter, but he in turn is being frightened by Mary Hale. She emerges from the bathroom ashen and perspiring. She sits heavily on the edge of the bed.

"Oh, Waltz," she groans, "I do need food."

She sits in her underwear and his white shirt in the chilly kitchen and complains of the heat while Waltz scrambles his last eggs. If she is staying, and she seems to be, he will have to shop. Out the window he sees the back yard has been sprayed with ice. The power lines droop perilously low under their breathtaking crystal weight.

He telephones Carla a third time while Mary Hale's eggs cook. He would not blame her if she did not answer but she is fearless and takes it up on the second ring. No response, though, she just waits in silence for the crack of disconnection.

He says, "Carla?"

"Daddy?"

"Yes, honey."

"Oh!" she exclaims, and laughs with great relief. "I've had someone calling all morning and hanging up when I answered. It was getting creepy."

"I'm sorry, Carla. That was me. Just as I called you something would come up. I'm sorry if I scared you."

"Four times something came up?" she asks.

He shivers, but says, "Yes, it was just one of those crazy sequences of events. I'm calling to invite you to dinner. You, Susan, Willy, Homer, too. I've got a friend here I want you to meet."

"Sure, Daddy. When?"

"Tomorrow night?"

"Tomorrow is O.K. with me. The roads are terrible now. Half of Ann Arbor lost power this morning. Luckily, it was the other half."

"Call Susan and Willy."

"Sure."

"How is that going?" he asks.

"It's a trial. Willy is going through a difficult time. He can't find decent work and he'll come and hide out here when he should be looking. Or he'll lose one of the peon jobs he does get just because he's too bored to show up."

Waltz grunts, not liking the sound of any of that. He has the canceled check for $5,000 he lent to Willy. Willy's signature across the back was quick and scrawling. He has not repaid a cent.

"Tell them they're invited, tell them it is important," Waltz says.

"O.K. Who's the friend?"

"Her name is Mary Hale."

"Is she a nun?"

"No." He laughs. "Why?"

"It's a nun's name. Mary Hale. Hail Mary. Get it?"

"Sure. You'll like her. Bring Homer."

"Homer's gone. The university canceled his grant at the semester. Evidently that was an option in the contract. He's taken his woodwinds and left town."

"I'm sorry, Carla."

"No problem," she says brightly. "There are other men."

"What's with Willy?"

"He says it's a phase of weakness." She laughs dryly, half to herself. "He says he is passing through a low esteem zone."

"Sounds like bullshit to me," Waltz says.

He remembers Mary Hale's eggs then, but she has already gotten them for herself; she has plucked the fork from his hand and scraped the eggs onto a plate. When he looks at her she makes a face of mild impatience. She gulps orange juice, which pleases Waltz.

"I've got to go," he tells Carla. "Call the others. Come at six-thirty or thereabouts. Tell Willy not to be afraid. I'll welcome him like one of my own."

"I can't promise anything."

"You'll be here, won't you?"

"I'll be there."

He hangs up on her. Mary Hale is gone, he hears her in the bathroom vomiting with such force he fears for the life within her.

While she sleeps again Waltz dresses and goes into town for groceries. The store is nearly deserted. The woman who rings his purchases confides that the people are afraid of going out and not being able to get home. A high, meager sun hangs in the overcast and cuts nothing of the ice that encases everything. There is a perilous beauty to the day, the sheath laid over the immediate world like the breathtaking skin of a snake.

The weather report calls for warmth, then rain, then bitter cold again. Marathonites fear the loss of power, the cashier tells Waltz as she puts his things in paper sacks, they fear hot wires falling over their shoulders or the roofs of their cars. They sit waiting for the worst in houses like boxes strung together with lines of electricity.

And as if touched by a prophet, getting home is indeed a struggle for Waltz. There is no getting a bite in the iced road. The hill up to his house rises like glass. He can see his house up there; he is so close he thinks he could hear Mary Hale moving around and being sick if he had the car window open.

On his first attempt he makes it halfway to the top and then a harrowing motionlessness takes over the car. He is hovering. The wheels spin in a fruitless harmony. He gives up and lets the car roll back down.

In preparation for a second run he positions the car a good distance from the foot of the hill. He seeks first speed, then momentum.

But it is difficult even to get moving on that horizontal plane of ice. The depth and thickness of the ice is daunting. As he covers the space he has allowed himself and moves to the foot of the hill he knows he is not going to make it. He barely climbs as high as his first attempt. The car skews sharply to the left and he slides back down sideways, helpless, watching out his side window as the ribbon of ice runs under him.

This problem has never confronted him before. All his winter lives in Marathon were cold and carefree times, as he remembers, when coming and going were routine. He lights a cigarette and peers out at the pearlish light. Where is the promised warming sun? Must he wait until the spring to get home?

He grimaces and thinks of Mary Hale kneeling piously over the toilet bowl. It is a messy sight; she objected to his presence, to his seeing her like that.

She has cloaked him in all this responsibility and for a long moment he is resentful. He had his life all to himself and then in a few months she changed all that. He moved in blissful emptiness until he saw this woman afloat on a river, and now he must get home to her.

There are roads he can take home the back way, he travels them in his imagination, but this circling would only delay the inevitable; there would still be hills to climb, the ice would lie as thickly.

A third try at the hill is a quick failure; his mind and heart are not in it. He is already looking ahead.

On the other side of Marathon he comes to the apartment of Joe Montague. Joe is surprised to see Waltz at his front door. He shakes hands, but with his other hand he surreptitiously shields his young and pretty wife behind him.

"Didn't you get my money, Mr. Waltz?"

"Yes, Joe, I did." He steps uninvited into the warm apartment. The TV is on. Joe's wife has straight blond hair and large, pale blue eyes. Waltz can't remember her name, though he remembers her growing up in Marathon. She is not yet twenty years old and watches Waltz with distrust and confusion. He smiles at her, wishes he had a hat to tip.

"You want some coffee, Mr. Waltz?" Joe asks.

"Yes, thanks. Call me Harry." He pounds his arms. His need to hurry has robbed him of all heat.

"The reason I'm here, Joe, is to make you an offer," he says. He takes Joe Montague by the arm and leads him to the front window. The car sits idling sleek and useless down in the parking lot.

"That is a 1981 LeSabre, Joe," Waltz says. "It has less than three thousand miles on it. A beaut."

"Sure is." Joe nods.

"How many miles on your VW?"

"Shit," Joe says, "close to forty thousand."

"And you still owe me about five hundred on it."

Joe swallows and nods.

"Here is my offer," Waltz says. "I'll swap you—straight up—that LeSabre for your VW. You just pay the rest of your note and we'll be square."

Joe Montague's eyes darken, he gives Waltz a small, sly, confused smile.

"What's wrong with the LeSabre?" he asks.

"Not a thing, Joe. Runs like a dream."

"Then . . ."

"Fact is, Joe," Waltz interrupts, "you're dealing with a desperate man. I'm in a big hurry to get home and that beautiful LeSabre out there can't get up the hill to my house."

"You're willing to trade for my Bug just because of that?" Joe Montague asks in bald wonder.

Waltz nods, rubs his hands together. He executes a small, nervous dance step, fearing Joe Montague's wife will return with coffee which he will have to drink out of politeness.

Joe Montague takes this all in. He is a witness to legend; this is a Harry Waltz story unfolding.

"Write it down," Joe says decisively, "and I'll sign it."

"Give me your keys. I've got some groceries in the LeSabre. I'll move them into the VW. We'll do the paperwork later." He puts out his hand and Joe Montague shakes it. "It's a deal then. The car is yours. It's a sweet runner, believe you me."

The VW, with its engine over the rear axle, is the answer. Waltz steers around the square, onto the street leading to the hill. He gooses the accelerator. The tires get a bite. He steers the car straight toward the hill. He notices the sun is out and everywhere he looks Marathon is blessed with a dripping jeweled crust. It is the promised warming.

The climb is so effortless he taps the brakes near the top, fearing he might fly right off the hill's peak.

In his house, everything is silent. The power is out. Light switches set in the walls have a touching uselessness. Cool shadows fill the kitchen and the downstairs rooms. The halls without windows are dark save for sunlight leaking under closed doors. Mary Hale is not in the bathroom, she is not asleep in bed. Waltz makes a pass through the house without finding her and fears for a moment he has lost her.

"Mary!" he shouts.

She answers him from the kitchen. Somehow she has circled around him, somehow they have missed each other. Her face is waxen. She is wearing one of Waltz's long winter coats and putting the groceries away.

"You have a flashlight?" she asks.

"Somewhere."

"Why are you smiling?"

"I'm relieved. I couldn't find you."

"You need a flashlight. Or candles. The electricity is off."

"All right." He nods.

"And where the hell *were* you?" she asks sharply, frowning at the fact her eyes have abruptly filled with tears. She puts a hand over her mouth. "I wake up and you aren't here," she says through her hand. A quizzical, sore look comes to her eyes.

"I had the damnedest time getting home from the store," he says.

But Mary Hale is not listening. She is intent on an inner storm. She spins on her heel and runs to the bathroom. Waltz follows. He is touched that she lets him stay and hold her white hair clear.

14

Carla and Susan come alone to dinner. They drive up together from Ann Arbor in Carla's Volvo and Susan is quick with an excuse for Willy, that he is playing basketball with some friends at the YMCA, that he is sorry he could not come. Waltz excuses himself after they have been there fifteen minutes and uses the phone in his office to call Susan's number. Willy answers on the second ring. Waltz hangs up without saying a word, wishing he had not made the call.

The electricity has been restored. The forecasted freeze has not materialized and the night is warm, breath-moist with fog. Everyone is oddly exhilarated; Waltz thinks it is because Willy is absent. Susan's belly is globular, she sits like a Buddha massaging it with her hands.

No one remarks on Mary Hale's flights to the bathroom.

"Isn't she lovely?" Waltz asks intently when dinner is over and Mary Hale is upstairs being sick.

"Why did you subject her to this torture?" Carla asks.

"What torture?"

"The torture of having us over for dinner. Of cooking a meal and being put on display when she has to run and puke every ten minutes."

"She wanted to," Waltz says.

Susan laughs harshly. "I'll bet."

Carla asks, "How pregnant is she?"

The question disappoints Waltz. He wanted to make a ceremony of the revealing of the fact. His daughters, and Mary Hale's nausea, have reduced the event to pure biology.

"Her doctor says nearly three months."

"You the proud papa?"

"Yes."

"My, my," Susan says. "This *is* a surprise."

"You going to marry the girl?"

Waltz hasn't a clue. He shrugs and wonders where Mary Hale is. A good five minutes have passed since the overhead churn of the plumbing. She might have fainted and cracked her head open on the toilet rim. She might have tripped on a snare in the carpet. The second story of his house is alive with mayhem. Any place out of his sight is armed.

But just as he is about to excuse himself, she reappears. She has changed into a pair of trousers and a white shirt; they are his clothes. The switch is startling: she is diminished, her arms poking out of the rolled sleeves are thin and white. She has tugged her hair back into a loose tail.

"They guessed," Waltz says petulantly.

"I knew they would."

Carla rises and hugs Mary Hale briefly, but with what Waltz thinks is warmth, and kisses her on each cheek. Susan smiles, then looks away.

"We figured you were pregnant," Carla says, "or else you had the plague, the way you've been throwing up. And if it was the plague, Daddy wouldn't be here. Hence, you were pregnant."

"Hey—thanks a lot," Waltz protests. But he feels better now

that they know. It is good that they are all smiles, that they assume the baby will be born.

"When did you say you were due?" Mary Hale asks Susan.

"Momentarily," Susan says, gripping her belly with both hands.

"Should you be here?" Waltz asks. When he does not see his daughters for periods of time they return in his mind to a previous state of innocence. Susan is not pregnant, Carla is not alone and in love with her sister's husband; they are both young, beautiful, and untroubled. He loses sight of them. He is always a little dismayed when they appear; it awes him that they are only nine years younger than Mary Hale, who looks wizened, toughened, alongside them.

The night breaks up too quickly for Waltz's taste; he was hoping something would be decided, some blessing bestowed. After a last cup of coffee Carla and Susan say goodbye. The fog swallows the Volvo ten yards from the house.

Waltz goes from room to room turning out lights and blowing out candles. Mary Hale has gone upstairs to bed.

He considers washing the dishes, but then decides he wants to be with Mary Hale, to sleep like the dead, and awaken in the light. He goes into the front hall and is on the first step going upstairs when someone raps on the front door. The sound scares him. It has to be Sam Boggins, he thinks; he knows no one else in Marathon except the people who owe him money, and they would not dare come to him unannounced at this hour.

He turns on the outside light and opens the door. His daughters have returned. Susan looks nervous, her coat pulled as tight as possible around her belly, and Waltz thinks the time has come for her. Carla steps in ahead of her, unbuttoning her coat, clapping her mittened hands.

"Pea soup, Daddy," she says. "Can we have our old beds back for the night? Until this burns off?"

"Of course you can," Waltz says. "How far did you get?"

Carla shrugs, unraveling garments. "A half mile, maybe."

"It was frightening," Susan says in a little voice. She looks uneasily around at the dark house, as though she has never been there before in her life.

"Are you O.K.?" Waltz asks.

She nods. "I was just looking forward to going home tonight."

"It'll be O.K.," Carla promises, like a mother. "We'll leave first thing in the morning."

"Call Willy so he won't worry."

"Think thoughts to make the baby want to stay inside for at least another day," Carla suggests. Everyone smiles at this, but Waltz wonders what those thoughts would be.

"I'll be O.K.," Susan says. "Don't worry about me." She goes into the kitchen to use the phone. She knows unerringly where the light switches hang.

"It was really bad, Daddy," Carla says, "or I'd have tried to make it."

"It's no problem, believe me."

"Well—we're a pain in the neck in the best of times. We know you like your privacy."

Waltz hangs up her coat, scarf, and mittens. He loves the smell: wool and Carla. She kicks off her heavy leather boots; the toes are wet, a darker brown. She bends to arrange them on the mat by the door, the spot his children have put their boots and shoes for as long as he can remember. He used to count the boots present to see who was home. He hates the idea of Carla thinking he likes the house to himself.

"It's no problem," he repeats, smiling down at her. He reaches out with his arms and wraps her in them. She feels chilly pulled against him, she has the feel of Louise and this so surprises him that he nearly cries. His penis, prodded by the memory of his wife's contours, warms with the first faint blood of erection. He kisses Carla on the top of the head and sets her free.

"Stay as long as you like," he says. "I often think all of you left too soon anyway."

"Nah." She smiles, then does a complete turn, a pirouette of uneasiness. He understands that they have no place to go. They are waiting for Susan to finish on the kitchen phone. Carla is made uneasy by Mary Hale's presence upstairs; she may think their return has surprised her father and his pregnant lover in the act of re-creating the moment of conception. Carla can't go forward and she can't go back.

"What's with them?" Waltz whispers to her.

Carla shrugs. "I don't want to get my hopes up."

"But?"

"But I feel it coming apart."

"You're not happy about that, are you?"

"Thrilled," she says, then grimaces. "She does nothing for him. Here he is in this horrible lost sequence of his life and she is helpless to do anything about it."

"What do you want her to do?"

"Nothing. Exactly what she's doing now. In a year he'll be all mine again."

"You don't believe that," Waltz says.

"I do. I've given it more thought than I would've thought possible."

"And what happens if he doesn't leave her? Where do you fit in there?"

"I'm already there," she says.

They hear the phone drop into the cradle. Carla is about to slide a last remark into the time left but then thinks better of it. She steps back, waits.

Susan appears and smiles at them with eyes that appear wounded to Waltz. "What are you two standing here for?" she asks.

"Rehashing the past," Waltz says. "You get hold of Willy?"

"I woke him up," Susan says. Waltz prays she will leave it at that, not fabricate a history of Willy's night of basketball, and she does.

Later, he thinks the house with its unexpected crowd of formed and half-formed souls has gone to sleep, he is working at his desk when Susan appears. One moment he is alone and the next she is beside him. She smiles down at him and rests a hand on his shoulder.

"When we were kids," she says, "we thought you must have been the most wonderful man in the world because all these people sent you money."

"But I am," he jokes, embarrassed by the money stacked by denomination on the desk, the pile of notes, his ordered books. It is his domain, nobody's business but his own, but he does not want to offend Susan by hiding it from her. He offers her a seat; while she gets comfortable he closes the ledgers. He lights a cigarette.

"You never explained who you were," she says offhandedly. "When the other kids bragged about what their daddies did, I couldn't say anything because I didn't have a clue."

"You just kept quiet?"

"Even at this very moment I'm at a loss to explain what you do," she admits.

"No!"

"It's true. I'm at a loss."

"I lend money, usually to people who would have trouble getting it any other way. They pay me back a little more than they borrowed." Waltz watches his daughter's eyes; she is not listening. She is looking ahead.

"I know you lent five thousand dollars to Willy," she says. "And I know he hasn't paid any of it back to you."

"Honey, it's all right. Believe me."

"But it's *not* all right. It's the reason he didn't come with us tonight. He sits home all day and frets. He says he is waiting but he can't say for what."

"Has he spent the five thousand?"

"Part of it," Susan says. "He hasn't wasted it, Daddy. Don't think that. He's not a drunk, or a gambler, or a womanizer. He's just lost."

"You tell him we love him," Waltz says, "and if you need more money, for whatever the reason, just tell me and it's yours."

"No. I just wanted to tell you that one thing. I didn't want you to think Willis was a deadbeat or something."

"Never crossed my mind," Waltz says. He again looks into her eyes. Again she is not listening. "This stretch of his life," Waltz says, "is not your doing. Don't blame yourself for it."

"I'm there, though. I'm a part of it."

"Sure you are. But you're not the reason. He'd be twice as bad off without you."

"We don't know that," she says.

"I'd bet on it." He wonders what she knows or suspects about her sister's love for her husband. Does she recognize Carla's patient, poised shadow over her troubled life?

"Are you going to marry Mary?" she asks.

"I want to," he says. "Right now she is the person lacking enthusiasm for the idea."

"Don't rush her." Susan stands and folds her hands atop her belly. "She strikes me as the type of woman who hates having a decision made for her."

"That *is* Mary Hale," Waltz agrees.

"Do you worry about the baby?"

"All the time," he says.

"You can have all kinds of tests done now. If there is something wrong with the baby you'll know soon enough."

Waltz nods his head. His insides feel packed with fear. He had put aside his image of the baby as an idiot; Susan's good intentions brought it back strong. He thinks of old come, old lovers, Mary Hale's white hair; he thinks of a news film he saw recently that made him weep, the Pope kissing a pinheaded boy.

"Mary has decided against all that," Waltz says. "She will have the baby, retarded or not. So she would rather not know. She just wants to have it."

Susan nods, smiles. "That's a good attitude. She'll make a fine mother."

She kisses him good night. Standing close to him, she is immense. He pats her belly. She walks back to her old room and after a while Waltz goes to his own, where Mary Hale sleeps snoring on her back and the silver fog stands nose to nose with the windows.

Waltz rolls onto his back. It takes him longer to get to sleep now, he thinks, with another body beside him. The balance and feel of his bed are all changed. He had gotten used to sleeping alone. Twenty years, it could easily have been a lifetime. He was that close to slipping irrevocably into the linear cool existence of the widower. Mary Hale appeared to rescue him. It amazes him, makes him smile up at the ceiling, makes him sleep.

The fog is gone in the morning but his daughters remain. They sit at the kitchen table in the sunlight retelling their childhoods. Waltz is the villain of their tales; Louise is the saint. He was the one always insensitive to their child's pain, he is the one with too many rules, he is the one who did not adequately love them. This hurts, when they tell him these things with smiles on their lips; they are just memory to his daughters, they have the time ahead to create an entire new set for themselves. For Waltz, they are final. He can't remember ever not loving them, his girls, Monroe, even Eugene, who proved so hard to love. As for rules, the girls especially are remembered in that time absolutely free, nearly airborne in their lack of restraints.

"You don't remember it clearly," he tells them. "Look at it as an adult. Somebody had to watch out for you."

They laugh, shake their golden heads, and drink their coffee. Mary Hale sits and listens. Waltz is made ornery with lust the way the sunlight will occasionally cut through the thin cloth of his shirt she is wearing and delineate the underslope of her breast. The sun falls on her white hair and makes it gleam. She has vomited twice already that morning. She sits poised uneasily in her chair, as though prepared to bolt. He wants to get her home sometime that day. He thinks she will do better in her own surroundings, wearing her own clothes.

"Should I tell him about Ray Packer?" Carla asks Susan.

"I forgot all about him," Susan says. But she does not supply an answer and Carla frowns and gets up to pour more coffee.

Waltz asks, "Who was Ray Packer?"

"A boy at school," Susan says.

"What's the story?" Mary Hale asks.

"It will only hurt Daddy's feelings."

Waltz says, "Fire away. You've hurt them irreparably already."

"Don't be a martyr, Daddy," Carla scolds.

"Tell me about Ray Packer."

"In 1963, two years after Mom died" (Waltz thought, hearing the date: the year JFK got it; he did not relate it to Louise's death) "a boy in our school named Ray Packer ran away from home. His parents were doing something to him, probably making him do his homework, and he just got fed up. He was a year ahead of us, tall and very cute. A basketball player. He ran away from home and got as far as the square. That's where we found him. He had a silly little suitcase, as I recall, and was sitting on a bench. We started to talk to him and he put on this big act about running away to New York. He told us he was waiting for the bus. Well, we left and went across the street and sat in the restaurant watching him. He knew we were watching him, too. He had this very intent, angry scowl on his face. We were in awe. We were sure he was going to run away to New York. Then, about two minutes before the bus gets there, he stands up and goes over to the drugstore. He's in there all the time it takes for the bus to arrive, see nobody was there, and drive away. Ray Packer waited until the bus was just out of sight, then he came running out of the drugstore, trying to flag it down. Pretending he had missed it. He kicked a stone. He kept an eye on us watching him from the restaurant." Carla shakes her head. She looks at Susan and they both howl. Mary Hale laughs; Waltz wants to laugh but he is uneasy, waiting for his feelings to be hurt.

"We walked over to him. He's back on the bench. He says he went into the drugstore to get something to read. He said the bus was early. Well, we say, he can always catch the bus the next day. No, he says, it's Friday, and the bus doesn't come on weekends. He is stuck in Marathon for the weekend. We told him he could hitchhike but he said that was dangerous. He told us about this guy who hitched to Flint and was never seen again."

"Barry Sweet," Waltz interjects.

"What?"

"He was talking about Barry Sweet. He was ten or twelve years older than you. When he was sixteen he disappeared hitching to Flint. Never found a trace of him."

Mary Hale shudders and clasps her shoulders.

"He was a bright kid," Waltz says.

"Anyway, Ray is moaning and groaning about his parents and missing the bus and having no place to stay until the bus comes again Monday. So we get the idea to have him stay with us."

"You never asked me," Waltz says.

"*That* is the heart of this story. We *didn't* ask you. You were so absorbed in yourself—your work, your money, your grief—we used to joke we could invite the high school band over for the weekend and you wouldn't be aware of it."

"I don't believe you," Waltz says.

"Believe it, Daddy. Ray Packer was all for the idea. He could spend a weekend with the two prettiest girls in Marathon. He wouldn't have to do anything about his future until Monday. We waited, just hanging around the house, like Ray was just visiting. When the coast was clear we hustled him up to our room. If anybody said anything we'd just say he went home. We took his meals up to him. We kept watch when he had to go to the bathroom. Remember, there was you, Daddy, but there was also Monroe, Eugene, Grandpa and Grandma, too. Ray even took a shower Sunday afternoon. It was the best weekend of his life."

"What happened Monday morning?" Mary Hale asks.

"We snuck him out and left him on the bench on the square. He said he was going to wait for the bus but about an hour later we saw him walking the halls between classes. He had this big grin on his face. He would see us and look kind of embarrassed. He thought he had let us down. He was in love with Susan the rest of the year. The best part was that nobody believed his story. He had all these corroborating details and it was just too much to believe. Spending the weekend in the bedroom of the Waltz twins, without anyone knowing? Who would believe a story like that? And when somebody came to us to verify the story, we denied it. The perfect crime."

Waltz is quiet. He smokes and drinks coffee. Carla watches him and he sees she is wondering if they have made a mistake. He is struck by the idea of a parallel life existing on the other side of walls; their bedroom abutted his office. He remembers rapping the wall when their stereo was too loud. What else had he missed?

"I don't know what I'd have done if I caught you," he says.

"Nothing," Susan says, kindly. She moves laboriously to her father's side and kisses him on the cheek. She smells of egg. "You were too sweet," she says.

"A pushover," Carla verifies.

"I don't know what I'd have done."

"Anyway, dear old Ray Packer lives in Ypsilanti now. He married Karen Bronson, I think."

Waltz asks, "Did you have sex that weekend?"

"No!" his daughters say together, smiling that they can give him that comfort.

"We necked a little," Carla says, "and one time Ray got too ambitious with his hands and Susan had to slap him. It was *so* loud. We thought we'd given ourselves away."

"But that was all, Daddy," Susan says.

"How old were you, Daddy? When you lost your virginity?"

Waltz blushes, laughs.

"I was twenty," Carla volunteers. She looks to Susan, who stares at her empty plate. Waltz does not want to hear; he has no curiosity beyond that one phantom weekend they have related.

"I was sixteen," says Mary Hale.

Susan says, "Twenty-two."

"Your turn, Daddy."

"I was twenty," he says, thinking: Twenty, both times.

"A good age," Mary Hale says.

He checks his watch. It is going on noon and he suddenly realizes he wants his daughters to leave. They have uncrated their old memories and left them lying around for him to fall over. They have been too personal. They have made him wonder what else he has missed in sixty-two years.

"Long drive ahead of you," he says, making no effort at craftiness.

"You trying to get rid of us?" Carla asks.

"Yes," he says, unblinking.

But still they do not leave. They drift through the house as though it is home again. Amazingly, at two in the afternoon, Waltz returns from a run into town to find Carla making a sandwich in the kitchen and Susan asleep on the couch in the den. She lies on her side under a light blue afghan Louise brought to the marriage, snoring deeply, her big, veiny hands laced beneath her ominous belly.

"The peaceful sleep of the successfully bred," Carla says from behind her father.

"Did she call Willy?"

"She told me to call him, the dummy."

"Did you?"

"Yes. I woke him up. He was asleep at noon. The slob."

"He wasn't worried about her?"

"He was asleep," she says. "How worried could he be?"

"What time do you plan on leaving?"

"Well . . . now there is talk of Willy driving up tonight."

"Was I to be included in this talk?"

She pinches his cheek. He winces and pulls away, though it does not hurt, he only wants to convey clearly his growing annoyance. He has grown fond of his house empty or full at his bidding. Now he wants it empty again. He wants to go to Mary Hale's house on Saginaw Bay.

"We would've told you eventually," Carla says.

"I was planning to drive Mary home tonight."

"No problem. We'll lock up after you."

They go back into the kitchen. Carla finishes her sandwich and delicately kisses her fingers clean. She washes and dries the knife she used to spread the butter, then drops it in the drawer. Carla always hated a dirty kitchen, Waltz remembers. The other kids forced her into doing the dishes time and again by letting them collect, letting their presence eat at her. He thinks it was the only time they got the best of her, the only weakness they could find in her to exploit. She was the cleverest, Monroe the sweetest, Susan the most effortlessly serene, Eugene the most like Waltz.

"Stay as long as you want," he tells her, and touches the soft hair at the back of her neck.

Mary Hale is asleep upstairs. She is still able to curl into a tight fetal ball, like a caterpillar that has been touched. The day is barely half expended and sleep is taking his house under.

He sits at his desk and tries to work. The mail has brought little business and he cleans it up in minutes. He is sad there is nothing from Willy, no first small chipping away at his debt. He misjudged the man; he did not see the deadbeat in him.

Something else troubles him. Two other men, both good customers, are late with the money they owe.

Downstairs to get a glass of water, he sees Carla asleep on another couch. A magazine is open across her thighs. He picks it up and sets it aside. Sleep, everywhere. His daughter will give birth in her sleep. His other daughter will dream of attainable love. Mary Hale will dream herself free of the life they have set in motion within her. Waltz, before he sleeps beside her, sets his dreams for a safe zone, tells himself to ignore his persistent sleep visions of deadbeats and goobies, and succeeds.

15

Willy at the front door awakens them all. He tells them later they frightened him, coming upon an absolutely dark house. They have shot the afternoon in sleep. Waltz, feeling drugged, moves through the house turning on lights to dispel the depression that has hold of him. All the lamps remind him of Louise because she selected them; all the shadows have her look to them.

Willy has come north in their battered Ford wagon. His arms are laden with groceries. Waltz sees by his uneasy but hopeful smile that he wants to make amends. He has no money, but he has food. He unpacks in the kitchen while Waltz and the three women watch silently, all still trying to wake up.

Waltz introduces Mary Hale. Willy comes forward and firmly shakes her hand. One side of her face is scarlet as a birthmark; her hair on the same side is matted.

Waltz wonders which of the two women who love Willy will go forward to save him. With all his food arrayed on the counter he has nothing else to do. He clearly wants somebody to offer to cook all this stuff; he is only the provider, he needs a woman for the rest. He bobs from foot to foot.

"Anyone hungry?" Waltz asks. He is not. More than ever he wants to drive Mary Hale home. He is tired of the house and of his family. If allowed, he would crawl back to bed and sleep the night through. Fatal lassitude lurks everywhere.

Susan gets gamely to her feet and picks through the provisions her husband has brought: tomatoes, cucumbers, celery, lettuce, ground beef, noodles, cheese, chocolate chip ice cream, three bottles of red wine.

Susan puts the ice cream in the freezer. She cuts the cellophane on the package of tomatoes with a fingernail and takes out three, then stuns all present by juggling them. Mary Hale claps her hands.

"You're *so* accomplished," Carla laughs.

Waltz says, "Bravo!" He is surprised, he would have expected Carla to be the one to free the room of its fatigue. Everyone is suddenly awake, even Waltz. The women jump with enthusiasm into the work of cooking the meal. Willy sits at the kitchen table. Waltz opens the first bottle of wine and pours five glasses. He says, "This was a good idea."

Willy's eyes brighten with surprise. "Thank you!" he says.

Beyond that, he has nothing to add. His state of mind will not permit harmless conversation. Every moment of these sad days seems limned with significance. He does not know what has happened to himself. Sometime in the past he lost that precious grain of confidence upon which everything turned. Now there is no getting it back. His wife tells him it is a passing thing but he does not believe her. She has no proof. She is only promoting the standard. He awaits the return of that confidence; Susan tells him waiting is fatal. He watched her belly grow day by day and wondered if it was the key; will the baby's birth mark the end of this terrible time? But it is too risky to put faith in that. He has seen too many similar signposts arrive and fall away; his thirty-fifth birthday, Susan's pregnancy, the first day of winter, the new year. Nothing turns it around. He can't relax. He avoids social functions; he was only able to make himself drive to Marathon because he would be bringing food. He would have value. He tries to tell a small joke and it is overwhelmed by the clatter of dinner's preparation. His father-in-law smiles crookedly at him. His timing is all off. He speaks into great clouds of noise that seem to roll up just as his mouth opens, his best thoughts are lost. He does not think enough of himself to repeat them; or he fears one person will have heard and know his desperation in his saying the words a second time. He is thirty-five years old and he has no work. His wife tells him this is a passing thing.

Waltz talks to Mary Hale alone after dinner. They hold each other in the shadows of a downstairs room.

"Do you want to go home tonight?" he asks.

"Yes. I want to sleep in my own bed. Wear my own clothes. But I'll stay another night if you like."

"No. I want to go, too. I'm not a good host."

"Yes, you are. You're putting everyone at ease. Talking to Willy. A born host."

Arm in arm, they return to the kitchen. Cool, strange, bluish smoke clouds the light. Willy and Susan and Carla are seated at the table. Carla daintily holds in two fingers a small, rumpled cigarette rolled in yellow paper. She holds her breath.

"We thought you'd gone to bed," Susan says, batting at the smoke with her hands. Waltz is not sure what is going on; Mary Hale stands with her hand tucked safe and warm inside the back of his pants. She makes a fist with this hand; he reads it as a signal to glide through this mysterious smoke and his daughter's unease and make tracks for Saginaw Bay.

"Mary has to get home," Waltz says. "I'm going to drive her and stay over a few days."

"Drive safely," Susan says. Carla nods. Her cheeks are round as balls. Willy will not lift his eyes from his glass of wine.

"You can stay or go," Waltz says. "Just leave a couple lights on, turn off the stove, and lock all the doors if you do leave."

They spend an hour getting all of Mary Hale's things together.

Waltz makes four complete passes through the house, picking up her possessions, books, a lighter, a sweater, a scarf, ballet slippers. She has brought so many bits of her existence, chunks of her work, an emery board, ring binders full of unattached papers, a beautiful maroon Parker fountain pen, that he can't believe she forgot clothes of her own. She will ride home in his shirt and trousers. He will launder them at her house and wear them himself. He packs a small bag. He has nothing to read, no hobbies or interests. He is amazed his days go so rapidly with so little on the surface to fill them.

Waltz kisses his daughters goodbye, shakes Willy's hand. Willy reminds him of business he will miss. The money will pile up beneath the letter slot. Waltz is proud he has created an oiled business of lend and collect. Business has never been better, yet the time he has spent on it lately seems fragmented, interspersed with events and emotions that wring the work dry of significance; he has trouble remembering, afterward, if he even worked at all.

There is a frost on the road; the long white dashes down the spine of the highway, the meadow-green road signs, the brushed-aluminum light poles, the stars, all appear coldly encased. The car holds the road well, its heater warms them. Waltz feels safe.

"Back there," Mary Hale says. "Do you know what they were smoking?"

"What?"

"Marijuana."

"Is that what that smell was?"

She laughs and squeezes his thigh; he jumps, startled, happy. "Where have you been the last ten years?" she asks.

"Here. Around," he says gruffly, playing the codger for her. "I've never smelled the stuff."

"You've never had it at a party or something?"

"Loan sharks, I should think, are not big partygoers."

"Anyway," she says, "that's what it was."

"Do you suppose Sooz was smoking it?"

"She was at the table. What can you draw from that?"

"I mean, with the baby practically on her front stoop," he says. "How healthy can it be smoking that stuff?"

"We didn't see her smoking it. I didn't get a look at her eyes. There's no telling. She isn't stupid, so maybe she refrained."

He drives for five miles without speaking. "Willy must have brought it," he then says.

"That was my feeling," Mary Hale says. "There was a definite link."

"He's out of work, he's got a kid on the way, he borrows five thousand dollars from me, and he spends it on marijuana."

"Some people smoke it like we drink beer," she says. "It's just a social thing."

"Let him earn his own social things," Waltz says.

"You lent him the money. You didn't think you could tell him how to spend it, did you?"

"No," he says, angry. "But I thought he'd make an effort to start sending some of it back my way by now. Even a token ten dollars. Something."

She asks, "Do you have it in writing?"

"I have the canceled check."

"That's no proof. He could say the money was a gift."

Waltz shakes his head. He does not like thinking of Willy in these terms. Ill at ease with deadbeats (they are paragons of awkwardness, to his thinking), it is so strange and unexpected having one in the family he prefers to ignore the situation until the fact of it is undeniable.

"He is going through a difficult time," Waltz says. "When he gets a job I'm sure he'll start to pay me back."

Mary Hale says, "Sure he will." A mile farther, she asks, "Where do we stand with each other today?"

He looks across at her. Her window is open a crack and the wind sings in through it.

"Well, I don't know," he says. "I'm just going along waiting for you."

"You've been so solicitous," she says. "Touchingly so."

"How about names?"

Mary Hale looks at him and makes a face. "How about careers?"

"Loan shark." Waltz laughs.

"No. Something respectable."

"That eliminates the law."

"Maybe a doctor."

"My daddy was a doctor. My brother Aaron is a kidney specialist. I had another brother who was a gynecologist before he died. Maybe it's in our genes."

Mary Hale nods distractedly. She holds three fingers to her lips like a secret sign, a pained look creased inside her eyes. It is a look Waltz knows. They are speeding down a stretch of dark highway. A Holiday Inn billboard lit like a small casino flashes past, telling them they are eleven miles from Saginaw.

"Feeling bad?" he asks softly.

Mary Hale nods. "I was doing pretty well," she says mournfully. "I hate this." She waves him over onto the shoulder of the road. He slows and eases the wheel over. He fears invisible slicks of ice that will send them whirling into the night. He activates the emergency flashers, gets out and goes around to Mary Hale's door. She is already out; she has moved to keep the door between them and vomits harshly while Waltz stands listening, staring into the dark roadway woods, his ungloved hand against the cold side of the car; his share of the burden.

A car whips past. The air smacks as the car goes by, all light, compactness, and violence. Waltz is amazed. He thinks about the day he was hit by one of those things, his leg breaking in the cold rain, and the car of poor Dick Finch had been barely moving. To be hit full-bore on a dark highway; he squeezes his eyes shut.

Mary Hale props herself against the car. Her eyes are shut and her breathing is deep and tired. She is aglow. Waltz moves around the door to help her back inside but she holds up her hand.

"I'm not finished," she says wearily. "I do believe."

A car coming up behind them slows and drifts over. Its headlights pick Waltz and Mary Hale out clearly; his eyes, as he looks back, Waltz wonders if they glow like cats. A bank of lights atop the car comes to life, twirling lances of red and white across everything.

He has Mary Hale by the shoulders and she is throwing up

vigorously. He thinks she is in the classic pose of the heedless drunk, vomiting the night's good times away at the side of the road.

The state trooper gets out, puts on his hat, and comes around to their side. Waltz can't see his face with the lights behind him.

"Having trouble?" he asks in a flat way, leaving the possible details to Waltz.

"A little morning sickness," Waltz says. "Carried to an extreme."

Mary Hale reaches into Waltz's back pocket for a handkerchief. She wipes her mouth and stands up straight out of the door's shadow. She squints back into the lights.

"You're pregnant, ma'am?" the trooper asks.

"Yes. Unfortunately, I must add at this particular point."

"Do you need an ambulance?"

"No, thank you. I live on Saginaw Bay. Once I get home I'll feel one hundred percent better."

The trooper looks from her to Waltz. Waltz takes her arm and helps her back into the car. She moves tentatively, like an old lady. She has white hair and the stark light puts age in her tired face. Waltz pushes down the lock and shuts the door.

"She really is pregnant," Waltz tells the trooper. "Don't let her white hair fool you. I'm the father. She'll make a fine mother."

The trooper smiles. "Stay on my tail," he says, "and I'll get you to Saginaw Bay in no time."

So they pass through Bay City behind an emblazoned police car. Waltz finds it a little embarrassing. The few people on the street turn to get a look at them.

"Maybe they think we're Jerry Ford," he says.

"Do you think he believes I'm pregnant?"

"I told him I was the father, too. He seemed to take it in stride."

"My motherhood shows in my face. I vomit a lot but my face is radiant when I do."

When he puts his ear to her smooth lank belly while she sleeps that night he imagines he hears through the fine web of cotton gown, through the muscle and sea fluid, the clear, effortless chemistry of division and growth. He lies listening for a half hour in the dark. Only when she rolls away from him, impatient in her sleep, does he leave her alone.

An hour passes and he remains awake. The strange house falls into place around him, transforming itself into its night shape. Through the wall there is the bay flat and cold. He knows nothing about it, if there is shipping on it, how deep it goes, the water could be salt and he would not be surprised. Michigan is a left-handed mitten; he lies awake at the base of the thumb.

He has spent too much of this day already asleep, he has done no work; he wishes he was home, where he could roam familiar halls, where he had his books to work in. He rolls on his side and a sharp ache passes through his chest, moving left to right, and disappears. Heart? Lungs? Some plug in his bloodstream? He has all this time left for things to go wrong with him. He thinks of Daddy Waltz in the outfield at ninety-seven. He thinks of Bernard dying young. And of Aaron out West knowing Waltz was back in Marathon looking for that key that would turn him loose for a full century, just as Aaron was looking.

Waltz stays four days, then dreams one night of his front hall so packed with envelopes no more can be forced through the mail slot. This dream awakens him at 6 A.M. uncharacteristically refreshed. He supposes this is guilt calling him back to work.

Mary Hale, glad to be home, has improved greatly. Her spells of nausea have diminished, she has learned to control them by eating several small meals a day. She has gained two pounds. She works a few hours in the morning, eats, naps, eats, then puts in two or three more hours in the late afternoon. She brings pies full of fruit home from work and cuts huge wedges for each of them. From the public library she gets a book of names.

"This is Monday," he says. "How about I come back Thursday night? Or Thursday afternoon? Spend the weekend?"

"Whenever," she says, shrugging with such subtle elaboration he barely feels it.

"Do you think I'm skipping on you?"

She moves away to stand leaning against the door. "No. The idea crossed my mind. You're too nice to make one clean cut. Too chickenshit, too. I foresaw a series of ever-widening gaps of time."

"What a thing to say."

"Forget it," she says. "I'll see you Thursday."

"Maybe."

"Can I make a request?"

"What?"

"On Sunday, can I go with you to visit Eugene in prison?"

She has conjured up Eugene for him in an instant and he hates her for it. Five months have passed since he last visited his son; he owes him a letter. A letter in a state corrections department envelope waits on his desk.

"I don't know," Waltz tells her, carefully poisoning his tone with annoyance.

"It's important to me," Mary Hale says.

"This is a touchy thing with me. When I go visit Eugene, it's nothing I plan ahead of time to do. Some Sundays I'll just wake up and some combination of courage, guilt, or pride all comes together in the right way and I just *go.* It's like a momentum builds while I'm asleep. If I think about it too much I don't go. Which I rationalize by saying: Well, it wasn't the right time. I could never plan a week in advance and then have to spend all that week looking ahead, *contemplating* it."

"Just for me?" Mary Hale says. She is smart enough not to ruin it by moving into his arms. "Couldn't you do it for me?"

"You go, I'll stay," Waltz says sharply. A cool veil falls over her face. "He'll be glad to see you. He doesn't get many visitors."

"Forget it," she says. "Forget I asked."

"It's no big thing," Waltz says. "You aren't missing anything, believe me."

"I said forget it. I've visited plenty of prisons. I don't want to see a *prison.*"

"Sure," he says. He has spoiled the parting. Absently he kisses her goodbye on the mouth, burrowing through her disinterest to keep his hand in, then drives all the way home thinking of Eugene.

Nothing has changed at home. His daughters remain, one still pregnant and looking even more swollen, ripe with possibilities he has no interest in being associated with, and Willy dressed in Waltz's bathrobe.

"I'm baffled," Waltz tells them all; they are lined up like suspects in the kitchen. "I honestly did not expect to find you still here."

"Sooz and I were discussing that," Carla says. "We decided it's because we feel safe here. We feel like little girls again."

"What about your jobs? Your homes? Who waters the plants? Who brings in the mail?"

"I go to work," Carla says defensively. "It's a long commute, I'll grant you that. But I work. I pick up clothes, food, money, whatever is needed, when I'm down there, then I hustle back up here."

"Jesus," Waltz says. He has them on edge; he has stepped on their childhoods all over again. Willy stands as if in secret prayer; Susan holds him in place. Waltz says, "This has me confused. Kind of angry, too."

Carla says, "It just reminded us of home. I think we needed that a little."

"All right. I can understand that."

Willy pulls free of Susan and leaves the room. Susan follows. Waltz listens to them climb the stairs and pass down the groaning hall over his head, he hears their door close. Waltz feels his presence has routed Willy; he is a deadbeat only in Waltz's presence.

"And you know, Daddy," Carla says, her voice strangely small and adolescent with excitement, "Willy took me aside the night before last and told me he loved me, that he made a mistake marrying Susan, that I'm the one he has loved all along."

An ache of disappointment and anger lodged in Waltz's chest. He has seen his children diminished so. "Come off it, Carla," he hisses. "When are you going to open your eyes?"

"My eyes *are* open."

"Honey, look what is happening to you. You're thirty-three years old, you're alone, you're mooning over your twin sister's husband. Doesn't that tell you anything?"

Carla says, "It tells me *you've* gotten old, dried up, and empty of any feelings."

"Have you slept with him?"

"No. Not since before she . . . We haven't had the chance. But the love is there. The rest of that will follow."

"Haven't had the chance?" Waltz says, incredulous, gored. "What happens when you do have the chance? You deceive your twin sister in the worst way possible?"

"That's it," she says, and leaves the room.

He hunts for Willy but Willy is cunning, he holds to Susan's side like a devoted husband, he won't let Waltz cut him loose where they would be alone. He knows Susan is his one hope. Waltz is patient, though. He kisses Susan on the forehead and puts a hand on her huge belly.

"What's taking this he or she?" he asks calmly.

"I wish I knew."

He turns to Willy. "How goes the search for work?"

"I'm being very careful," Willy says. He has shed Waltz's robe and put on blue jeans faded almost white and a gray flannel shirt. His hair is wet and curly from a shower. He is handsome, Waltz thinks, but with the deadbeat's face smoothed of worry and conscience.

"We put your mail in your office," he says.

"Come and see me," Waltz says to Willy. "When you've got a spare moment."

The accumulation of mail over the time he was away is stacked on his desk. There is less than he expected. He takes out his books and begins to work; he is at it a full three hours and nobody interrupts.

Finished, he is confused. Three men are late with the money they owe: Paul Rivers, Glen Empire, Al Rudyard. Good customers, he knows them well, they were previously punctual and uncomplaining. Paul Rivers lives in Flint, he is in his mid-forties and out of work, he spends his time fishing and looking for jobs. He has been on the string with Waltz since 1972, when he borrowed $1,000. Through the years he has borrowed more and paid it back, his payments arriving within the same three-day span each month, but now he is eight days overdue. Glen Empire lives in Kalamazoo and hates being in debt. He regularly pays more than is required each month, trying to get free of Waltz. Al Rudyard had come all the way from Marquette in the Upper Peninsula, right to Waltz's door, pounding furiously on it an hour after midnight. He had heard Waltz loaned money to people the banks would not touch. Waltz fixed him a cup of coffee and a plate of bacon and eggs. They talked on and off, mostly an exchange of life's information, and in the early morning Waltz copied Rudyard's name, address, and phone number off his driver's license onto a slip of paper, added the figure $10,000 and the agreed-upon interest, and passed the note to Rudyard to sign. When the bank opened at eight o'clock they went together and drew out the money. That had been six years ago. In all that time Al Rudyard had never missed a payment, until now, and he was far from being off the string. He, too, was eight days late.

Waltz rose from his desk and went to the window. He thought of Eugene and his brisk, violent side. Would Eugene beat up these three men for their tardiness?

He pulls the three men's notes from his files. The signatures of indebtedness are clear and strong. He has their good names; this comforts him. The vital honor of their business will hold.

Paul Rivers lives the closest of the three. A family man, Waltz recollects, with a wife and a half-dozen children. A woman answers Waltz's call on the first ring. Kitchen noise, the roar of a TV, hit Waltz in the ear. He asks for Paul Rivers and fully five minutes elapse before Paul Rivers gets to the phone.

"Sorry," he says, a little out of breath. "I was in the crapper. Who's this?"

"Harry Waltz, Paul."

"Hey! Eth!" the man shouts away from the phone. "Turn the fucking set down, will ya? Put the kids in the other room! I'm trying to have a conversation here! Who'd you say you were?"

"This is Harry Waltz. I haven't gotten your money this month, Paul, I wondered if there was a problem."

"Harry," he says. He pauses. "Look, Harry, I'm a little slack this time around. O.K.? I'm sorry. I'm good for it. We've been doing business a long time, you and me. You'll get your money. And I wish you wouldn't call me here."

"Paul, you signed the note," Waltz says. "You forfeited the right to be 'a little slack' when you signed the note. Put that money in the mail tonight—tomorrow at the latest—and we'll forget you were late. O.K.?"

"You'll get your money, Harry. I just don't got it right now."

"Paul, you've got to follow the rules. Up until now you've followed the rules. Now this. You've been out of work for months. Why are you dry now? I've got your note right in front of me. Your signature is very clear. Get that money in the mail tonight and this will never have happened."

He hangs up before Paul Rivers can respond. Carla is at the foot of the stairs calling him to dinner but he stays at his desk for long minutes shaking and wondering and thinking of Eugene.

Susan has her baby in the dead of night. A panic of bells awakens Waltz. He is out of place, he doesn't know where to turn. The phone that is ringing is not his, he is in bed in the house on Saginaw Bay. Mary Hale reaches and answers the phone. She holds the covers to her. She listens a moment, then hands the phone to him, saying, "It's Carla."

"Carla?" he says.

"Daddy?"

"Yes. Is everything all right?"

"Susan's in the delivery room. Willy's with her."

"Where are you?"

"The hospital."

"In Marathon?"

"Ann Arbor. Susan was saying earlier this afternoon she had a feeling the time had come. Her water broke at six-thirty, so we all piled in the car and drove right down here."

"That's terrific," he says. He wants to ask her if they remembered to lock the house.

"So don't worry," she says. "Everything's fine."

"O.K. Thanks. Call when you know anything."

"I will."

They hang up and Waltz passes the phone back.

Mary Hale asks, "Why was she crying?"

"Who?"

"Carla, on the phone."

"She was crying?"

"Yes. When I answered, she was crying."

Carla calls again in four hours. The day has broken open around them, golden and sweet with warmth. Waltz and Mary Hale have moved to the kitchen, they eat sweet rolls and drink coffee and ice water and Waltz smokes cigarettes.

Carla is curt, reporting, "It's a boy. Eight pounds eight ounces. No names yet. I'll see you later."

Just like that, he is a grandfather. The boy could live to a hundred, father twins, anything is possible. Waltz wishes his grandson had a name. He feels it is bad luck not to have one; the kid has no protection. With a name, he takes on a weight, something to hold him to the world. And with a name, Waltz could attach characteristics and qualities to the name. He smiles, puts out his cigarette, accepts kisses of congratulation from Mary Hale.

Again, he does not remember if Carla had been crying.

16

Waltz feels something going awry in his business life. Chinks in the honor system, he thinks; but this is too unfathomable and he pushes it to the rear of his thoughts, from where it worms forward like a lengthening crack in the ice that holds him.

He says to Mary Hale, "I got in touch with all three of them.

Nothing I said seemed to matter. They said very arrogantly that I'd get the money."

"Maybe they're having a tough time of it."

"Everyone's having a tough time of it," he says. "You still have to pay your bills." He thinks, shakes his head. "I couldn't believe the *arrogance* of them."

They are driving south in Mary Hale's car, Waltz at the wheel. She sits awaiting the worst; any bump in the highway could set her off, any dip of motion could produce the need to stop along the roadside. Her obstetrician is full of good news when she visits him. Everything is fine. The sickness will stop soon. The baby will be healthy. Still she waits.

Not unexpectedly, Waltz awakened that Sunday morning with a desire to visit Eugene. Mary Hale was delighted and even claimed to be surprised. She had spent an easy night; she said she slept through the night when Waltz was there. Lying in bed that morning Mary Hale wanted to make love to Waltz; as a reward for taking her to see his imprisoned son, he surmised a little bitterly. But he kissed her mouth and held her off. The momentum of travel and confrontation was fragile, he knew, and sex could easily ground it. He might fall back to sleep when they were finished, or lose the precious combination he temporarily possessed in the emptying.

"I owe him a letter," Waltz says. A green rectangular sign anchored on poles at the side of the highway informs them they have forty-four miles to go. It is a comforting distance; they will not be there soon. He says, "All the time he's been in prison I can't seem to come to grips with it. The first letter he sent me, I didn't even open. I put it aside, then read it when his second letter arrived. It's worked that way ever since. I'm always a letter behind. I'm always hearing old news from him."

"That's safe," says Mary Hale. She has put on faint make-up. She has an appearance of competence. Dressing that morning, she took his hand and pressed it to her abdomen, asked, "Feel anything?" He told her then about listening to her stomach while she slept, hearing the chemistry at work.

They don't speak again until they have parked in the prison's visitors' lot and Waltz reaches to shut off the engine. She touches his hand.

"Let's sit a minute," she says. "Let me have a cigarette."

People move between the parked cars toward the visitors' entrance. Although the air is cold, they move with a stunned sluggishness. Many are black, nobody looks at anyone else, some carry babies bundled like laundry; Waltz wonders if they hide files deep inside all those blankets.

Mary Hale removes a manila envelope from her bag. Waltz sees the seal of the Michigan Department of Corrections in one corner.

She says carefully, "Eugene is getting out today."

"Out?"

She nods, her eyes gravely on Waltz, wondering how he is going to take this and where this all will lead.

"How?" he asks in a voice small and tight.

"Legal wrangling," she says, a proud smile faintly illuminating her face, then falling away. "I started looking into it right after you told me he was in prison. I truly like him, Harry. I had to tell him my plan because I needed his cooperation. I told him not to tell you. His first parole hearing is in three months anyway. He'd be sure to get out then. He's been a model prisoner. I know a judge who has a rotten son I've quietly pulled out of the morass on two occasions, free of charge; just to have a judge owe me. He was glad to help. I told the parole board Eugene would be living and working with his father, a respected businessman, when he got out."

"Did you tell them I was a loan shark?"

"They *knew*, Harry. But for some reason you are viewed in a good light."

She smiles, but he is not taking. "What if I don't want him?" he asks.

"In all my plotting," she admits, "that is the one eventuality I prayed would not occur."

"What happens if I don't want him?" he repeats, harsher.

"Then you can refuse to sign his release as his guardian and he will remain where he is."

"For how long?"

"Three months. Until his first parole hearing. The fact that you were willing to look after him helped me get him out early." She takes a deep breath. More visitors drift past. "You put him in there," she says. "You can keep him there."

"He was engaged in criminal acts," Waltz blurts. "I witnessed one. He would have been caught eventually. Or shot. Something *bad* was going to happen."

"I'm not talking about that, Harry. This is now. Your oldest child is thirty-six years old and he's sitting in prison. Do you still want that? Are you going to let him sit in there when you have been given the chance to let him out?"

He holds a match to another cigarette. "It's tempting," he says.

"I never thought it would come to this."

Waltz says, "Fact is, I don't much like the kid . . . man. How does that strike you?"

"What's not to like about him?"

"He's got a mean streak."

"So do I. You do, too, I'll bet. These three guys who haven't paid you this month. What happens if they just never pay?"

"It won't be that way," he says.

"Don't count on it," she says. "One thing leads to another, they find out nothing is going to be done to them if they don't pay, do you think they'll pay?"

"They signed the notes."

"The answer is *no,*" she says. "And word will get around to all the other people who owe you money, and none of those people will pay either. Watch. They're only human."

He waves her away; this is not something he wants to hear.

"How long will I have to be in charge of him?"

"Just a little while," she says.

"Too long."

"Jesus Christ, your own flesh and blood. What does that tell me about this baby you want me to have?"

Waltz turns to her. "The baby will be perfect," Waltz proclaims.

"Maybe for the first two breaths. Not after that. He will start collecting flaws like all the rest of us."

"No," he says.

"And twenty years from now, when he's a young man with a young man's troubles, are you going to have him sent to prison, too?"

He would have to wait until then to know. He would be eighty-two years old, a true fossil of fatherhood to his young son.

She holds an official form out to him. At the bottom is an empty line marked with a small black *x*.

"Sign this, Harry." She uncaps her fountain pen for him.

"I can't do that," he says.

She sits silently a minute, then says in a low, cold voice, "I've learned to like Eugene. I've worked hard to get him this close to being free again, and I won't see him remain in prison just because of you. So here is my final offer. You sign this release and bring Eugene home with you, I'll keep this baby you seem to have such ungodly hopes for. If you refuse to sign, I'll have the baby aborted." She holds the pen and paper out to him again. "It's that black and white, Harry."

"You wouldn't do that," he says. His senses have gone dry. He sees this woman now in an edging of stone, on the dark ice of resolve.

"Believe me," she says, "I would. There's still time. Right now this baby is just a lot of discomfort to me. I'm not attached to it, yet. Eugene, however, is real to me."

Waltz slams open the door and heads across the parking lot, gliding between cars. The cold makes him stiff; he feels old, his JFK leg an ache that prods a vain limp. Young black men in a tight knot, dancing with their heads down and their hands in spring jackets, trying to keep warm without resorting to the tainted heat of the prison, look up and stare in evident wonder at his swift approach. Mary Hale shuts off the engine and takes the keys and chases after him. She holds the release form in one hand, the uncapped fountain pen in the other, a cigarette clamped in her teeth. Sparks caught in the wind swirl back into her eyes and blind her. She has to stop. The form cracks in the wind.

Waltz sees her there and for a minute his temptation is to leave her. Trust her to the care of the young black men. He can disappear efficiently while her vision is watered.

But whether gooby or genius or something between, the child she is carrying is his and he badly wants that child. He retreats to where she stands trying to rub clear her eyes. She flinches when he touches her; he gives her his handkerchief, his arm. In the entryway just inside the first door, a chamber so tropically hot Waltz begins immediately to sweat, there are chairs to sit down in to ease the decompression of passage into prison. Waltz and Mary Hale sit side by side while she dabs at her eyes.

He says, "When Eugene was a boy he did a cruel thing to a retarded man and since then I haven't quite liked him."

"That's no reason to keep him in prison," she says.

"And he reminds me of myself," Waltz says. "Why would I want him around?"

"Set him free," Mary Hale pleads. "You don't belong in prison, and neither does Eugene."

He grasps her wrist. "I won't be blackmailed," he says. "I want that child you're carrying, but not under those terms. My name is all I have—I've learned that in my business—and I won't be threatened into signing anything."

"It was the only tool of negotiation I had," she says. "It was my last chance."

"You know me better than that."

"Not on this," she says. "You and your son, what goes on in your mind, you're a different man there. You're so flat and ugly when the subject comes up. I thought I could be, too."

"You wouldn't get an abortion?" Waltz asks.

She shakes her head, her head bowed and her face hidden in white hair, and her admission frees him to be gracious. They have reached a place of understanding. He will do this for her. He smooths the form across her slim back and with her fountain pen signs his name alongside the *x*.

He has his eldest and sole surviving son back again.

And on the ride home Eugene drops immediately to sleep in the back seat. Waltz, driving, envies him. It looks so easy and affordable. In the mirror, Waltz studies his sleeping son. The tension of release, the understanding they will be living in the same house again, the nut-like bunches of muscle in the jaw, have fallen away. Eugene had shaved, leaving a blue cast to his jaw. His face is leaner, the eyes sunken, dark, alluring in their mystery; prison has made Eugene handsome.

When they stop in Fenton for gas Eugene awakes and goes inside to use the washroom. Waltz watches him go; maybe he will climb out the bathroom window and sprint across the frozen Michigan ground, heading for the woods, a farmhouse, freedom. Two separate women, strangers to Eugene and each other, study him with casual interest. His son is slim, tall, with a shock of dark hair falling almost to his eyes. When he returns from the washroom one of the women, paying for her gas, smiles at him but he walks by her, oblivious. Soon they are on the road and he is asleep again.

Mary Hale rides quietly. She looks pleased with herself.

"You look very smug," Waltz observes in a lowered voice.

"Do I?"

"Like you pulled a fast one."

"I'm glad he's out. I'm glad I'll be having your baby."

He is content. A bargain has been struck between two people of reciprocal honor. More than at any other time since he met Mary Hale he feels full of love for her.

Eugene diffuses the uneasiness of the first hours of his presence there at home by leaving. He borrows one of his father's white shirts, his father's dark burgundy necktie with thin diagonal white stripes, a pair of his father's trousers. He borrows forty dollars and the keys to a repossessed Firebird and goes out.

"Is he allowed to do that?" Waltz asks.

Mary Hale says, "Yes. Why not? He's thirty-six years old."

"Is it in the terms of the parole?"

"About the only thing he can't do is own a gun."

"He's not forbidden to associate with his low-life friends?"

"No."

"I counted fourteen words he spoke since he got out."

"What do you expect? You sent him to prison. You wouldn't answer his letters. What does that tell a man?"

"That he's not wanted."

"Precisely."

"And that's precisely right."

"Please, Harry."

"What did he expect? What did *you* expect? Sure, you can negotiate a trade with me. But that doesn't change my feelings for him. I still think he's a bad apple."

"Give him a chance. That's all I ask." She gathers up her gloves, her scarf, her coat.

"Where are you going?"

"Home," she says.

"Stay the night," he begs. "I'll need you to talk to later."

"Talk to your son."

"He'll come home and go to his room," Waltz says. "Not one word will pass between us."

"Nonsense. *You* start the conversation."

"Don't go."

"I have work to catch up on," she says briskly. "I want you to get comfortable with Eugene on your own. If I stayed I'd be a buffer of pleasantries between you two. You'd drive me nuts. Good night."

Mary Hale kissed him goodbye, then called when she reached home; she sounded so hopelessly distant. Eugene had not returned. Waltz reported that he had fixed a small dinner and taken it upstairs to his office to work.

He says, "I didn't want Eugene to think I was waiting up for him."

"Did you leave a light on?"

"Yes. Although he is probably at this very moment pulling another job for spending money."

"Harry Waltz," she growls, "don't say that even in jest. He needs you more than anyone else right now. He hasn't had an easy life. Did you know he hated Monroe?"

For an instant Waltz can't place the name. "My Monroe?"

"Yes."

"Why?"

"Because Monroe was talented, a success at an early age, then dead in an honorable fashion before anything happened to take the shine off him."

"I see," Waltz says, thinking of the clusters of young girls camped in the house waiting for Monroe; where was Eugene in all those memories?

"Just give him a chance," she suggests. "He's a stranger and so are you."

"I was doing my books from yesterday's mail. Two more people are late."

"Did you call them?"

"I'm afraid to, I think," Waltz says.

"You've got to call them. Just like they have to pay."

They hang up soon after, Waltz promising to call the laggard debtors, promising to try with his son. But he stays at his desk for another two hours, accomplishing nothing, sketching three-dimensional block numerals on a note pad. The tenets of his life feel shifted and abused. Men no longer honor their signatures. Fathers and sons are cool strangers to each other. Old men father children. At this late date he has been put in charge of a grown man, and in scant months he will begin all over again with an infant.

Waltz is in bed when Eugene gets home. His son comes up the stairs but instead of turning into his own room he comes down the hall to Waltz's room and stands in the doorway, looking in. Waltz suffers a chill of poor judgment, watching his son's squared shadow. Should he have locked the door?

"Daddy?" Eugene asks clearly.

Waltz waits a minute, then replies. "Yes."

"Can I talk to you?"

"O.K."

"I'm sorry about the time. But it's important to me."

"No problem," Waltz says. He turns on a light, hiding his eyes. His son still wears his father's white shirt with the tie loosely knotted and the sleeves rolled up, reminding Waltz of a young clerk home from work. His son's eyes have been watered with doubt since the last time he looked into them; either doubt or knowledge. Eugene carries a chair to the edge of the bed and they both light cigarettes. He sits down, crosses his legs, his top leg bobs, he picks a white thread away.

"I've been to Flint," Eugene says. "I knew they would learn soon enough that I was out and I wanted to tell them I wouldn't be interested in their company in the future." He takes a deep breath; this last has come out in a rush, rehearsed. Eugene smokes a moment. His face is free of calm. His eyes are dark and sad and moist. He might have escaped from prison, rather than being freed legally.

He continues. "I understand that you are not happy I'm here. Mary has been good to me in that way. She refused to allow me to have any fantasies about myself. I'm grateful for that."

"I'm glad you're out, Eugene," Waltz says in a low, shamed voice.

"I hope I can make you really feel that way sometime," Eugene says. He stands abruptly and jabs out his cigarette. "In the morning I'd like you to explain what you want me to do. I'm here to work. I'll do anything you want."

Waltz says, "I don't have any work for you."

"I could take some cars to Flint."

"Winter is a slow time. I've got a guy who comes and gets them for me."

"I could collect for you," Eugene says.

"It all comes in the mail." Waltz hates this efficiency he projects; his son is so nakedly in need of feeling useful Waltz wishes he had a hundred tasks he could heap upon him.

"How *is* business, Daddy?" Eugene asks almost absently.

"Business is O.K."

"I was talking in Flint, and I heard there were some problems."

"Problems with me? You heard my name specifically?"

"They know I'm your boy. Yes, they mentioned my father, Harry Waltz, was having some problems."

"Who told you this?" Waltz asks.

"Nobody. Punks. Guys who used to be my friends. They

didn't know any more than what people had told them: that you were having some problems."

Eugene's dark eyes fixed on Waltz. Doubt was gone; sadness, too. They were eyes fired with information and the scent of opportunity and trouble. Something in his words had touched his father. Eugene's fingers picked the knot out of the borrowed tie. Maybe the idle Flintian talk of trouble in the empire of Harry Waltz had some bone to it after all. He took the tie into his father's closet and hung it with the others. While in there he lit another cigarette, then returned to his father's bedside. His father was sleepy and pale in his rumpled white hair and naked feathery chest, sitting up in bed, looking at something in the distance, then like a seasoned killer flicking his eyes on Eugene and asking, "Did Mary tell you I sent you to prison?"

"She didn't have to."

"How did you know?"

"From talking to people. Prison is a great place for talk. There is almost nothing else you can do that isn't against the rules. I was kind of shy, a loner, when I went in. Once inside, though, I came out of my shell. It was against my nature, but I became an outgoing guy. I talked to all kinds of different people. One day I met a fella, I introduced myself, and he said, 'Oh, you're the chump whose pop sent him up.' I'd been in about four months then. It was, believe me, news to me. At first I thought he was just playing with my head. But I talked to other people and I kept getting the same story. Mary confirmed it to me, but I knew the fact of it long before that."

Waltz says, "You were a punk."

"True." Eugene nods. "I don't hold any ill will, Daddy."

"I don't believe you."

"I can't help that," Eugene says. "But I don't."

"I was told by someone back then that you were heading for trouble. That you might be killed."

Eugene says easily, "I know all that. Forget it, Daddy. What you say is true: I was a punk and sooner or later someone was liable to shoot me in the back. I was that kind of man."

"Just like that you change? Forgive?"

"No." His face darkens. "I haven't been out long enough to know what kind of man I'm going to be."

His son has been free less than a day and it seems like forever. He might never have been away. He has taken his place in the chair pulled up to the foot of the bed, cigarette going, nervously running his hand the length of the weak crease in his father's trousers. Waltz sees him as unformed, cut off from the life he knew, but with nothing to move toward.

"I'm having a small problem with some people on the string," Waltz admits, doubtful of the wisdom but liking the feel of his motives for doing so. "In the last several days five usually very conscientious people have missed payments. Three of them I've talked to."

Eugene sits forward. "What did they say?"

"That times are hard. That I'd get my money."

"That's it?"

"Yes. I'm bothered because they've been good customers in the past. One has been with me for years. I don't understand it. It's like they all went nuts at once."

"Hey," Eugene says brightly, seriously, "they've got to pay."

"I'd say so, too. But they don't seem to care."

"Let me go talk to them," Eugene says. "That can be my first assignment for you."

"I can't let you do that."

Eugene holds up his hands. Palms purest white, unhealthy-looking, stains like soft boot leather color the inside of his first two fingers. "No rough stuff, Daddy. I promise." He winks. "You'll know that, and I'll know that, but these five guys won't know that."

His son's intent comes clear to Waltz. His son is smiling for the first time since he got out of prison.

"You have a reputation—"

"Exactly," says Eugene. "I'm known for punching out guys who don't pay. Who's to know I'm not that type of man anymore?"

Waltz shakes his head. "No, Eugene. I can't work that way. These are all decent men. They'll pay. In the morning I'll think up something to keep you busy. Go to bed now."

Eugene says sullenly, "I won't sleep."

"How do you know?"

"Too quiet. There aren't three hundred guys all around me in the dark snoring and farting and crying out in their sleep. I need that noise to sleep. It's spooky quiet."

"Promise me you won't go off and do anything about this problem of mine on your own."

"I promise," Eugene says. "Promise you won't send me to prison again."

Waltz nods sheepishly. Eugene comes forward and hugs his father. Waltz awakens a number of times in the night and hears Eugene pacing like a wolf; he hears music playing faintly, bugle music coming through the walls, and once Eugene is standing quietly in the room's darkness, motionless and silent as a sentry, and Waltz feels safe.

In the morning Waltz explains to Eugene, "I can't permit you to use your reputation as a tough guy, an ex-con, to intimidate my clients into paying their debts. It would be no different than if you actually beat them up. I'd never do such a thing myself and you'd be acting as my emissary if you did."

Eugene glances up from his coffee. His face is tired and sad. "Suit yourself," he says.

"I must continue to believe in the individual's respect for his or her own good name," Waltz says, sounding as though he is apologizing.

"Sure," Eugene says. He gets up. He has not changed clothes. He stands with his hands thrust deep in the pockets, clenched, his head down with an electric exhaustion. Waltz prays his son can go to sleep soon.

"Why didn't you answer my letters?" he asks curtly, his eyes rising to Waltz.

"I don't know. I was ashamed."

"Of me? Or of what you'd done?"

"Both. I guess I thought if I didn't answer your letters right away I wouldn't have to face the fact I'd put my son in prison. Or the fact that he belonged there."

"For the longest time after I learned you'd sent me up, I planned to murder you," Eugene says in a frank, conversational tone. He is only relating the truth. "There was no way, of course. Fortunately . . . for both of us. I could've had it done easily enough. But that would have been missing the point."

"Did you get any sleep at all last night?"

"I didn't even try."

"Why don't you try now?"

"It would be useless," Eugene says. "For weeks after I got to prison I couldn't sleep because I wasn't used to the noise and the tension. Then I became a part of it and slept straight through every night. Now I have to unlearn all that conditioning and get used to the quiet." He smiles blankly at Waltz. "You didn't think this would be easy, did you?"

"When did you stop wanting to kill me?"

"It came to seem pointless," Eugene says. "It would only compound my trouble. I was proud of that attitude. It seemed very mature on my part."

"I'd say so." Waltz stands to leave. He has no plans for the day but to flee his son's dangerous presence. "Try to get some sleep."

"It's no use. I won't sleep at least for another two days. Give me something to fill the time."

"I've got no work for you, Eugene," he says, holding out his hands to prove they are empty.

"Let me go talk to those guys," Eugene suggests. "I'll just introduce my—"

"No."

"You can't let them sucker you like this, Daddy. Word will get around. Pretty soon everybody will be doing it."

Waltz says, "It's my business."

"O.K., Daddy. But I've got to get out of here. I feel more

cooped up than when I was in prison. Let me borrow a car."

"Where will you go?"

"I don't know. Somewhere. Not Flint. I'll never get to sleep this way."

Waltz gives him the key to a car. He follows Eugene upstairs and watches while he packs a suitcase with his father's clothes. He wears prison-issue shoes.

Waltz asks, "Where are you going?"

Eugene winks. "Maybe I'll go to Detroit and get laid."

Waltz writes a series of phone numbers on a slip of paper. One is the number to his house, in case Eugene forgot, another is Mary Hale's house, a third is a man Waltz knows in Detroit.

"He's a customer," Waltz explains. "He can get you tickets to the Pistons. Maybe he can help you with the other thing."

Eugene thanks his father, embarrassed that he is procuring for him now, too.

"Please check with me every night. I'll be here or at Mary Hale's. It's a condition of your parole that I know where you are. You have money?" He goes to his office and returns with three hundred dollars in cash. Eugene sees this, says, "You'll be burgled if you aren't careful."

"I am, though. I only deal with gentlemen."

"Upright souls," Eugene observes, and he is gone in a moment.

In the time his son is first gone Waltz feels the earth shifting beneath him. Four more customers turn up tardy, and insolent when he telephones them. The lucrative efficiency of his business feels snagged on the world's collective dishonesty. In town, at the bank, he drops the pen when he is filling out deposit slips and is amazed when its fall is jerked short by the chain holding it to the desk. For the first time in his life he feels doddering, genuinely old. He notices crumbs on his sweater. Dust on his cuffs. His trouser knees are worn thin, and faint white spots of dried salt have splashed as high as his knees.

And everywhere he looks, deadbeats.

17

Sam Boggins' shop is closed at noon but Waltz knows better and hurries across the alley ice to the back. He made this trip once and spied Sam's hairy buttocks churning between Melody's clutching legs on the cot in the back. Looking in, Waltz thought his eyes locked with the woman's, but maybe not. She was elsewhere, and Waltz left feeling lonely and excited.

The curtains are drawn on the window this winter day and frost ferns coat the glass. He puts his ear to the window and hears nothing. He goes to the back door and knocks. Nobody answers. Waltz is afraid Sam has gone home.

Then the door opens and Waltz notices for the first time a peephole like a small round eye.

"What's that?" he asks Sam, stepping into the warm back room.

"It was Melody's idea," Sam Boggins says. He is studying Waltz. Sam does not see him much anymore. Waltz puts his eye to the peephole. A part of the alley opens to him.

"Did you check to see who I was before you opened the door?" Waltz asks.

"Yes. Melody's idea wasn't a bad idea. Tom Bitely got robbed last week. Two men tied Jill Pentwater up in her shop and stole one thousand four hundred dollars the week before. I carry a gun and I'm only a barber."

"I didn't hear about any of that," Waltz says.

"It's kept quiet. Also, you're removed. If you were a part of the business community you'd hear these things."

"Did they catch anybody?"

"No. Might be the same guys both times. Or it might be a trend. Both times they were black. Probably from Detroit or Flint. In and out."

Sam moves to the front of his shop. Waltz follows. He passes down a shadowed room and looks into a wastebasket full of dark, moving water. Then he realizes it is cut hair. The front of the shop smells of hair oil, a creamy scent, and the burned-engine smell Sam's clippers give off. He has the Marathon High School basketball schedule in the front window. A pair of binoculars stand out among the neat ranks of equipment on the shelves behind the two chairs.

Waltz points to them. "What are these?"

"Binoculars," Sam says. From somewhere beneath his chair nearest the window he pulls out a black revolver. Waltz can see gray bullet noses in the cylinder.

"This is what the world has come to, Harry," Sam says in a faintly alarmed voice. He looks at the heavy machine in his hand with disbelief that he is a part of the world that has come to this.

"You don't need that, Sam," Waltz says softly.

"If a bunch of Detroit tigers come through that door after my money, I guess I will need it."

"What will you do?" Waltz asks. "Get in a gunfight with them? Tell them to step outside and draw?"

"I'll shoot them."

"If they take your money you can earn it back. It's not worth dying over."

Sam Boggins sniffs proudly and puts the revolver away. "It's easy for you to say something like that." He picks up the binoculars. "You want to know what these are for? My customers—and other laggards with nowhere to go—like to sit here and spy on your house with them. Can you believe that?"

"Why would they want to do that?"

"Because you're the richest man in Marathon," Sam practically yells. He is full of a ceaseless agitation Waltz doesn't understand. Waltz takes the binoculars and goes to the front window. He is surprised how large they bring in his house, the front porch, the roofs of a few parked cars of unlucky debtors, the very tip of the gazebo roof, the peak of the State Home bell tower.

"These poor clucks with nothing better to do than sit and look at your big damn house, and dream about having your money,"

Sam says. "Sometimes I want to box their ears and tell them to go out and work for their own money."

"That's right," Waltz says. "I earned my money. I didn't inherit it, or steal it."

Sam Boggins gives Waltz an odd look of distaste. "You're a shylock," he says curtly.

Waltz thinks then that he does not come to see his friend often enough; he has allowed the friendship to sour.

"Don't say that," he says. "Not you, Sam. It doesn't do you justice."

"You're a shy and I'm a barber. You're rich and immune. I'm just scraping by and for that I've got to carry a gun. Hell, Harry, you're one of them!"

"No, I'm not," Waltz says. He has made a mistake coming here, compounding an earlier mistake he did not realize he had made. He wants to get to Mary Hale's house as fast as he can.

"I didn't tell you to be a barber, Sam. You didn't tell me, 'Harry, don't lend money.' Don't start crying about it now. Of all of them, I thought you'd be the last one to say I was immune."

Sam looks away, not easily convinced. He watches Waltz out of the corner of his eye. "I hear you're having some problems," he says.

"Who told you that?"

"I just heard it around. Said with a certain glee, mind you, so there was probably a degree of wishful exaggeration to the reports. I see your boy is home."

"Eugene," Waltz says, thrown off. "He's driving me nuts already. Wants to collect on my bad debts."

"So you have bad debts."

"A few. The times, I guess."

"We've had bad times before. You've never had bad debts, though."

"Oh yes. There's always one or two who can't pay."

"But never so many it gets out into the mainstream of public conversation," Sam Boggins says.

Waltz says, "I don't know, Sam. Suddenly nobody honors their notes. Most everybody pays on time, true. But lately there have been good customers going bad. Turning into deadbeats before my very eyes. And what's worst: they're arrogant."

"And for a while your daughters were staying in your house. Twins. One pregnant. A man," Sam Boggins relates, and smiles mischievously when Waltz looks surprised. "You see the fascination people have with the richest man in Marathon?"

"I suppose," Waltz says, "though I don't understand why."

"Easy for you to say," Sam replies flatly, looking away. "One guy—you remember Norm Cleveland?—he swears your friend Mary is pregnant. He swears her belly has grown in the time she's been showing up with you. What do you think of that?"

"I think it's nobody's business." Has he missed something in Mary Hale's growth? Her belly still looks planed smooth and loose to him, with a cavernous navel and pelvic bones that stab him if he lies atop her the wrong way. Is he looking at her from the wrong angle? Strangers watching from a distance through binoculars see it. Is he too close?

"No offense intended, Harry," Sam says airily. With a brisk snap he unlocks the front door and turns the OPEN/CLOSED sign. Within moments a man rushes in off the cold street, bundled, his head down to cleave the wind. Waltz doesn't know the man but the man knows Waltz, his eyes shoot open and he adopts a studied, nervous nonchalance.

Waltz shakes Sam Boggins' hand and goes out the back. He had hoped he could hide out there all day with his friend, play chess, or just talk. Now he feels he is on the run. He doesn't want to go home; it is haunted with deadbeats, they slither daily through the mail slot, like ghosts, absence creating presence.

He dances back down the iced alley, feeling watched. At the mouth of the alley he remembers the car he had repossessed that Hesperia had shot like a common dog. Waltz had left it on the street in front of Sam Boggins' shop and forgotten it and now it is gone.

He leans in through Sam's front door. "Sam, do you remember that car Hesperia shot?"

"I do."

"Whatever became of it?"

Sam Boggins snaps a pinstriped white cloth out before him with something Waltz takes for anger. Sam is hidden behind this billow for a long moment, it drifts down before him like a woman's skirt, and he adjusts it and pins it snug around his customer's neck and shoulders.

"I had it removed," he says.

"Why?"

"Why? It was an eyesore, Harry. It was rusting and leaking fluid and taking up valuable parking space in front of my shop."

"One whole space?" Waltz teases.

"One *entire* space, Harry. Parking is tight. No reason you should care. It's not your bread and butter. I couldn't afford to give up one parking space to your museum piece."

"O.K., Sam. I'm sorry. What did it cost you?"

"Never mind."

"No," Waltz insists. "I want to pay you."

"Forget it, Harry. Can't you see I'm busy here?"

"When did you move it?"

"It sat there two weeks," Sam says. "Come in or out. I can't heat all of Michigan." Waltz steps in and shuts the door. "All the time it was out there," Sam goes on, "I couldn't believe you were just going to leave it there. I said to myself, 'Harry isn't that stupid.' Finally, I had it towed myself. It's over. O.K.?"

Waltz backs without a word out the door and into the cold. The square is full of empty parking spaces. He counts five vehicles in all, four drawn up close to the warmth and smells of the Marathon Restaurant, the fifth a sheriff's car with its squarish blue star on the door and cap of snow on the red dome light.

He must get to Mary Hale's.

Climbing the hill to his house he knows he is being watched. His back will be wide in the eyepieces. The weave of his coat will be porous as screen. He stops and turns. He picks Sam Boggins' window out of the flank of storefronts and waves exaggeratedly to it. He might be signaling from one mountain to another. He is not the least embarrassed, he has scored a phantom point from a distance.

Waltz pushes through his house's front door, really hurrying now, and there is Carla sitting on the stairs. Her coat is unbuttoned and her scarf and mittens are in a careful pile beside her. She sits tucked into herself like a porcelain cat. She smokes and uses a soiled coffee cup as an ashtray.

"Hi," she says in a scratchy voice. She takes a photograph from her pocket. It is a picture of a bloody baby boy moments from the womb; the umbilical cord is shiny blue and slick, the boy's testicles look gargantuan and purplish bunched between his fat, flexed legs.

"Susan asked me to give you this," she says. "She says you can keep it. She has others."

Waltz grins down at the picture. "Do I have to?"

"He *is* a beautiful baby. Once he got cleaned up he's a real hunk."

"Did they ever give him a name?" Waltz asks.

"Jesus, you *are* out of touch. Harry Willis."

"You're kidding," he says.

"No. Wish I was."

"He still has to pay me the money he owes."

"Ever the loan shark," she says.

"How'd you get here?"

"Hitched. Took me seventeen rides, if you can believe that. Everybody was going about a mile down the road. It was very frustrating. I'd just be getting warmed up when I had to get out again. The ratio was ten women and seven men, if you're interested. I'd never have predicted that."

"Why?"

"Oh, a woman alone. Hitchhiking. I thought it would put ideas in men's heads. Maybe it's too cold for those ideas. Everyone was a perfect gentleman."

"You sound disappointed."

She shrugs and drops her cigarette in the coffee cup. She removes her stocking cap and shakes out her hair.

"I was looking for romance and adventure," she says. "Something unexpected and different." She sighs. "If one of the men—one of the men *was* sort of handsome, but I could see in his eyes that he was stupid—if that man had suggested I go to his house and live with him a while, I would have gone."

"No," Waltz says skeptically, alarmed.

"I was prepared. I told myself that at the worst I'd wind up here. And maybe I'd end up in the home of some mysterious man."

"And maybe you'd end up dead on the side of the road."

"Oh, Daddy. Always expecting tragedy," Carla says. "He would have money and buy me new clothes. I would stay in his house all day while he went out to work. Nobody would know where I was."

"But here you are," Waltz says. "The worst has happened."

"Nah," she says, smiling, getting up off the stairs, kissing him on the cheek. "I'm glad to be here."

Waltz helps her off with her coat. "Eugene is home," he says.

"Not now. I checked the house."

"No. Home from prison, though. He's out driving somewhere. He could be home in ten minutes, or tonight, tomorrow, in a week. I don't know."

"How is he?"

"He says he can't sleep. He's already been to Flint once, he said he went to tell his old friends he was out and to leave him alone. I don't know, does that ring true with you?"

"It might," she says. "It doesn't do anybody any good to doubt him from the start."

"So wise," Waltz says, and touches her cheek.

She says, almost to herself, "Eugene."

Waltz says, "He wants to collect for me. He says he has a violent reputation and can use it to collect my late payments without actually being violent."

She smiles. "It has a logic."

"But it's not my way. Do you see? I don't want him representing me. I don't want—I will not be linked in people's minds with my son the thug. It would be no different than if he actually beat people in my name. So I have this thirty-six-year-old son who can't sleep. I don't know what to do with him."

"Let me stay a while," Carla says. He had understood this as her goal from the start. Sitting on the stairs she had looked rooted, comfortable; this was the house she had grown up in, after all.

"What about your place?"

"No problem. I can keep Eugene occupied. Keep him out of your hair."

"All right. Stay as long as you like." He longed to ask her about Willy, father of the bloody boy, but hadn't the nerve; it was enough that she was there and Willy elsewhere. She was for the time being beyond his range.

While Carla fusses in her old room, hanging up her coat, putting a brush and comb out on the dressing table that needs a good dusting, Waltz calls Mary Hale from his office.

"What are you doing?" he asks.

"A nice mixture of working and vomiting."

"I'm sorry about that. Can you come see me?"

"Are you kidding? I don't plan to leave this house until it's time to have the baby. I must be near a bathroom at all times."

"You went with me to prison," Waltz notes.

"That was a mission. How's he doing, by the way?"

"He can't sleep. He's out somewhere driving now. He feels a need to be moving."

"He'll work that out," she says.

"So you won't be down?"

"Why don't you come up here?"

"Carla just arrived. She hitchhiked from Ann Arbor. She seems blue and I don't want to leave her right away."

"All right. Then I suggest we return to our separate pursuits and try to see each other later. Agreed?"

"No, not agreed. I went to see my only male friend today. I think I've lost him. He's bitter because I'm rich."

"I don't blame him," Mary Hale says. "If you had more contact with the human race you'd run into even more of that. Aren't you lucky?"

"He implied—he practically said it right out—that there was no difference between me and a common liquor store holdup man."

"Because you're a loan shark?"

"Yes. He called me stupid."

"Did you ask him why you were rich, then?" she asks. Her voice is quick and bright, lively in his ear. He can see her at her desk, in her robe, bundled against the bay chill with her legs tucked under her. He momentarily resents his sad daughter because he wants to be on the road north to this woman.

"They watch my house through binoculars," he tells her.

"You're a celebrity."

"I'm a loan shark, for God's sake. They'd seen you and said you looked pregnant."

"They did?"

"Are you showing?"

"A slight protruding," she admits.

"Drive down here and let me see for myself."

"I'm sorry, Harry. One episode of vomiting along the roadside is all I care to experience. Call me tomorrow. After Carla is settled in, come see me. And keep the blinds down."

Eugene does not return home that night. No phones ring to tell Waltz what has happened to his son. Carla, her face chapped from a day on the road, her eyelids heavy, kisses him good night and climbs the stairs to bed. He hears her get fresh bedding from the linen closet, he hears the rectangular pattern of her footsteps as she moves making the bed. She lets water run in the bathroom sink with the door ajar, her mother's habit. She hums while brushing her teeth. He thinks this could be his chance. Carla will be asleep soon and Waltz can be at Mary Hale's house by midnight. It is not lust that drives him, but loneliness. After twenty years it has wormed into him like an itch more surprising than sad.

But he imagines Carla waking up and finding him gone. She

would be unprepared for that. A note would not be enough. She can't seem to keep a man, and he is her father, and he won't subject her to his disappearance.

At noon the following day Eugene is still gone and the front doorbell rings and there is Paul Vermillion. He chills Waltz with a hearty handshake and smooth words of friendship.

Waltz invites him in and follows him down the hall to the kitchen. There is snow in Paul Vermillion's hair and on the shoulders of his camel's-hair overcoat. He accepts with a polite nod Waltz's offer of coffee.

"How are things, Harry?" Paul Vermillion asks when they are at last settled at the kitchen table.

"No problems. What can I do for you?"

"You've been in the news, Harry. Your name is on the wind. Everywhere I go the name Harry Waltz is on people's lips."

"The world is a pretty boring place right now," Waltz says, wanting time, and information. "Soon someone more exciting will come along and you won't hear about me ever again."

Paul Vermillion laughs carefully and blows across his coffee to cool it.

"Don't diminish yourself," he says. "You're a legend in Michigan. Hell, the entire Midwest."

"Thanks."

"In Flint, you're downright famous. They say you singlehandedly keep the auto workers afloat."

"Not true," Waltz says. "They're good men at the mercy of less-good men. I just lend a little money."

Paul Vermillion says, "Everybody in Flint has owed Harry Waltz money at one time or another."

"Not everybody."

"Just about. Just about."

Waltz asks, "Why are you here?"

"I heard your boy Eugene is out of prison."

"Yes."

"What's in his future?"

"A good question."

"Does he know about our little business years back?"

"He knows I sent him to prison. As to whether he knows your part in it, I couldn't tell you."

"Where's he staying?"

"Here. He's away now, but this is his home."

"That's good of you, Harry."

"Now I'm trying to find him work."

"I hear your business is not so good," Paul Vermillion says.

"Where do you hear this?" Waltz asks. "All day I meet people who know my business better than I do. Who are these people who know so much?"

"Just acquaintances. Men in the same line of work as you and me. Somebody told me—I told them this was a lie—but they told me you were carrying people who don't pay their way."

Waltz says, "A few laggards."

"That's true?"

"It's true."

"You want me to talk to them?"

"No, thanks," Waltz says. "Eugene has already offered. They're on my string and I'll take care of them myself."

"O.K.," Paul Vermillion says. "You know best. But those guys will eat you alive. They get a taste of getting off and it's like a cancer. It'll go right through your organization."

"No problem," Waltz says, his eyes cool, his spine stiff. "Thanks for your concern."

Paul Vermillion touches the side of his nose, as if thinking. "Another thing, Harry. I know this has *got* to be a falsehood. I heard you just *gave* a guy five thousand dollars. Is that true?"

"That's family."

"The way I heard it, you wrote the guy a check and it just—"

"Family," Waltz repeats. "Please stay out of it."

"Sure, Harry." He finishes his coffee in a gulp and stands.

Waltz asks, "Why are you here?"

"I heard these crazy stories. It didn't sound like the Harry Waltz I know. I thought I might be of help."

"Have you seen Eugene since he got out?"

"Me? No. I'm not looking to, either. Between you and me, I still think the lad's got a lot of violence in his soul. Sorry, Harry, but I think he'll be back inside before long, probably for good."

Waltz says, "No."

Paul Vermillion shrugs and smiles. He is at the front door. "How old are you, Harry?"

"Why?"

"What are you? Seventy?"

"Why?"

"I heard this other story and it was just too crazy to be believed. A guy told me you traded a new LeSabre straight up for a six-year-old VW. Now, is that true?"

"What's that got to do with how old I am?"

"Then it's true?"

"There were circumstances," Waltz says, "but, yes, it's true."

"Jesus. That trade, plus the five thousand you threw the other guy, plus the customers that are reaming you, I believe we're talking way over ten thousand dollars that you're out. Can that be right?"

Waltz asks, "Do you know Paul Rivers?"

Paul Vermillion blinks. "Paul Rivers? No. Who's he?"

"Do you know Glen Empire?"

"No," he answers firmly.

Waltz's element of surprise is spent but he pushes on through the list. "Al Rudyard? Dom Prince? Leo Mesick? Joe Gladwin? Charlie Radlett?"

"No, Harry. Why do you want to know?"

"Why do you want to know how old I am?"

"Because you don't seem like yourself," Paul Vermillion says with grand solicitousness. "I thought you might be losing interest in your work. I thought you might want to farm some of your problem accounts out. I'm in awe of the network you've built over the years. I just want you to know I'm available. I'd be honored."

"No," Waltz says, "I'm not losing interest." He does not mention he is going to live to a hundred. It seems boastful and remote, like loving a woman you have never met. He tugs open the front door and the cold feels wonderful swirling in around him. "Thanks for your concern," he says. He shakes Paul Vermillion's hand and it is gloved and the feel of alien hide disgusts and frightens him. He has a point to make. He tells Paul Vermillion, "Stay away from my son. And stay off my property."

Carla has been watching from the top of the stairs. When Paul Vermillion is gone she comes down, holding something wrapped in a towel.

"Who was that creep?" she asks.

"That, my dear, was a gangster."

"Really?"

"Small-time, polished, possibly well educated, but still a gangster," says Waltz. He touches her bundled towel. "What's this?"

Carla smiles sheepishly and unwraps a petite silver pistol. "I've seen *The Godfather* too many times," she says.

"Where did you get that?"

"I bought it. You think I'd hitch alone?"

"Hell, first Sam Boggins. Now my own daughter. Put it away."

"I want you to know where it is," she says. "In case that gangster comes back."

"No. I want nothing to do with it."

"It's a fact of life, Daddy."

He leaves her. "Put that thing away," he calls back.

Work awaits him. Climbing the stairs to his office, he picks up the towel Carla had wrapped her pistol in. He carries it into the office and shuts the door. He recalls his conversation with Paul Vermillion; nothing of the structure remains, only the feeling of it. He tries to hear the man's voice, and does, but it does him no good.

He wraps the towel once around the phone receiver, having no idea what this will do to his voice; it is only something he has seen done. He must stay on only a moment. It is an attitude he must project. He dials a number in Flint and Paul Rivers answers on the second ring.

"Rivers?" Waltz says sharply through the towel. "This is Paul Vermillion."

There is a hesitation of just an instant and Waltz thinks he has missed. Paul Rivers really doesn't know the gangster.

But Paul Rivers says, "Sure, Paulie. What can I do you for?"

"You going to be home a while?"

"Sure."

"I want to drop over."

"Sure, Paulie. When?"

"Three-thirty. I'll see you then." And Waltz hangs up right away, thinking that is how a gangster would handle it.

18

Waltz next calls Mary Hale. Thrilled by his detective work, he wants to tell her all that has happened because it will have a firmer existence in two people; alone with it, he fears he may drive off and never be seen again and his information will vanish with him.

But there is no answer at her home or office.

Carla is in the kitchen eating a sliced-turkey sandwich. A drop of mayonnaise squirts onto her hand when she bites down and Waltz watches her shy juggling to get everything cleaned, in order, eaten. When she finishes and goes to the sink to wash her hands Waltz starts when he sees she has the pistol stuck in the waist of her jeans. He wants to say something but is afraid she will draw on him.

"I'm going to Flint," he tells her. "Will you be O.K. by yourself?"

"Sure. What's in Flint?"

"I've got to talk to a customer."

She winks. "Want to take my gun?"

"No."

Twenty minutes before he leaves he goes upstairs to change clothes. He takes a quick shower, shaves, brushes his teeth. His hair is pure white, he is not sure when that happened. He brushes the dust from his only suit and puts it on. He knots a burgundy tie with a white silhouette of Michigan sewn into it. He feels proud, in control. He squares his shoulders in the mirror and combs his hair. He gets no answer from Mary Hale. Then he is running late and there is nothing for him to do but go.

Waltz parks his car (the VW he got from Joe Montague for the LeSabre, he wants traction on the roads in case he has to run for it, or give chase; he feels pinched in his suit and drives with his shirt collar and trousers unbuttoned) a block over from Paul Rivers' house. The street is quiet in the middle of the afternoon, kids in school, fathers at work. But on Rivers' street Waltz sees a man in his middle thirties, dressed in a letter jacket and Lions cap, out shooting a basketball at a netless rim. The ball is so cold the man can't dribble it, when it falls through the rim it hits the driveway like a rock and dies. Another man is chipping at ice on the sidewalk with a long-handled tool. A third man jogs past Waltz and looks away; he is young and unshaven, his breath coming easily.

Were all these men out of work? Four, including Paul Rivers, on one block? One industrious, one childlike, one seeking improvement, one a deadbeat. He wonders if any of the others need to borrow money.

Waltz slips up on Paul Rivers' house from the side. He doesn't want to be seen coming up the walk, he doesn't want Paul Rivers to have a chance to hide. In the front door are set three thin windows of ridged, milky glass, useless and unattractive, and a peephole. It is exactly three-thirty. He pushes the bell and turns his back on the spyglass, backing up close to it so only his back will be visible. Paul Rivers won't see his white hair.

Waltz hears a scratching at the other side of the door, hears a chain swing loose. The door opens. Waltz turns and smiles.

Paul Rivers blurts, "Huh?" His breath clouds a spot on the storm-door glass. Waltz gets this door open before Rivers has a chance to lock it. He glides inside and lets his momentum pull the door shut and pull Paul Rivers in his wake.

"I—I'm sorry, Harry, but I'm expecting someone."

"You're expecting Paul Vermillion, and he's not coming," Waltz says. "That was me on the phone. You want to go in the kitchen? I want you to be comfortable."

"I thought our business was settled," Paul Rivers says.

"No. You owe what you've owed all along, plus a little more."

Paul Rivers has shaved for Paul Vermillion's visit, his smooth cheeks glow pink, a mist of sweat rests on them, and on his forehead. He has pushed the kids' toys to the side, turned off the TV, hidden his wife and children somewhere. He looks guilty, pasty, spending too much time indoors.

"I promise, Harry," he says. "I thought we were square."

"Relax. I'm the same man you've dealt with all along. I just want to talk to you."

"Somebody's making a big mistake. Let me give you ten bucks today," Rivers says. "Earnest money. The rest in no time at all."

"Shut up," Waltz snaps, angry at the fear his appearance has put in this man. He is five inches taller than Paul Rivers, but he is outweighed by sixty pounds and is fifteen years older. Nevertheless, he puts his hand flat on Paul Rivers' chest and pushes him back toward the kitchen. "In there," he orders. "Make us some coffee. Then sit down and shut up. I only want to talk to you."

Waltz sits and smokes and watches Paul Rivers.

"What did Paul Vermillion offer you to ignore your debt to me?" Waltz asks.

The man has a tiny yellow scoop in his hand. Nervous, he digs instant coffee out of a jar and empties it into cups. Coffee falls to the floor grainy and distinct as sleet.

"I'm not armed, Paul," Waltz says. "Would you please relax?"

"I can't relax, Harry," Paul Rivers, his back to Waltz, says. His is a broad-shouldered back with a generous circle of fat at the waist. "You being here has put me in a real bind."

"You put yourself in the bind," Waltz says. "Did you think you could just stop paying and never have to answer for that?"

"Paulie said he'd pay you what I owed."

"Why did he come to you in the first place?"

"He said you were getting old," Paul Rivers tells Waltz, giving him the coffee. "He refinanced my debt at a lower rate. He's been talking to a lot of people, giving them the same pitch."

"What's my age got to do with it?"

"To me, Harry, nothing. But Paulie said you were getting old and could be had. He said he knew you weren't the type who'd make trouble. You'd never hurt anyone over money, Harry."

"So you know I won't beat you up," Waltz says. "For that reason you break your word? You go against your signature?"

Paul Rivers lowers his eyes. "He gave me a better deal, Harry."

"So?" Waltz snarls, rising to take the coffee to the sink to throw away the awful stuff. "You signed the paper. *Before* you signed—that was the time to shop around for a better deal."

"Harry," Paul Rivers says, "your pants are undone."

Waltz looks down and laughs. He forgot to fasten his trousers before he got out of the car. He turns his back on Paul Rivers to arrange himself, and to compose himself.

When he turns back, he smiles and says, "So Paul Vermillion may have a point."

Paul Rivers says, "I'm not saying you're old, Harry. You'll always be smarter than me. But I know you aren't mean and you said you aren't carrying a gun and Paulie saved me a chunk of money. For all those reasons I'm willing to ignore that note I signed with you. A lot of other guys are willing, too."

"How many?" Waltz asks.

"I couldn't say for sure. I just know Paulie Vermillion's been showing up in the strangest places."

"O.K.," Waltz says, lighting a cigarette, plotting. "So you break your word to me and you go under Paul Vermillion's thumb. What do you think will happen if you come up a little short with him? With me, you could talk to me. I know you're out of a job, money's tight, I'll listen. I'll give you a little extra time. You think Paul Vermillion will?"

"He gave me such a good deal I don't ever see a problem meeting my obligations," Rivers says.

"Paul Vermillion *is* mean," Waltz says. "And he *does* carry a gun. He'll beat you up if you don't pay on time. That's how he runs his business."

Paul Rivers picks up the phone on the wall and dials. While the number rings he says to Waltz, as though he is proud, "It's a decision I made, Harry. A chance I'll take. . . . Hello, Paulie? Is he there? . . . Yeah. This is Rivers. He told me to call right away if Harry Waltz ever showed up here. . . . Yeah. He's standing right in front of me. Big as life. O.K. Just tell Paulie, O.K.? . . . No. He's not making trouble. . . . I know. That's what they said. I'm just doing what he told me. O.K.? So long."

Waltz asks, "Did you sign a paper?"

"Who needs to sign? Me and Paulie both know we did business with each other."

"How do you know when your debt is paid? You've got no record. With me, you knew where you stood. You'd just about climbed out of your hole, Paul. In a year you'd be just about clear."

"Paulie and I have an agreement."

"You shook, right?"

"Yeah, we shook."

Waltz puts on his gloves and his coat. "I'm not through with you, Paul. You signed the note and you have to pay. I can't help that you've compounded your problems. But you've still got to pay."

"Get out, Harry. *I'm* through with *you.*"

Waltz leaves and gets lost going back to his car. It takes him a half hour to find the VW and he comforts himself thinking he has much on his mind, that the light is failing, that the car is strange. He wants to have a talk with his son, but more importantly he has to see Mary Hale. His son, he believes, will only bring bad news. In Mary Hale there is hope for a cessation of his confusion and pain; he believes in the power of her answers.

He reaches Mary Hale's house but she isn't there. She once showed him where she kept a key hidden on a ledge above the back door and Waltz uses this key to let himself in. A storm of howling dimensions has risen and his eyebrows and hair hold gobs of snow that melt into his eyes. He has great, forming hope for this storm; he likes the apocalyptic feel of it. There are portentous winds, a sheen of ice on the roads, thick snow that seems to originate at the bottom of Saginaw Bay and then storm inland in gusty waves. He desires the state to be encased and immobilized. He wants to be held a willing prisoner in this house. Nothing will move across the great Mitten, no business will be transacted, no deadbeats will surface, no promises will be broken. He wants time to stop.

He searches through the house for Mary Hale, remembering how they missed each other once before. He calls her name, expecting her to be there. He has counted on her presence. He does not want to be responsible for getting her home safely. The last time she counted on him he made a sucker deal out of necessity and it returned to him later as evidence of advancing age, of his inability to function in his chosen line of work.

He calls her office and they tell him she left for home a half hour before. Already she is late. Waltz is content to wait and worry, the responsibility for action removed. Mary Hale might now be anywhere in the storm and he thinks of his need for her as a taut string upon which she slides toward him like a bead.

It takes another hour for her to get home. He doesn't hear her car in the snow or the scratch of her key in the lock. She is just suddenly in the kitchen shaking snow onto the tile like a dog. When she removes her coat Waltz studies her. A soft swelling of her abdomen startles him. He thinks he has been missing something all along. Her breasts hang heavier. Her face is a little fuller, with a chapped blush to her cheeks and a cold crimson dot at the tip of her nose.

"Hello, there," she says to Waltz, with a full smile that delights him. He gets up and kisses her. He puts a hand on her belly.

"Why are you here?" she asks.

"To be with you."

She wipes her face dry with a dish towel, faintly smearing eye shadow. He wishes she would ask him to stay.

"Why were you at work?" he asks. "You should be taking better care of yourself. Fewer risks."

"I'm fine," she protests. "I refuse to sit around the house all day. It's bad for me, hence it's bad for the kid."

"How *is* the kid?"

"Passable. I still throw up, but I can handle that."

"Get out of those wet clothes," Waltz tells her.

"Make some coffee. Put whiskey in it. That's what I want," she orders.

He makes the drink and brings it to her in her bedroom. She has hung her clothes neatly from hangers along the top of the bathroom door.

"Put that here," she says from the bed. A hand comes out of the covers and touches the nightstand. He lands the cup and saucer safely on the spot. She cracks the riddle of covers bunched at her chin long enough to show him her cooled, dark-nippled breasts, and to smile. She coughs delicately and her breasts quiver.

She commands him, "Get out of those dry clothes."

Her coffee and whiskey has gone cold by the time they have finished making love but she drinks it right down and wipes her mouth with the back of her hand. She sits up against the headboard and a trickle of liquid escapes from the corner of her mouth and rolls between her breasts. She smiles, "Get that, will you?"

He licks it away in a nursely fashion, promising nothing. She has drained him of everything but his problems.

He says, "I went to see a customer of mine. One of the new breed of deadbeats. He said he was offered a better deal elsewhere, so he took it."

"From Paul Vermillion," she says.

"How did *you* know?"

"Asking questions. My need to know, Harry. I have a wealth of inside information. What else do you want to know?"

"What *do* you know?"

She says, "You're important to me, Harry. I knew you were troubled by these things, so I made some inquiries. That's what I've been doing most of today."

"And what did you find out?"

"That a small-time hood named Paul Vermillion is interested in taking over your business."

"He told this guy I saw today that I was too old."

Mary Hale nods. "I heard that. He also believes that you are a pushover . . . that you lack a necessary hardness."

"I've heard that, too. Does that bother you?"

She says, "It's in you somewhere, Harry. It doesn't bother me that you don't break your customers' legs, no. I wonder how you feel, though. What do you say to all this?"

"I feel deserted by my own values."

"You've still got your values," she says. "Others may have abandoned them, or never held them in the first place. But *you* still have them."

"They signed the notes. They have to pay."

"Says you," Mary Hale replies with mild reproach.

"What else is there, then?"

"You tell me."

"Come on, Mary," he complains. "I don't have the temperament to harm these people. If they decline to honor their own signatures I can't be bothered with them."

"Think of all the money you're out."

Waltz huffs, "Money."

"Paul Vermillion won't stop with a few customers," she says. "When he sees nothing from you in the way of a response he'll just go right down your list. He puts the deal to them in a businesslike fashion. He simply offers a better rate. He promises to settle their debt with you. No one questions where he makes his money in this scheme. No one thinks beyond himself. They see that lower rate and they're all for it. He doubles his money by not paying you off. Everyone is instructed to tell you the money is on the way. Paul Vermillion is the man you have to worry about here, Harry."

"He has cleared their consciences," Waltz says.

"For the time being. This sort of scheme catches up to them, of course. But by that time it's too late. So what do you do about it?"

"Do I hire my son the thug?"

"Do you?"

"My daughter carries a gun," he says. "She might be the answer."

"Is she?"

"Damn it, I don't have answers to these questions."

She rolls away from him in bed. She is hunched deep in the covers with only her white dome of hair for him to see by. She puts forward her suggestion in a whisper, "Get rid of Paul Vermillion."

Waltz draws air. "Did I hear that?"

"What did you hear?"

"Did you say kill Paul Vermillion?"

"No," she says, rolling back toward him, suddenly lively, with a hard gleam in her eye, a lawyer's love of a fine point. "I said get rid of him. I didn't say anything about kill."

"Short of killing him," Waltz says, "how can I get rid of him so he won't be around to torment me?"

"You tell me."

"Prison?"

"Prison?" she says. "You interested in that?"

"No."

"You sent your son. But you won't send a man who is blatantly threatening your livelihood."

"With Eugene . . . I thought there was a good purpose to be served. No. No prison. No killings. No beatings."

She gets up and goes into the bathroom. Waltz hears running water, teeth being brushed. Calm sounds of the everyday. He has laid down the law and nothing has changed.

She returns to bed and warms her cool buttocks against him. She adopts the curl of sleep.

"I'm not tired," he complains. "It's early."

"I'm exhausted."

"I've got to come to a decision on this."

"Your mind is made up," she says. "You may not realize it yet, but your mind *is* made up."

"Tell me why."

"You've made your choice," she explains. "Ideals versus material wealth. It's the classic question. I admire you. Go to sleep."

19

But sleep is elusive and as Mary Hale falls away from him he has nowhere to go, nothing to hold on to. He gets up and dresses and sits in an armchair by a window. Light from the snow comes in. There is a table to his right and a telephone on the table.

Answers come to him but he dodges them as they approach, or he holds them for a moment before discarding them. Nothing fits his image of the way he is. His life divides into halves as clean as good debts and bad debts. Any way he figures it, the worst he sees happening is he will lose money that is rightfully his. He will be a fool in some eyes. He will count on the honor of other men to stay in business; that is as it has always been. That assumption has brought him to this point of trouble.

He runs a finger along the cool plastic back of the telephone. An ordered cluster of twelve square lights comes on when he picks up the receiver. A dial tone purrs in the distance. The number jumps into his mind; for a moment it clears everything away with how long the number has stuck with him for all the infrequency of his use of it. He punches it, bringing the operator in first, so that while he tells her to charge the call to his home number he can hear the circuits, the phantasmal technology, falling into place and opening like electric gates all the way to L.A.

It is earlier there; he does not even know the time in Michigan. He hears a bell ringing, tries to picture the phone and where it sits. It might be sitting in the sun out by a pool, the receiver water-spotted. Another bell and then a third and then the tiny seizure of excitement above his heart when the phone is answered. Waltz longs to hear Aaron's voice but he has never once in all the years been first to answer the phone; he sends Molly ahead of him like a hated king's food-taster, and this time is no different.

She says, "Hello."

"Molly, it's Harry," he says.

"Harry—" she utters, then stops. She will turn the phone in against her body to block him while she calls for Aaron.

"Harry," she says, "it's so strange. You calling like this. Just now."

"Why?"

"Aaron's dead, Harry," she relates. "He mentioned he hadn't talked to you in a long time and then here you call."

Waltz wants to pull the phone across the room to lay beside Mary Hale's warm length while he hears this. In the dark he feels he is floating, held to Earth by a curled cord, the air illuminated by stars on snow.

"Dead?" he says.

"Lung cancer," Molly says. "He's had it for two years and smoked right to the end. That's just the way he was. Didn't fight it, didn't change. He just said that's the way it was meant to be."

"I just called to talk," Waltz says. "About some things going on out here."

"What things, Harry?"

"Oh, nothing—"

"Please, Harry. Tell me. It'll be nice to think about something else for a minute."

"Business problems. A guy is trying to take over my business. I'm at a loss how to respond."

Mary Hale rolls over in bed. He prays she will awaken and reel him in.

"Don't let yourself be pushed around," Molly says, with the firmness of a long-held philosophy.

"I won't," he assures her.

"I'd like to be of more help but I don't know how you think about things. It's hard."

"I'm probably . . . if you got to know me I'd probably remind you a lot of Aaron."

"Do you think so?"

"Yes, I do. I'll come out for the funeral," he says. "You can see for yourself then."

"You know, Harry, that's the oddest thing. When Aaron was

getting very sick near the end he had me collect all his papers together, his important papers. And he told me very adamantly that he wanted to be buried back there in Marathon."

"You're kidding."

"No. It's in the will, too. He's very clear on that point."

"Why would he want to be buried here?"

"Something about you. He told me he wanted to get you." He heard her chuckle.

"For what?"

"That I don't know."

"The ground is like stone now," Waltz frets. "They'd never get him in the ground."

Molly says assuredly, "They have machines now that can dig through anything."

"Bury him out there," he says angrily. "I don't want him."

"Harry"—she begins to cry—"I'm ashamed of you."

"You can't be. You don't know me. I haven't seen Aaron in forty years. I can only guess what he looks like now because he's my twin brother. If I had died before him I wouldn't have myself shipped to California to be on his hands."

"Marathon is Aaron's birthplace," Molly says.

"Big deal. He ignored it. He ignored his Daddy."

Molly says gently, "He hated your father."

"No!" Waltz exclaims. Mary Hale rolls over in bed, her thin hand snaps on the light and Waltz has to throw a hand over his eyes, which leak tears like faulty drums. Aaron's death has not touched him so much as Aaron's posthumous hatred of their father.

"It's true," Molly says. "For forty years it is the one topic of conversation that never died, never dried out, never tired him. He was bored with his work, with me, with L.A., bored with everything in his life at one time or another. But he was never bored with hating your father."

"Why did he hate him?"

"Because your father had a favorite," she says. "You."

"No."

"It's true. Why do you think he hid out in California for forty years?"

Waltz takes a breath and tells Molly he will call her back. No machines exist, he thinks, that can penetrate the iron winter ground. The teeth of backhoe scoops, the work-shined blades of hydraulic shovels, would spark against the earth and snap off.

"For forty years he's a rumor out in California," he complains to Mary Hale. "Then he dies and suddenly he's all over me. He couldn't even be bothered to come back for Daddy's funeral. Molly says he hated him."

"You've got to do this thing for him," Mary Hale says evenly. She has killed the light and settled him alongside her in bed; she slowly brushes his hair with her electric fingers. "It's unfair, looking at the logic, at what is deserved. But it's death, too, and if you shortchange the dead chances are you'll be shortchanged when you die. Call it superstition. Call it good manners. But you really don't have a choice, Harry."

"Watch me. I can refuse."

"Call her back and tell her you'll be happy to do whatever needs to be done."

"No."

"It's your place, Harry."

"The guy is a stranger. Let him bury himself."

But he calls her, again in the dark, punching the little squares of light and letting the cost hang as a petty punishment on Mary Hale's bill. "What do you want me to do?" he asks.

"I'll be flying in with Aaron's body to Detroit," Molly says. "Meet us with a hearse. Make the funeral arrangements. I'll pay the bill when I arrive. Don't scrimp. Put a death notice in the Marathon and Flint papers. Aaron had a number of friends who will want to attend. I know this is a lot of trouble for you, Harry, but Aaron will be pleased."

Waltz throws in, before Molly is gone, "I'm going to be a daddy."

"What?"

"I'm going to be a daddy," he says. "There is a woman here in

Michigan, she's right here in the room with me, who is going to have our baby."

"Why, Harry . . . I'm stunned. Is she our age?"

"Almost," he says proudly.

"Aren't you afraid?"

"Did Aaron tell you about the State Home?"

"Yes, he did. It sounds awful. I would think a memory like that would make you be more careful."

"The place is closed," he says. "I miss them since they're gone." The globy white faces pressed to the fence watching him pull weeds from the flower beds or smoke a cigarette in the gazebo, the men-children who engaged his children in a snowball fight through the fence, the solitary applauding figure watching him masturbate in the gazebo shadows, they were easy company and always happy.

"We aren't worried about the kid," he says, lying for his own part. "His or her mother is a lawyer and his or her father is a famous loan shark. What mix of genes could slide easier through life?"

"Do you love her?" Molly gently inquires from L.A.

"A tough question," Waltz says. "There's hope."

With his new responsibilities he feels trapped by the storm. The wind and snow that warmed him and set him free to hover in Mary Hale's good graces now block his return to Marathon.

"When do they arrive in Detroit?" Mary Hale asks.

"Day after tomorrow," Waltz says. He examines the lethal winter air through the rear kitchen window. "I may not make it."

Mary Hale encircles him with her arms. She is warily encouraged, for that morning she was not sick.

"Sure you will," she assures him. "You don't have to be in Marathon to make the arrangements."

He telephones the funeral home in Marathon that handled the death of Daddy Waltz. His brother will be waked for one day only at Waltz's house, in the room where his father had lain.

Someone will meet the plane in Detroit to transport the coffin to Marathon. Waltz will meet the widow.

"Shall we place the death notice for you?"

He calls out names and relationships, they have the ring of notoriety and fame to him, he has known them so long and their concerns seem so magnified. Marathon will rise and notice the passing of a Waltz, he thinks, but he has no confidence in this.

"Put it in the Flint and Marathon papers," he says.

"In a death of this stature," Waltz is told, "the Detroit papers will want something, too. Is there some way I could contact his family in California to do a more complete obituary?"

"You have his family," Waltz says.

"We were thinking of his professional life. Often that is of more interest to the general public. Also, might we not have a recent photograph?"

He almost tells the man he does not have one. Then it occurs to him to just send a picture of himself. Paul Vermillion will see it and feel momentarily touched with boundless luck.

He gives them Aaron's number. Let Molly fill in the holes in her husband's life. It is enough for Waltz that he is coming back. If he hated Daddy Waltz for his favoritism, Waltz thinks, he must have hated the favorite, too.

The momentum of the occasion fills their day. When darkness falls the snowstorm stops for Waltz because he can no longer see it and in the morning the sun is out and the roads look passable.

"Come back to Marathon with me," he says to Mary Hale.

"I've got to work yet, Harry," she says, giving him a lawyerly kiss on the lips. For a second day she has been free of nausea, it fills her heart and eyes with hopefulness. Her breath smells of egg when she sees him off.

Slow going home, he sits for three hours in a sun-shot plane of white, progressing not one inch. Cars in front and behind him pin him to the spot. He is chilly in the VW. But then a plow materializes and leads them south. He reaches home fearing Aaron has beat him there; maybe he is still alive, the punch line to an elaborate macabre joke to hide the emotion of his return.

But only Carla is there. She is reading the paper by sunlight in the kitchen and Waltz has to explain to her the death of her Uncle Aaron. Surprising tears come to her eyes.

"He called for you here sometimes when nobody was home," she tells him. "He never left any messages. We would just talk. Mostly about me. He had a nice way with people he didn't know. He was sweet."

Waltz asks, "Any sign of Eugene?"

"Not a word."

Waltz is certain something has happened to his son; he has run afoul of the law, formed a new gang, been shot for some past slight.

Toward the end of the afternoon the sun is so round and warm Waltz thinks a false spring has come to see Aaron safely into the softening ground before closing up again like a vault. This brief chink in winter is there strictly for his brother.

He walks with overcoat unbuttoned down the hill to the square to buy the newspapers that contain Aaron's obituary. He stacks the Flint paper, the Marathon paper, and the two Detroit papers on the counter and atop this formidable mound of paper and ink puts his money.

Branch is the druggist's name, Waltz thinks he remembers. His weak jaw is obscured with a silver beard. Branch pushes the money back at Waltz.

"We're all deeply sorry about the death of your brother," the druggist says. "The papers are on us."

Waltz looks the druggist in the eye, sees that a brief word is expected of him. He says thanks, snatches the money back, and beats it out of there with the papers under his arm.

A perfect stranger waylays Waltz on the edge of the square and pinches his arm painfully while expressing condolences and offering to be of any help at all. Waltz nods, grimaces, and spins free. He should never have chanced the walk. The metallic anonymity of an automobile would have gotten him in and out of town without incident, none of this immersion in sunny air and grim society.

Two more Marathonites see him out in the open and change directions to intercept him. He thinks of swatting them with the papers, which are so heavy they numb his arms if he doesn't alternate the load. The weight would drop one in his tracks and divert the other, Waltz could break free, and run for it.

But he halts like a citizen and shakes hands, he even makes small, pained talk, answering questions, trying to feel a part of this ritual. Everybody knows more about Aaron than Waltz does. He suspects his twin brother might have been living in town all along for all the details he hears. Some older men spin anecdotes that ring true even for Waltz; and he realizes the old men are confused, that they *are* talking about him, that for forty years he has been mistaken by some for Aaron.

He finally panics and bolts, though, when he sees more people coming toward him. They swarm like tacklers, buzzards of sympathy, and it is his challenge to thread through them, to reach the home ground up on the hill.

It takes him an hour. The fingers and soft pads of his hands are stained black with printer's ink, there are smudges of it on his shirtfront. He has shaken a lot of hands, been kissed on the cheek and on the mouth by solemn-faced women he did not always know. He would not be surprised if told he had shaken the hand of every single male Marathonite except Sam Boggins, whom Waltz kept watching for in the informal attack of well-wishers, but who never materialized.

The obituaries have nice sounds to them. They run to impressive lengths. Waltz's picture runs with the Detroit papers' obits, his brother's name beneath it; he is serious, bright-eyed, handsome, and young. No one knew the difference.

A headline in the Flint paper draws him to it:

"MISSING" MARATHONITE HID
INSIDE HOME FOR TWO YEARS

Accompanying the story is a smudged likeness of Elaine Schoolcraft, whose refrigerator he repossessed the day Hesperia shot his car. Standing beside her, unable to conceal a smirk of wise-ass triumph, is the woman's husband, missing in Lake Superior and presumed dead, who lived in the basement and came up only long enough to help Waltz with the refrigerator.

He recalls that day with the clarity of delayed embarrassment. The woman had sworn him to a secret he did not understand.

Even then, he thinks, he was getting old; it is a slip he is surprised Paul Vermillion did not learn of and capitalize on.

Waltz reads the story in his kitchen. The man had no debts, he was not on the run from the law, he was not in any trouble. "I was tired," he is quoted. "I wanted to be free."

His wife had no comment. She had brushed her hair for the newspaper's photographer but her face is not amused, or relieved, only her eyes have any life in that blurred reproduction. Within Elaine Schoolcraft lies the heart of the story, Waltz thinks. All that time leading the life of the grieving woman, the potential widow, no life outside the house but the jobs she would have to take to support herself and her husband. No men (her husband was not dead, only missing; to date would be out of the question) except the one hiding in the basement, turning toadstoolish in the skin, milky in the eyes. Waltz can recall the bleached, strong arms of the man who helped him.

The woman would have the story to tell. Of the two, she has the more palpable depth. Why did she put up with him? And did she in turn live a life secret from her husband, who had selected his boundaries for their obscuring properties, one facet being his inability to know where his wife was when she was away from home? Someday Waltz will see her on Marathon's narrow streets and speak to her of his admiration.

Mary Hale calls that evening to say she will not make it there that night. Waltz is just as glad. The warm break in the cold has produced fog that scares him with its impermeability and gives him hope Aaron's plane will not make it through until he feels better prepared.

Carla washes and Waltz dries the dishes both for that night's dinner and for the previous two days of meals. The job takes more than an hour, there is grease to be cut, water to be redrawn.

"I talked to Susan today," Carla says. "They're coming up for the wake."

"All right," Waltz says.

"I'm not crazy about it."

"Because of Willy?"

"Didn't you ever wonder why I came here that night? And why I've stayed?"

"Oh," he says, "details intrigued me. But I think I guessed the basics."

"The baby—dear Harry Willis—changed him. I guess I expected it, too, but I was still surprised how *completely* he made up his mind. Suddenly there was no ambivalence, no weighing of twin sisters." She runs water over her soapy wrists and hands, then shakes them out. "He was a father," she says, "and fathers didn't sleep with their wife's sister."

"You slept with him?" Waltz whispers.

Carla looks at her father and smiles sadly. "Does that detail intrigue you? Nine times after they were married. The times before she took him away I didn't need to count."

"And Sooz never knew?"

"I don't know. We *are* twins. She'd get looks in her eyes sometimes. She never made me lie to her, which I appreciated."

Her dark face turns to Waltz again, her voice perks up with information she thinks will please him.

"Sooz said he got a job. He'll be teaching history at a high school in Ann Arbor. Someone quit on short notice and he will fill in. He'll also teach the second semester; then, who knows?"

"Good," Waltz says.

"He knew a man in the district. He knows everybody. It's a wonder he's not a millionaire."

"Too nice, maybe," Waltz says, not convinced.

"So he really is on the right track, Daddy," Carla says earnestly. "I'm positive you'll start getting your money back from him anytime now."

"You shouldn't worry about that. Let *him* worry about it." He is angrier with Willy than he has ever been with anyone before. It is not the money. He is angry in behalf of his daughter Carla, that this man has set her on the run from her home, driven her back to the soft place and memories of her childhood; that he has deceived this woman's twin, also. Maybe there is an element in their beautiful faces only potential lovers recognize that signals gullibility and makes them desirable.

Carla in her baggy clothes, her dark golden hair in a silk scarf, wringing out the dishcloth, deserves better. She deserves a man who knew his mind and honor before a child forced him into it, who would recognize pain and spare her beforehand.

"When do you think you'll go back?" he asks.

"I've got no plans," she says. Her hand dives into the gray scummed water and yanks the drain stopper. The act is out of sequence. She has to wash and dry her hand all over again. Out the window, Waltz can't see a thing. Is Aaron's body flying through that stuff? He checks the time. The plane won't leave California for hours. Waltz prays for some saving confusion that will delay the body even getting to the plane, and thus into his care.

"Come to Detroit with me tomorrow," Waltz says. "I foresee a long and laughable day."

"Why laughable?" Carla asks.

Waltz shrugs. He was being snide.

Waltz is showered, dressed, and ready to leave for the airport the next morning when a man from the funeral home calls. The fog, he reports, is lifting in Detroit, but very slowly, and flights are running two to three hours late. Waltz asks the man to call him when they are leaving.

He had been ready for the drive, the day, and now he must wait. Out back he can just see the gazebo's peaked shape, but that's all. This is an improvement over the previous hour. He has put on his suit, knotted his tie, put cash in his wallet.

He checks the exterior world once more; he no longer expects to see Eugene again.

Carla wears a long-sleeved green dress that is snug at the hips then swirls loosely to below her knees. The dress once belonged to Louise. A coral heart hangs on a chain around her neck. She has filled in the sad pockets of her grieving face with make-up and lipstick and planted a copper comb belonging to Louise in her hair.

"You look terrific," Waltz tells her.

"Thanks. What was the call?"

"The funeral home. The planes are running a few hours late. We have to wait."

"All dressed up with nowhere to go."

"How about breakfast in beautiful downtown Marathon?"

She looks out the window. Waltz thinks he sees a bird shoot past, even Carla flinches. "Can we get there through this?"

"Sure," he says. He selects a fancy LTD with amber quartz lights from the vehicles parked in front of his house. The seats are cold and moist and for a minute he thinks the thing won't start; he cranks it tenderly, then ferociously, and only when he gets tough does it come to life.

Looking back through the fog he gets a shock: His house is gone. No, he looks steadily toward where he knows it must be and its faint shape swims out stately as an ocean liner.

"You think we should try it?" Carla asks. The question comes swirled in her breath.

"Sure we should try it," he says; though now he would rather be warm in his house making his own breakfast, this short plunge through the fog looms like a test of youth.

"We don't have to go," she says.

He winks over at her. "No problem."

He puts the LTD in reverse, it jumps back like a frightened cat, sputters, decides to work, and they back out into the road and are off.

The trip is brief. The road is empty; they are sheltered in their foolishness by being the only car out. They park on the square and step inside the Marathon Restaurant. Nobody there. Not a single soul occupies any of the tables or booths. The door sets off a small trio of brass bells when it opens and closes and this music of potential commerce brings the owner out of the back. His hair is askew, his eyes are large and watery and confused.

"Oh—Harry," he blurts loudly, snatching two menus from the box rack built onto the counter beside the cash register. He gets a coffeepot from a waitress station as they move past to a booth by the window, the same booth Waltz and Mary Hale sat in to discuss the fact of her pregnancy.

The man pours them coffee. He has rough, nicked hands, yellowish nails, a scratched wedding band; his hand shakes a little pouring coffee. Waltz thinks: This man is my age.

The man says, "You been in a lot, Harry."

"It's a nice place," Waltz says. He has been in the place three times. Is business so bad that makes him a regular? There never seems to be anyone in the restaurant. No business, hands that shake, wet sad eyes, these things are important to this man Waltz's age. He wears a name tag: VIN.

"Did you go to Marathon High, Vin?"

Vin smiles as though being teased. "Come on, Harry. Course I did. I was in two classes with you. Gym and Speech."

"Sure." Waltz smiles. He taps his head. "Memory, huh?"

"Mine, too. Some days there's nothing there. Other days, I can remember the taste of Mom's milk."

"Sure," Waltz says. He and Carla place their orders.

"You weren't worth a dime in Gym," Vin remembers when he brings water, grapefruit juice for Carla, and a stainless-steel pitcher of cream. "But you sure could talk."

His daughter laughs and Vin's face breaks open happily, that he has somehow done this.

She says to her father when Vin is gone, "That is the source of your fortune. You could talk people into thinking they needed your money."

Waltz shakes his head. "No, I was able to talk people into believing there was nothing wrong with them taking my money. *That* is the source of my fortune." He sits up straight. "I brought honor and gentlemanliness . . . and seemliness to loan sharking."

"And we're proud of you, Daddy," Carla says. He thinks he is being mocked but her eyes are serious and caring.

"You never brought your school friends home," he says.

"You were always there," she protests cheerfully. "Who wants to spend time in a house where a parent is always around?"

"That's true, I suppose. I thought you were ashamed."

Carla bows her head. "We were, I was, a little. Everyone talked about you like you were a criminal. I tried to balance that idea with this picture of you at home. You were always kind of baffled. Trying to figure things out. Eugene. Monroe. Me. Susan. Remember that show, *One Step Beyond?*"

Waltz does not, but nods to urge the flow of the story, he loves to hear about himself, the way he was.

She says, "We nicknamed you 'One Step Behind.' "

He laughs sharply, hurt, his wince interior. His recollection of that time, his children's childhoods, strangely jibes with Carla's telling. He was at a loss much of that time. He was lucky that money was not a worry, he does not dare think how he would have raised four children and sweated the bills every month, too; maybe he'd have done better. That prospect makes him shudder with retrospective relief, though; it would have squeezed him dry.

"Think it's breaking?" Waltz asks, nodding out the window at the fog. He can see clearly to just beyond their car.

"No," Carla says. "If it's like this in Detroit I doubt Uncle Aaron will get in today."

"Keep talking. You're getting my hopes up."

"It's only a brief delay," she reminds him. "Sooner or later you've got to do this."

"You sound like Mary Hale," Waltz says. "Don't you believe in eternal delay?"

Carla laughs. "No."

"You kids," Waltz scoffs, a mock old-timer. "How can you expect to get through life if you don't hold out hope for eternal delay?"

"Tell me about eternal delay."

"It is the hope," he says, "that something unpleasant will be forever put off by benevolent outside forces. For instance, that this fog is permanent, that planes will never fly and cars will never move. And Aaron will have to be buried out in sunny California because there is no getting into the big Mitten." He spreads his hands. "That is the concept of eternal delay."

"What an awful way to live," Carla says.

Waltz shrugs. "Hardly a philosophy," he says, but when he looks out the window the fog gives him hope.

At one o'clock in the afternoon the funeral home calls with word they are leaving for Detroit. Waltz puts on his tie again and Carla, in a slip and robe, goes upstairs to get back into her mother's green dress. On the road there is a raveled edge to the fog not present earlier. Visibility is a good hundred yards and the sun, earlier just a cool dime high in the sky, looms larger, embracing, and indomitable.

"This looks like it," Waltz says when they are miles from home.

Carla reaches over and squeezes his arm, says in a voice like an announcer, "This is *not* a test."

Cars coming up on their left hang for long moments beside the repossessed LTD so the male drivers can shoot glances in at Carla. She is so beautiful. Waltz is proud, she is his daughter, she is with him. Her serenity fills the car and leads Waltz not to worry. This time is only something he will look back on, this reunion with his brother, as something painful gracefully handled.

Aaron's plane is already in when they reach the terminal. Hurrying down the concourse they meet the passengers coming toward them, Waltz looks into the faces of women, trying to divine Molly. No one stops him. He is Aaron's twin, it should be up to her to pick him out.

"See her?" Carla asks, her breathing quick.

"I never *have* seen her," Waltz complains. He never sounded Aaron's taste in women. Does he look for a woman like his mother? Will Aaron's desires parallel his own? He has no idea.

But they reach the gate and there she is. Her back is to them, she stands alone except for ticket agents finishing their jobs. She is short, a compact woman with one hand resting on a shoulder bag, the other on a cocked hip. She looks through the greened glass down at the jet that carried her and Aaron. Men in airline coveralls roll a bronze coffin out of a dark slot in the underbelly of the plane.

Waltz wants to circle her to read her face. There is nothing to be seen in the glass she watches through. But he stands silently behind her and to her left. He watches over her shoulder as the coffin is rolled easily into the rear of the funeral home's beige hearse. One of the men on the unloading detail exaggeratedly wipes his hands, cleaning them of some symbolic taint. The others look at each other, one speaks, they all laugh. It is great to be alive. The hearse backs up, pauses to change gears, then heads for Marathon.

"Molly?" Waltz says.

He wonders if she will faint, thinking he is Aaron's ghost there in the airport. He notices that when she turns from the window she keeps a hand on the railing. She, too, might be afraid of falling.

Molly looks at Carla first. A polite smile on an oval face, blue eyes made large with shadow, whether of grief or cosmetics Waltz can't tell. These eyes move on to Waltz; he gets the idea she has been watching him at the edge of her vision all the time she looked at Carla, she might have watched him come up behind her in the glass. She was getting ready.

"Harry," she says, in the voice on the phone all those years. "I'm amazed."

"Why?"

She takes his hand like a man, allows him a soft, quick kiss on the powdered plane of her forehead, cups his elbow in her hand.

"All these years Aaron said he had a twin. Deep down, I was skeptical. It turns out he was telling the truth."

"Do I really look like him?"

"Do you?" She laughs. "My God. You're one and the same." She steps back appraisingly. "He looked ill at ease in a suit, too."

He introduces Carla, then they head without a word back

through the long tunnels and sliding doors, the three of them arm in arm, to where her bags wait. Outdoors, Waltz is startled by the cold. Winter still reigns in Detroit. In Marathon, a false spring has arrived to welcome Aaron home.

20

They all sit up front in the LTD, Carla by the window, Molly between her and Waltz, who drives relaxed, showing off. She is so little, like a girl riding alongside Daddy, but her legs are tapered and in stockings, she possesses low-slung, soft breasts, and there are shoots of silver in her clean brown hair. Tiny feet, too. Her wide hips press against him and he feels a little kernel of lust pop open in him, such a surprise.

All through the maneuvers of vacating the airport she did not say a word. She rode along between Waltz and Carla; he did not dare look into her face. Was this her way through life? A silent floating on the good graces of others? Her silence kept the world guessing. Why had Aaron hidden this woman from him for so long?

Waltz remembers a letter coming in the summer of 1946, the year Monroe was born. It was addressed to no one in particular. The letter was from Aaron in L.A. with news he had met a woman; no name, just a woman. Through infrequent correspondence over the next three years Waltz learned the woman had a name and it was Molly. In 1950 came word of marriage. But no sight of either of them, ever.

"We had hoped to get you out here before this," Waltz says to her, his words feeding into the silence. He wonders if she notices how warm it is getting as they approach Marathon. The day is clear and nearly spent.

Molly says, "Aaron always wanted to bring me. He had such nice things to say about this part of the country."

Waltz, flabbergasted, says, "You're kidding!"

"No. He was always talking about the white Christmases and the town square and the friendly people."

"Where the hell was he, then?"

She smiles patiently. "I've told you, Harry. And he *was* very busy."

When she tilts her head up to talk to him he receives soft gusts of lavender and mint. He can look down at the tiny silver hairs standing delicate guard at the entrance to her nose and the powdered, maintained slackness of her face. Her lips have been carefully painted a faint pink.

"Aaron left something for you in his will," she says. "Not money. He said you didn't need that. It was just an envelope attached to his will with a paper clip." She takes it out of her bag. It is a simple brownish envelope with Waltz's name and instructions to open it upon Aaron's death written in his brother's careful script. The envelope when Waltz takes it in his hand has a dry, papyric feel. He thinks the glue must hang on out of memory.

"Thank you," Waltz says, unsure whether he means it. He slides the envelope into his coat pocket. He is afraid of it just like he was afraid of letters from Eugene in prison. There is information in the world he has no use for and he resents people springing it on him without his permission. Dead, Aaron keeps trying to get in touch with him, while alive he didn't have the time.

Waltz puts the envelope from Aaron on his desk in the same slotted block of polished wood that held the letters from Eugene.

What message does Aaron want to convey at this late date? Their voices went out to each other all those years, usually late at night in sleeping houses, the things they said to each other nothing special. Waltz talked always in the belief Aaron's stay in L.A. was temporary. He would come home sooner or later.

The only calls of real moment, he realizes, were to report deaths: Bernard's, Monroe's, May's, Daddy Waltz's. To report and to request his presence. Maybe he was just a beacon of bad news to his brother.

Throughout the shared fixing of supper (Waltz, his daughter, this quiet fragrant stranger who has changed into a black kimono and small rustling sandals, weave among each other in the kitchen) Aaron's letter haunts him. Its smooth paper hide watches him when he sits down at his desk to work. He is pleased the river of deadbeats has evidently run dry; the payments coming in are on time, exact, and comforting. The nation's backbone, Waltz thinks with pride, are men who honor their word and pay what they owe. Now and then he picks up Aaron's letter and plays it through his fingers. He holds it up to the light and sees within the dry paper shell a darker square of folded paper. No words are clear, though. He puts it away quickly, then, before he is face to face with his fear of opening it.

Mary Hale calls with her regrets.

"You been busy all day?" he asks.

"Extremely. A very busy day. You're waking Aaron tomorrow, right?"

"Three to five. Seven to nine-thirty. They're bringing him over at noon."

"I'll try to get there at seven," she says. He hears the soft mutter of her yawn. He wants to say something but he doesn't want to get her riled, though she has no history of this. It seems to him she is holding back from coming to his house, as though knowing that once there it will be difficult to leave.

"What's his wife like?" she asks.

"Very small. Tiny. Blue eyes. Some gray in her hair. Quiet. She didn't say ten words at dinner."

"Maybe she's sad," Mary Hale suggests.

"I guess." Waltz sighs. "Come down here tonight, Mare. I miss you."

"I can't. It's not a good time."

"I could go for this Molly," he says, "if given half a chance. We already know she likes my type."

Mary Hale laughs. "Do what you like. I still can't come tonight."

"Aaron left me a letter in his will. A strange little letter."

"What did it say?"

"I'm afraid to open it."

"He's dead, Harry. How can he hurt you?"

This is such a dumb question he is nearly crushed by it; he expected so much more from her.

"Oh—" she says quickly. "I saw your son."

For an instant Waltz hopes she means Monroe, come to her in a dream, and in perfect health. But it is only Eugene, she tells him.

"How's he doing?" Waltz asks. "He have any plans?"

She says, "He's coming around."

"What does that mean? Where's he been?"

"Traveling, I gather. He suddenly appeared at my door and only stayed an hour. He was very nervous and—"

"Probably tense about some job he was getting ready to pull," Waltz says.

"Be kind," she warns. "He knew your brother was dead. He saw it in the papers. He didn't say when he was coming home. He wanted me to tell you not to worry."

"O.K. Thanks," he says without spirit.

"Harry, have a heart for the man."

"Sure." But he is doubtful; he wants Eugene home, to hear the words from him.

Molly asks Waltz about Aaron's letter the next morning at breakfast. Waltz smiles shyly and rubs his eyes. The night before, he could not sleep.

"I haven't opened it," he says.

"Oh, come now, Harry," Molly teases.

"I'm a little afraid."

"What's to be afraid of?"

"I didn't see him for years," Waltz says. "Only an occasional letter or phone call. And then from beyond the grave he suddenly has this message for me that he doesn't want me to read when he's alive. It's spooky. It could be anything."

She huffs with disappointment and drinks her coffee.

"How do you think it will go today?" he asks, to be polite.

She says firmly, "It will go fine."

"I don't know what to expect. There might be a lot of people here, or nobody."

"He's a Waltz, right? People will come out of respect for the name, for your father, for you. I'm looking forward to it."

"Jesus, I'm not."

She pats his arm. "You'll do fine."

"How do you know?" he asks eagerly.

"I can tell" is all she says, disappointing him. She stands. She is in a chocolate-brown robe with ballet slippers on her feet. He sees she will leave him alone if he doesn't snare her quickly.

"What was it about Aaron that you loved?"

She looks sharply at Waltz. Through their brief acquaintanceship he has not seen her cry, has not seen any of the mystique of grief he expected. She is only a contained woman. Something that is of no concern to him is held effortlessly within her. A mere stranger, even a twin stranger, will not draw it out.

But she gives his question thought; she even sits back down.

"He was a good, sweet man," she says. "I liked best that for all his accomplishments, for all the arrogance he occasionally exhibited in public—and he could be a perfect *snoot*—when he was with me he didn't think he was anything special. You can fake arrogance. Many people do. But you can't fake humility, not for thirty-six years."

"What accomplishments?" Waltz asks.

"Physician. Kidney specialist. A pretty good tennis player. Good golfer. Good sailor. Good chess player. Poker player. Flute and piano player. Built high-rise birdhouses. A good cook. An expert at baseball. Good in bed. Handsome. He grew handsomer by the day. He was unbearably handsome the day he died. I think it was the pain he was in that gave a special lining to his face. It made him irresistible."

Waltz says, in a hushed way, "He did all those things?"

"Yes. Aaron never wasted time. A quality I hated only because it made me feel guilty."

"Why did he hate Daddy?"

She holds her hands out wide. "It was diffuse, Harry. Like a cloud of gas. He didn't say: 'Well, Daddy beat me.' Or 'Daddy beat Mommy.' It was just there. It's in the blood. The blood of sons. It's the father's lot."

"I don't buy that," Waltz says.

"That was another thing. He said you were more a twin to your father than to him. He said that was why you were the favorite. You were the mirror."

"Did he hate me, too?"

"Harry, I'm tired. He never said he did." She stands again, smooths the robe down her thighs. She is getting away again.

"What about our mother?" he asks.

"What about her?"

"Did he hate her, too?"

"No. Well, only in her ties to your father. A mother, when she's married to a man her son hates, ceases to exist in the eyes of the son. It's not a question of not loving. The love is so natural it's unquestioned. It's there and it doesn't require a lot of thought or analysis. But hate—well, hate has to be turned over in the mind and picked apart and built back up and . . . embellished. You see?"

"No," says Waltz.

"Don't worry about it. You can't change the way he was."

"Did he—" he begins to ask; she had turned away from him, but now she turns back. "Did he ever speak to you about a secret ambition?"

"If he talked to me about it, how could it be a secret?"

"I mean, something that was above everything else he wanted to accomplish?"

She thinks a minute. "Nothing comes to mind."

"He never said he wanted to live to a hundred?"

"Like your father?"

"Yes. He never said that?"

"I don't remember him ever saying that," she says.

"I just wondered," Waltz says, and lets her go.

He stacks the breakfast dishes in a quick, clattering motion. A sticky fork pinwheels off a plate and he grabs at it in midair, and misses.

Two hours remain before the arrival of Aaron, Waltz plans to fill the time with sleep. A long day of grim ceremony stretches ahead of him and seems impassable without rest beforehand.

But the morning light in his room is fresh and prodding and spills in through the drapes and still he can't sleep. Without any sort of conscious decision (it is like going to visit Eugene in prison used to be, an inexplicable momentum he does not question) he gets out of bed and scurries naked to his desk for Aaron's letter. He takes it back to bed with him.

The envelope comes open easily and the crisp sheet of paper unfolds. All this has a smoothness he finds amazing. He feels the perfect time for unsealing his brother's secret has arrived and he is merely passing into it.

The note is dated (he is further amazed) at the top of the page: October 18, 1970.

> You're reading this, Harry, so I have died before you, you lucky stiff. I plan to remove this from my will should you die before me. From the date above you can see that you are fifty years old today; I turned yesterday. It is just after midnight now. Happy birthday! What are you thinking on this day? I bet I know: Halfway there. You more than any of us always seemed to think a race was on.
>
> Bernard is dead. And because you are reading this, I am, too. So now it's you alone in the field. You've had twins and now you will live to a hundred.
>
> Congratulations, bitterly. Because you are going to live to a hundred and I'm dead at the unsatisfying age of ____ (fill in, please), I am going to take out my disappointment on you. My last request will be to be brought back to Marathon to be buried.
>
> Aren't I a pain in the ass?
>
> Also, I do this to at long last bring you out into society. I will force this on you. My one recurring image of you is as an

awkward boy standing off to the side with money in your pockets. I don't recall you talking to anyone unless it was to arrange a loan.

I know you will do your best despite what you think of me or my request. In the time I lived with you I was always amazed at the evident effort you put into everything. I searched for that quality in myself (being twins, I thought it must be in me somewhere) but never found it. Nothing ever came easy for you, Harry. That's why Daddy loved you. And nothing ever came hard for me.

Say hello to Daddy. The late, great Aaron.

And in a different hand, a different ink and pen point altogether, this was added at the bottom:

So strange to read this after all this time. I will let it stand. You called today and told Molly that Daddy was dead. He made it, though. I knew the momentousness of this day and was waiting. He made it just like he knew he would. More than ever you have the clear field and the inside track. You sounded good on the phone; angry with me. I can understand that. Can you understand me? I don't care.

This trick I mean to play on you has made me sad. I should never have opened this letter again. It's like teasing a man you'd be wiser not to.

Why don't you die so I can destroy it?

A.

Waltz runs a hand along the cool bronze shell of Aaron's coffin. It arrived while he was asleep; Molly signed for it and directed its placement. Now she sits in a chair against the wall. In a black suit with a blouse of white like froth at her throat, she seems more businesslike than grieving. He thinks her eyes drill into his back as he moves down the coffin toward where Aaron's head lies. He glances at his brother like a man testing a hot stove, ready to jump away.

Finally, he looks full at him and lets his eyes rest on him. The combed white hair, the artificial sunned color of the skin, the loose vertical thrust of the jaw, they are elements of another man. He looks closer; he wants to see the eyes, hidden now behind dusty-looking lids, for he thinks they will hold the answers.

But, no. Minutes pass and Waltz looks carefully and there is no question it is Aaron there after all this time. Waltz does not cry. The other man he at first thought Aaron might be was himself.

Waltz takes a seat beside Molly. The wall is cool. He wants to light a cigarette but supposes that if he is to make it to a hundred he should think about quitting.

"What was in the note?" Molly asks.

"A practical joke," Waltz says evasively, but only because he does not want to go into what it really means to him.

"That's all?"

"He said it was a trick."

Shy debtors approach Waltz in the cool shadows of the house to press envelopes of cash into his hand. It is seven-thirty and the town of Marathon has seized Aaron's wake as license to visit Harry Waltz's house. The lamps burn and the curtains billow gently in and out, pushed by the breezes of this false spring. Waltz expects baseball games to come out of the radio. The front door remains open.

Attendance from three to five was sparse. Sam Boggins came early and stayed until the end and seemed amazed anyone else came at all. At the end of the first shift the guest book provided by the funeral home contained seven names.

Sam Boggins signed the book on his way out; he was the last to leave. Waltz walked with him halfway to the square.

"You coming back tonight?" he asks.

"You think I should?"

"You're welcome."

"Why did he come back here to be buried?"

"To bug me," says Waltz. He took the letter from his pocket for Sam to read.

"He's mad because he didn't live to a hundred?"

"Basically, yes. I love the whole idea of it, though," Waltz says. "In 1970 he planted this note like a little time bomb and then he was patient enough to just let it tick. Knowing he'd never see it explode. He had the right frame of mind to live to a hundred. And now that he's not, I just know I will."

"O.K., Harry," says Sam Boggins without skepticism, which Waltz appreciated.

"Come back tonight. Bring Melody. Have a drink with us. You may be alone or you may have to fight the crowds. O.K.?"

"O.K."

"We'll make it a night," Waltz promises.

People begin arriving at the stroke of seven. Waltz has created a bar in the kitchen of cold beer in a steel tub, bottles of cheap liquor, plastic glasses, water the only mixer.

He is busy pouring drinks at eight o'clock, when he looks up (a cold diamond of ice melting in one cheek) there is Mary Hale. She wears a loose black dress and a loop of pearls.

"You came," he says.

"Did you think I wouldn't?"

"I haven't seen you in so long."

She smiles and kisses the cool bulge in his face. Her eyes have been faintly lined with eye shadow, a circled, sore redness. She yawns when he kisses her. Waltz puts his hand on her belly, as though searching her for weapons, and there is a hard mound growing under the black cloth.

"Day by day I'm becoming more misshapen," she says in a tired, resigned voice. "I can't sleep. Then I sleep for fourteen hours at a stretch. I've gained eleven pounds."

"That's great," Waltz says.

She orders a beer and he pours it for her. His mind has settled, having her there. He need not worry about a number of things for the duration of her presence.

"Nice party," she says.

"Does this seem like a party?"

"Strange but true," she says.

He takes Aaron's note from his shirt pocket. All day he has waited to show it to Mary Hale. The envelope has a damp backing to it where it has pressed against his chest; it is warm in this winter pause and he is perspiring.

"This was my brother's message to me," he says, unfolding the lank paper.

She reads it quickly. "Very sweet," she proclaims, handing it back. "Very sly. Very sad."

"Don't you just love the idea of it?" he asks, wanting so badly for her to get it.

"Of you living to a hundred?"

"That . . . but of Aaron setting that note there for me so long ago."

"You called it," she says. "A voice from the grave." She takes a long swallow of her beer and this annoys Waltz; it feels dismissive. He is alone in his appreciation of Aaron's gesture.

Flowers keep arriving, tall sprays wrapped in green and silver foil like slim women in elegant gowns. The deliverymen put them where room permits, then steal through the house to the kitchen for a beer before exiting.

The rumor that the Aaron Waltz wake is not a bad party drifts down through Marathon; Waltz imagines people rousing themselves, throwing on a tie or a decent dress, and getting up the hill. He wishes he had more beer.

It has become an easy party to get lost in. Waltz is its conscience. If people can stay clear of him there is a chance they can have some fun. There is no hint of grief anywhere but around him. Men and women laugh and drink for free until they move into the small column of space he occupies. Then their eyes turn solemn and their voices speak platitudes of sorrow; he has long since stopped listening. He nods and accepts their handshakes or quick, moist kisses on the cheek. He is eager to free them back into the swirl of gaiety he encourages. Everywhere there are hiding places. He floats like a pig in a river. He is an island of implied grief, he fears that as the night wears on his guests will begin to resent him, the way he appears and reminds them of why they are there. So he travels with his vision lifted an inch above everyone else, where no one can catch his eye. Everyone seems to appreciate this.

Sam Boggins has come back. His wife, Melody, is with him. She is a tiny woman, smaller than Molly. Bones like twigs, he imagines, even the big ones, the femur and the tibia. The rapt expression on her face when he spied her making love to her husband in the back of his shop stayed with him; succeeding smiles and frowns can't push it away, it is something of hers he can hold untouched. She kisses Waltz quickly on the cheek. He remembers her in high school, a year older than they, the way she ran and laughed in the halls following the final bell, pursued inexorably by Sam Boggins.

Sam holds a glass of whiskey. He has to shout, "What happened here, Harry?"

"It's a wake," Waltz says, shrugging, even laughing. "It's better than I ever thought possible."

Melody frowns, she disapproves. She says something Waltz can't make out, but he doesn't ask her to repeat it. His greatest fear is that at nine-thirty all these people will feel the hour of termination and leave. He does not want this party to end.

Mary Hale touches his arm. "Eugene is here," she says. "Don't give him a hard time."

He excuses himself from Sam and Melody, but Melody is persistent about some point. She pulls Waltz's ear down close to her warm mouth and speaks clearly, the words coated in clean spray, "Did you hear about the new couple moving into town?"

He straightens and shakes his head. He feels uncomfortable up close to this woman. He is friends with her husband; he sees her in only a single light.

"What couple?" he asks Sam.

"A retarded couple," Melody says, glancing at her husband for corroboration. "The state is renting an apartment for them right downtown. On the square."

Sam says, "They both have jobs with GM."

"Husband and wife," Melody says. "They're both only marginally retarded, evidently, able to hold jobs, take care of themselves. Someone from the state will stay with them, but on the whole they will be on their own."

"Well, great," Waltz says.

"I don't know that it's so great," Melody says. "What if they reproduce? Who takes the responsibility for that? And if they need someone to stay with them, that's just admitting they aren't quite able to live like normal people."

He can't answer this. His impulse is to encourage the couple to go at it, rut unprotected and produce a gooby or two. He thinks of this mating in selfish and statistical terms; that their retarded offspring might reduce the chance of Waltz's child turning out the same way.

Willy and Susan arrive, holding a blue-hooded bundle that emits a serene silence in the center of all the smoke and outlandish good times. Willy has cut his hair, it gives his face a swollen look. He is paler, Waltz thinks, plumper around the jaw, his eyes a little baffled.

Waltz looks for Carla to protect her, but she is out of sight somewhere.

Susan kisses her father and delivers the baby into his arms. "This is Harry Willis," she announces proudly.

He looks under the hood, in at a wry, gremlin face, asleep. "He's a doll," Waltz says. Susan's face breaks into a smile. Did she think he would not like his grandson? Exhaustion sits in her eyes. Her face has thinned between the twin sheaves of dark gold hair. She looks taller and less healthy.

Later he is cornered by Willy in a dark nook of the kitchen. Willy has the grave nervous air of a man about to ask for a daughter's hand.

"I've got this for you," he tells Waltz. He holds out five twenties, fanned like cards. "I was going to write you a check but I thought maybe you'd question its mettle. It's just a start, I know. But I want you to know the intent is there."

Waltz takes the money and folds it out of sight.

"Thank you, Willy," he says softly. He clears his throat, sips his beer. He wants to get these next words exactly right. He puts a hand on Willy's shoulder and draws him close. Willy's eyes turn warm and yielding; he expects good news, an exchange of affection, perhaps the good-hearted cancellation of his debt.

"You stay away from Carla," Waltz warns, his voice husky with anger. "You keep your hands off her and every other woman except your wife. If you don't, I'll come talk to you again. From now on, you're just another customer. I want the money on time every month—a hundred, fifty, five hundred—whatever you can afford. But something. You pay me five thousand and we'll be even. There is no better deal in the universe.

"You touch Carla," he repeats, "or anyone else, you asshole, and I'll kill you."

He spins away, leaving Willy looking shot. He hurries through the thinning knots of people; it is near the time of dispersal. His hands shake and his heart sings with what he has just done.

Eugene has entered the house, people keep telling Waltz. Carla whispers this in his ear. Minutes pass and Susan tells him the same thing. He rewards each with a kiss.

Still, he does not see his son. There are forty pounds of fresh ice in sweating bags and a case of beer in the kitchen, but no sign of Eugene. He may be moving a room ahead of his father as he searches.

Mary Hale stops Waltz in the kitchen. "Eugene is here," she says again.

"I've heard that rumor," Waltz says.

"He went out to his car."

"That's my car. He's probably still wearing my clothes. Spending my money."

"Hush," she says, looking over Waltz's shoulder at the door, "Here he comes." She leaves the kitchen, turning when only Waltz can see her in the doorway to blow a kiss.

Eugene has grown a sparse flanking of beard while on the run, it has come in nearly golden, for some reason he reminds his father of Carla.

"Hello, Daddy," he says. "I'm sorry about Uncle Aaron. I don't have a feel for the guy, but I'm sorry all the same."

"He sent me this," Waltz says, handing the letter over. "It was attached to his will."

Eugene reads it. "Nice," he says, handing it back. He looks nervously around. "You really want to live to a hundred?"

"You bet," Waltz says. "It's a cinch now."

"Why?"

"I'm all that's left."

"That doesn't mean anything."

"You'll live to a hundred, too," Waltz maintains, saying this with conviction because he thinks it will irritate his only son. "You'll jump at the chance, too."

Eugene puts ice in a cup and pours whiskey over it. Waltz tells him, amazed, "I'll have another kid your age before I reach a hundred, too."

"Maybe that kid will live to a hundred," Eugene says. "Maybe it won't be me at all."

"No." Waltz takes Eugene's arms, grasping the biceps, pinching in a judging way. "You're strong and good. You have the feel for the long haul."

Eugene pulls away, embarrassed. "That's such bullshit," he says scornfully.

"No, no." Waltz blinks. He feels emotion open up within him, a space enlarging that his son will fit within. "Monroe was a good boy but I always sensed a frailty in him. I can recognize that now. Back then, it was just one more thing to be afraid of. You, though, you've got that stony heart your granddaddy had. I've got it, too." He blinks, winks, taps his son's chest. "That's what you've got to have to make it all the way through."

Eugene nods stiffly, looks for escape. Waltz understands it is something his son will have to grow into. Eugene was always in trouble; Monroe always had a head full of music. Is it any wonder, Waltz longs to ask, that he had a favorite?"

"2045," Eugene says, half to himself.

"That's the year to shoot for. It's not so far away. Your granddaddy played center field at the age of ninety-seven. Don't think it can't be done. He was on his feet at the turn of his century."

"I'll remember that," Eugene says.

Waltz gets himself another beer, to pass time, to signify he is prepared to move on to something else.

"You learn anything while you were gone?" he asks.

"No. Didn't expect to."

"That's why you didn't, then," Waltz says. He feels his anger at this waste rise suddenly in him. He has long wanted a sabbatical to roam and watch and question. He is tethered by debt as much as those who owe him. Here his son has returned from just such a journey and professed to have learned nothing.

"Are you home to stay now?" he asks.

"This isn't my home, Daddy," Eugene says. "It would be easier if I stayed somewhere else."

"Easy?" cries Waltz. "You want ease? You want leisure? I thought you'd want to get out and *go* after being in prison."

"No," he says carefully. "I want to stay at rest, but know that I'm free to go. That's what I want to savor. I thought it was motion I wanted, at first. But actually it's motionlessness, with the option of motion. Do you see?"

Waltz says, "I guess."

Eugene says, after a moment, "Mary loves you."

"Does she?"

"Oh yes. I remember Mom, and she was fine. But I don't remember having the feeling she loved you like Mary loves you."

"Your mother loved me," Waltz says, feeling Louise in the room, protecting her still.

"I know," Eugene says. "But I was a kid. What did I know then? I was watching out for myself. You know—you'll hate me for this—when Mary started visiting me in prison and working to get me out, I had the idea she was coming on to me. I pictured me getting out and right away slipping it into her. Now I know better. Nothing in her in the way of sparks for any man but you, Daddy. What is it about you? I see all these qualities in you through her. It makes me wonder what you're holding back from me. What I'm holding back from you."

"I don't know," Waltz says. "Who can talk to their father?"

Eugene says, "Nobody. I'm convinced."

"Yeah," Waltz says, though he only agrees for Eugene's sake; he could always talk to Daddy Waltz, he was the one to stay in Marathon, he became all his father had. Eugene and Aaron would have gotten along, each ill at ease in their father's shadow.

"Where will you stay, then?" Waltz asks.

Eugene looks at the floor. "I've got a place in Flint," he says.

"You said you'd stay away from Flint."

"I know I did, Daddy. But it's where I feel most at home."

"What about the terms of your release?"

"Will you send me back?" he asks, his eyes flaring.

"You can't live in Flint, Eugene," Waltz says. "They don't like you there. You'll get hurt."

Eugene smiles and puts a hand on his father's shoulder. "Come with me," he says softly. "There's somebody out in the car I want you to see."

"He's been out there all this time?"

"Believe me," Eugene says, "he'll wait."

The strange warm air enfolds them when they step outside. Eugene leads Waltz down the driveway, then he stops and turns to face his father. There is money in his hand.

"Before . . ." Eugene begins. "I want to explain something, Daddy. You remember when I was a kid, that night you found the gooby caught in the fence?" Waltz nods. "And I had loaned some money to a guy who said he wouldn't pay me back?"

"Yes," Waltz says.

"His name was Lou Basil and he did pay me back," Eugene says. "It took a while, but he paid me back. You know why he paid me back?"

Waltz shakes his head.

"Because I beat him up," Eugene says. "I went to his house the next day and waited for him to come out and when he came out I punched him in the face three times. Then and only then did he pay me the money he owed." His eyes fill with quick tears that he touches, daring them to roll free. "That was the beginning," Eugene says.

"You should have talked to him," Waltz says.

"There are some people you can't talk sense to, Daddy. It was my misfortune to meet such a person early in my career."

Eugene takes the money and folds it and puts it in his father's shirt pocket.

Then they walk on down a line of cars. At the end of the line is the car Waltz loaned Eugene. Someone is in the front seat.

"There's a hundred and fifty dollars there," Eugene says to his father.

Waltz asks, "What did you do?"

"I did what you should've done when these guys started to fuck you over," Eugene says. Paul Rivers is in the front seat of the car. He sits with his head tipped back to keep blood from his nose from running free onto his shirt, already darkly spotted. His right eye is swollen shut; in the shadows it reminds Waltz of a plum.

"Tell him, Rivers," Eugene snaps.

"You won't have any more problems with me," the man says weakly, speaking to the car's ceiling. "I'll pay on time from now on."

He touches his eye with a rag. He moves it down to his nose, then to a smudge of bruise at the corner of his mouth. Waltz takes the money Eugene has given him and reaches in through the window to put the money in Paul Rivers' shirt pocket. Blood comes off on Waltz's fingers.

"We're finished, Mr. Rivers," Waltz says in a low voice. "You belong to Paul Vermillion now. I had nothing to do with you getting beaten. I'm sorry it had to happen, but I never want to see you again."

"I can pay," the man cries. "I'll never be late again."

Waltz straightens up. His bad leg gives him a shot of pain. His son leans against the car, smoking. His eyes hold a miserable, sad light.

"It's time for you to go away now, Eugene," Waltz says.

"They're making a fool out of you, Daddy. You should hear how they talk about you in Flint. They say you're too old, a touch. That's why I did it. I couldn't let them talk about you like that."

Waltz says evenly, "Those men who went with Paul Vermillion are aberrations, Eugene. I'm glad to be rid of them. Maybe you can get a job with him."

"Daddy . . . they'll ruin you!"

"Go on, Eugene," Waltz says patiently. "Go back to Flint."

21

An accord is reached and Waltz begins, little by little, to move north to the house on Saginaw Bay. The house in Marathon makes him too sad. Too many people have died there, too many moved away. Following Molly's departure for California three days after Aaron's funeral, Waltz never spends another night in the house. He gratefully sleeps at Mary Hale's side and drives to Marathon in the afternoon to pick up his mail. Each return trip, he fills the car with his clothes, books, foods that will spoil, a favorite lamp or clock, though these are few. He has loved the people of the house, but the house's inventory otherwise has barely touched him.

Mary Hale clears a room for him and says it can be his office. It is off their bedroom, with a window overlooking the bay.

"I'll have to tell my clients where I am," he says.

"That would be a good idea," she says. Her belly grows, seemingly expanding perceptibly day by day. She spends the evening hours massaging it with her hands, sometimes smearing a cream that smells of bananas over it, to prevent stretch marks. Something within her flutters, or she claims it does; but when Waltz drops his ear to her to listen, nothing stirs, as though they know he is spying.

They invite Susan and Willy to dinner, but only Susan and the baby come. She has an excuse ready for her husband. Harry Willis cries throughout the evening and soon Waltz's daughter repacks her arsenal of equipment and departs. The night brings Waltz close to tears. He regrets having put Willy at that distance hostility creates. He is thinning the ranks of people he can love, or learn to love.

But he doesn't regret it enough to bring Willy back into the fold he perceives himself the head of. Willy has become merely a debtor in Waltz's mind; another string to tend.

Willy must not have told Susan about her father's ultimatum. Of course, how could he? She viewed her husband's absence at the meal as strictly Willy's problem, with no rancor toward Waltz deeper than a vague irritation at owing him money. She brought good news when she came: Willy's teaching contract would be extended another year, and this fragment of security brought color and life for a minute to her drawn, tired face; a beautiful face made nearly plain by the demands of a cranky baby. Waltz helped her cart her supplies out to the car. Mary Hale wrestled with the squawling, squirming Harry Willis, and Waltz loved the sight—the way she seemed expert at turning him and changing his position and warding off the mindless thrashing of his legs, as if he were a volatile chemical that must constantly be moved or risk explosion.

Susan regarded her ornery son a moment, her eyes deep, tired spots of sadness.

"He's a better baby than he's shown tonight," she told her father.

"I know he is, honey. Maybe he's catching a cold. Maybe he misses his daddy."

"Maybe," she said. She shook her keys like a cheerleader's pompon.

"Has Willy started paying you your money?" she asked.

Waltz cupped her shoulders. She felt all bone, the bones sagging with an exhaustion she saw no end to. "Yes, he has. And don't you give it another thought. Everything will be fine."

He wanted to tell her to let Willy worry about it, but she would only take it on herself; she would fear her husband folding under the weight. Waltz kissed her goodbye, then helped get Harry Willis into his car seat. The baby boy, in a blind expression of rage, lashed out with a small fist and hit Waltz with surprising force in the eye. Jerking his head with its poked eye clear, Waltz cracked his head on the doorframe and he laughed at the image of the son already doing what the father should have done: tell Waltz to mind his own business.

Carla comes to dinner on her own. She, too, looks tired. But it is a different sort of fatigue from her twin sister's. They barely look alike sometimes. His family is getting old, running down on him. Only Waltz feels ready to go.

Carla is intrigued by the empty house in Marathon. She tells her father she wants to get out of Ann Arbor, she is tired of living in an apartment, she will move back home.

Waltz immediately accepts her offer. "It would be nice to have a Waltz in there," he tells the women. "I think Marathonites expect it."

The rest of the evening turns on this idea. Carla plans the move, where she will put her books, where the best light for plants falls, whether she should get a dog. Waltz wonders if she will take her old room back, or become head of the household. It is a big house for one woman; it was too big for him. He is glad to be free of all that emptiness. He hasn't the heart or the gall to ask Carla why she is still alone so late in her life.

Waltz has a telephone installed in his office overlooking the bay. The man who puts it in is full of loud, empty chatter and Waltz fears for Mary Hale asleep in their bedroom. The phone man, despite a good job, still spews gloomy words about the state's economy that Waltz longs to grab as they emerge from his mouth and shove back where they came from. He is a young man with a mustache like misplaced food. He makes a call to a test number on Waltz's new phone, and everything evidently works, because he speaks for several minutes to someone, running up Waltz's tab.

Waltz sees something good in the fact that his new number is the same forward and backward.

When the phone man leaves, Waltz watches through his office doorway as Mary Hale sleeps, then awakens, then dresses. She sleeps a great deal now. Her face has taken on weight. Her back and legs are constantly tired. She says she hates the way she looks, but Waltz has surprised her smiling at herself in the mirror. When she is newly awake she sits a minute or two on the edge of the bed calmly stroking her rounded abdomen. Something may have wrinkled in the hours of her sleep, something that desperately needs smoothing. Her head is tipped forward and her eyes are closed while she does this. Her lips move; she might be singing. Waltz thinks she knows he is watching. When they sleep Waltz fits himself against her back, one hand draped around and across the globular weight she carries. Her navel is pushed out like an acorn. The rooted exhaustion she sees in Susan's eyes, and the implacable tyranny of Harry Willis, seem to be nothing more to her than inevitabilities she has decided she can live with.

Waltz calls the people he has on the string. His new phone works perfectly; it always reminds him of gates opening all down the line. His customers are almost universally nervous to hear from him. He is bad news to all but a handful of friends and relatives. The ravaging by Paul Vermillion of his list of clients has not taken place. He has lost a few, but gained more, and this warms his heart so much he sometimes can't sleep.

He had told Mary Hale of the time with Eugene in the driveway of his house; of the beaten man; of the blood that came away on Waltz's fingers. She had made no judgment. She went to Flint once on business and upon returning said she had spoken to Eugene.

As when his son was in prison, Waltz still felt the need to know how he was doing.

"He said you had exiled him to Flint," she said. She sat soaking her feet in hot water, rubbing her belly with a cream that smelled of coconuts. "He seems to think you will someday call him back."

"That might happen," Waltz said, though he knew it never

would. Doubted it, anyway. His son was free to go, the exile all in his mind.

He gives his customers his new address and phone number. Some he has to remind to write the information down. No one remarks on the palindromic phone number.

Days later, right on schedule, envelopes full of cash begin arriving at his new home.

Carla moves into the Marathon house. On her days off she cleans the large rooms, shampoos rugs, throws open windows to let in air where none seems ever to have existed. It is April, and very warm. The daily drive to work in Ann Arbor doesn't seem to bother her. She talks about a summer lawn party centered on the gazebo.

Waltz comes down on a Saturday and she is on the phone with somebody. She shoos him from the room with a wave of her fingers. He goes out to the garage and starts up the lawn mower. It has a rattle deep in its heart he thinks is new. But the blade is sharp and cuts the first high grass of summer cleanly. He pushes this machine around his property, close along the stone wall in front, in between the repossessed cars, around the gazebo's octagon walls, next to the high State Home fence along the back property line. He does a passable job; he likes the smooth burr look the mower leaves in his wake; he likes the smell of the cut grass and the mower's gas.

Later he helps Carla rearrange furniture. She has taken down drapes, or moved bulky items of furniture, and in so doing allowed light into rooms he remembers as always being dark. She has made it into a new house. She has taken her old room, but removed her and Susan's twin beds and moved her double bed in. The twin beds she has broken down and stored in the attic. He wonders who helped her with all this lifting. She fixes him supper and sends him home, where Mary Hale, round and growing, awaits him.

On another day Waltz is in Marathon to pay a surprise visit to Carla, and stops first at Sam Boggins' shop. The front door is locked. Waltz knocks in back; Sam will see his old friend through the fish-eye peephole and welcome him. A smell of lanolin, tobacco, and dust blows in Waltz's face when the door is opened. Sam Boggins holds a broom, leans on it.

"Melody's waiting, Harry. I'm sorry."

"Can't you tell her you'll be a minute late? I haven't talked to you since Aaron died."

"You moved away," Sam Boggins says, almost reproachfully. He moves to let Waltz in.

"Yes," Waltz says. "That house is too full of sadness for me."

"You're living north of here?"

"On Saginaw Bay. Mare's house. I'm still in business."

"I'd heard that, Harry. That's good." He puts the broom away. "How's Mary doing?"

"She's fine. She'll be a wonderful mother."

Sam Boggins says, "Now Carla's in your house."

"It's nice to know she's there," Waltz says. "What would Marathon do without a Waltz?"

"It would do without," Sam Boggins says flatly.

The binoculars are on the shelf and he finds his house with them. The western windows have caught the sun, setting the house afire. A movement just out of the field of vision catches his eye. Waltz swings the glasses to see. It is a car pulling into his driveway, and for an instant he feels that burn in his heart he had when he followed Eugene that night long ago. He can set the glasses down and never know. But he can't do that, and watches Willy get out of the car. A golden-haired woman comes out of the house to meet him. There is a happy spring in her step, a smile on her face, she runs down the yard and kisses Willy hard on the mouth.

Only then does he drop the binoculars back on the shelf. Must he live a hundred years before he will learn? He guesses the woman was Carla, but he will never know for sure. Twins run in his family.

• • •

Waltz returns home and Mary Hale is there in his office. She is in her eighth month and hugely round. He tells her of seeing Willy at his old house, of his threats to Willy at the wake, of his doubts.

"It probably was Carla," Mary Hale says.

"But after everything I told him, he still goes back to her!"

"He knows you won't kill him."

"How does he know that?"

She laughs faintly. Her head is against his chest. "You can't dictate, Harry. They're big boys and girls now. He owes you money. That's all." She touches his face. "Harry, listen. I went to see my OB today. He told me to expect a caesarean."

"Why?" he asks, frightened by the word.

"The baby's large," he says. "And the opening is small. He doesn't think my pelvic structure will accommodate a baby this size."

Waltz nods and swallows. The bay through the window is gray-blue, still winter there, although it is nearly hot, and Mary Hale's face and arms are wet with perspiration. She goes to get a glass of water in the kitchen and Waltz follows.

"You can be there," she tells him. "The hospital will let the father in to view the C-section if you take a class. It's just one night. Ninety minutes. There's a film."

Waltz laughs. "You don't have to sell me. I'll take the class."

She drops her head to his chest again. Even talking makes her tired. "I know you will," she says. "Something else . . ."

"What?"

"I'm ready to get married, if you are."

"Are you sure?"

"I think it's the perfect time," she says, watching him closely. "It's the next step. I don't want this baby to be illegitimate even for a minute." She returns her face to his chest. "I love you, Harry. I love you for bringing me along like you have. For giving us this baby. This baby means the world to me, Harry. I love you for that. And I love you for letting me get to this point on my own terms. Now I want to go from here together."

• • •

They are married on the beach, down from the house by the lifeguard tower. It is a warm evening and children dance shrieking in and out of the bay's cold water; their parents sit on blankets and keep one eye on the kids, one eye on the odd ceremony unfolding before them. A tall old man in a new suit with his pregnant bride, no child herself, seemingly on the brink of delivery. Two white-haired figures in the dusk. Carla is there, and so is Susan and Willy and Harry Willis, and Sam and Melody Boggins, and even Mary Hale's brother, the man who brought Waltz and Mary Hale together; he uses the occasion to pay Mary Waltz part of what he owes.

While they wait for the minister to park his Volvo and clamber in beach thongs and summer suit down through the sand to where they all stand, Waltz works off nervous energy throwing stones into the bay. He considers saying something to Willy, but will not ruin the day. He considers simply peppering him with stones. His arm feels strong and true; he guesses he would need only a few throws to do the job. But Willy isn't in the mess alone. Carla welcomes him; it might have been her only reason for moving to Marathon.

The guard chair is empty when the ceremony begins. The beach is closed. Swimming is at one's own risk. But the chair's tall, derrick shadow falls on the sand; this cheers Waltz, reminds him of that long climb up there with Mary Hale, and how he flew coming back down.

He puts a ring on Mary Hale's finger when instructed to do so. This is witnessed by bathers, his family, friends, a debtor. Mary Hale folds her hands peacefully atop her belly, waiting to be kissed.

He is a spy again. Maybe for the last time. Maybe not. Soon he will have a new child to watch over, protect, and enlighten.

Waltz sits on a four-legged stool at Mary Hale's head. Her line of sight is blocked by a cloth barrier. Her white hair is bound within a blue paper cap. She looks younger, tired. Waltz can see over the barrier to the mound of her belly made reddish yellow with antiseptic solution. It is a taut hill framed in sterile cloth, and her obstetrician makes a long horizontal cut in it four and one-half inches below her navel. Waltz follows this procedure in a mirror suspended at an angle from the ceiling at the foot of the table. A line of blood follows behind the blade, and a second surgeon dabs at this blood with a cloth. They proceed down through Mary Hale without drama or violence, through skin and muscle and yellow bulbs of fat. The process reminds Waltz of a package being opened, each layer of wrapping is carefully set aside for later use. The doctors make small talk with the two nurses, flirting; one even whistles. They ignore Waltz, who feels hidden and safe in a mask and cap and gown, even boots on his shoes, everything made of paper spun like cotton. He is older by far than anyone else in the room; almost twice as old as the doctors, he judges. If they were his age they would be thinking about retiring, where he is just starting all over again.

In the mirror he thinks he sees the slick dark hair of the baby pushing through the opening in Mary Hale. But it is the wall of the placenta; it is the winter color of the bay's water, with a fine random network of threads of blood stitched in it. A cut seemingly no more than a shaving nick is made in this sac and the amniotic fluid gushes out. There is so much of it, Waltz nearly shouts. The pace of the event quickens; danger and the need to hurry have come into the room. The fluid, smelling of the sea, splashes over the edge of the table and onto the operating room floor. An instrument is produced to pry open the hole in Mary Hale's belly. The doctors work with deliberate speed. Waltz thinks he hears someone cry.

He looks at Mary Hale. Her eyes are closed but she is smiling. What does she sense of the events taking place below her heart? His grip on her hand has turned her fingers blue.

"Something's in there," the OB says. Mary Hale's eyes open. The doctor finds time to wink at Waltz. "We're in the right place today. This is a big baby. Normal delivery wouldn't have worked." Waltz has the impression he is trying to sell the procedure, when Waltz was long ago sold.

As Waltz watches, a tiny slick head appears in the opening in Mary Hale's belly. It is purple and outraged, with a pucker of distaste on its lips. A nurse reaches through the tangle of arms and hands with a bulb syringe to clear the baby's mouth.

Instantly, Waltz knows the baby is a girl. There is already a feminine attitude to the face, the delicate mouth and lilac eyelids, and an undercoating of shy beauty. Then the rest of the baby emerges and Waltz's first knowledge is confirmed.

"It's a girl," he says to Mary Hale. "She's a beauty," he adds.

Then he almost asks if they are sure there isn't another child still inside.

MORE ABOUT PENGUINS, PELICANS AND PUFFINS

For further information about books available from Penguins please write to Dept EP, Penguin Books Ltd, Harmondsworth, Middlesex UB7 ODA.

In the U.S.A.: For a complete list of books available from Penguins in the United States write to Dept DG, Penguin Books, 299 Murray Hill Parkway, East Rutherford, New Jersey 07073.

In Canada: For a complete list of books available from Penguins in Canada write to Penguin Books Canada Ltd, 2801 John Street, Markham, Ontario L3R 1B4.

In Australia: For a complete list of books available from Penguins in Australia write to the Marketing Department, Penguin Books Australia Ltd, P.O. Box 257, Ringwood, Victoria 3134.

In New Zealand: For a complete list of books available from Penguins in New Zealand write to the Marketing Department, Penguin Books (N.Z.) Ltd, Private Bag, Takapuna, Auckland 9.

In India: For a complete list of books available from Penguins in India write to Penguin Overseas Ltd, 706 Eros Apartments, 56 Nehru Place, New Delhi 110019.

SMALL WORLD

David Lodge

Philip Swallow, Morris Zapp, Persse McGarrigle, the lovely Angelica – all these jet-propelled academics are on the move, in the air, on the make in *Small World* . . .

'Academic infightings, couplings touching, funny and frightful, set pieces, dark humour, sharp wit and plain farce – here is everything one expects from this author but thricefold and three times as entertaining as anything he has written before' – *Sunday Telegraph*

'A wonderful tissue of outrageous coincidences and correspondences, teasing elevations of suspense and delayed climaxes' – Anthony Thwaite in the *Observer*

'Ingenious and proliferate plotting . . . a new comic débàcle over every page' – *The Times*

LEGS

William Kennedy

Legs inaugurated William Kennedy's brilliant cycle of novels (including *Billy Phelan's Greatest Game* and *Ironweed*) set in Albany, New York. True to both life and myth, *Legs* brilliantly evokes the flamboyant career of the legendary gangster Jack 'Legs' Diamond, who was finally murdered in Albany. Through the equivocal eyes of Diamond's attorney, Marcus Gorman (who scraps a promising political career for the more elemental excitement of the criminal underworld), we watch as Legs and his showgirl mistress, Kiki Roberts, blaze their gaudy trail across the tabloid pages of the 1920s and 1930s. Diamond and his gangster entourage emerge as emblematic figures from an era of American innocence – and corruption.

'Pure literary excitement . . . easy to read and hard to put down. I enjoyed it from the beginning to the end and wished it were longer' – Joseph Heller

STICK

Elmore Leonard

Stick was at a temporary low point. As an ex-con he wasn't exactly supplied with life's little bonbons. He reckoned that if intelligence and all the rest of the straightarrow stuff didn't put him on the fast track, he could always fall back on the bullshit.

Stick decides to drop in on Florida's Gold Coast, a nasty, glitzy, gold-plated world of dirty deals and easy death . . . and finds the perfect scam. The target is a big, monied, junked-up wheeler-dealer. The scenario is perfected by a sweetly bodied blonde, expert on men and money. The prize is seventy-two thousand perfectly rounded dollars.

'A cracking thriller' – *Observer*

'Irresistible' – *The New York Times Book Review*

'Compulsive' – *Sunday Times*

ANGELS

Denis Johnson

Jamie meets up with Bill Houston on the Greyhound bus going from Oakland, California. They've both got time and a little money to burn. So they decide to burn it together . . .

In *Angels* Denis Johnson sends us on a nightmare odyssey through motels, sleazy juke-box bars, white-hot afternoons and failed relationships. It's the flipside of America – the America that runs concurrently with *Dallas* and *The Johnny Carson Show* – portrayed with wit, anger and startling originality.

'A dazzling and savage first novel . . . whether the characters are conversing with a dark angel or ordering a platter of french fries, they are people who can't be ignored' – *The New York Times Book Review*

KING PENGUIN

☐ ***The Stories of William Trevor*** £5.95

'Trevor packs into each separate five or six thousand words more richness, more laughter, more ache, more multifarious human-ness than many good writers manage to get into a whole novel' – *Punch*. 'Classics of the genre' – Auberon Waugh

☐ ***A Confederacy of Dunces*** **John Kennedy Toole** £3.25

In this Pulitzer Prize-winning novel, in the bulky figure of Ignatius J. Reilly an immortal comic character has been born. 'I succumbed, stunned and seduced . . . it is a masterwork of comedy' – *The New York Times*

☐ ***War Music*** **Christopher Logue** £2.50

An account of Books 16 to 19 of Homer's *Iliad*. 'Stunning . . . an explosive re-living of the splendours . . . with its sweating, bloody battles' – *Spectator*. 'A small triumph of skill and beauty . . . the perfect introduction to Homer' – Lawrence Durrell

☐ ***The Samurai*** **Shasaku Endo** £2.95

In 1613 the unlikely contingent of a Catholic priest and a small group of Japanese Samurai set sail for Mexico, Spain and Rome. A double-sided mirroring of East and West, by the author of *Silence* – 'one of the finest living novelists' – Graham Greene

☐ ***The Book of Laughter and Forgetting***
Milan Kundera £2.95

'No question about it. The most important novel published in Britain this year . . . A whirling dance of a book . . . a masterpiece full of angels, terror, ostriches and love' – Salman Rushdie in the *Sunday Times*

☐ ***A Midnight Clear*** **William Wharton** £2.50

Six men – the crack bridge-players and poets of a US Army Intelligence squad – spend a nerve-shredding Christmas in a château in the Ardennes Forest during the Second World War. 'The most original war book I've read since *Catch 22*' – *Guardian*

KING PENGUIN

☐ ***Keepers of the House*** **Lisa St Aubin de Terán** **£2.50**

Seventeen-year-old Lydia Sinclair marries Don Diego Beltrán and goes to live on his family's vast, decaying Andean farm. This exotic and flamboyant first novel won the Somerset Maugham Award.

☐ ***Cal*** **Bernard Mac Laverty** **£2.50**

Bitter, tender and passionate, this love story is set in Ulster and has been acclaimed by the *Observer* as 'a gripping political thriller and a formidable fictional triumph'.

☐ ***The Memory of War*** **and** ***Children in Exile***
James Fenton **£2.25**

Including 'A German Requiem' and several pieces on the Vietnam war, this collection of Fenton's poems 1968–83 is a major literary event. 'He is a magician-materialist . . . the most talented poet of his generation' – Peter Porter in the *Observer*

☐ ***Store Up the Anger*** **Wessel Ebersohn** **£2.50**

Lying in a South African prison cell, Sam Bhengu struggles to recall his past. In its eloquent violence and sadness, this outstanding novel 'grips like a vice' – *Observer*

☐ ***The Game*** **A. S. Byatt** **£2.95**

Cassandra is an Oxford don; Julia, her sister, a best-selling novelist. When Simon re-enters their lives via a television programme, all three remember a strange childhood game they used to play. This time, the game is played out to a fatal finish . . .

☐ ***Cards of Identity*** **Nigel Dennis** **£2.95**

At the newly renovated country house of Hyde's Mortimer, the 'Identity Club' meet for the reading of three extremely bizarre papers . . . 'One of the funniest, most intelligent and far-reaching pieces of satire' – *The Times*